FRACTURED SLIPPER

PRESENTED BY FAIRY TALE INK

ADRIENNE MONSON   ANGELA CORBETT
LEHUA PARKER   ANGELA BRIMHALL

D1518247

TORK MEDIA

CONTENTS

INTRODUCTION

Fairy Tale Ink is a group of independent authors who write in different genres. But we have a couple of things in common: we love fairy tales and have always wanted to write our own retold versions. Since our desires lined up perfectly, we decided to do a series of anthologies. That way, readers can find one set of their favorite fairy tale, and read a few different versions of it.

We look forward to retelling more classic fairy tales and would love to hear what you think of the stories we have published so far. Please post reviews on any channel you frequent. If you'd like to learn more about the authors and their other works, or would like to see more information on our other anthologies releasing soon, please visit our site www.FairyTaleInkBooks.com.

RELL GOES HAWAIIAN

LEHUA PARKER

RELL GOES HAWAIIAN

Magic Realism

by

Lehua Parker

For island girls who wear a different kind of slipper.

CHAPTER 1

The guy in the cargo shorts and polo shirt shakes his head. "No matter how hard you cram, it's not going to fit."

I'm standing in the rental car parking lot at the Honolulu International Airport trying not to cry. Next to me are twin stacks of boxes piled higher than my shoulders, each stamped with Watanabe Global—Rush Delivery—Extremely Fragile. Looking at the orange Mini Cooper Convertible in front of me, I'd be hard pressed to fit even my single carry-on in the trunk.

I have less than two hours to get everything across the island before my wicked stepmonster erupts and rains hot lava all over me.

Who am I kidding? Even if I pull off this this miracle, she'll still blow her top.

The rental agent shrugs his shoulders. "You're going to need something much larger. Why'd your company reserve this?"

I sigh. "Because I asked for it."

"A Mini?"

"A convertible. I had this image of driving through paradise with the top down."

"You didn't know about the boxes?"

"Nope. This is Regina's way of getting back at me."

"Regina—"

"Regina Watanabe."

"Of Watanabe Global?"

"Yep."

"You're her assistant?"

"Stepdaughter."

He checks his tablet. "The reservation is for R. Watanabe."

"That's me. The R is for Rell, not Regina."

"Got it. You're here for the auction?"

I nod.

"The whole island's talking about it. It's a big deal," he says.

I wave my hand at the boxes. "There's not going to be an auction unless I can get these boxes to the venue. Talk to me about renting a truck or van."

He tippy-taps on his tablet for a moment and frowns. "We don't have anything on the lot. I have a van due back in six hours, but that's no help." A few more taps. "Looks like none of the other agencies have trucks or vans available, either."

I feel tears start to well again, but there's no way I'm going to let something Regina did make me cry. When Daddy died six years ago, I swore whatever happened, I'd never give her that satisfaction again. She thinks banishing me to a tiny all-girls prep school is torture, but I know the Christmases and summers I spent on campus with the headmaster's family were warmer than any celebration at home.

Wherever that is.

I almost feel sorry for my ten-year-old stepsisters, Zel and Ana.

Almost.

Today's date is just a coincidence. I should've known when Regina sent me the ticket to Hawaii that this trip wasn't about me. The car and boxes prove that.

Stepmonsters never change their stripes.

I bite my lip hard. There's got to be a way.

"What about a delivery service? Can I hire someone to take the boxes to Lauele Town?"

The attendant uses his stylus to push back the brim of his cap.

7

"You mean the pavilion above Keikikai Beach, right? Where they're setting up the tents for the auction and luau?"

I nod.

He looks at the ground for a moment and makes a decision. "Look, I know we just met, and I don't want you to think I'm some kind of creeper—"

Said every creeper ever.

I take half a step back.

He sees the look on my face and laughs. "Which is exactly what a creeper would say?"

I shrug.

Pretty much.

"Just hear me out. You don't have many options, and there are a ton of boxes."

"What do you have in mind?"

He points toward the monkeypod tree in the employee lot. "Take my truck."

What? He can't be serious. Who does that?

"Take your truck?" I say. "I can't do that."

"Why not? I'm offering."

I raise an eyebrow, considering. He's about my age, maybe a couple of years older. He's taller than me, the kind of taller where you can wear fancy heels on a date, but don't have to stand on your toes to kiss.

Kiss? Right. Like I'd know anything about that.

What I read in books and magazines doesn't count.

My eyes travel across his broad shoulders, down to his slim waist, and quickly back to his face.

Get a grip, Rell. Look at his eyes, not his body. You're the one who's acting creepy about this.

His green eyes widen when I meet them.

Oh, great. He knows I've been checking him out.

His uniform is hardly stylish, but he makes it work. Wisps of sun-streaked hair peek out from the edges of his cap.

My stomach flips. He's cute. How did I miss this?

Oh, yeah. The boxes.

Focus, Rell!

I swallow and point. "That truck?"

"Yeah. The Datsun with the surf racks. Don't laugh. It's paid for."

I feel the blush rise. "No! I mean, it's great—"

He laughs again. "Relax. I'm just teasing. It may not look like much, but it runs well. You can drive a stick, right?"

My heart sinks.

"No."

"Good, because it's an automatic. You have no excuse."

His eyes are full of mischief. This is too easy. Nothing involving my stepmonster is ever easy. I'm missing something.

"Why are you getting involved? This isn't your problem."

He flicks his stylus against his tablet. "I'm from Lauele, born and raised. Watanabe Global is a major sponsor of the new International Abilities Surf Camp."

"I think they're announcing some kind of partnership with Get Wet Prosthetics tonight," I say.

"Get Wet started the International Abilities Surf Tournament. Jay Westin—you know Jay?"

"No."

"He's a close friend. I've surfed with him since boogie board days. The surf camp is Jay's idea. He wants to make it easy for kids with disabilities to learn to surf."

"That's amazing," I say. "I don't know much about the camp at all."

"When I left Lauele this morning, the crew from Get Wet was already busy setting up. They're probably waiting on this stuff."

"Regina's text said I had to get the boxes delivered before noon."

He reaches out and pats a box. "Take my truck and get your boxes delivered. If makes you feel better, I'm not helping you; I'm helping my friend, Jay."

There's something wrong with this. Finally, I see it.

"But if I take your truck, how will you get home?"

"Me? Bus. With stops, it's only a four hour trip."

My mouth drops. I can't let him do that.

Laughter bubbles out of him like water from a fountain.

"I'm not taking the bus, Rell. I'll drive the Mini Cooper home and meet you later. I'm off in a couple of hours."

He pauses, waiting for me to agree.

I stand in the sunshine looking at the stacks of boxes. I so want to leave them. I'm tired of Regina's passive-aggressive crap.

"Of course, if you have another option..."

All those boxes.

He's right. Leaving the boxes would only hurt the auction, not Regina. The truck's old and worn, but it should do the trick. As weird as this is, I don't think it's a scam.

Okay. I'm doing it.

I fumble in my purse. "I don't have a lot of cash with me—"

He pushes my hand away from my wallet.

"Nonsense," he says. "I'm not taking your money." He crosses his arms and frowns. "Stop trying to make this complicated, Rell. It's very simple. You need to get those boxes to Lauele. I have a truck. It's cool."

I throw up my hands. "This is insane."

He laughs. "Insane is trying to shoehorn those boxes into a Mini Cooper. It's really no big deal. I'm happy to help. C'mon. Let's finish up the paperwork, load the truck, and get you on the road."

CHAPTER 2

*B*ack at the rental office, he runs around the counter and brings up the forms on a monitor.

"Where are you staying? Waikiki? I know it's not in Lauele. There aren't any hotels out there."

"We're staying somewhere close. It's the private residence of someone my stepmother knows." I grab my phone and pull up the address. "It's called Hale O Ka Poliahu."

"No way. You know Poliahu?"

I blink, wondering at his tone. "Uh, no. I think she's someone my stepmother met while skiing in Switzerland. When news got out about Watanabe Global sponsoring the auction for the surf camp, Poliahu offered us her home. She said staying there would be easier than driving back and forth across the island."

"She's right. Lauele is not a tourist-y kind of place. Not a lot of services out there. But, wow. You hit the jackpot. Poliahu's estate is legendary."

"You know it?"

He shakes his head. "By reputation only." He hits enter a few times as the screen flashes. "The house sits upcountry in the mountains above Keikikai Beach. It's usually empty. I can't remember the last time Poliahu was home."

The printer under the counter whirls, spitting out the rental contract. "Okay. One Mini Cooper Convertible. Two day rental. Aw, seems like a shame to fly all this way and only stay two days."

"Believe me, two days with my family is long enough."

He pauses, then lightly touches my hand. "I'm sorry," he says.

I shrug. "It is what it is. It's fine."

With a highlighter, he marks up the contract. "Since it's a corporate rental, here's where the collision insurance and extra driver fees are waved. Be sure to bring it back full or we'll have to charge you extra for the fuel. Initial here, here, and here. Sign there. I just need your driver's license, and we're done."

I really don't want to hand him my license, but I have no choice. Reading the signs posted all over the office, I realize why the reservation's under R. Watanabe and booked under Regina's account. This is the moment when he tells me I can't rent a car at all. One last calculated humiliation by Regina, I'm sure.

Maybe he'll tell me how to catch the bus.

I keep my finger over my birthdate as I slide my license across the counter, but when he picks it up, he sees it anyway.

"Hey! Today's your birthday! Hau'ole la hanau."

I blush.

Again.

"Thanks," I mumble. "Is this a problem?"

He double-checks it. "For a regular rental, you're underage. We make exceptions for corporate rentals."

Hallelujah!

I let the air I was holding out in a rush.

He hands my license back with a sympathetic smile. "It's a silly rule. Most of the guys who work here are under 25, and we drive the cars all the time."

He throws me the keys from his pocket and grabs the keys to the Mini off the rack. We walk back through the rental lot to his truck parked in shade of a big monkeypod tree. He opens the door for me, and I climb in.

"Don't worry. It's rusty and a little dinged up, but my truck's safe. Just make sure you brake extra hard and pump 'em a bit before you stop."

"What!"

"Kidding, kidding! The brakes are fine. Man, you make teasing too easy." He slams the door and the whole cab rattles. I start the engine. Warm air blasts from the vents. I look for the button to roll down the widows.

He taps on the glass and points.

It's a hand crank.

I roll the window down.

Literally.

It takes forever.

The whole time he's grinning at me.

"Good," he says when the window's open. "I wasn't sure if you knew what that was. There's no air-conditioning, so you'll want keep the windows rolled down. Just think of it as driving a convertible with a roof." He pats the hood. "Meet me at the boxes."

I adjust the rearview and figure out how to put it in gear. When I'm at the far side of the parking lot, I surreptitiously test the brakes.

No problem. The truck's bigger than what I'm used to, but it handles well.

I pull up next to the boxes and leave the truck idling. It doesn't take long to load them. Rather than stick my bag next to me, I slip it in the back behind the cab and in front of the boxes.

For a moment, I stand there a little dazed and overwhelmed. I'm not quite sure how all this came together.

"Know where you're going?" he asks.

I hold up my phone. "I've got the address. Google Maps should get me there."

He holds up a finger. "I almost forgot. Wait just one sec."

He dashes back inside and comes back with a business card and a lei made of shiny black seeds. "Here's my phone number. Call if you have any problems. I can leave work early if you need me."

"My number is—"

He wiggles his phone. "Got it off the paperwork. I'll text when I get back to Lauele this afternoon."

I look at the neatly stacked boxes and shake my head.

"Is this what they mean by the aloha spirit?"

He gives me a look like he's not sure where I'm going with this. "Isn't this just doing the right thing? That's universal, no?"

No. But thank goodness I'm in Hawaii.

"I don't even know your name," I say.

He holds out his hand. "Jerry Santos."

I take it. It's warm and strong and slightly rough.

"Rell Watanabe."

He grips my hand tighter and pulls me a little closer. He places the lei around my neck. "Aloha, Rell," he says, pecking me on the cheek. "Welcome to Hawaii."

CHAPTER 3

"*You're* late."

When I step out of the truck, I ignore my stepmonster for a moment and take in the view. From the driveway, I can see all the way down the mountainside to the beach and out to sea. Waves that look like squiggly lines roll to the sand. If I squint, I can see surfers riding to the shore. The air is chilly, far chillier than I ever imagined Hawaii would be. I puff out a breath, expecting to see it turn to frost like it does back home in winter, but it doesn't.

"What happened to the convertible you insisted on? Don't tell me you'd rather drive this—" I don't have to look. I know how her mouth twists over these words—"whatever it is."

I turn to her and force a smile. "Hi Regina. It's nice to see you again."

She snorts, but keeps her eyes from rolling. "Those boxes don't belong here. I told you to take them to the venue. That means the place where the auction is being held, not the house where we're staying. I'll try not to use such big words in the future."

"I know what venue means, I just—"

She sighs. "It's hard for you to think of others, I know, but please remember we're guests here. No doubt that jalopy is leaking oil on Poliahu's beautiful driveway."

"If it's leaking oil, I'll scrub it."

"With what? Your toothbrush? Honestly, Rell, if you'd use your brain for once—just move the truck. Don't be so dramatic."

The front door crashes open, and Zel and Ana come tumbling out, chasing a gray tabby.

"Get him!" Zel shrieks.

"I got the rope. You tie the noose," Ana shouts.

Noose? No way. I didn't hear that right.

Zel lunges for the cat, but misses. "I told you I'm not doing the noose again, Ana. You have to learn how to tie it yourself."

"But you know what happened last time, Zel. You do it."

"No."

The cat starts left, then jukes right, fleeing between Ana's legs.

"You're letting him get away!" Zel says.

"Anastasia! Drizella!" Regina shouts. "I told you to leave that filthy animal alone. You'll get fleas."

The cat escapes over a rock wall and disappears under a bush.

"Aw, Mom," they chorus. "You never let us have any fun."

Good grief. My stepsisters are monsters.

"Enough. I am not getting held up in customs again because you two have fleas."

Zel pouts and scratches her arm. "It wasn't fleas, it was—"

Regina holds up her hand. "Don't argue. You want fun? Fine. Go change. Rell's taking you to the beach."

What?

"Me?"

"Yes, you. You're already dressed for it in those ragged shorts and t-shirt. I hope you didn't embarrass yourself by wearing that on the plane."

Zel snickers. "I bet she wore that on the plane."

Ana says, "Not in first class!"

Brats!

I look at my cut-offs and tee-shirt. "What's wrong with my clothes?"

"Rell, the real question is what's right?" Regina snips. "They're hardly couture. They're fine for cleaning house, I suppose, although I don't really know."

"Or going to the beach," Ana says.

"You promised fun, Mom," Zel says.

I look at the twins. Growing up under Regina, they really didn't stand a chance.

It's not their fault.

I can play nice.

"You really want me to take them to the beach?"

Regina says, "Yes. But first move the truck and sign the papers."

"What papers?"

"Why must you question everything I say? Get a move on. You haven't got all day."

She spins on her heel and heads to the house.

"Girls, let's go. Mommy has lots to do. Unlike Rell, Mommy's busy, busy, busy. A lollygagger, that's what Rell is. But she's here now to take care of you."

"Is lollygagger French for nanny?" asks Zel.

"No, dummy," says Ana. "She's not our nanny. She's old Papa Watanabe's daughter."

"But he's dead."

"Yeah," says Ana, picking at a scab on her arm. "He's worm food now."

"So if she's not our new nanny, why is she here?" Zel asks.

Ana shrugs. "I dunno. Maybe she wants something."

"My new iPhone? She can't have that."

Regina grabs each of the twins by the arm and hisses. "Rell is nothing for you to worry about. She wants nothing; she gets nothing. She's just here for a couple of days, one night only, then she's going back to school, and you'll never see her again. Now go change!"

She marches them to the door and shoves them into the house.

Pausing on the threshold, she points to the truck and then to the street before slamming the door hard enough to rattle the glass.

I close my eyes. "Two days is an eternity."

"Meow?"

I bend down and look under the bushes. "Kitty-kitty," I say. Gray fuzz peeps out at me. "It's okay, sweetie. They've gone. I won't let them hurt you."

"Prraow?"

I hold out my hand, and the cat slinks over and rubs against me. I pick her up, and she melts, her purr vibrating so deeply in her chest that it tingles against my shoulder.

"At least somebody's happy to see me."

The cat snuggles deeper, warming me until I'm no longer shivering. I need to get my jacket out of my bag.

A red cardinal swoops by, flitting from branch to branch in the tree above me. "Look at you! You're gorgeous," I say. He preens and trills. I laugh. "Now you're just showing off." He bobs his head and shakes his tail.

A monarch butterfly lands on the roof of the truck, the black and orange patterns of his wings blurring in the sunlight like—

"Oil!"

I put the cat down and hurry to park on the street.

Jerry's truck runs fine, but I'm not chancing it.

I only have one toothbrush.

CHAPTER 4

I set the parking brake, grab my jacket from my bag in the back, and walk slowly up the driveway. I hesitate, then enter the house through the servant's side door.

"Hello?" I call.

My stepmonster answers from the dining room. "We're in here." She sighs. "Waiting on you, as usual, Rell. But take your time. It's not like we've other, more important things to do."

At one end of a long dining table sits three men, two in crisp aloha shirts and khakis and one in a three-piece wool suit and tie. There are stacks of papers piled high on the table and several pens lined up next to an empty chair.

Regina nervously hovers, fidgeting with her pearls.

I narrow my eyes. She's never nervous.

On the table are official-looking stamps, seals, and ink pads. Behind the men on the buffet table are more file boxes stuffed with millions of folders.

Except for the warm wood furnishings, everything is in shades of white. White gardenias float in crystal bowls, their scent cool and clean. Snowy linens cover the table.

Even wearing my jacket, I shiver. Somehow the beautiful room comes off as cold as a mountain peak. The vibe is Hawaiian-Eskimo, something weirdly anti-tropical. Looking out the window I half-expect to see a snow-dusted coconut tree.

At the far side of the room in front of a fireplace are two chairs and a table arranged for a cozy tête-à-tête. The fireplace is big enough to roast an ox.

We need a fire to warm things up. Heaven knows we have enough paper here to burn down the house.

Twice.

Regina places her palm on the back of a chair and raps her ring against it, the sound like a judge's gavel.

"Sit here, Rell. Let's get started."

I pull out the chair. It's heavier than it looks and slides awkwardly along the thick carpet.

I sit, and the man in the three-piece suit turns to me. "Rell, we've met before—"

"When I was twelve. I remember."

He continues as if I'm invisible. "My name is Michael Lucius. I'm an attorney with Lucius, Griffin, and Melton. These are my associates, Avery Meʻe and Mark Andrews. Do you know why you're here?"

"No."

"Yes, you do," Regina says. "It's your birthday."

"It is? Wait. Are you throwing me a surprise party? Is that why you brought me to Hawaii?"

"No."

"It's the luau tonight! I knew the charity auction couldn't be real."

Regina's lips press into a thin white line.

Awesome. Now if I can just get her eye to twitch…

I say, "Oh, no. Did I ruin the surprise?"

The corner of her eye jumps.

Yes!

"Rell, not everything is about you. The auction tonight has nothing to do with your birthday."

Of course not. I know better than to expect a party. But the surf camp doesn't make sense. Charity's not Regina's thing.

I wink. "Got it. No birthday luau."

Regina takes a deep breath. "You're here to sign papers, that's all."

"And deliver boxes. Don't forget that part."

She squints and pinches the bridge of her nose. With any luck, I've given her a migraine.

"That's enough," she says. "No one likes a drama queen. You sign papers every year on your birthday."

Yeah, in the school secretary's office. It's no big deal.

This feels like a big deal.

"Not in Hawaii."

"You're complaining about a trip to Hawaii? Unbelievable. Nothing I do makes you happy. You even disliked the convertible."

"Yeah, thanks for arranging that. So thoughtful."

Regina throws her hands in the air. "See? Do you see what I deal with? Clearly, this is why we're here today, gentlemen."

Mr. Lucius delicately coughs. "If I may? Rell, it's exactly as your stepmother said. You're here to sign a paper. The process today is much like what's happened in the preceding years, but with a little more formality. Mr. Andrews is a notary. As Regina is your guardian, Mr. Me'e and I will serve as witnesses to your signature. Everything is in order."

Mr. Andrews nods and holds up his notary seal. "I need to see your driver's license for my records. We all know who you are, but contracts are contracts. We must obey the law."

For the second time today, I hand a stranger my ID and watch as he copies information from it. Stamp, stamp, sign, double-sign, date, and he's done.

"As a Notary Public, I certify that the young lady in front of me is Rell H. Watanabe," he says.

"Thank you, Mr. Andrews," says Regina. "Let's get on with it."

CHAPTER 5

*A*s I slide my driver's license back into my wallet, Jerry's business card falls out.

"What's that?" Regina asks.

"Nothing," I say, tucking it back in as my heart beats wildly. "Just a card from the rental place."

To hide my reaction, I reach for the stack of papers nearest me. "Do I have to sign all of these?"

Mr. Lucius chuckles. "No, my dear. That would take hours. We've simplified it for you. You just have to sign one document." He takes the papers from me and flips to the back where a post-it flag sticks out. "We only need your signature here. I've already dated it."

I pick up a pen and scan the page.

"Mr. Me'e and Mr. Lucius already signed the witness lines," I say.

"Of course. Unlike you, they are sensitive about wasting other people's time," Regina says. "Sign and let these good people get on with their day, Rell."

Her tone is annoyed, but her face is eerily blank.

Something's off.

I flip a couple of pages.

"What am I signing?"

Regina rolls her eyes, but her facial expression doesn't change. "I told you. Papers that allow me to continue to pay for your schooling. You want that, right?"

I turn and look up at her. "Smile," I say.

"What?" she sputters.

No change.

"Smile."

"You ungrateful little—"

No change.

"Are you upset with me?" I ask. "I really can't tell if you're mad or happy or sad—"

The penny drops.

Her face has been Botox'd to the max. I peer closer. That's a new nose. The flab under her chin has definitely been tightened, too.

She's not happy or sad. She's annoyed as always, but plastic surgery has taken care of both the wrinkles and the emotion. Even her skin looks waxy.

Whatever.

I turn back to the document.

"Mr. Me'e, does signing this paper allow me to graduate high school in the spring and start college in the fall?"

Mr. Lucius shoots him a look and says, "This is not a negotiation."

Negotiation? It's a simple yes/no question.

Mr. Me'e says, "It allows—"

Regina snaps, "Do you want me to pay your tuition or not? That's what it comes down to, Rell. Sign it and things go on exactly as they have before."

"It that correct, Mr. Me'e?"

Mr. Me'e says, "Signing will—"

"Yes," says Mr. Lucius. "If you sign the document, Regina can continue to pay for your schooling."

"There are other options," Mr. Me'e says.

"Yes, she can be homeless. She can get a GED. She can get a job as fry cook. Or she can complete her education in comfort. It doesn't matter to me. I try to do a good thing, and it's turning into a mess.

Typical. Sign or not, but stop wasting everyone's valuable time, Rell," Regina says.

"But with all these papers, it seems like—"

Regina shakes her head as she reaches over and snatches the pen out of my hand. "I'm sorry, gentlemen. This has been a colossal waste of time. Apparently, Rell feels the need to read each and every scrap of paper before signing."

Wait a minute.

"I just want to know—"

"We told you, but, as always, you're not listening. You're complaining that I brought you to Hawaii instead of letting you stay at school and sign the papers there." She turns to Mr. Lucius. "You're right. I should've anticipated this. She was always such a difficult, suspicious child."

"I am not."

"See?" Regina says.

Mr. Me'e says, "Do you want me to explain—"

"Lucius," Regina interrupts, "contact her school this afternoon and tell them next month's tuition and dorm fees can't be paid."

"Yes, Regina."

Mr. Me'e starts to speak, but Regina stops him again.

"She's stubborn and foolish, Mr. Me'e." Regina waves her hand at all the mountains of paper. "There's no way Rell can read through everything before the payments are due. As you know, without her signature, my hands are tied when it comes to disbursing funds on her behalf."

Mr. Me'e says, "That's true, however—"

Regina cuts him off again. "I appreciate your concern for her welfare, even if she doesn't. Your heart is in the right place, Mr. Me'e, but if Rell insists on being uneducated and out on the street, it's her choice."

Mr. Lucius stands. "I think we're done here today, gentlemen."

Regina shakes Mr. Lucius's hand. "Thank you again. I'll be in touch. Rell, see them out. It's the least you can do."

Regina pivots and exits the room.

I look at the document.

Homeless and uneducated.

I'm not going to cry. She can't make me cry.

Life doesn't have to be like this.

Next year, I'm going to college. I'll get out from under Regina's thumb. I'll scrub dishes and wait tables if I have to.

But first I have to graduate from high school.

The pages blur, but I manage to pick up a pen, find the signature line, and scrawl my name across it.

The men stand up. Mr. Me'e sighs as he picks up the papers. Regina rushes back into the room.

"She signed?"

Mr. Me'e holds it up.

"I want a copy of that for my records. Several copies, in fact," Regina says. "Put the original in the vault."

"Avery?" Mr. Lucius says.

Mr. Me'e places the signed paper in his briefcase and locks it. "Consider it done. I'll have the copies delivered tomorrow."

"Mommy," says a voice, "I thought Rell was taking us to the beach."

Zel and Ana stand in the doorway, wearing the most hideous swimsuits I've ever seen, all ruffles and bows.

With their frizzy hair, they look like overdressed poodles at a clown convention.

Ridiculous.

The stress gets to me, and I can't help it.

I laugh.

"Mom!" yips Ana. "What's wrong with Rell?"

Yips. Like a poodle.

I throw my head back and howl.

"Nothing, dear. She's just deliriously happy to see you." Her tone is angry, but Regina's face doesn't change.

Oh, man. She has resting witch face. And she did it on purpose.

I almost fall out of the chair.

Mr. Lucius reaches for the pitcher on the sideboard. "Maybe a glass of water would help?"

Laughter burns the anger and sadness away. I feel much better.

"No," I say. "It's okay. I'm fine."

Snort, giggle.

I swallow hard.

Get a grip, Rell. Keep it up and the next thing you know you'll be locked away in an insane asylum.

I rub my eyes and take a breath. "Those boxes need to get to the *venue*. The rental car guy told me that's at a pavilion above Keikikai Beach. Is that a good place for the girls to swim?"

"Yes. It's one of the best on the island," Mr. Me'e says.

I open my mouth and a hiccup escapes. "Excuse me. That red-eye flight was long. But flights are cheaper after midnight, right?"

The barb goes right over Regina's head. I've been dismissed and forgotten like yesterday's dishes.

It's not worth a sigh.

"Zel and Ana, let's give Regina some peace and quiet so she can get her work done before the party. It's beach time. Not even paperwork can ruin a day at the beach."

CHAPTER 6

The girls don't say anything until after they climb in truck, and we head down the mountain to the beach.

"Ana says you're not our new nanny."

"No, Zel, I'm your big sister," I say.

"Stepsister," Ana says.

I shoot her a look. "Right. Stepsister. I know it's been a long time since we've seen each other. I think you guys were just four—"

"If you're not our new nanny, why are you taking us to the beach?" Zel asks.

"Don't you want to go to the beach? It's fun."

Ana shrugs her shoulders. "Whatever."

"Whatever," says Zel.

"Your mom told me to take you to the beach."

"Whatever," Ana says again. "But remember, just because you're driving, you're not the boss of us."

"Yeah. The last nanny thought she was the boss of us," Zel says.

"Nanny Bossy didn't last long," Ana says, staring out the window. "We Nair'd her."

"Nair'd her?"

"In her shampoo."

"You didn't!"

Zel nods. "We did. Now she's Nanny Baldo."

Ana scrunches up her face. "More like Nanny Patches."

I give them another look. "So how bossy was she?"

Ana turns to me. "She wanted us to pick our clothes off the floor."

"And read books."

"And took away our candy."

"We NEED our candy."

"So don't try to take it," Ana says.

"Okay," I say and try not to scratch my suddenly itchy head.

When we hit the highway that circumnavigates the island, I turn right and follow the signs to Lauele Town. The ocean peeps through the ironwood trees on the left, but it's not until we come to a two-story building with a big sign saying Hari's on the front that the view really opens up.

Across the street from Hari's is a beach pavilion with a sign that reads Keikikai Beach. Big delivery trucks fill the parking lot. In a grassy field people are setting up a big event tent and an on-site catering kitchen.

"Must be the place," I say, pulling into the parking lot.

Zel points to the big banner across the front of the tent: International Abilities Surf Camp Charity Auction & Luau.

"You think?"

Ana rolls her eyes. "You're right, Zel. She's too stupid to be our nanny."

"Hey!"

They jump out of the truck and start heading toward the beach.

"Zel! Ana! What about all the boxes?"

Without stopping, they wave at me.

"Not my problem," Zel says over her shoulder.

"That's why you're here," Ana says.

"And your truck smells like old feet!" Zel shouts.

I scramble out of the truck. I almost forget, but at the last minute I grab my purse off the seat and whip it over my head and across my body. The girls are striding across the sand now. "Zel! Ana! Get back—"

"Jerry, you can't park here."

I whirl around. Nobody's there.

"What?"

I hear a tongue click and a sigh. "Down here."

I peer over the hood of the truck. "Oh. Sorry, I didn't see you."

Near the license plate, a tiny man with a clipboard adjusts his hat and frowns. "Why are you driving Jerry Santos's truck? Where's Jerry?"

"I—"

"Never mind. You have to move it. We need the entire parking lot for the event tonight."

"But—"

"Eh, Luna. Check out the back. The wahine brought the boxes we've been waiting for." Two thick brown hands reach over the side of the truck and lift out a box.

The guy with the clipboard grins. "Why didn't you say so? Hui! Eh, gangies! Come kokua!"

In an instant, one by one the boxes begin to rise out of the truck and float toward the tent.

What the what?

I walk around the front of the truck and into a scene from *Willy Wonka*. A fireman's brigade of men no taller than three feet are unloading the boxes and handing them down the line and into the tent.

The one lifting the boxes out of the back taps the side of the truck. "Eh! Das the last one," he says. "All pau!"

I peek into the back to check, but when I turn around to thank them, they've disappeared.

The first guy rips something from his clipboard and holds it out. "Your receipt."

I glance at it. "Menehune Inc.?"

He grins. "We're Local 808. No job too big or small. We specialize in rock walls. I'm Luna. You a friend of Jerry's?"

"Sort of."

"Ah," he nods. "That kind of friend."

"No!" Heat pinks my cheeks. "He just lent me his truck. That's all."

He cocks his head. "Oooh! You're THAT kind of friend."

I adjust my bag over my shoulder and glare. "I don't know what you're talking about."

"Relax, titah. I'm just joking with you. You work for Watanabe Global, right?"

"Sort of. I'm Rell."

"Ah-ha! I thought I recognized that smell."

"What?"

I fight an impulse to sniff my arm pit. Instead I surreptitiously rub my cheek on my shoulder and breathe deeply.

Flowers and laundry detergent.

This guy's nuts.

He flicks his wrist. "Nothing. You remind me of your mother."

"You knew my mom?"

"Oh, yeah. She was a Ha'awina. The Ha'awinas go way back in Lauele. You never know?"

I shake my head. "No."

"Your family owns land around here. It's just mauka of the land where they want to build the surf camp. See?" He points uphill. "That's where the road will go. You seen the designs, yeah?"

I shake my head. "I don't know anything about the project."

"Well, go park Jerry's junkalunka truck in front of Hari's store—he won't mind—and come to the tent. We'll show you everything."

"Thanks, but I can't. The twins took off down to the beach, and I need to keep an eye on them."

Luna whistles. "Makani!"

"Yeah, Luna?" a voice answers.

"Girls. Beach. Now."

"On it!"

I don't see Makani, but I hear feet thunder across the pavement. A heartbeat later, little puffs of sand rise from the beach.

Luna smiles. "No worries. Makani will keep an eye on them."

My stomach clenches. "I don't know Makani."

"No worries. He's like the wind. He'll make sure they don't get into trouble."

"I think I better—"

He taps the side of the truck. "I need you to move this first. After you park the car, go into Hari's store. Tell him Luna wants a sprunch. Put it on my tab."

"Luna, you sly dog. Tell Hari yourself. Don't let this guy fool you, Rell," says a voice behind me.

"Jerry! Don't spoil my fun," Luna says.

My heart skips.

Jerry!

He startled me.

That's it.

That's all.

It has nothing to do with his deep surfer's tan or eyes like green beach glass.

Right.

Jerry holds out his hand. Reflexively I hold mine out, too. He drops keys into my palm.

"I hoped I'd find you here. Your rental car's across the street at Hari's. Are my keys still inside the truck?"

"Yes."

"I'll get my truck out of Luna's hair."

"Thanks so much for loaning it to me. I couldn't have done this without you."

"No problem." He opens the door and climbs in the cab.

I grab the open window before he can shut the door. "Hey. You said you were involved with the surf camp. Luna was just going to show me the plans. Wanna come see?"

I groan.

That sounds desperate. Needy. Guys hate that.

"I'd love to. Be right back."

I watch as Jerry backs up and parks across the street next to an orange Mini. I can't stop smiling.

"Oh, yeah," says Luna. "Totally a friend like that."

CHAPTER 7

When Jerry jogs back, he's holding a hideous ruffled floral beach wrap. "I think this belongs to you."

I want to die.

"Actually, I think it belongs to one of my step-sisters." I quickly stuff it in my purse. "I really should go check on them."

"Makani's with them," Luna says. "They're fine."

I hesitate.

Jerry comes to my rescue. He jumps up on the rock wall separating the grass from the sand and scans the beach.

"Luna's right. The girls are fine. See for yourself."

He reaches down and pulls me up next to him. He puts a hand on my shoulder and leans close as he points toward the ocean. His after-shave reminds me of cedar and cinnamon.

I breathe deeply.

And a touch of clove.

I shake my head.

This is ridiculous, Rell. You're acting like a love sick puppy. Knock it off.

Jerry mistakes my headshake for a no.

"Can't see them? Look a little more to the right."

He leans closer until his breath kisses my cheek.

Wintergreen mint.

All I have to do is turn my head, and we'll be kissing for real.

Ah! Focus! Ana and Zel. Where are they?

I follow Jerry's arm as it points out along a lava outcrop. The girls are still close to the main beach, splashing in a shallow tide pool. A few feet away, a medium-sized yellow dog approaches them, wagging its tail.

A dog.

The girls wanted to hang a cat.

This can't be good.

I step away from Jerry, so I can think.

"I see Ana and Zel, but I don't see Makani," I say.

"He's out there. Guaranteed," Luna says.

"Makani's a dog?" I ask.

Luna cocks his head. "A dog? No, Makani's a—"

"She's talking about Ilima," Jerry interrupts.

"Ilima? Who's Ilima?" I ask.

"That yellow poi dog next to the girls is named Ilima. Between Ilima and Makani, the girls are in good hands. There's no need to worry about them," Jerry says.

"Everyone keeps telling me that I don't have to worry because Makani's out there, even though I can't see him. Are you telling me now that Ilima's a lifeguard? She'll jump in and rescue the girls if they get swept out to sea?"

"Ilima's Ilima," Luna says, scratching his head. "Makani's Makani. I'm Luna. He's Jerry. You're Rell. Why is this so confusing?"

Jerry laughs and jumps down from the wall.

"It's not, Luna. The reef's scary when you're not from Lauele. Rell just wants to make sure the girls are safe."

"Didn't we just say so?" Luna says.

"Yes, but she needs to understand things for herself." Jerry jerks his head toward the tent. "If Ilima's here, Uncle Kahana is, too. Why don't you come in and meet him? He can show you the plans. It will just take a minute and then we'll walk down to Piko Point."

"Piko Point?"

He points towards the girls again.

"Piko Point is at the end of the lava outcrop. From there I can show you where the surf tournament's held and tell you all about the surf camp."

From the ground, Jerry reaches up and places his hands along my waist. Without thinking I lean down and put my hands on his shoulders as he lifts me off the wall. On the ground, I have to look up a little to see his eyes. I know with just a little stretch, our lips would meet.

Cedar, cinnamon, cloves, and wintergreen mints.

Jerry clears his throat and smiles as he releases me, taking a half a step back.

"We are friends," sings Luna. "Friends, friends, friends! We are friends."

I turn toward him, but Luna's gone.

"What's that all about?" Jerry asks. "Why is he singing an old Cecilio & Kapono song?"

"Who knows," I say. "He's a little—"

"Strange?" Jerry raises an eyebrow.

I roll my eyes. "I was going to say quirky."

"You don't know the half of it," Jerry says, taking my hand. "C'mon. Let's check out the tent."

CHAPTER 8

*I*nside the tent, a young woman with long hair piled on top of her head is smoothing tablecloths over a row of tables. Head down, she says, "Stack the brochures on the end, Luna. I want people to see the full list of auction items before they come in to bid." She looks up. "Oh, Jerry! I thought you were Luna."

"He's around here somewhere, Nalani. I just saw him," Jerry says.

"Luna!" Nalani shouts. "I need—"

"Already pau, Nalani!" says Luna's voice.

I turn, and a table that I swear wasn't there when I walked in is now next to the door and covered with artfully swirled stacks of brochures.

"What about the flowers?" Nalani says, placing her hands on her hips.

Like magic, a vase filled with purple bougainvillea appears.

"And pens!" Nalani says.

A woven basket of pens quivers next to the vase.

Nalani cracks her gum. "Why do I have to remind you buggahs about everything?"

"You're welcome," says Luna, but I can't tell if it's coming from under a table, behind the stacks of boxes, or outside the tent.

She cracks her gum again and smiles at us. "Who's your friend?"

Jerry says, "This is Rell Watanabe."

"Hi," I say and hold out my hand.

"As if." She ignores my hand and kisses my cheek. "Aloha, Rell. Strangers shake. Ohana honi—kiss."

"Ohana? You mean family?"

"Don't look surprised. The word ohana existed long before *Lilo and Stitch*. And, yeah. We're second cousins on your mother's side. The last time I saw you, you were busy eating sand on Keikikai Beach."

"Ew!"

She shrugs. "It's what babies do. You don't remember coming to Lauele?"

"No."

Nalani puts her arm around my shoulders. "It was a long time ago. If your mother was still alive, I'm certain you would've been back many times. Let me get Uncle Kahana. He'll want to meet you."

"I have an Uncle Kahana?"

"Oh, Honey! Everyone has an Uncle Kahana. There he is," she says. "E hui! Uncle Kahana! Someone to see you."

At the far end of the tent, in front of a massive stage, a slightly built elderly man in a faded t-shirt and worn board shorts turns toward us. He raises his brown arm and waves.

"Send 'em over, Nalani. It's too far for an old broke okole man to walk all the way over there."

Nalani gives me a little nudge, and Jerry and I thread our way through the tables.

Panic bubbles.

I have an Uncle Kahana.

People I don't know call me family.

My mother's family was from Lauele.

I give Jerry a side-glance.

I have to know.

"Are we related?" I whisper.

He pauses for a minute, considering. "Calabash cousins for sure. My great-great grandfather's aunty was hanai to your fifth cousin's mother, and she married my third cousin's nephew, so yeah, we're ohana."

Family.

My heart sinks.

"You know what calabash means, right?" Jerry says.

"No."

"It's an old Hawaiian idiom. Basically, it refers to all the people who make sure you never go hungry as well as the people you feed. It's less about sharing physical blood than sharing experiences and responsibilities."

I feel a sharp tug on the bottom of my shirt. When I reach back, I feel Luna's thick hand squeeze mine.

"Don't worry," he whispers. "Calabash cousins can *date*."

I spin around, but all I see is the edge of a tablecloth settling against the floor.

"Did you say something?" Jerry asks.

"Me? No."

I hear a giggle, and then Luna's voice sings, "Friends, friends, friends."

"It's just Luna singing again," I say.

"Luna. What a pest!" Jerry says.

"So, we're calabash cousins, but not blood."

"Right," he says.

Calabash. The butterflies settle. It might not make a difference to him, but it does to me.

Wait a minute.

I touch his arm. "Is that why you lent me your truck?"

Jerry shakes his head. "Of course not. I didn't know you were ohana until I saw Luna talking with you. One of his quirks is he only talks with family."

"But I'd never met him before. How could he possibly know me?"

Jerry shrugs. "I don't know. But no one outside of family ever sees him or his crew."

Luna giggles again. From somewhere around my knees, he singsongs, "First comes love, then comes marriage, then comes Rell with a—"

I smack the tabletop.

"Cockroach?" Jerry asks. "They get pretty big in Hawaii."

"It's nothing."

Luna giggles again.

Imp.

"Close," says a voice in my ear, "but not quite."

CHAPTER 9

$\mathcal{I}$t doesn't take us long to reach the far end of the tent where Uncle Kahana is standing next to a table with an architect's model.

"Uncle Kahana, this is—"

"Rell Watanabe." He leans over and kisses my cheek. "You look like your mother."

It's so unexpected that I have to catch my breath.

"You knew my mother?"

"Of course. And your father. And your grandparents—"

"Yeah, Uncle Kahana is real old," says Jerry.

Uncle Kahana narrows his eyes. "Don't you have cars to park?"

"Nope."

"You sure? I hear you college boys are good at that."

"The best! We learned from old futs like you."

Uncle Kahana snorts and wags his finger. "One of these days, Jerry, if you're lucky, you'll get to be as old as me."

"I hope so, Uncle, I hope so."

"But for now, Jerry, let me show Rell the surf camp. It's because of Watanabe Global that it's possible." Uncle Kahana motions for me to come closer. "This is why we're here."

The model shows six cabins connected by paved trails with ramps and handrails. Near the parking lot are outdoor showers, racks for storing surfboards, and a covered pavilion with cooking facilities. Uncle Kahana opens one of the cabins like a dollhouse.

"Four beds in each cabin's main room with a separate space for aides or camp counselors. No bunk beds. Everything's extra-wide for wheelchairs, and the bathrooms have rails and chairs in the showers. The goal is to allow campers to live as independently as possible."

"You should see the zip lines and towers. Awesome," Jerry says.

"That's not until Phase Two, when we add the obstacle courses for strength and agility training." Uncle Kahana shoots me a glance. "You know about the tournament?"

I shake my head. "I don't know anything. Tell me."

"When the Abilities Surf Tournament went international and got corporate sponsorship, Jay and Nili-boy came up with the idea to add a summer surfing camp. When they started, the whole thing was sponsored by Get Wet Prosthetics and some grants, but frankly they can't do it without the support of businesses like Watanabe Global. This camp is going to be life changing."

I run a finger over a cabin. "It's a camp for kids who want to become pro surfers?"

Uncle Kahana's head snaps toward me. He frowns and opens his mouth, but doesn't speak. I look up from the model and catch his eyes. He reads something in my face and softens.

"The camp is for more than just kids, Rell. Adults, too."

"But the goal is to win the competition, right? It's a surf tournament."

Uncle Kahana chuckles quietly. "No. The goal is to heal. When bodies, minds, hearts, and souls are healed, they have a desire to test themselves. Competition is the natural result, that's all. You've been to Piko Point?"

Jerry says, "Not yet. She just got off the plane this morning."

"Take her, Jerry. Tell her. It will all make sense then." He cocks an eyebrow at me. "You surf?"

I smile and echo Jerry. "Not yet."

He pats my arm. "No worries! With a name like Rell, you'll be a natural."

CHAPTER 10

*a*t the edge of the sand near the showers, Jerry stops. He steps out of his shoes and pulls off his socks.

"No shoes. Only tourists walk on beaches in shoes."

"We're supposed to carry them?"

He takes my shoes from me and sets them next to his on top of the short rock wall.

"You want me to leave my shoes here? Are you nuts? I only have one other pair. Someone will steal them."

He looks at me, amused. "This is Lauele. Nobody'll bother them. Promise."

The sand is warm on the top and cooler underneath as it squishes between my toes. There's a light breeze coming off the ocean. It's not enough to chop the water, just enough to keep things from getting too hot. At Keikikai Beach, the water is bathtub calm and clear as glass. A little ways down the beach, a young mother is splashing with her toddler, but other than them, the beach is empty.

"Where is everyone?"

He cuffs my shoulder. "It's Friday. Most people work for a living."

"I mean, where are the girls?" Panic rises. "I don't see them."

Jerry shades his eyes. "There. Walking out to Piko Point. They're on the Nalupuki side."

I follow his arm to the lava outcrop stretching out to sea. On the far side I see waves splash as they hit the rocks. This side is calm. The other is wild. I have a vision of the girls tumbling into the rough water, followed by my head on Regina's wall.

I shift my weight and run.

"Rell! Wait!"

At the start of the rocks, Jerry catches my arm, forcing me to stop.

"Slow down. Makani's with them, remember? They're just exploring."

"I have to get out there."

"Okay, but don't run. You're barefoot, remember? Parts of the reef are slippery. Other spots are sharp. Let's go slow. Step where I step."

His hand travels down my arm to grab my hand.

"We have to wade just a bit to get to the first rock. It won't get as higher as your knees, promise. But keep your eye on the water. You never want to turn your back to the ocean."

I tell myself it's the shock of the water that makes me squirm and not the feeling of holding a boy's hand.

Good grief. Maybe an all-girls prep school isn't everything it's cracked up to be.

We step out of the ocean and onto the lava. It's rough and rippled like water and dotted with pockets of salt, but it feels warm under my toes.

I raise a hand to my eyes and peer out toward the point. The girls are sitting down near a big saltwater pool, watching something in the water. Ilima is sitting a few yards away, chewing her tail.

"It's easy," Jerry says. "But watch where you step. It's low tide, so there might be some wana exposed."

"What's that?"

"It looks like a black ball of spikes. It's a sea urchin. Nothing to worry about, but you really don't want to step on one."

"It's like a sea cactus?"

Jerry snorts. "Good one. Just don't let them hear you say that."

"Wana are sensitive?"

His eyes twinkle. "Totally!"

When we get near the girls, I hear them arguing.

Ana says, "It's a killer snake."

"You're lying," Zel says.

"I saw a video about it. One bite from a sea snake and you're dead before you get back to shore."

"Nuh-uh."

"Put your foot in the water and wave it around if you don't believe me."

"You do it."

"Hi girls," I say.

Ana looks up. "Let's make Rell do it."

"Yeah. Rell, put your foot in the water."

"So a sea snake can bite it? That's not very nice."

Ana's eyes flit to Zel. "There's no snake," she says.

"We just want to know how cold the water is," Zel says.

Jerry squats down next to the girls. "Put your own hand in the water. Rell can't tell you if it's cold."

"Who're you?" Ana asks.

I say, "This is Jerry."

"Is he your boyfriend?" Zel asks.

I shoot Jerry a look.

Why? Why do I do this? He's not my boyfriend. I don't have to check with him to see if he agrees.

"No," I say evenly. "But he is my friend. We drove to the beach in his truck."

"Ugh. That old thing? You need a better truck," says Zel.

"Yeah, your truck smells like seaweed."

"And stale burritos."

My face turns purple.

Let a wave take me now.

Please.

I can't look at Jerry.

The girls are beyond rude.

Jerry throws his head back and laughs.

"Of course it smells like seaweed and burritos. It's a surf truck."

Zel and Ana's eyes bug out of their heads.

"Are you crazy?" Ana says.

"Or just weird?" Zel says as she stands.

She moves toward a rock the size and shape of a basketball perched near the edge of the biggest tide pool.

"Careful!" Jerry says. "That rock is called Pohaku. It's part of an ancient fishing shrine. Be respectful and don't get too close."

"What?"

"Stay away from that rock," Jerry says. "It's not something you touch or play with."

"Come on, Ana," says Zel. "Let's leave the love birds alone."

"Yeah, love birds." Ana rises and makes kissy noises as she walks over to another tide pool. "Ooo! A crab! Let's catch it!"

Jerry stands. "Charming. Your sisters?"

I sigh. "Stepsisters."

"Wicked little demons, aren't they?"

"I don't really know. I haven't seen them in years. But you're probably right."

The water in the saltwater pool is deep, but I can see all the way to the bottom and through a large archway that leads to black water.

"Is there a sea snake?"

He shrugs. "It's possible, but highly unlikely. Sea snakes are really rare in Hawaiian waters. I've never seen one. It was probably an eel."

I bend down and run my fingers along the surface of the water. "It's colder out here than near the shore."

"Right off the point is deep water. There's a channel between us and the other side. That's what makes Nalupuki a great surfing beach."

Beneath my fingers, the water stirs. A thin rope peeks from a crevasse, then shoots out to wind between my fingers. I'm too surprised to jerk my hand away.

"What's that?"

Jerry gasps. "It's a baby snowflake eel. They're usually really shy. I've never seen one do this. It's like he's happy to see you."

More fish rise from the bottom and head to the surface. I see yellow tangs and purple damsel fish, striped sergeant majors, and others I don't recognize. I pull my hand out of the water.

"They must think I have food," I say. "Do people come out here and feed them?"

The look on Jerry's face is odd. It rolls through different expressions until it lands on something between sheepish and puzzled.

"Nobody I know," he says.

I stand and look at the strip of sand off to the right. Just past it is the hillside from the architect's model.

"That's where the surf camp is going?"

Jerry nods. "Yeah. That's Kaulupali land over there. Your family owns a few acres just above it. Uncle Kahana is gifting some of his Kaulupali land to Jay's foundation to use for the surf camp. Come out to the very edge of the lava with me, and I'll tell you the whole story."

"There's a mystery?" I tease. "A deep, dark secret?"

But when Jerry reaches for my hand to help me over a slippery patch, I see the pain in his eyes.

"There's a reason for the surf tournament and the camp." He sweeps his arm out over the bay.

"It all began here during our freshman year of high school."

CHAPTER 11

Out at the very edge of the lava outcrop, the waves splash against the rocks, sending a fine mist toward us. In the water just off the point, a guy on a green surf board and a girl on a cream one wait for the next set. The guy waves at Jerry.

"Santos!" he shouts. "Where's your board?"

"Home," Jerry says.

"Brah! Better hurry. Kids will be out of school soon," calls the girl.

"Can't," Jerry says.

"You snooze, you lose! The waves wait for no one," says the guy.

Like magic, a gentle swell forms off the point. The surfers swing their legs onto their boards and paddle into position where the wave suddenly builds four feet higher.

"Chee-hoo!" the guy calls.

"Laters, Jerry!" says the girl.

Jerry's eyes are on the surfers as they head to shore.

"You surf here a lot?"

He nods, but doesn't look at me. "From the time we could walk, we were in the ocean. Like I said, the International Abilities Surf Tournament, Get Wet, the surf camp—it all begins here."

He tugs my hand until our shoulders touch.

"Our freshman year, Jay Westin and I were competing in a surf tournament. Jay was the favorite." His lips twist wryly. "In those days, Jay was always the favorite. When the heat started, we all raced from the beach, paddling to get to the sweet spot just there," he points, "right where those surfers were. The waves were bigger that day. We were jockeying for position when someone yelled, 'Fin!'"

I look back to the beach and shiver.

It's so far.

"But it was just a dolphin, right?"

"No. Sharks. I saw them."

"Them?"

"Two. One the size of Jaws and the other his littler brother. Jay was out farther than the rest of us. From Piko Point, the shark fins made a beeline to him and disappeared."

"They left?"

Jerry shakes his head. "They dove. Sharks ambush. The biggest one rocketed from the bottom and came up underneath Jay's board, knocking him off and into the water. I saw the other one circling below."

I squeeze his hand. I have no words.

"When Jay came up for air, he shouted at us to go—to head back to shore."

"But you didn't."

"I couldn't. I knew he'd never leave me. I heard sirens and jet skis start up on the beach. I tried to paddle toward Jay. I thought if I could get him up on my board, we'd be okay. I knew help was coming, but before I could get there— "

He swallows and presses his lips tight, the horror of that day as fresh as a minute before him.

"The smaller shark bit Jay."

"You saw that?"

"Yeah. In all its technicolor glory. Red blood in blue water looks purple. Seafoam turns pink. Bone is whiter than white." Jerry reaches down and touches his shin a few inches above his ankle. "It ate his foot."

"My—"

I can't even say it.

Jerry tugs my hand until I look him in the eye.

"Jay lost his foot, but more importantly, he lost himself that day. Before the attack, being in the ocean was like breathing to him. People think losing a limb is about what someone can or can't do, but that's the smallest part of it."

"Jay Westin. You said he started Get Wet Prosthetics?"

Jerry nods. "That came later. After it happened, Jay filled his empty surfing space with hate. It took a lot of time, but the ocean eventually healed him—body, mind, heart, and soul. He figured out how to surf again. To forgive himself."

"Himself?"

"You sound surprised."

"But it's the shark who took his foot."

"It's complicated." Jerry rubs his face. "Anyway, Jay and his cousin Nili-boy started Get Wet Prosthetics to help others reconnect with the lives they were meant to live." He gestured toward the beach. "This camp is the next step. Watanabe Global is doing a lot of good by supporting the auction. That's one reason why I helped you."

"One?"

Jerry presses his shoulder against mine. "Don't push it," he says.

I watch the surfers pull out of the wave and head back out.

"After what you saw, you still surf?"

"Every day I can. Rain or shine, big waves or glass."

I look at the waves crashing against the lava and think about pink foam and white bone.

"I'd never get in the water again."

"You only say that because you've never surfed."

"What about sharks? They're still out there."

Jerry gives me a side-glance. "We worked it out. It's all cool now."

"What—"

Bark, bark, bark, BARK, BARKBARKBARK!

CHAPTER 12

$\mathcal{W}$e whirl around in time to see the girls rocking the round stone perched on the edge of the biggest tide pool. Ilima's dancing around them, her jaws snapping like a shark.

BARKBARKBARK.

"Come on, Ana! One more push and we'll get it in the water!"

"No!" shouts Jerry as he lurches toward them. He slips on the lava and falls to his knees. "Stop it! You don't know what you're doing!"

The stone starts to tip.

"Girls," I say as I scramble around Jerry.

Ilima leaps and bites one of Ana's ruffles, tugging the back of her suit off her hips.

"Eeee!" Ana shrieks. "I'm being attacked!"

The stone tumbles.

Zel pumps her fist. "Yes!"

Ilima releases Ana's suit and rushes to the edge of the tide pool. As the stone sinks to the bottom, big silver bubbles rise like jellyfish and pop at the surface. Ilima collapses on the lava, raises her head, and howls.

"Stupid dog," Zel says, marching over. "Nobody bites my sister, but me!"

She swings her foot, kicking Ilima squarely in the ribs.

Ilima's howl turns into a yelp. She leaps to her feet, saltwater dripping off her chest. Pinning her ears back, she growls.

"Zel! Ana! Don't move!" I say.

"That dog pantsed me!" Ana says, pulling her suit up over her butt. "Kick it again, Zel!"

"Ana, are you hurt? Let me see."

I spin her around, but she covers her backside with both hands.

"Don't! You're as pervy as the dog."

There's not a mark on her.

Zel draws back her foot again. "Don't you growl at me, crazy dog. I'll kick you again."

"No, you won't!" I grab each of them by the arm. "Stop this right now!"

It's not until I turn back to Jerry that I see the tears in his eyes. He's kneeling at the edge of the pool, staring at the bottom in shock.

"Jerry?"

No response.

"Jerry, your knee is bleeding. Are you okay?"

At the sight of blood, the girls still.

He raises his eyes from the water and looks at the girls. "Why?" Tears spill down his cheeks. "That was a sacred aumakua stone. A guardian of this place for hundreds of years. People come here to pray, to meditate, to leave offerings. I told you it's an ancient shrine. I told you to leave it alone."

Zel scrunches up her face. "It's just a stupid rock."

Ana says, "Yeah. If it's so important, why did people leave it here?"

Ilima lowers her head and growls deeper.

Jerry stands and pulls his shirt over his head, tossing it on the ground. The sunlight glistens on his surfer's broad shoulders and trim waist.

"Go," he says. "Get them out of my sight."

His hands move to his belt.

Ana pulls her arm out of my grasp.

"You're not the boss of us," she says.

Jerry unbuckles his belt and moves to the top button of his cargo shorts. "Leave before I'm temped to use my belt to do more than hold up my pants."

"I'm tell—ow!" Ana says when I grab her by the ear.

"You can't—ow, ow, ow!" chants Zel.

I twist their ears a little harder.

"I'm not your nanny. I'm your big sister and that does make me the boss of you! We're going home. Now."

Ana and Zel try to plant their feet, but I twist relentlessly and force them to stumble back to the beach.

I hear a splash and look over my shoulder. Jerry's pants are on the ground near the big saltwater pool. His feet sink below the surface.

After what the girls did, he'll never speak to me again.

Goodbye, Jerry's feet.

Zel realizes I'm distracted and tries to pull away, but I grip harder.

"Stop it, Rell! You're hurting me!"

"Good."

At the rock wall near the showers, I let go of the girls long enough to grab my shoes.

Jerry's shoes.

I run my fingers over them.

Goodbye, Jerry's shoes.

It's been real.

I turn on the shower and rinse my feet.

"Into the water," I say.

"No."

"It's too cold."

"We'll shower at home."

"You're not getting sand in the car and making more work for Jerry. Rinse."

"No."

Oh, yes. Yes, you will.

I grab ruffles.

"Let go!"

I twist for a better grip.

"Hey!"

"Rinse the sand off your feet or I'll dunk your whole body under the spray."

"You can't make us."

"You're not the boss!"

I yank, pulling their legs into the spray.

"Cold, cold, cold!" they shriek.

"Good," I say.

"Ha! Fooled you. It's not that bad."

"Yeah, we wanted to anyway!"

"Let's get really wet and soak the car!"

"Yeah! Water's way worse than sand."

Out the corner of my eye, I spot Ilima limping around the showers and slinking behind the trash cans.

She's following us.

That can't be good.

"Let's go," I say.

Ilima trails us all the way past the event tent and across the street to the rental car. I unlock it and push Zel toward the backseat.

"It's too small," she whines.

"Complain to your mother."

"It's too hot," Ana says.

"Get in."

"I want to sit up front."

"No, I want to," Zel says.

I grit my teeth. "You both get in the back right this minute or so help me, I'll leave, and you can walk."

"I hate you!" Ana says.

"Right back at ya," I say.

"I'm telling Mom," Zel says. "She'll punish you for being mean to us."

I count to three, then slide the driver's seat all the way forward. "Get in."

They grumble, but finally climb in. When I get in, I feel their knees and feet pushing against my back.

They want to be that way? Fine.

I turn all the air conditioning vents toward me and start the engine.

"Hey! What about us?"

"Can we put the top down? It's hot."

"No. Be quiet."

"I want a drink."

"Me, too."

"Let's go in the store."

"No way," I say.

"Come on, Rell. Buy us a drink."

"It's hot, and we're thirsty."

I adjust the mirrors. "You can get one at the house."

"You're so mean, Rell."

"Mom was right about you."

When I put the car in reverse, Ilima steps out of shadows to watch us leave. I roll down my window.

"I'm sorry," I tell her. "I hope your ribs are okay. I won't let them hurt you again."

"What's Rell saying?"

"She's apologizing to the dog!"

"That dog attacked me!"

"It should be put down!"

"She's crazy. I can't believe Mom sent us with her."

Ilima locks eyes with me.

My eyes dim like I'm going to faint. I take a deep breath and try to shake the ringing out of my ears.

I smell sandalwood and lemonade.

Ilima tips her head to the side and chuffs.

The taste of lemons fills my mouth, sweet and sour and a little salty, just the way Mama used to make it.

In an instant, I'm three years old again, running through the back-yard sprinklers. Mama says, "Rell! Time for lunch, sweetheart."

Mama?

"What are we waiting for?" Ana whines.

55

"It's so hot!"
I swallow and the memory's gone.
When I look back, Ilima isn't there.
"Mom is so going to hear about this," says Zel.
"Uh-huh," says Ana.

CHAPTER 13

$\mathcal{I}$'m so angry that I don't consider parking on the street when I get to the estate and pull all the way to the back of the house. I grab my purse from the seat next to me, throw the keys inside, and hold the door open for the girls. They climb out acting stiff and sore, like I forced them to ride twisted like pretzels in a box. A door opens, and Regina stalks out.

"My precious," she says, throwing her arms wide.

"Mommy!" the twins shout and rush to her, crocodile tears falling like rain.

"My lambkins! What's wrong? Are you hurt?"

"Mommy, Rell yelled at us."

Regina's jaw clenches as her eye starts to twitch. "I'm sure it was just a misunderstanding. Rell knows better than to yell at you."

"Regina—"

"And Mommy, we were thirsty, but she refused to let us drink!"

"What! In this heat?" Regina pulls the girls close. "That's cruel, Rell, even for someone as thoughtless and uncaring as you."

"She made us ride in the back without air conditioning!"

"That's not all! She twisted our ears! Look!" Ana flips back her hair.

Regina looks at Ana's ear, then Zel's.

"Oh, my babies! Your ears are all red and swollen!"

"Regina—"

Regina rises to her full height and squares her shoulders. "I am so disappointed in you, Rell. I wish I could say I was shocked, but I'm not."

"The girls pushed—"

She holds up her hand. "I don't want to hear it. Clearly, this is my fault. I thought if you spent some time with your sisters, you'd love them as much as they love you. I thought you'd decide you missed us and would want to be part of the family again. But I see my hopes were misplaced. Your father was right about you."

Her words stop me cold.

Victory shines behind her eyes. She's daring me to ask.

I won't give her the satisfaction.

It's a stare-down until one of us blinks.

She holds out her hand. "Keys," she says.

I blink.

"What?"

She wiggles her fingers. "Give me your keys. After the way you've behaved, you're not going anywhere."

"But the auction—"

"I don't want you anywhere near the auction. You've proven you can't be trusted. You'll spend the night in your room."

"I—"

Faster than a snake, Zel reaches out and tugs my purse off my shoulder.

"Got it, Mommy! Her keys are inside."

"Give that back!" I reach to swipe it from her, but Regina sweeps Zel protectively behind her.

"Don't you touch her. You've done enough damage."

Zel unzips my purse and pulls out my phone. "We got her cell, too!" she crows.

"Give me Rell's phone," says Ana.

"Why?"

"I want to send text messages to her friends."

"She doesn't have any friends," says Zel, pushing buttons. "Oh, man! Her phone's locked! We can't text from it."

"Let's throw it in the toilet!"

"Yeah!"

"Come back here," I say and move towards the door. Regina blocks me.

"Run along and get ready, dears."

"But we don't want to go to the auction."

"Bor-ring!"

Regina pats their heads. "You're not going to the auction, sillies. That's for grownups. I've arranged for all the good girls to spend the night at the fabulous Princess Party at Disney's Aulani Resort."

"Rell's not a grownup," Zel says.

"She's not a good girl either," snickers Ana. "At the party, I'm going to be Jasmine."

"No, I am!"

"Too late. I called it."

"You're Olaf!"

"Olaf isn't a princess!"

The girls bicker all the way into the house.

They still have my phone!

I better not find it in the toilet.

Regina says, "We need to talk."

I scowl. "I've nothing to say to you."

"Then listen." She steps close, so close I can see the makeup spackled under her eyes. "We can do things the easy way or the hard way. It doesn't matter to me. If you want to keep going to that fancy school, you'll do what I say. Otherwise, I'll cut your funding, and you'll be out on the street."

"Why can't I go to the auction?"

"Because I said so. This deal is bigger than you know. You've proven that you can't handle taking two little girls to the beach. There's no way I'm letting you near something this important."

"Funding a surf camp for disabled people is big? That makes no sense, Regina. What's your angle?"

"No imagination. That's what your father said about you. Rell wears her heart on her sleeve, he said. There's no way she could ever play poker."

"Regina—"

"Get your things. I'll show you to your room. In the morning you can drive yourself to the airport."

Oh, no.

My bag.

In my mind, I clearly see it in the back of Jerry's truck.

She sees the look on my face. Her eyes widen like it's *her* birthday.

"You don't have it?"

"It's—I think I left it in the back of the truck."

"You have no clothes."

"No."

Regina throws her head back and cackles. "No car, no phone, no clothes! How utterly perfect. There's no way for you to go now."

CHAPTER 14

On my way to a tiny room just off the kitchen, I discover the laundry room. After Regina and her entourage leave, I toss my clothes in the washer and take a long, hot shower. With no one else around, I pour myself a glass of guava juice, make a peanut butter sandwich, and scrounge up a bag of chips. Shivering, I take them outside to sit in the twilight while my clothes dry.

Wrapped in a big, fluffy towel, damp hair hanging down my back, I sit on a chaise lounge on the patio and sigh. Even though the sun has gone down, it's far warmer outside than in the house. Regina must have the air conditioning cranked. I could almost see my breath when I got out of the shower.

My dinner sits next to me on a small side table.

I need to eat. That iffy breakfast burrito on the plane was hours ago.

I take a bite of sandwich, but I can't swallow past the lump in my throat.

Accentuate the positive, Rell. Don't let Regina get you down.

Bright side: At least I'll have clean clothes for the plane ride home.

Clean clothes. Big whoop.

I force the down the bite of sandwich and wipe my eyes on a

corner of the towel. Time to suck it up. Only babies cry. Big girls pull up their panties and problem solve.

Even if their panties are still in the dryer.

Identifying the problems is always the first step in dealing with Regina.

Problem one: car keys. I'll search the house. I doubt Regina took them with her.

Problem two: a phone. There's got to be a landline for the house. Find it and call Jerry.

Problem three: I need my purse. It has Jerry's business card.

Problem four: find a phone book or computer. Call the rental company. Somebody there can give me his cell.

Call his work?

Gee, Rell, that's not stalkerish at all.

Oh, Jerry.

What would I even say? Sorry my wicked stepsisters pushed your special rock into the ocean? Hope you were able to get it out?

Unbelievable.

I can't forget the look on his face.

I should've stayed and helped him instead of running away like an idiot.

He's wondering why I'm not at the party.

He probably thinks I'm mad at him or something.

Who am I kidding? He's relieved I'm not there.

I look at my sandwich and soggy chips and wrinkle my nose. I bet they're having dinner now. Luau food like roast pork and fresh pineapple.

Bright side: peanut butter's okay. A little sticky. Filling. The bread's fresh.

Hey, another one: The surf camp will be built. That's a good thing, right?

But it makes no sense. Why would Regina care about a surf camp? There's no margin in it.

Jerry—

Stop it. Just stop it.

A guy like that probably has a girlfriend. The way Luna talked, probably several *friends*.

Cedar, cinnamon, cloves, and wintergreen mints.

The sunlight on his bare shoulders when he took off his shirt.

Should've kissed him when I had the chance.

Just one dance at the party. Is that so much to wish for? It's my birthday, for crying out loud.

I'm not going to cry.

Not going to.

Dang it!

Through the tears, I see a star peeking over the mountain top.

The first star.

No candles on my birthday cake. Heck, no birthday cake! I'm not wasting this chance.

"Starlight, star bright; first star I see tonight; I wish I may; I wish I might; have the wish I wish tonight."

I close my eyes and wish.

"Woof."

I whip open my eyes. In the shadows on the far side of the patio is a yellow dog.

"Ilima?"

She limps towards me until she is standing in a pool of moonlight. I rise from my chair and lean forward, one hand clutching my towel, the other outstretched.

"Hey, girl. What're you doing here? That's a long walk from the beach. How're your ribs?"

She sits and cocks her head at me. Her tongue drops out of her mouth as she pants.

"Thirsty? Be right back."

In the kitchen I fill a bowl full of cool water and bring it out to the patio.

I set it next to her. "Here you go."

She glances at it, then bats it away with her paw.

"You don't want it?"

Her eyes lock like laser beams on my sandwich. She smacks her lips.

"Sandwiches aren't for dogs."

She whines and lies down, resting her head on her paws. Her eyes never leave my sandwich.

"Really? You like peanut butter?"

"Woof!" She sits up, ears forward.

I shrug. "Okay."

I tear off a chunk and toss it to her.

She catches it mid-air and gulps it whole.

"Careful! You keep eating like that and you'll choke."

Her ears droop as her body shakes, quivering in the moonlight. The air fills with the scent of sandalwood and lemons. Sparkles of silver light cascade down her body like glitter as she bows her head. I hear chanting or drums—a rhythmic beating that pulses like ocean waves against the shore. A gust of wind swirls around the patio, blowing the bag of chips to the ground.

"Ilima?"

The high, clear note of a conch shell echoes against the house, a wall of sound so loud I cover my ears.

"Ilima, what's going on?" I shout. "We better get inside."

Her limbs and torso elongate as she rises.

Before me stands a beautiful Hawaiian woman.

"I—I—Ilima?"

"Woof," she says.

I step back and almost trip over my own feet. My heart is pounding. I can't get enough air to breathe, let alone scream.

The woman laughs, and it is the sound of wind chimes and beach glass. "Relax," she says, rolling her shoulders and neck. "I'm just playing with you." She touches her ribs and grimaces. "Although I could've done without the kick in the ribs. What's the matter with those two? Are they retarded?"

Reflexively, I say, "Don't say retarded. People aren't retarded."

She smiles without showing her teeth. "My mistake. It's tough to

64

keep up with your human terms; they change so often. What should I say?"

"Intellectually disabled or differently abled."

This conversation is surreal. I shake my head to clear it, but the woman is still there.

"Are they?"

I blink. "What?"

"Intellectually differently abled?" she says.

"No." I cock my head to the side. "At least I don't think so."

"Ah. Just plain mean, then. Good. That makes this easier." She stares at the rest of the sandwich still in my hand. "You going to finish that?"

"Uh, no. Knock yourself out," I say as I hand it to her.

Her fingers brush mine.

Oh, man. She's *real*.

Ilima the woman takes dainty bites, but finishes the sandwich as fast as a dog.

"Oh, that's better," she says. "Changing form always makes me hungry!" She points to the glass of guava juice. "May I?"

"Be my guest."

Like I'm going to say no.

She drains the drink in one great swallow. "Umm, that's good," she says.

She sees me watching her.

She deliberately raises the glass to her lips.

She raises an eyebrow.

And takes a bite.

Glass crumbles and falls to the ground.

What the?

She chews.

Crunch, crunch, crunch.

She smiles, this time showing her teeth. There are little bits of glass clinging to her lips.

The world starts to dim. There's a buzz, buzz, buzzing in my ears.

This time I really do faint.

CHAPTER 15

$\mathcal{W}$hen I come to, I'm laying on the chaise lounge. Ilima is holding out a glass of water.

"Don't worry. It's a new one from the kitchen. I didn't even lick it."

I sit up too fast. The blood rushes from my head.

Don't faint. Don't faint.

It's all over if I faint.

Ilima puts a hand on her hip and waves the glass near my face.

"Take it. Drink. Trust me. It's all going to be okay. I promise."

The water is cold against my tongue as I gulp it. When it hits my stomach, I feel more awake.

"Better?"

I nod.

"Good." She holds out her hand and pulls me to my feet. The towel starts to fall, but I catch it and wrap it tighter against my chest.

"Jerry, huh?" She circles behind me. "A girl could do a lot worse."

She snorts bitterly. "Many have."

She prods my back.

"Tall, but not too tall. Slender, almost willowy."

She runs her fingers through my hair.

"Good girl," she says with a snicker.

Is she *petting* me?

I bite my lip.

Don't lose it, Rell. Don't laugh.

"Nice hair. You've given me a lot to work with."

"Work how? What're you going to do with me?"

"Give you a birthday present, of course. What did you think was going to happen?"

"I have no idea."

She faces me again. "Look," she says, holding up a mirror.

"Where did—"

But then I see the girl in the mirror, and it doesn't matter where the mirror came from.

"That can't be me!" I say.

Ilima smirks. "Of course it is."

"It can't be."

"How do you know? Have you ever seen the real you?"

It's me, but a me I've never seen before.

I'm wearing a silk floral shift tied over my shoulder. My hair is swept high and to the side with cascading curls. The smell of the gardenias in my hair mixes with the twisted lei of tiny white flowers around my neck.

I reach up to touch them.

"Pikake," she says. "A kind of jasmine. Don't touch or they'll brown."

My makeup is subtle. Just a few sweeps of mascara on my eyelashes, a kiss of blush along my cheekbones, and a light coral lip stain. My skin looks radiant. Dangling from my ears are simple gold drops in the shape of the flowers in my lei. On my feet are thin leather flip flops that show off my newly manicured toes. A glance at my fingers shows the same finishing touch.

Oh, no.

I reach down and run fingers over my shins.

Smooth as a baby's bottom.

Ilima smirks. "Pits, too. I'm guessing your razor is in your bag."

"How—"

"Granted, Jerry probably would have preferred you in the towel, but let's not throw ourselves at him any more that we already have, shall we?"

"Why—"

"So you can go to the party and dance with your beau. That's what you wanted, right?"

I turn sideways in the mirror. "But this—"

"You were expecting a poufy blue dress and impractical heels? Mainlanders," she scoffs. "No sense of style."

"How—"

She lowers the mirror and tsks. "Good grief, child. Speak in complete sentences. I know you can."

She raises the mirror again, holding it in front of me like a wish.

"See? Perfect. Jerry is waiting. You want to go or not?"

I swallow.

"Yes."

"Good."

"But I don't have my car keys—"

A car pulls into the driveway and beeps its horn.

"Gecko," she says. "Much better than your Mini pumpkin coach, even if we had the keys. Come along, Rell. We don't have all night."

As I get in the car, the driver doesn't say a word, just twitches nervously. In the rearview mirror I see that his eyes are slit like a reptile's. He sees me watching and quickly slips on a pair of dark glasses. His fingertips are odd, too big and puffy for his hands. Before I can look further, Ilima pushes the door closed and stands outside the car twiddling a finger at me. I roll down the window.

"Here's the deal: The car and driver will be waiting for you as soon as you step back into the parking lot. No need to call. The driver will only bring you back here, so don't bother trying to get to the airport or some place crazy like that. You kiss that boy, the one you wished on, the car won't come. In fact, if you kiss him, you'll go back to standing in a towel with wet hair dripping down your back. Transitions are funny. The towel may shrink a little, too, so keep that in mind."

I reach through the open window and touch her arm. "Thank you, Ilima. It's a wish come true."

She lifts my hand off her arm and gives it a little squeeze. "I'm not a fairy godmother, Rell. I don't grant wishes; I pay my debts. That's all this is."

"Who are you?"

"Don't look a gift horse in the mouth." She sees the look on my face and softens. "It's your birthday, Rell. Go have fun."

CHAPTER 16

The tent at Keikikai Beach glows like a candle. As we pull up, I hear live music; guitars and ukuleles strum as a velvety voice caresses a melody filled with Hawaiian vowels. The driver takes me all the way to edge of the red carpet where a perky young man in a blue aloha shirt opens my door and presents me his hand.

"Aloha!" he says. "Do you need parking assistance?"

"Um," I mumble as I exit the car.

"No," croaks the driver.

As soon as I'm standing on the edge of the carpet, the driver hits the gas. The valet barely has time to get the door closed.

"Whoa!" yells the valet. "Where's the fire?" He turns to me. "Are you okay?"

I take a deep breath. "Yes. Thank you."

"That guy's crazy. Do you know him?"

"No. He's a hired driver."

He pulls out a cell phone. "Which company?"

"Gecko."

"Gecko? Never heard of them." He raises an eyebrow. "You sure he's legit?"

I stifle a laugh. "He was provided by my—"

By my *what*? My dog? I shudder. Ilima's not my dog. Definitely not my fairy godmother, either. My gift horse? I bite my lip to keep from laughing.

The valet's eyebrow goes higher.

I'm taking too long to answer.

I cover my hesitation with a cough.

"Oh, excuse me. Sorry, got a frog in my throat. The driver was sent by my, um, *benefactor*. He came highly recommended."

The valet holds out his phone. "You should report him. There's no excuse for that."

"I will."

Although I don't think a dog who isn't a dog is going to care very much.

The valet wiggles his phone.

Oh, no. He's still waiting for me to make the call.

"But thanks. I'll call later," I say. "No need to spoil the evening."

He slips his phone back into his pocket and holds out a hand. "Your invitation, miss?"

Invitation?

Crap.

I'm not carrying a purse. I run my hands down my sides, but the shift has no pockets. I hold out my empty hands, give a weak smile, and shrug.

His eyes do a quick sweep from head to toe, assessing. He must like what he sees, because he smiles and says, "It's okay. Just tell me your name so I can have it announced."

Double crap!

"That's not necessary," I stammer. I try to step past him, but he takes a step sideways, forcing me to stay on the edge of the red carpet.

"I know it sounds silly, but it's an old-fashioned tradition the organizers are insisting on."

This is the last thing I need.

"I don't want to bother everyone," I say. "After all, I'm late. The event has already started."

"It's not a bother. Look, other people are waiting to be announced."

I peek around him and see a short queue of guests lined up at the top of the red carpet. At the archway leading into the tent stands a seven foot mountain of a man in silver brocade livery. Two teenage boys in loincloths block the doorway with crossed wooden staffs topped with white cloth balls.

At the giant's nod, a couple hands a gilt-edged card to him. He regards it for a second, then nods again. The couple steps forward, the staffs are uncrossed and whisked aside, and another man in a loin-cloth and a short feathered cape softly blows on a conch shell. As the echo dies, the giant announces the couple's names and ushers them in. Once the couple enters the tent, the wooden staffs are crossed again, and the whole thing starts over.

I sigh.

Only Regina would insist on something so pompous and ridiculous.

Inside the tent, nobody seems to be paying much attention to the guests' arrivals. The music doesn't pause, and I can see people talking as they wander between the tables filled with auction items.

Maybe it's no big deal. Even if he announces me, it's unlikely Regina will hear it.

"Your name, miss," the valet prods. "Tell me quick, and it will be over before you know it."

Fine. Here goes nothing.

"I'm Rell," I say. "Rell Watanabe."

The valet jumps back. "Rell Watanabe! I'm so sorry, Ms. Watanabe! Your driver should've brought you to the special VIP entrance! Let's get you right to the front!"

He gestures frantically to the giant. VIP, he mouths. BIG TIME!

The giant looks startled, but bows to the couple next in line, executes a snazzy military turn, and starts toward me.

I want to die.

My cover's blown before I can even get into the party.

I look at my feet still on the edge of the red carpet. Should step back onto the parking lot? How long will it take for the car to return and whisk me away?

I lift a foot and hold it over the pavement as I scan the parking lot. I spot the Gecko car barreling towards me. While I can't see his eyes through his dark sunglasses, I can feel his lizard's gaze lock onto my foot, the heel of my flip-flop perilously close to touching the road.

Go or stay?

One shot, one dance. That was my wish.

I risk looking back. The giant is almost to me when another man sidles next to him.

"It's okay, Moki," he says. "The lady is with me."

The mountain pauses mid-stride. "You sure, Jerry?"

"I got this. Thanks, guys," Jerry says and holds out his arm.

The valet nods and moves to the next car at the curb.

When I slip my hand into the crook of Jerry's elbow, he tucks it tight. From the corner of my eye, I see the Gecko car swerve away.

"Okeydokey," says the mountain. His eyes widen when they meet mine. "Wow, laulau, Jerry. She's cherry like a '57 Chevy. You're a lucky man."

He snaps off a salute. "Ma'am."

One complicated three-step about-face and he's striding back to the archway.

I feel the laughter Jerry's fighting to stifle as it rumbles in his chest. He turns and leads me away from the red carpet.

"Cherry like a '57 Chevy?" I say. "Really?"

He shoots me a look. "It's a compliment."

"Cherry like a classic car?"

"Moki works in a body shop straightening fenders all day. To him, something particularly fine is cherry." Jerry takes my hand off his elbow and twirls me around, giving a low whistle.

A potted hibiscus lining the walkway twitches.

I snatch my hand away. "Women are not dogs to be whistled at."

Ilima pops into my head.

Maybe some of us are.

Can't think about that now.

Jerry cocks his head to the side, a slow smile pulling at his lips.

"Moki's right. You look cherry—like you stepped out of an ad from the 1960s."

"You and that wolf-whistle belong in the '60s."

"This is Lauele. Sometimes there's not much difference."

"Cherry and Jerry, sitting in a tree, k-i-s-s—" sings a voice from the behind the potted plant.

"Knock it off, Luna!" I hiss.

"What?" Jerry asks.

"Nothing," I say.

I hear Luna giggle as his footsteps retreat.

CHAPTER 17

*J*erry leads me around the back of the tent to the area near the makeshift kitchen. There's an open doorway, and we pass through it and into the main tent. As I look around, I realize we're standing behind the stage.

Wires and cables run everywhere. Off to the side is an audio mixing board and monitors, the dials bouncing to the rhythm of the band playing on stage. Standing behind the loudspeakers that are pointed toward the crowd, it's surprisingly quiet backstage.

Jerry says, "Don't worry. This is one of the servers' entrances. You really didn't want to be announced, did you?"

I shake my head. "My stepmonster didn't want me here tonight."

"No! Not want you? Impossible." He clutches my hand to his chest like a B movie hero.

My heart leaps.

Chill out, Rell. He's joking.

Ilima's right. I can't make this too easy.

I pull away.

"You mean the boxes at the airport weren't a big enough clue that I'm not the favorite daughter?"

"They did make me wonder."

A waiter with a loaded tray rushes through the door. "Excuse me," he says. "Pupus coming through!"

"Oh, sorry," I say and step aside.

The waiter rolls his eyes at me. "The party's on the other side of the stage, people. This area is for staff only. If you love birds want a little privacy, head to the beach."

"Lighten up, Renten," Jerry says. "No act."

Renten sniffs. "Some of us are working, Jerry. Don't you have cars to park?"

Jerry stamps his foot and fakes a charge. Renten squeals and quickly rounds the stage.

"Yeah, that's what I thought," Jerry calls.

Cedar, cinnamon, cloves, and wintergreen mints.

I lace my fingers so I can't reach out and run my fingers through his hair.

Do I really need the car to bring me back to Poliahu's? Maybe walking home wouldn't be so bad.

Maybe I don't have to go back there at all.

I glance at my dress. I'm on borrowed time.

But how short could that towel be?

Naked and in public, Rell. Keep that in mind. Do not kiss him!

When Jerry turns to me, his wide grin fades when he sees the look on my face.

Awesome!

I probably have crazy stalker woman tattooed on my forehead.

"Rell—"

"I'm sorry, Jerry." The words rush out like a train wreck.

He purses his lips. "You say that a lot."

He's got great lips. Soft and pillowy and firm like—

"Rell?"

"What? Oh. Sorry."

"Stop saying that. I'm the one who's sorry about how I behaved at Piko Point."

I look down, confused.

Piko Point?

He tips my chin up. "You don't have anything to apologize for."

He's talking about the rock.

This conversation is going to suck.

I take a breath.

"No, I do. I was supposed to be watching Ana and Zel. I'm responsible for the disrespectful and disgraceful way they pushed—"

He places a finger against my lips. Warmth spreads like butterscotch from the pit of my stomach to the ends of my toes.

"Shhhhh. I was there, too," he whispers. "It's not your fault."

"But the rock?"

"I got it back where it belongs. I actually think Pohaku enjoyed the swim."

He brushes a strand of hair from my cheek. My knees go weak. Those lips look so soft.

"...Ilima?" he asks.

Crap. I missed something.

"Ilima the dog?" I say.

It's his turn to look confused. "Yeah, the yellow dog at Piko Point. I haven't seen her. That sister of yours—"

"—stepsister—" I say.

"—Ana—" he says.

"—Zel—" I say.

"—whatever. One of those demons kicked Ilima really hard. I went to check on her later, but I couldn't find her. Uncle Kahana says she's missing. Have you seen her?"

"Uh, no," I say, eyes wide and face blank.

I should get an Oscar.

On stage, the song ends. The room applauds. Someone calls, "Hana hou! Hana hou!"

I raise an eyebrow at Jerry.

"It means they want more."

The singer says, "Ah, mahalo plenny, everyone. On behalf of Uncle Tiko, Uncle Butchie, and the rest of the band, I want to thank Get Wet Prosthetics for having us here tonight."

"Hana hou, Tuna! Hana hou!"

The singer turns to the band. "You guys wanna do one more?"

"Shoots," says the bass player. "Let's do *Ahe Lau Makani*."

Back into the microphone, Tuna says, "One last song. Everybody out on the dance floor. Shake some loose change out of your pockets for the surf camp. Uncle Butchie, take us home."

The lead guitarist counts off. "One-two-three, one-two-three." The band swings into the intro.

"Is that a waltz?"

"Yeah," says Jerry.

"That's going to get everyone dancing? Not *YMCA* or *Boot Skootin' Boogie* or—"

"This is Lauele, remember?"

Through a seam in the backdrop, I see people grab partners and head to the area in front of the stage. Young, old, and everyone in between shuffle in modified boxed-steps.

In the soft glow of lantern light, it's magical.

Jerry takes my hand, the challenge clear in his eyes.

"No way. You waltz?" I say.

He puts his left hand on my waist. "Don't worry. I'll be gentle."

"Ha!" I put a hand on his shoulder. "Try to keep up."

We sway for a couple of beats, then his palm gently presses me backward and we're off. He leads me in a few simple steps, and I follow with ease.

"You've done this before," he says.

"Six years of dance lessons."

"I thought you went to a fancy all-girls school."

"Yep. That means I can lead, too. Need a few pointers?"

He pulls me closer. "Oh, no, babe. We're just getting started."

He lengthens his stride, and we glide and swoop, my heart pounding one-two-three, one-two-three. He spins me in double-time, and I keep my eyes glued to his face, the one thing in sharp focus as the rest of the world whirls by. He pulls me tighter to his chest. I inhale cedar, cinnamon, cloves, and wintergreen mints.

One-two-three, one-two-three.

Ocean waves. Sand between my toes. Sunlight and tradewinds caressing my hair.

One-two-three, one-two-three.

Stepping over tide pools at Piko Point. Yellow tangs and snowflake eels. Feathery corals and translucent fins.

One-two-three, one-two-three.

As the song reaches the chorus, he signals for a dip.

One-two—

CRASH.

We tumble to the floor, the strands of my lei tangling between us.

CHAPTER 18

"Rell! Are you okay?"

I feel a tug on my foot. I try to lift my leg, but my flip-flop is caught on a cable. As I kick it off, I realize my dress is riding high on my thighs. I quickly sit up and tug the hem down.

"Oh, yeah," I mutter. "This is much more practical than high-heels and poufy skirts. Bloody Ilima!"

"Ilima? She's here?"

"No, she didn't get in the Gecko car with me."

"Rell, look at me. I need to check your eyes. Did you hit your head?"

"No. Just injured my pride." I gather my flip-flop and slip it back on. "Are you okay?"

He rolls to his side and props his head in his hand. "It feels like the scrape on my knee might be bleeding again."

"Oh, Jerry! I'm—"

He shakes his head. "Nope. You're not allowed to say that anymore. The tragedies of the world aren't your fault."

"Tragedies of the world?" I grin.

He sits up and bumps my shoulder with his. "I meant comedies of the world. If it makes you feel better, you can take the blame for the trip. See you next fall."

"But you were leading!"

"I accept your apology," he says.

I punch his shoulder.

"Abuse! Abuse!"

"Right."

He laughs and wiggles his fingers menacingly. "Tickle retaliation!"

"Don't you dare—"

"Here's your mic, Ms. Watanabe."

Three people enter backstage and stand by the audio board.

"Call me Regina," says my stepmonster. "Like Cher or Beyoncé."

"Oh, like in that movie—"

"I have no idea what you're talking about," she says in a voice icicle cool. "There's only one Regina."

Regina?

"Eep!" I squeak and dive under the stage. Jerry hesitates for a split second, then slides next to me.

"They can't see us," he whispers.

I'm too afraid to do more than nod.

Regina and Mr. Lucius stand near the stage stairs. An audio tech fiddles with Regina's mic. At the audio board he says, "Can you give me a little test?"

Regina says, "Test one, two, three."

Mr. Lucius says, "Eeney, meenie, miny, mo."

The audio tech watches the dials and frowns. "Mr. Lucius, could you repeat that please?"

"Catch a tiger by the toe."

The audio tech pats his pockets and looks around. "Your battery is low. I'm going to have to get a new one from the truck. Be right back."

As he disappears outside, Regina puts her hand on her hip. "The incompetence of these islanders is stunning."

I feel Jerry bristle.

Sorry, Jerry. My stepmonster's a jerk.

"A few more hours," Mr. Lucius says, "and it will all be over. Once the deal's done, you don't have to stay on this rock."

Regina lowers her voice. "The bribe worked?"

"There are no bribes, Regina. Only meaningful campaign contributions."

Jerry and I exchange a glance. He pulls his phone out of his pocket and hits record.

"And was our contribution meaningful?"

"Very. Once the permits for the surf camp's access road and utilities are filed with the county, the planning commission will be forced to approve our development behind it. It's just a matter of paying the filing fees. We're prepared to cover whatever doesn't get raised tonight."

From her purse, Regina pulls out some lipstick and starts smearing it along her lips. "Don't be too hasty, Lucius. Let them sweat and be grateful when we save their project. Public gratitude now will make it impossible for anyone to believe they didn't know about the eighty story high-rise we're building on the property behind them."

Jerry sucks in his breath so fast, I'm afraid they'll hear us. He holds the phone closer to them.

Mr. Lucius says, "Marketing is ready to go. Did you see the mock-ups of the sales campaign? We're positioning it locally as bringing jobs and technology to a blighted economy."

"Technology? That sounds expensive," says Regina.

"We're donating a few computers and upgrading the internet connection to the high school. That's it."

"Because we care," Regina says.

"Of course."

I want to smack the smirk right off his face.

"In the Euro and Asian markets we're positioning the development as the perfect island escape—a real life Bali Hai. We've already shot the beauty scenes of the beaches for the media campaigns." He sighs. "But have you thought this through, Regina? Do you really want an ugly, low budget surf camp of cripples to be the first thing your clients see?"

Regina laughs, and it's the sound of nails on a chalkboard and the last wormy apple as it falls off a tree.

"You're funny, Lucius. The camp is never going to be built. With my development, taxes and land values are going sky high. My analysist predicts that most of the land will be in foreclosure in less than five years. I'm going to own all of Lauele."

"I still don't understand, Regina. Other than the beach, there's nothing here. The only store or restaurant for miles is Hari's."

She puts away her lipstick and rubs her lips together. Her mouth is shiny and red, like she's chewing glass.

"The first thing I'm going to do is knock down that ugly convenience store across the street and build a nice, modern natural foods kind of place."

"The lot's too small. You won't have parking."

"We'll raze the beach pavilion and expand the parking lot on this side. Once everything's private, there won't be a need for public works anymore."

Mr. Lucius holds up his hand. "The beach laws are ridiculous in Hawaii, Regina. You have to allow public access—even through private land."

"People won't come if the entire area's gated. We'll keep the riffraff out. Even the beaches will belong to the Bali Hai tenants."

"I don't think we can make that—"

"You can and you will. Increase our campaign contributions if necessary," she snaps.

Waving a black box and cord, the audio tech slips through the doorway. "Got a whole new set-up right here, Mr. Lucius."

"About time," mutters Regina.

The audio tech replaces Mr. Lucius's mic and pack.

"Let's test again," he says.

"If he hollers, let him go," Mr. Lucius says.

"Perfect." He places the old set next to the audio board. "Regina? Can you give me one last check?"

"Eeney, meenie, miny, mo."

CHAPTER 19

*A*bove us, the waltz fades. As the applause dies, the band scurries down the stairs and exits backstage. Tuna's voice says, "Mahalo, gang. Before we get started with the auction, Uncle Kahana wants me to introduce someone who has become dear to our hearts: Regina Watanabe. Aunty Regina!"

"Aunty Regina?" Regina hisses. "Cow, I'm not related to you. These people!"

"Mic-ay on-ay," whispers Mr. Lucius. "Smile!"

Regina's fake smile doesn't reach her eyes.

Maybe it's not Botox.

As Tuna exits stage right, Regina and Mr. Lucius climb the stairs and enter stage left. The audience is still applauding when Tuna stops backstage and bends down.

"Howzit, Jerry," she says.

"Hey, Tuna," he says. "This is Rell."

"Aloha, Rell. I like your lei. Don't stay under the stage too long. Get plenny spiders. Laters, gangies." She waves with just her thumb and pinky outstretched as she heads outside.

I turn to Jerry, eyes wide in the darkness. "How—"

He shrugs. "It's Tuna. We used to call her Tunazilla when we were kids. Voice of an angel, body of a linebacker. She just knows things."

Above us, Regina begins speaking.

"As you know, Watanabe Global has deep roots in this community. From the first moment I heard about the International Abilities Surf Tournament and its goal of expanding into a surf camp, I knew this project was exactly aligned with everything Watanabe Global stands for. Its value is immeasurable—"

"My father would never have torn down a community for money," I say. "She's going to ruin Lauele."

"There won't be a Lauele," Jerry says.

"This is my community, too. I've got to stop her."

"Rell—"

I grab Jerry's cell phone, crawl out from under the stage, pick up the abandoned mic set, and switch it on. There's enough juice in the batteries to make the needles bounce.

Suck it, Regina!

I hold the mic next to Jerry's phone and press play.

Nothing.

I press again.

Nothing.

I look closer.

Locked!

"Jerry, what's your password?"

"Ua mau ke ea o ka 'aina i ka pono."

"What?"

"Just hand me my phone."

Jerry stands next to me, flicking his fingers over his phone screen.

"Ready," he says.

"Let's do this!"

The file starts to play, but nobody can hear it over the loud-speakers.

"The battery's too weak," Jerry says. "Cut the other mics and boost it through the board."

I pull down the audio faders for Regina and Mr. Lucius's mics, cutting her off mid-sentence.

This is for you, Mama.

For you and our ohana.

I twist a dial and bring up the volume on the mic I'm holding above the cell phone.

"Is this better?" my voice booms over the loudspeakers.

"Rell?" shouts Regina from the stage.

Over the speakers Regina's voice says, "The camp is never going to be built. With my development, taxes and land values are going sky high. My analyst predicts that most of the land will be in foreclosure in less than five years. I'm going to own all of Lauele."

Chaos.

The audio tech comes flying backstage. "What are you guys doing?" he shouts. "Get away from that equipment!"

Jerry steps in front me. "Just listen, Darin! The whole thing is a scam."

"Jerry—"

"LISTEN!"

Darin pauses.

Regina's voice says, "We'll keep the riffraff out. Even the beaches will belong to the Bali Hai tenants,"

Darin mouth drops. "Oh my—"

"Stop this immediately!" shrieks Regina. Her lipstick's smeared in a long red streak across her chin. Her hands go to her hair. "I demand that you give that illegal recording—"

"Fake illegal recording," shouts Mr. Lucius. "This is a fraudulent attempt to malign my client!"

Darin stands next to Jerry, blocking access to the cell phone.

"Play that again, Jerry," he says. "I wanna know which politician we're impeaching."

Regina spots me cowering behind the guys.

"This is all your fault, Rell! When I get through with you—"

I turn and flee.

CHAPTER 20

*M*y foot barely touches parking lot before the Gecko car screeches up. The valet runs up, but I'm faster. I fling open the door and jump into the backseat.

"Rell!" shouts the valet, "Is it true? Is Watanabe Global planning to build a huge—"

"Yes!" I say. "Sorry!"

I slam the door shut.

"Hit it!"

The driver snaps my head back as he accelerates out of the parking lot, smoke billowing behind.

The whole way to the house, I shake.

I stare out the windows at the empty beaches and modest homes that line the main road. The moon shines over the ocean, the light reflecting off coconut trees and hibiscus hedges as we speed by. I burn each image into my brain, trying to create a lifetime of memories in just a few minutes.

I can never come back.

None of this is real. It's all a giant chess match to get a high-rise development approved in Lauele. My father's company is planning to turn sleepy Lauele into an exclusive version of Waikiki. Regina never planned to support the surf camp. She just wanted the infrastructure permits approved so she could build her high-rise condominiums.

They must hate us.

I hate us.

Even if Jerry convinces people that I had nothing to do with it, there's no way I can show my face around here again.

Goodbye, Jerry.

It's probably best we never kissed.

The driver doesn't bother pulling into the driveway. He just whips up next to the gate and slams on the brakes. The locks on the back-doors pop open when I touch the door handle.

"Thanks," I say as I swing my legs and step outside. "I appreciate—"

SLAM!

The door rips out of my hand as the car takes off like a cockroach when the kitchen light comes on.

"Hey!" I'm so angry, I step out of my flip-flops and fling them after the car.

They miss by a mile.

Story of my life.

"Happy eighteenth birthday to me. It's all downhill from here."

CHAPTER 21

*A*ll the lights are on in the house. It should be cheery and bright, but it feels cold and sterile. I shut the front door and blow on the decorative glass pane set in the middle. Mist coalesces, the patterns as delicate as a snowflake.

That's frost, I swear.

Inside the house is the faint scent of smoke. As I walk through the entry, I hear wood crackle and snap. I follow the sounds to the dining room and discover a roaring fire in the fireplace. Two white wingback chairs flank the fire on either side. Between them is a small table overflowing with a coffee service and trays. Ilima the woman is sitting in the chair to the right, a teacup and saucer balanced in her lap.

"Back so soon?" she says. "He must've not been a very good dancer."

"Can you get me to the airport?"

She takes a sip from her cup and watches me over the rim. "Where are your shoes?"

"Really? That's what you're concerned about?"

She shifts and curls her feet beneath her. "Come sit by the fire. Poliahu loves the cold, but she's mindful of the comfort of her guests."

She gestures to the coffee service. "There are cookies, cake, sandwiches. Have a bite of something. Your blood sugar's low."

"How would you know?"

"Your smell."

"That's ridiculous."

She shrugs. "It's true. You haven't eaten a meal in hours. Your body tells me it's hungry by the sickly-sweet smell that's coming off you in waves."

"It's probably the flowers you're smelling."

"Nope. It's you. I've learned a lot about humans living with Kahana."

"You and Uncle Kahana?"

"Get your mind out of the gutter. It's not like that." She takes another sip, her eyes never leaving me. "Sit," she says. "You're making me nervous."

When I sit down, she hands me a plate of cookies and a teacup. "Lilikoi biscuits. I think you call them passion fruit cookies. Hold out your cup, and I'll pour."

"That's okay. I don't like tea or coffee," I say.

"Good, because this is hot chocolate." When she tips the pot, the chocolate pours out as rich and thick as molten lava. She fills my cup only halfway. "So you can dunk," she says.

"What—"

"Uh-uh. No talk. Eat."

I'm too tired and hungry to argue.

The cookie is crisp like shortbread with a thin layer of passion fruit jam on the top. I dunk one into the hot chocolate, and it clings to the cookie like a hug.

I gently blow, then bite.

Ohhhhh," I moan. "I forgive you everything."

She grins like the Cheshire cat drinking cream. "Eat, child. We'll talk later."

I'm not sure how long I sit there, but when I'm done, the platters are empty. Little pies filled with coconut pudding, rolled pastries filled with cream and candied pineapple, tiny sandwiches filled with watercress and cucumber—I eat them all.

"More?" Ilima says.

"I couldn't."

She wrinkles her nose. "Well, at least you don't stink of hunger anymore." Setting her cup down, she sits forward and leans close.

"Bali Hai," she says. "The name isn't even Hawaiian."

"I didn't know about the development."

"But now you do." Ilima leans back in her chair. "Regina's bringing modern jobs and prosperity to backward Lauele."

"No, she's not."

"Are you sure? You're Rell Watanabe of Watanabe Global."

"My mother was a Ha'awina. This is my ohana."

Ilima's eyes narrow. "Ohana is an easy word to say when you'll get on a plane tomorrow."

I rock back in my chair. Ilima's words sting as harshly as if she'd slapped me.

Oh, come on! What am I supposed to do?

"I'm only eighteen!"

She picks up her cup and takes a sip. "Yes, you're not a child any longer," she says.

"You mean I'm responsible?"

"When you claim the privileges of ohana, you also accept the responsibilities."

Jerry's words pop into my head.

"No one goes hungry," I say. "That's what you're getting at?"

Ilima smiles.

"Jobs feed people. You think the jobs are important. You think what I did tonight to stop the development was wrong."

Ilima takes another sip, her eyes never leaving my face.

I take a deep breath.

"I know you're powerful. You can probably turn me into a frog or something. But I don't agree. Jobs are not more important than people. There is more to life than money. Regina may still find a way to build her high-rise, but I'm going to do everything I can to make sure it's not on my mother's land in Lauele."

Ilima's eyes crinkle. "A frog? Is that how you see yourself?"

"I...no," I say.

"Say ribbit."

"No!"

Ilima's mouth quirks. "C'mon. I want to hear you say ribbit."

"I'm not going to say it."

"Why?"

"Because I'm not a frog!"

"Because you're not a frog. I wonder, Rell, if I held up a mirror in the moonlight now, would you recognize the real you?"

Seriously?

We're back to mirrors and moonlight?

Shoot me now.

Ilima takes one look at my face and bursts into laughter.

"Ah, child. Clearly you're not made for poufy dresses, even if you don't realize that yet."

"Is Bali Hai the reason you did all of this?"

"Oh, no. That's merely a bonus."

Bonus?

The fire crackles. Ilima reaches out with the poker and pushes a log deeper into the flames.

"That's better. Nice and hot," she says. "You danced with the boy."

"Yes."

"But you didn't kiss him."

"No."

Her eyes gleam. "Then where are your shoes?"

I take a deep breath. "Out in the middle of the street."

"Why?"

"I threw them at the car."

"Why?"

"Because the driver almost ran me over when I was getting out."

Ilima sits back and bites her lip. "You left my birthday gifts in the street?"

I rise. "I'm sorry. That was thoughtless. You've been very kind to me. I'll go get them now."

She crosses her legs and rests her head against the chair. "There's no need," she says, "since you've shown me you've no use for my gifts."

I flinch as wet hair tumbles down my back. In my hands is a washcloth. One side of my body is warm from the fireplace, the other is freezing.

Freezing because I'm naked.

I flip the washcloth, pulling it this way and that, trying to cover all of my bits and pieces, but it's no use.

Ilima rolls her eyes. "Modern humans are so uptight. You would've thanked me if you'd kissed him."

I step behind my chair. "Where are my clothes?"

"Where did you leave them?"

"In the dryer."

"Then that's where you should check."

I spin around and head to the laundry room.

Bloody, bloody dog!

As I put on my clothes, I hear her chuckling. Yanking my shirt over my head, I storm back into the dining room.

"You think this is funny?"

"Are you mad because I didn't fold and iron your clothes?" She sniffs. "I'm not your maid."

"Or my fairy godmother. You said that. Who are you? Why are you doing this to me?"

Ilima stands. In the flickering of the firelight, she grows, filling the space around her until her head brushes the ceiling. "I do things to achieve my own purposes," she says. "I pay my debts and collect those owed to me. This night isn't over."

CHAPTER 22

$\mathcal{T}$he front door swings open with a force that shatters the glass pane in the center.

"RELL! You will come here this instant!"

The last word is a hiss no human can make.

I have just enough time to see Ilima shrink back into a dog and curl up beneath a chair before my stepmonster stalks into the room.

"Traitor!" she shrieks. "After all I've done for you. I paid for your schooling, your room and board, and the clothes on your back!" She grabs a vase from the sideboard and throws it at me. I duck, and it shatters against mantel. "No more! Do you hear me? No more!"

I square my shoulders and pull my head high. With nothing left to lose, she has no power over me.

"Go back to the hell you crawled from, Regina! I don't need you or your money."

"Oh, no? Your fancy school has been cancelled. You have nowhere to go."

"I can stay with the headmaster and his family. I've done it before during the holidays. They won't mind. I can stay with then until I get a job and can pay my own way."

Regina cackles. "You think you stayed with the headmaster's

family because they liked you? No, Rell. I paid them to take you in. They don't care about you. You're just a paycheck to them."

"I don't believe you. When I fly home—"

"You won't."

"What?"

Regina grins and my blood chills. She wags her manicured finger at me and speaks so softly I can barely hear her. "You're not going back to school, Rell. You're not well. After the way you treated your sisters today and the lies you told at the auction, well, it's obvious you're a very troubled girl. I have a very special place in mind, a place that will heal your damaged mind. It's a lockdown facility in Taiwan. We'll reassess after the second or third round of electric shock therapy, but the doctors are very keen on some new brain surgery techniques they'd like to try out."

My mouth goes dry.

"You wouldn't."

She crosses her arms. "I already have."

"You can't."

"I can. I did."

Her phone beeps, and she glances at the text message.

"The medical crew is on its way. I just received confirmation of straight jacket restraints and meds to make you compliant. See for yourself."

She holds out the phone, but when I move to take it, she yanks it away.

"You really think I'd give you my phone? That's your problem, Rell. You think everyone is as stupid as you."

"No. She thinks everyone is as kind as she is," says Uncle Kahana from the doorway. He steps to the side. "Watch out, Avery. There's glass on the floor here."

Mr. Me'e walks into the room, a folded paper in his hands. "Hello, Rell. Remember me?" he says.

I nod.

"What are you doing here? You work for me!" Regina says.

"I quit."

"You can't quit. I have your firm on retainer. Nobody treats me like this." She punches buttons on her cell phone. "I'm calling Lucius right now."

"Knock yourself out," Mr. Me'e says.

"And I'm calling the police! You are all trespassing!" Regina flounces to the other side of the room. "Lucius? I need you immediately!"

Uncle Kahana says, "Is she always like this?"

Mr. Me'e nods.

"I think the surf camp dodged a bullet."

Ilima thumps her tail.

"Ilima! I've been looking for you everywhere!"

Ilima chuffs.

"Fine," says Uncle Kahana. "We'll talk about it later."

Mr. Me'e hands me the paper. I unfold it. It's the paper I signed in this very room so many lifetimes ago.

"Rell, I didn't make copies of this document like Regina and Mr. Lucius wanted. That's the original. You have no idea what you signed, do you?"

"Something that allows Regina to pay for my schooling. If I don't sign these papers every year, she can't pay my tuition. I don't earn enough cleaning the school kitchen to pay for more than half my board."

Mr. Me'e sighs. "That's what I was afraid of. Rell, those papers you signed every year were your consent—your permission—for Regina to continue to act as your legal guardian."

"Isn't that what I said?"

"No." He turned to Uncle Kahana. "It's as I suspected. She really doesn't understand."

Uncle Kahana comes to me and kneels at my feet. He takes my hands in his and looks me in the eye.

"Rell, when you signed those papers every year, you told the courts that you wanted Regina to be in charge of you and your estate. Your father set his will up so you could choose. Regina was not your guardian until you chose her."

In an instant, I'm twelve years old. Daddy is dead. The house is full of somber people wearing black. Regina and Mr. Lucius take me into Daddy's office. Regina hands me a brochure with pictures of horses and smiling girls.

"Wouldn't you rather be there? Look at this school."

I can't think. The black lace on my dress is itchy, and my shoes pinch.

Mr. Lucius says, "All you need to do is sign right here, Rell. You can be there tomorrow."

I pick up the pen and scrawl my name.

I blink back the tears. "All these years I could've had another guardian? But no one wanted me!"

Mr. Me'e says, "That's not true, Rell. Lots of your father's friends and family wanted you. Your mother's family, too. Before anyone had a chance to talk with you, you disappeared. When people pushed, Mr. Lucius just showed them the paper you signed naming Regina your guardian. Regina forbade anyone from contacting you at school."

"Rell, lots of people have been waiting for this day," Uncle Kahana says. "Do you know why?" I shake my head. "Today you turned eighteen. You no longer need a guardian. Anyone who wants to contact you can."

I can't breathe.

Mr. Me'e nods. "I have a stack of birthday cards in my car dating back to when you turned thirteen." He looks down. "But I didn't given them to you because you signed that paper today giving Regina power of attorney over you and your estate."

"This paper makes her the boss of me?"

"Yes. And your estate."

My head is spinning. It's too hot near the fire.

"You said my estate. What's my estate? Money? Did Daddy leave me enough to finish school? Is there enough for me to go to college?"

Mr. Me'e and Uncle Kahana exchange a look.

"Rell," says Uncle Kahana, "your estate is Watanabe Global."

Mr. Me'e nods. "You control the whole thing."

CHAPTER 23

*S*irens wail in the distance, getting closer as they climb the
mountain. It's either the police coming to arrest Uncle
Kahana and Mr. Meʻe or the Taiwanese doctors with straightjackets
and needles coming to take me away.

Before I can say anything, Regina rushes back across the room,
waving her cell phone at me.

"I hope you're satisfied. Lucius is filing so many charges against all
of you, you won't see daylight for a century."

"You planned to steal my mother's land and build high-rise condos
on it. You were going to raise the taxes so high, people would beg you
to buy them out for pennies on the dollar," I say.

"Rell—" Regina says.

"You were never going to build the surf camp," I say. "You just
wanted the permits. But the joke's on you, Regina. Because of what
you said tonight, the auction was never held. Without the auction,
there aren't any funds to pay the fees."

"You see what I mean, gentlemen? Rell is delusional. She thinks
there's a big conspiracy. The truth is, as a show of good faith,
Watanabe Global just paid the fees for the surf camp's permits. Everything is in order."

"Not quite." I stand and hold out the paper. "Do you see this, Regina? It's the paper I signed this afternoon. It's the only copy."

Regina lunges at me.

I yank the paper away.

"Did you really think I'd let you touch it? That's your problem, Regina. You think everyone is as evil as you."

I wad up the paper and toss it into the fire.

"NOOOO!" Regina screams, pushing me aside and plunging her hands into the flames.

"Grrrr," growls Ilima as she shoots out from under the chair and chomps down on Regina's arm.

Regina screams and pulls her charred hands out of the flames.

Uncle Kahana grabs a bowl filled with floating gardenias and dumps the water over Regina's hands. Regina falls to her knees, sobbing. Ilima retreats under the table, spitting and rubbing her tongue along the carpet.

All of this goes on, but I never take my eyes off the charring ball of paper until there is nothing left but ashes.

CHAPTER 24

I'm sitting on Poliahu's front steps when Jerry walks up and sets my bag down beside me.

"Thanks," I say.

"I was going to give you your bag earlier, but you left in such a hurry."

He tosses a pair of flip-flops at my bare feet.

"I found these out in the road. I think they belong to you."

As I bend to put them on, he kneels at my feet.

"Let me." He cups my heel in his hand and slips the strap between my toes. "Perfect fit. They must be yours."

"Because they wouldn't fit anyone else?"

He laughs. "Don't be silly. Slippahs fit everybody. That's why they're the official non-shoe of Hawaii." He nudges my leg. "Scoot over."

I slide over so he can sit next to me, and we watch as the EMTs load Regina into the ambulance.

Bright side: they got to use some of the sedatives she ordered for me.

Waste not, want not.

"Where are the twins?" Jerry asks.

"Aulani. They're enjoying a Disney Princess Sleepover Party. I'll pick them up tomorrow."

"What're you going to tell them?"

I sigh. "I don't know. That's tomorrow's problem."

"You're staying here alone?"

I shake my head. "No. Once Regina's on her way to the hospital, Mr. Meʻe is taking me to a hotel in Waikiki."

"Or you can stay with me."

I look at him.

"I mean, with my family. My mom said to ask you. She's worried."

"Ohana," I say.

"Of course."

"Calabash."

Jerry puts his arm around my shoulders. "Calabash," he says.

Uncle Kahana comes over and pecks me on the cheek. "Happy birthday, Rell."

"Thanks."

"I'll see you tomorrow. Come on, Ilima. Let's go home."

Ilima rises slowly from the lawn, limping a little.

"Hey, what happened to you?" Uncle Kahana says.

She chuffs and jumps into his car.

"Kicked in the ribs?" Uncle Kahana says. "Who?"

Ilima sits up on the front seat and locks eyes with me through the windshield.

I pay my debts and collect those owed to me.

I shiver.

I'm never getting on her bad side.

"Cold?" says Jerry, pulling me closer.

I bury my nose in his shirt.

Cedar, cinnamon, cloves, and wintergreen mints.

"Rell?"

I raise my chin and capture his lips. At first, they're soft with surprise, but firm enthusiastically as our kiss deepens.

Cedar, cinnamon, cloves, and wintergreen mints.

And something a whole lot more.

He breaks the kiss and takes a deep breath. I snuggle back down, and he rests his chin on my head.

"I know who I am," I say.

"Oh? Is this a game? Am I supposed to guess?"

"I'm Rell Watanabe."

"Nice to meet you, Rell. I'm Jerry."

"And I know what I want."

I feel him hold his breath.

"I'm afraid to ask," he says.

I sit up and look him in the eye.

"I want to build a surf camp."

THE END

ABOUT THE AUTHOR

LEHUA PARKER is the author of the MG/YA magical realism series, The Niuhi Shark Saga, and other companion stories set in the fictional town of Lauele, Hawaii. In addition to the series, she publishes short stories, poetry, plays, and essays in magazines and anthologies, often under a different pen name.

One Boy, No Water; Book One of The Niuhi Shark Saga; was nominated for 2017 Nene Award by the children of Hawaii. Other titles in the series include *One Shark, No Swim; One Truth, No Lie;* and *Birth: Zader's Story.* The Niuhi Shark Saga tells the story of two Hawaiian brothers—one a surfing star and the other allergic to water. *Rell Goes Hawaiian* brings back many of the characters from the series.

Originally from Hawaii and a graduate of The Kamehameha Schools, Lehua is an author, editor, public speaker, and business consultant. Trained in literary criticism and an advocate of indigenous cultural narratives, she is a frequent speaker at conferences and symposiums. Now living in exile on the mainland, during snowy winters she dreams about the beach.

Aunty Lehua loves to talk story with students and is available for school and classroom visits.

Catch up with her at
   Blog & Website: www.LehuaParker.com

Niuhi Website: www.NiuhiSharkSaga.com

www.LehuaParker.com

facebook.com/LehuaParker
twitter.com/LehuaParker
instagram.com/LehuaParker

SCATTERED CINDERS

ANGELA CORBETT

SCATTERED CINDERS

Urban Fantasy

by

Angela Corbett

Published in the United States of America by Tork Media

PROLOGUE

$\mathcal{M}$y bare feet hit the cold tile floor as I ran down the hall, my toes curling for grip. Star, my little grey kitten with a soft white ring of fur around her neck, was running after a toy ball and we were racing to see who would get to it first. She glanced at me and I returned her determined gaze…right before she abruptly skidded into a stack of pillows. I stopped running and fell into the pillows after her, giggling as I searched for her through the fabric. After a few seconds she emerged from her plush cave, toy in her mouth. She shot me a gloating look before she started to take off back down the hall again, pawing at her ball as she went. I followed her, starting the chase again.

I was cut off by a blur running out in front of me. It was about the size of a ten-year-old boy. I frowned. My cousins, Mark and Kory, were visiting and I'd never gotten along with them. They were two spoiled boys and they both had mean streaks. Mark had run into the hall from where he'd been hiding in one of the bedrooms. A cruel look covered his face as he tackled my sweet Star, grabbing her by the neck. Star started crying in protest. Anger bubbled within me. "Put her down!" I yelled.

Mark's face twisted into a sneer. "No," he said, and pinched Star tighter. Star yelped again and tried to squirm away.

"You're hurting her!"

An awful smile spread on his lips. "I know."

My simmering anger turned to a boil. I loved animals, and Mark was harming mine. That made him my enemy. I loved my kitten more than anything and knew it was my job to protect her. I gave a comforting glance at Star before I turned my eyes on Mark, concentrating on his face. I repeated the word "drop" over and over in my head. My eyes focused with the precision of a laser as an orange light tinted my vision. Within seconds, smoke started percolating around Mark. A glowing flame circled his legs and started to flicker. Mark looked down, screamed, and dropped Star. The kitten ran over to me, her little eyes still wide with terror. I scooped her up into my arms, holding her like a baby as Mark started yelling, "You burned me! You *burned* me! I'm telling!"

Mark ran off. I didn't care. Star was safe and that's all that mattered. But I'd only meant to scare him, not burn him. A twinge of regret wound through me and I pushed my brows together at the emotion. Mark had hurt Star, and he would have kept hurting her. He was mean. I'd had to save her. It was my job, and I'd done it. If I'd hurt Mark a little in the process, it was okay because I'd saved Star. I felt better after I'd rationalized it all out in my head.

Mark was a bully and a tattle-tale so I knew I'd have to deal with my parents and uncle soon. That was fine. I hadn't done anything that they could prove. My eye caught a black smudge on the rug. I wrinkled my nose and went to investigate it. A scorch mark. I looked around for something to cover it with and grabbed the curtains in front of the window, adjusting them to hide the mark.

A concert of footsteps sounded down the hardwood hallway and my mom, dad, and uncle Robert came into view, Mark in tow, smiling like the cat who got into the cream.

My dad gave me a reproachful look. "Sweetheart, Mark said you hurt him. Do you want to tell us what happened?"

I steeled myself against my dad's gaze and shot a glare at Mark. "I was playing with Star. Mark jumped out and grabbed her by the neck, and then started being mean to her. She was crying and he was hurting her. So I made him stop."

"You made him stop," my dad said, making it part question, part statement.

I nodded and toed the floor with my bare feet. I didn't like being the center of attention, especially when I was in trouble.

"*How* did you make him stop?" My uncle Robert and Mark's dad asked, his tone a combination of anger and curiosity.

I looked at him and shuddered. Uncle Robert had never been my favorite. He was cold and I hardly ever saw him smile. "I told Mark to drop her."

"And he just dropped her?" Uncle Robert asked, disbelieving.

I lifted my shoulders. "I had to say it a lot."

My uncle hadn't taken his eyes off of me since he started talking. I shifted, uncomfortable with his assessment. "Mark says you burned him."

I had. I wasn't sure how, but ever since I was little, I'd been able to start fires with my mind. I'd never told anyone, but I practiced with my fire when no one could see me. My emotions affected the strength of the flame. Sometimes my emotions got the best of me, and I wasn't as careful. Mark had made me really mad, and he'd been hurting Star so I hadn't been as cautious as usual. My fire was still a secret though —I just had to convince my uncle. I looked up at him with wide eyes. "How would I do that, Uncle? I'm not allowed to play with matches."

My uncle gave me an appraising look, and then his eyes went over my head to my dad's. My dad held his gaze for a moment like my uncle Robert had issued a challenge and my dad was responding with stares instead of words. My dad bent down and took my hand. "I don't know what happened, but it's not okay to hurt someone else. You need to apologize to Mark."

I narrowed my eyes. Mark got hurt because he was hurting my defenseless kitten who hadn't done a thing to him. I was *not* apologizing unless he apologized too. "Mark was hurting Star. Does he have to apologize for that?"

My dad glanced up at my uncle. "Yes, he does."

My eyes went from my dad to my uncle and I watched as my uncle's jaw clenched. "Say you're sorry for hurting the cat, Mark," Uncle Robert said.

Mark scowled and folded his arms across his chest.

"Now," my uncle said in a tone that brokered no argument.

Mark made another face. "Sorry," he said, his voice bordering on mocking.

My dad took my hand, his eyes soft but ringed with authority. "Now it's your turn to apologize, El."

I didn't want to apologize to Mark when I'd done nothing wrong. I'd made him stop hurting my cat. I never would have burned him or hurt him for fun like he'd tried to do with Star. I burned him in kitten-defense, but my explanation wouldn't matter. It took everything in me to say the words, but I knew my parents would insist. "I'm sorry," I said, trying to make it sound like I meant it when I totally didn't.

My dad squeezed my hand.

"I think it's time for us to go. We'll see you soon," my uncle said, putting his hand on Mark's back and guiding him down the hall.

My mom reached down and put her soft hand on my shoulders. "I think you should spend some time in your room thinking about what you did," she said. My dad nodded in agreement and I knew I wouldn't get out of some sort of punishment. My parents both followed my uncle and I went down the hall to my room, leaving the door slightly ajar.

About fifteen minutes later, I heard voices coming from the hall. I snuck to my door and saw my parents standing in the hallway, near where Mark had been tormenting Star. I crept closer so I could hear them, and stood in the shadows, listening to their conversation and watching them.

"There hasn't been a magic user in either of our families for generations," my mom said, worry creasing her forehead. "Why did it have to happen to our little girl?"

My dad bent down, his hands going over the black mark on the carpet that I'd covered with the curtain. He looked up at my mom. "No one can ever know she's a mage, Rose."

My mother sighed, concern lining her forehead. "I know."

My dad reached out his hand and took hers. Her shoulders slumped a bit like his touch had visibly taken away some of her stress. "We'll figure it out."

"How?" My mom asked, her tone sounding defeated. "She's already exhibiting her power. And we have no idea what her power actually is. She starts fires, but is there something more to it?"

My dad stood up and pressed his lips together. "We knew this day might come and we put precautions in place. We won't know the extent of her talents for years. It's something we'll have to figure out with time."

My mom worried her hands together. "We need to teach her to control her magic and keep it a secret."

My dad nodded. "She's smart. We'll explain it and she'll understand."

My mom shook her head as she bit her trembling lip. "If someone knew what she could do—" my mom's voice trailed off and was replaced by a heaving sob.

My dad reached out and pulled her to him, wrapping her in his arms. "They won't find out," he said, his face against her head as he whispered into her ear. "No one will."

I didn't tell my parents my secret—that this wasn't the first time I'd played with my magic fire, practicing it, and trying to get better at controlling it. I knew mages were rare, and those mages who lived in the open often lived in danger. I'd been careful about keeping my powers a secret, but I wasn't certain that I'd always been alone and unseen during my trial sessions. I would have to be more careful in the future; my parents seemed worried.

That night, I climbed into my warm, safe bed in my room, the soft touch of my parents' good night kisses lingering on my cheek. I fell asleep with Star cuddled around my arm, and dreamed of our next adventures.

It was the last time I saw my parents alive.

They were found by our housekeeper on the floor of their bedroom, sprawled out next to each other, my dad's body covering my mom's like he'd tried to shield her. Three streaks of glittering teal that almost looked like claw marks were torn across each of their chests. The same claw marks were also slashed across my bedroom door. Like someone, or something, had tried to get in but for some reason, couldn't.

The police never found my parents' murderers.

But I would.

I'm Cinder, a fire mage, and my flames are fueled by vengeance.

CHAPTER 1

The streets of Everly were quiet as I walked home from my shift at the shelter. I'd been working there for a little over a year. It paid the bills, and kept me safe, which were things I'd learned not to take for granted. I was proud of myself and how far I'd come—on my own, because that's the way it had been ever since I'd run away from my caregiver to save my life.

Memories of what it was like when I was younger and had a home and parents who loved me stabbed at my heart. Now, life was a struggle; I didn't know any other way. I'd struggled at first to find food, then I'd struggled to make money and stay safe. It was in my darkest hour when I finally found my tribe—the people who were like me: magic users in hiding, protecting one another.

The world was full of magic. Some people were open about their abilities. They were the people who came from a long line of magic users and had resources, money, and ways to protect themselves from those who would try to take advantage of their skills. They lived public lives, had huge houses with expensive cars, and were treated like celebrities within the mage community. Others, like me, didn't have any of those advantages and lived in fear of anyone finding out who we actually were, or what we could do. We were constantly looking over our shoulders, hoping someone wouldn't identify us and try to use us. The fear didn't stop me from utilizing my magic for my own purposes and trying to help others, but it made me very careful about who I helped, and who I trusted with my secrets.

Magic is passed down through families at random. No one knew when it would happen, why, or what the variations of a person's powers might be. One family might produce magic users in every child, another family might skip mages for five generations. And others still, could never have magic at all. Then there were the people who had gone so long between magic users being born in their families that when the power manifested in someone, they didn't realize what it was and often brushed it off as some sort of quirk.

There were several theories about why magic existed, and why some people had it, but others didn't. The idea that made the most sense to me was that for some reason, mages had the ability to tap into a part of the brain that most people couldn't access. Essentially, mages were able to utilize their brain and subconscious in ways that gave them superpowers. Some genetic lines produced offspring more capable of this than others.

In addition to the public world of mages, there was an underground world where magic users were highly sought after, both to hire, and to use. These were people who wanted to find mages, take them, study them, and harness the magic for their own gain. They would do almost anything to gain access to magic and especially to mages who had a lot of power. When I'd first developed and started playing around with my powers as a child, I hadn't known what my powers were. I'd learned quickly, and also learned that my magic made me prey for some very influential people and I should trust no one.

In the underground, magic users without family and protection were traded and sold like objects. It was horrifying, and something I was constantly aware of, and knew I had to avoid. As soon as I was able, I dedicated my life to finding other magic users who needed protection, and helping them to stay safe. Without the benefit of family, money, and security, we'd had to create our own. My little tribe lived in the tunnels beneath Everly, where the people society didn't want to see, stayed. It was a good place to hide—people like to pretend things that make them uncomfortable don't exist, and burying them in the tunnels is a good way to make that happen. We weren't the only mages hiding there, but mages weren't the most dangerous things lurking in the darkness either. We tried to stick together, and watch out for our own.

"Hi, Kerry," I said, slowing to check on one of my favorite people. He was sitting on a chair outside of his house, watching people come and go.

His eyes lit up when he saw me. "Hadley Scott!" Kerry said. "I haven't seen you for a couple of days."

"I was on a long shift at work."

He nodded and leaned back against his chair, getting comfortable. Kerry was about six feet tall, a burly guy in his fifties with a golden beard, kind eyes, an easy smile, and the frame of a lumberjack. He lived in an old shipping container at the entrance to the tunnels, and acted like a sentinel for everyone who passed through. He knew more about what happened in the tunnels than almost anyone, and he kept me in the loop. He also made sure the people I cared about stayed safe, and that mattered a great deal to me. I handed him some food. I always tried to bring him something on my walk home from work. "How are things today?" I asked, holding out the sandwich I'd grabbed for him.

"Good, good. Sway's been keeping me entertained."

I raised a brow and wondered what she'd been doing...hopefully not playing with her magic in public. She liked to use it to freak people out. It was going to get her in trouble one of these days. "She is pretty entertaining."

"What's this?" Kerry asked, tilting the wrapped sandwich and trying to peer inside at the contents. "Turkey with cheese?" His voice carried a hopeful note.

I nodded. "Your favorite."

His mouth spread into a wide, grateful smile. "You're too good to me."

I shook my head as I kept walking. "Don't be silly. You deserve all the goodness in the world." I gave a little wave as I continued through the maze of tunnels. The tunnels were originally built as ways for stores to have deliveries made to their basements easily without disrupting the businesses. As time went on, the tunnels that offered basement access to the buildings above also became another access point to the businesses and several stores were robbed. As a result, most of the businesses sealed off their basement tunnel access doors long ago, but the tunnels and their various offshoots remained. Some of them even had doors that still opened into the basements of old, abandoned buildings.

One of those buildings was where my people stayed. The door offered an extra layer of protection, but the magic users who resided there were the best defense against any one intruding. Mages alone could be dangerous depending on their powers, but mages working together were a force. The concentration of my friends all in one spot did carry some risks, however. While it gave us more defenses to have multiple mages with various powers in one area, it would also make us a target if anyone was trying to find us. Luckily, the tunnels were full of all kinds of people, and everyone generally kept to themselves and protected those that they knew could help them. I was one of the people others came to for help.

I continued down the tunnel, watching animals that were hiding in the shadows scurry away at my footsteps. Some of the people lingering there in the dark did the same. The realization that they were all scared because they'd been treated poorly in the past squeezed at my heart. I knew what it was like to be afraid and alone. Even though I knew I couldn't save everyone, it didn't stop me from wanting to take them all under my wing and make sure they had refuge and weren't being hurt anymore.

As I came around the corner, I heard voices. The tones were heavy, and sounded menacing. My heart sped up and I stopped walking. I listened for a few more seconds, and then crept forward slowly. Two figures were locked in a fight, arms swinging and legs kicking as they each tried to gain the upper hand. They were grunting and growling as they grappled, and I couldn't tell which one of them was winning. In the blur of movements, I couldn't identify much about them aside from the fact that one of them had blonde hair and the other's hair was a deep black that reminded me of charcoal.

The guy with dark hair twisted, trying to get in a better position and that's when his face came into focus and I lost all train of thought. He had glittering cobalt eyes that contrasted against his tan skin and hair, full lips, a carved jaw, and cheeks that were currently dimpled with strain from the fight. The blonde guy reached his arm around, shifted, and flipped the dark-haired guy over on the ground, hitting the back of his head on the pavement. I winced and hoped he would be okay.

The guy with blonde hair rose with a sharp smile on his face as he towered over his spent opponent. The toothy smile that looked like a row of small daggers in his mouth instead of teeth is what made me recognize him, and my stomach immediately clenched. Grog. He was well-known in the tunnels—a wraith who needed fresh blood to use his magic. Taking the blood from his victims wasn't pretty, or painless. Everyone knew to stay away from Grog. The dark-haired guy must have wandered into the tunnels by accident—or he was just exceptionally stupid. No one was coming to save him. The tunnels had been forgotten by normal law enforcement long ago; we had to police ourselves.

The guy on the ground made a groaning noise and shifted his head. At least he wasn't unconscious. Grog moved into his strike pose and I was racing forward before I'd even made the conscious decision to do it. And I shouldn't be doing it. Using my magic in public with no disguise went against everything I'd taught myself in order to survive. But I couldn't stand by and do nothing while Grog killed someone defenseless. It wasn't in my nature. The dark haired guy needed help. I would help him.

"Grog," I yelled, rushing toward him, my chestnut brown hair swishing around my shoulders as I ran. I could feel my golden eyes darkening as my adrenaline and anger increased.

He looked up and narrowed his eyes at me. We'd had run-ins

before. The guy on the ground focused on me too, his sapphire eyes bright. I willed him to take advantage of the distraction and get up and run. He just laid there, about as helpful as a sack of flour. Maybe he was more hurt than I thought. "Leave him alone," I snarled.

Grog looked from me to the guy on the ground. I could practically see his thoughts moving, and knew just as certainly when he'd made his decision. "No," Grog said. "He's mine."

Grog leaned down, talons that looked like needles stretching from the tips of his fingers. I had mere seconds before he'd push those talons into the man. I stopped about ten feet from Grog, planted my feet, put my hands up in front of me with my palms out facing him, and concentrated all of my attention on the wraith. My vision sharpened and took on an orange hue as flames rose in my irises. I watched as the smoke started to twirl around him.

Grog halted his attack on the man and started yelling at me to stop instead. I just needed him to back off and then I'd let him go before the smoke turned into flames. "Are you done, Grog?"

"No!" he roared, and turned back to the guy on the ground.

I increased the pressure of my magic and in seconds, the smoke that had been circling around him flared to life, flames rising from the ground. Grog screamed and took off down the alley.

I dropped the flames and released a breath I hadn't known I was holding, and then turned my attention to the guy on the ground. He was looking at me. I'm not sure what I'd been expecting as a reaction...relief maybe, perhaps a thank you for not being turned into Grog's dinner. I got neither. The guy's eyes flashed and fury drenched his features. His wrath was totally focused on me. "Why did you do that?" he growled as he pushed himself up off the pavement, his body rising like a finely tuned machine.

I stared at him, stunned. After several seconds, I finally found words, "Are you kidding me? Do you know where you are? Or did you wander into the tunnels by accident?" I pointed toward the alley where Grog had retreated. "That wasn't some random person who lives down here for fun. It was a wraith who needs blood to fuel his magic. He was about to kill you! I saved your life!"

They guy reached down, brushing dirt off of his jeans and black shirt. "I know exactly who that was. And I had it handled." His skin was pulled tight across his face and his tone was very precise. He seemed livid.

I snorted a laugh. "You were on the ground, frozen and helpless."

A muscle ticked by his eye. "I wasn't helpless."

I raised my brows and crossed my arms over my chest. "A toddler would have had more defense skills than you."

His shoulders went rigid and his cobalt eyes flared with intensity. He focused on me as he closed the distance between us. In my haste to help save him from having all his blood leeched away, I hadn't totally noticed his aesthetics. He was huge. And I was suddenly very aware of how incredibly attractive this idiot was. His dark hair swept over his forehead in messy chunks. He had a straight nose, full lips, and a jawline that looked like it had been chiseled by a master artist. And all of that sat on top of a body that looked like it was ninety-nine percent muscle and as hard as titanium. I narrowed my eyes. Why did all the hot guys have to be dumb?

He stopped less than a foot in front of me. I glared at his invasion of my space and held my ground. His lips stretched and suddenly, his powerful arms were locked around me, holding me in place. A spark rushed through me at his touch. I immediately explained it away as anger for the arm prison he'd put me in. I looked down to analyze his hold and how I could escape it and got distracted by his thick arms, corded with ropey muscles. I wrinkled my nose at my reaction. That kind of distraction was not an option because number one, this imbecile was ungrateful at best, and dangerous at worst. He was here. In the tunnels, where he clearly didn't belong. He'd been fighting Grog for some unknown but incredibly stupid reason, because you only fought something like Grog if you had no sense, and I couldn't trust that he wasn't insane. And number two, he'd just watched me use my magic and could now identify me—that was *not* a good thing. I'd spent years cultivating disguises and making sure my powers were used as stealthily as possible. The only people who knew who I was, and what I could do, were the people I trusted implicitly. "Let me go," I hissed, wriggling in his hold.

"Oh no," he said, his arms pulling me tighter to him. "You just screwed up everything, and we need to have a chat."

Fear rushed through me. I had no interest in spending any more time with the hot idiot currently trying to abduct me. Someone being able to identify me and turn me over to the Magic Harnessers for ransom was one of my biggest fears. I was not inclined to spend any more time with this stranger who seemed to be more enemy than friend. "I'm not interested in talking."

"Guess how much I care," he said. He voice was deep and his breath hot on my neck. The sensation shot traitorous electricity through me and made me really mad.

The skin on my face pulled tight with anger. "Probably about as much as I do." I lifted my leg and stomped down on his foot as hard as I could. His grip loosened enough that I was able to move my arm and jam my elbow into his side. I heard him groan, and his grip loosened a little more, enough for me to twist out of his grasp. I turned and started to run. Just as I thought I was getting away, he reached out and grabbed my leg and we both went down on the pavement. Hard.

I caught myself before my face hit the ground, but my hands were already burning from the fall. I reached up, brushing the hair out of my eyes and turned to look back at him. He only had my ankle; I could still get away. I started kicking with every bit of strength I had, using my anger at the whole situation as fuel. He couldn't hold on, but somehow, by some ridiculous twist of fate, he managed to grab my shoe. I scrambled away from him, one foot naked. I stared at him, my eyes wide and a baffled look on my face. That jerk took my shoe! I stalled for half a second, wrapping my head around that information and trying to decide my next move. Demand it back? Fight him for it? No. That would be dumb. I'd just outed myself as a powerful magic user to an unfriendly stranger in the tunnels. I wasn't in the mood to stay and fight this barbarian for my footwear. I gave him a glare as I pushed myself off of the ground, got up, and started to run.

My mood was foul as I looked over my shoulder. He was kneeling on the pavement, his expression one I could only describe as grim curiosity as he watched me flee. My heart was pumping with adrenaline and frustration. I was angry at myself for letting my guard down and being identified. And I was furious with the jerk who had done the identifying and, to add insult to injury, took my freaking shoe!

I ran for several blocks, taking paths I normally wouldn't just in case he was following me. When I was certain of my safety, I went home. I came to the curved arch alcove that led to Haven, the building my people stayed in. Ancient red brick crumbled around the foundation. It was hundreds of years old and I was surprised it had held up this well with no real maintenance. The tunnels protected the basements of the buildings from weather though, so that helped. I came to the large metal door, pulled out my keys, and unlocked five different locks. Some might call the security paranoid; I called it thorough. Anyone who thought the locks were overkill hadn't spent much time in the tunnels. I slipped inside, shut the door behind me, and relocked all of the locks. Then I leaned against the back of the door, breathing a sigh of relief.

I thought about the man. Dark hair falling over his face, all hard lines that projected testosterone, full lips that should be illegal on a man, and piercing blue eyes. My mind wandered to his big arms and large hands...hands that had been wrapped around me trying to submit me, and the same hands that had stolen my shoe right off of my foot. I narrowed my eyes at the negative turn of my thoughts, and then welcomed them because it broke the spell I'd been putting myself under about the attractive and dangerous thief.

I furrowed my brow and grumbled under my breath. Now I'd have to find another pair of shoes and I really liked those! Breaking shoes in is hard, especially when you run as much as I do.

CHAPTER 2

Sway was watching the news and I stood in the doorway, watching behind her. Another terrorist attack, fires destroying hundreds of thousands of acres of land, earthquakes crumbling cities and killing people. She flipped off the news as I sighed and leaned against the exposed brick wall that matched the red brick on the outside of our home. She heard me and turned her head around. "Things keep getting worse," I said, motioning to the TV. I was concerned about the rise of violence I'd seen recently. It felt like we were on the verge of something—something terrible and terrifying. I just didn't know what it was. Part of me wondered if mages might be helping to cause the problems—or fight them. Mages were incredibly powerful and unless they had protection from their families or other magic groups, people kept their powers a secret.

Sway leaned forward and grabbed her drink off the table. She loved soda, and loved it even more when it was flavored with extra sugar. "You worry too much, Hadley," she said, sipping her sugar water as she twisted on the couch so she could see me better.

"Someone has to," I answered, plopping down next to her. "Where is everyone?"

She waved her hand toward the doors. "Out. Perry had a party to go to. Lauren and Lexi had a swim meet, Jeb is working, and Monty had a date."

My eyebrows went up. "Monty had a date?"

"I know," she said, her eyebrows creeping up. "We were all stunned."

"I didn't know he was interested in dating. Who is she? Does she have magic?" I frowned as various scenarios flooded my brain. "Do I need to be worried?"

Sway gave a hefty sigh. "He's fine. He met her at school."

That didn't make me feel much better, but at least I had a way to track her down if he went missing. Abductions were a cruel reality of our world. Unless you had someone protecting you, you had to constantly be on the lookout for people who wanted to use you. Magic Harnessers—people who tried to steal magic and use it for their own purposes—were real, and they were petrifying.

Sway looked at me from the side. "You put everyone else's needs in front of your own. You need to start taking care of yourself first."

I shook my head, snorting a laugh as I realized how much I'd fooled her. Did I like helping other people? Sure. Everyone does. Did I want to make sure people I cared about were safe? Of course I did. But she was making me seem far more altruistic than I was. My main motivation, and the reason for almost every decision I made, was to find the people who had murdered my parents, and kill them. It had become a personal mission that had turned into an obsession the longer it went on without resolution. Someone had taken my family from me, along with my only hope for a normal life, and stolen it. I was on a personal vendetta, and I would get retribution. "I'm not as self-sacrificing as you make it seem."

She shifted and moved to the floor in front of the couch, stretching a leg out. She'd been practicing yoga and karate for years and I seriously envied her flexibility. She bent at the waist and grabbed her foot with her hand and then her face contorted into a weird expression as she inclined her head to look at me. "Why are you only wearing one shoe?" she asked, her tone full of confusion.

I screwed up my face. I was still so shocked by what had happened that I'd forgotten I only had one piece of footwear. The thief's infuri-atingly handsome face flashed in my thoughts and I scowled. "It wasn't my choice."

"Whose choice was it?"

I had a slew of colorful names for him, but tried not to swear around my friends who were younger and impressionable. "A jerk's. I met him on the way home in the tunnels on Vine Street. I thought he needed help. Turns out, he didn't. And then the dummy attacked me for trying to save his butt."

She looked as offended by the whole thing as I had been. "That's not very nice. Did you ask him why?"

I pressed my lips into a line. I'd been trying to escape the chat he wanted to have, not prolong it. "He was aggressively persistent about not letting me leave. I decided not to stay and have a discussion."

One of Sway's eyebrows went up and she looked at me like she was seeing something other than what I was trying to project. "Was he hot?"

His dark hair, deep blue eyes, and wide shoulders flashed into my mind. So. Hot. And I wasn't going to admit that to a single soul, ever. I had a hard time even admitting it to myself. "I'm not going to answer that."

Her lips spread into a grin. "So he was *way* hot!" she paused, her head tilting and eyes going up to the ceiling like she was weighing her options. "I think I would have stayed to see where things went."

I waved a hand in front of me like I was giving her permission. "Feel free to try it if you're ever being accosted by a dimwit the size of a gorilla."

She gestured toward my foot. "So why are you walking around half barefoot?"

I narrowed my eyes as the scene replayed in my head. "Because the jerk stole my freaking shoe."

Sway gave me a look. "He *stole* it?"

I nodded.

"Like, off of your foot?" she asked, a wrinkle forming between her brows. "You let him get that close?"

I glared. It wasn't that hard to imagine. Hand-to-hand combat wasn't easy. You used the weapons you had available. "I was trying to get away from him and he grabbed my leg. We both fell. I kicked at him, but he was able to hold onto my foot and pull my shoe off."

She frowned. "Why didn't you take it back?"

"Because he'd seen me use my powers and could identify me. I thought I should get away as soon as possible."

"Why didn't you just start him on fire?"

I'd asked myself that same question. Thanks to my stupid heroics, the stranger knew I had elemental fire magic and he could easily give someone my physical description. I should have neutralized the threat. But I hated hurting people. It wasn't in my nature unless the person had done something to deserve it. I still didn't know what the shoe thief's motives were. "It's a shoe. It wasn't worth the energy."

She rolled her eyes. "You could have just singed him a bit."

I shook my head. "He'd already seen some of my powers. I wasn't going to show him anything else, or give him any additional information."

She made a hmmph noise. "Fair enough. Hopefully you'll never see him again."

I nodded in agreement. "Fingers crossed." A heavy weight seemed to settle on my chest as I said it, and I had a feeling that wouldn't be the case.

It had been three days since the incident with Grog and the shoe thief. Despite feeling like I constantly had to look over my shoulder, which wasn't an unusual feeling for a rogue mage anyway, things had been normal. I'd been busy at the shelter on a forty-eight hour shift. The long shifts always wiped me out and I was happy when I got to go home where I could relax. It was getting colder outside at night so the shelter was overwhelmed with people looking for a hot meal and a warm bed. I hadn't run into Grog since I'd set him on fire, and neither had Sway, Perry, Lauren, Lexi, Jeb, or Monty...that I knew of. I hadn't been home to talk to them, but none of them had texted me about it.

At the entrance to the tunnels, I said hello to Kerry and made my way down the wide pathway. I glanced in the direction of Grog's makeshift house, various metal pieces in different states of decay patched together to make a living space. I didn't see him there, but I still watched my back as I continued to Haven.

I opened all five locks on the front door and breathed in the scent of sugar as I pushed into the house. Someone had been baking something. I shut the door behind me, locking us all in, and walked across the painted concrete floor into the kitchen. I grabbed a chocolate chip cookie off of the counter and broke it apart. The inside was still gooey and the chocolate melty—my favorite. I was about to take a bite when I heard a commotion from somewhere down the hall and I was accosted by Sway, Perry, and Lexi, who came from the other room at a run, and barely stopped before plowing me over.

"Whoa," I said, jumping back and then trying to regain my balance. "What's going on?"

"We met the jerk," Sway said breathlessly, a coy smile playing at her lips.

An uneasy feeling immediately rose in my chest as I asked, "What jerk?"

"The jerk who took your shoe," Lexi answered, wiggling her eyebrows.

"You weren't kidding about him being hot!" Sway reached out like she was touching something invisible and then quickly pulled her hand back like she'd been burned.

I put a piece of cookie in my mouth and it tasted like heaven. "I didn't say he was hot," I mumbled between bites.

Sway rolled her eyes. "You didn't say he wasn't, either."

Lexi started bouncing from foot to foot. "He's been in the tunnels asking about you!"

My eyes widened and the cookie suddenly felt like lead in my stomach. "What do you mean?"

"He brought your shoe," Perry said.

I blinked. "He what?"

"He thought a girl running around with only one shoe might be something people noticed—"

"I *totally* noticed," Sway interjected.

"—and he wanted to find you. We nicknamed him OWWLS," Perry said.

"OWWLS?" I asked.

"For the Old Woman Who Lived in a Shoe," Perry said.

I laughed out loud. "Good grief, I love you guys. I hope you told him that name. And I hope you didn't tell him anything else."

They all looked at me like I was an idiot. "Of course we didn't tell him anything about you," Perry said.

"That would be *so* wrong," Lexi said. Her tone sounded like she'd just eaten something disgusting.

I leaned a hip against the counter. "Did he seriously go through the entire tunnel system asking everyone if they knew a girl missing a shoe?"

Lexi nodded. "I wanted to text you but Sway said not to bother you at work."

Anticipation zinged through me and I immediately quelled the traitor emotion. I had no business being excited about the dangerous idiot who was using my shoe as an identification device. I frowned. Now I'd probably have to change my appearance or something stupid like that. I'd done something similar once before, and didn't look forward to doing it again. I liked my dark brown hair and bright blue eyes. "Well if someone is ever looking for me in the future, feel free to text—even if I'm at work."

Sway eyed me closely and bit the corner of her lip. "Do you know who he is?"

"The shoe thief?" I asked, pushing my brows together. I walked past the three of them to get some milk out of the fridge. "Yeah, he's some guy with an ego and a fondness for feet."

Sway pressed her lips together and shook her head slowly. "He's a lot more than that. Do you have your phone?"

I nodded.

"Do a search for the Oklahoma City tornados two years ago," she said.

I did. She took the phone from me, scrolled through the videos and then clicked one. As the video pulled up, I saw a man standing on the screen and immediately recognized the dark hair and wide shoulders. He was alone in the middle of a city, the sky a strange greenish grey color. A tornado was whirling in front of him; it couldn't have been more than a few blocks away. The entire area looked like it had been deserted as people tried to escape the path of the storm. The shoe thief was in the middle of the road, in the direct path of the tornado. The lines of his face were hard with determination as he raised his arms above him—the same way he'd done the night I'd tried to save him—and faced the storm down. Hair on the back of my neck prickled and I wanted to yell at him to run away. The tornado moved closer and closer and then it abruptly stopped in front of him, like it was a dog obediently listening to commands. Over the course of a few minutes, I watched as the storm started to collapse in on itself, getting smaller and smaller until it had completely dissipated. I stared, dumbfounded. He had stopped a tornado—rain, sleet, and wind—and controlled the weather with nothing more than his magic. And not only had he stopped it, but he'd made it submit to his will. Which meant he was an incredibly powerful mage. I'd never seen anything like it.

"Why wasn't this all over the news?" I asked.

"People thought it was digitally altered," Sway said. "The only people who really believe he did that are those of us who know magic exists—and those who want to use it."

Like the Magic Harnessers. They'd love to get their hands on someone with his power. Imagine what people could do if they could control the weather. It could be used to make tsunamis, hurricanes, tornados, and take out entire cities and states in a covert way because it would seem natural. It could also be used as a profitable venture for everyone from farmers to ski resort owners. And since you can't mess with the weather in one area without it affecting other places as well, it could seriously screw over entire countries and economies. His power was impressive, and he was even more dangerous than I'd originally assumed.

"He's powerful. If he's being this brazen with his magic, I'm surprised he hasn't been taken by Magic Harnessers. Who is he?" I asked.

"His name is Storm," Sway answered.

Storm. Because he could control the weather. I rolled my eyes. "That's adorable. Did he pick that name himself?" It sounded like something someone with a lot of muscle but not much intellect would do.

"I think it's his given name, but most people don't call him Storm," Sway said. She paused, seeming to choose her words carefully. "His last name is Hurston."

I froze with my glass of milk halfway to my lips, my mouth gaping. "As in *the* Hurstons?"

Sway nodded slowly. "The same. Everyone calls him Charming."

Of course they did. And I'd heard of Charming Hurston and his antics. He was well-known for being an egotistical, self-centered player. I wrinkled my nose, annoyed that I'd tried to help him when he certainly didn't need it, and even more so now that I knew who he really was—a pretty boy with an attitude. "Well, I can attest to the fact that he's anything *but* charming."

"He looks pretty charming," Lexi offered, resting her chin on my shoulder as she looked at my phone and the video paused on his sculpted face. "He's like a real-life prince in the magic world."

She was right about that; the Hurston family was legendary. I bit the corner of my lip and shook my head slightly. Good grief. Of course I'd had to save the notorious Storm Hurston—a man with a super stupid name who could have easily saved himself. Why couldn't I save a normal dude? The Hurstons were one of the most powerful magic families and their lineage went back for centuries—an anomaly since no one really knew how magic was passed genetically and some families skipped having magic users for decades. Shoe-stealing Charming didn't have to worry about being targeted, abducted, or having his magic stolen. He had protections with his family—a lot of them—and people to cater to his every whim. He was basically magic royalty. Which begged the question: what was he doing in the tunnels, fighting a wraith? And why was he looking for me now?

"What did he say when he told you he was looking for me?"

The three of them glanced back and forth at each other like they were trying to decide how to answer.

"Just tell me," I said. "There's no need to sugarcoat it."

"He said it was very important that he find you," Lexi answered carefully.

"Okay, that's not so bad."

"I told him there was a good chance he wouldn't get what he wanted," Perry said.

Nothing wrong with that either. It was true.

Perry gave me an uncertain look. "He said he always gets what he wants. And he wants you."

So that was bad.

Perry kept going, "He said he'd clear the tunnels with a windstorm to get you out if he had to."

And now he was threatening my home, and innocent people, including my friends—the people I viewed as family. Anger punched my chest. So the very *un*-charming Charming was hot, dumb, and had an ego the size of the Arctic. We both had element-based magic. I wondered who would win if we squared off. "I told you he's a massive jerk," I said, tipping my glass toward them.

"But still *super* hot," Sway said dreamily.

A knock sounded on the front door and Perry jumped up. "I'll get it."

"You said he's been looking for me for a couple of days?" I asked Lexi and Sway.

Lexi nodded. "We've all seen him wandering around, holding your shoe like a little lost puppy."

"It wasn't lost," I said, my tone infused with anger, "it was stolen."

"It was stolen after you tried to kick me with it. Repeatedly," a deep, slightly familiar, and irritatingly attractive voice said from behind me. My whole body came to attention and I was intensely annoyed at the betrayal.

I turned and saw him standing in the middle of our kitchen. All muscle, irises I could drown in, and some serious boundary issues. I narrowed my eyes, pushed my shoulders back, and folded my arms across my chest. "I kicked you because you were attacking me and trying to drag me off to whatever cave you crawled out of. I wasn't going with you, shoe or no shoe. What the hell are you doing here?" I asked, then turned to glare at Perry. "Why did you let him in?"

Perry put his hands up in defense. "He said he saw you walk in here and if I didn't let him talk to you, he was going to conjure up some wind and rip our house apart. I decided not to risk it."

If I could have shot daggers at the shoe thief with my eyes, I would have. "I didn't want to talk to you during our last meeting and I told you so. In response, you threatened my friends and our home. Twice. Do you really think that makes me want to talk to you now?"

He gave me a blank look. "I don't care whether you want to talk or not, that's exactly what's going to happen."

Grrrr. He was pompous and entitled, two of the things I hated most. "No." I pointed toward the door. "Get out."

He ignored my command like I hadn't even spoken and it aggravated me even more than I was already aggravated. I hadn't thought that possible.

"I've been looking for you." The frustration was evident in his tone.

Yes. How dare I not come immediately when he'd started wandering around with my shoe in tow. He probably wasn't used to not getting exactly what he wanted, whenever he wanted it. "I've heard."

"And you didn't respond." His voice was tight.

I crossed my arms over my chest. "I know. While my curiosity can get me in trouble sometimes, when I heard some weirdo was wandering around aimlessly, trying to identify me via shoe, I decided that was a path I really didn't need to explore. You could be a serial killer obsessed with feet for all I know."

Dialing up the notorious Charming wasn't a good idea for someone like me. Hearing that he was looking for me hadn't been an invitation, it had been a warning to run. One that I hadn't considered heeding because I'd been running my whole life and I was sick of it. And aside from that, I knew Charming's kind—privileged and arrogant humans who thought the world bowed to them. I wanted nothing to do with him. "I know you're probably not used to this, but not everyone falls all over themselves when you walk into a room."

He cocked a brow and looked thoroughly amused. I wanted to punch him. "Do you know who I am?"

Do I know who he is? Like everyone should fall down at his feet and worship him. I rolled my eyes. "Yeah. You're the ungrateful princess who instead of saying, "Thanks for not letting Grog suck my life away," got pissed, attacked me, and took my property."

"Princess?" he said the word slowly, enunciating each syllable like no one had ever insulted him before. I found that extremely hard to believe.

I nodded. "If the shoe fits. Did it?" I asked, raising a brow. "Have you been wandering around in my shoe and composing odes to my shoelaces?"

His tongue went over the inside of his cheek as he studied me. "Do you have some sort of deep devotion to your footwear?"

"As a matter of fact, I do. It takes a long time to wear shoes in and those were some of my favorites. Now I only have one of them and blisters from the other shoes I've been wearing since you stole mine. You can give my missing property back any time."

He watched me, assessing for several seconds. "You kicked me with it. I feel like that makes it mine."

"If I'd known you had a foot fetish, I would have kicked you with something bigger."

His eyes flashed with mirth. "And if I'd known you were going to run, I would have captured you faster."

He had no idea what I could do. Someone like him would be so full of themselves that if I unleashed all of my magic, they'd be sick for days—provided they didn't flat out suffer a psychic break. "Try it," I said through my teeth. "I dare you."

His eyes darkened this time. "Next time I capture you, it will be because you want me to."

I managed to look indignant, though his proximity to me and the lines of his shoulders were making that outrage hard to muster. "You're confident."

"Yes. I'm excellent at what I do."

"Ego?"

"No. Magic."

Perry, who was older than Sway and Lexi, coughed. I'd forgotten they were even there. I turned to see the three of them, watching with rapt fascination, like they were seeing a soap opera play out in real time. That was all I needed. Witnesses to this fight. They'd already been here too long. "I need to deal with *un*-Charming. Will you three give us some privacy, please?"

Sway's face fell and Lexi looked like someone had just stolen her puppy. I sent my eyes to the ceiling and shooed them off, hoping they'd respect my wishes and not just eavesdrop down the hall. They sulked out of the room. I had no idea why Charming had been looking for me, but I didn't want my friends to be concerned with it. If it was something they needed to know, I'd tell them.

I turned my attention back to our visitor. His lips slid into an amused expression.

"Why are you looking at me like that?" I asked, warily.

"Because you called me Charming. So you *do* know who I am."

Of all the conceited... "First, I called you *un-Charming*. Second, don't flatter yourself. I had no clue who you were until my friends told me you'd been here threatening them while I was at work during the past couple of days and they recognized you. Until thirty minutes ago, the only thing I knew about you was that you were the most aggravating and bristly human being I'd ever met. My initial assessment of you was spot-on. Why are you here, and what do you want?"

He leaned against the kitchen countertop and studied me for several seconds. "We have a mutual enemy, Hadley."

Great. So someone had told him my name—or the name I used at least. I'd taken on a new identity after I'd run away and no one knew my real name.

I raised my brows. A mutual enemy was news to me. "You don't even know me. How do you know who my enemies are, or that we share one?"

He licked his lips and my eyes couldn't help but follow the movement. They lingered there a little too long before snapping back up to meet his gaze. He grinned, totally aware of the affect he was having on me. "Your reputation precedes you," he said.

I thinned my eyes. That sounded ominous. "What reputation is that?"

He studied me, his eyes full of interest—for what, I wasn't sure. "I know about the fire on Clayborne Avenue, and the inferno on Green Street. There were others too, but those are off the top of my head. It took me a few hours to put things together, but I did. You're Cinder, the arsonist, and you're practically a legend."

I pursed my lips and my heart sped up. I'd been careful to keep my identity a secret my whole life, and then I threw it all away by fighting Grog in front of Charming. I hadn't taken my usual precautions and now I was paying for it. Anger at my own stupidity coursed through me. The fires on Clayborne and Green had both happened when I was younger and still trying to learn to control my magic. I'd had years of practice and now when I burned something down, I was more underhanded about it—and made sure I wasn't ever caught. Cinder was a name the press had given me, but no one had ever identified me in person. I was careful to take out any video feeds, and to keep myself covered with a hooded cape so I couldn't be easily recognized. I wasn't about to tell him any of that though. I simply stayed silent, not wanting to give anything away.

"On Clayborne, you destroyed a sweatshop. On Green Street, you stopped a human trafficking ring."

I'd been given a gift and had decided long ago to use it for good, as well as for my own purposes. No one was injured in the fires on Clayborne and Green, or in any of my other incidents, but I wouldn't have felt too bad if the people exploiting others *had* been hurt. They were bad people doing bad things and I was happy to have the chance to stop them. But again, not information I needed to share with Charming so I kept my features neutral and said nothing.

He leaned against the counter, the seams of his shirt straining around his biceps. "It was noble," he said, admiration in his voice. "I was impressed."

I rolled my eyes. "I imagine someone like you is always impressed with destruction."

"No," he said, watching me closely. "Power. Few people in the world use it for good. You appear to be one of them. And I'd like you to help me take down someone completely vile."

I arched one of my eyebrows. "Who would that be?"

His eyes narrowed and he stared at the wall, his mind going to a totally different place than the photo of the beach he seemed to be focused on. "I don't know. That's why I need you."

He didn't know? What the... "You don't know? It sounds like you need a private investigator."

The crease between his eyes deepened. "We already have those. They're not helping."

"Okay. Then why me?"

He looked directly into my eyes and the sincerity there was unmistakable. "Because you're exceptionally powerful, and I need the help of another strong elemental mage. Your magic would work well with mine in a fight."

Technically, rain could put out my fire, but his wind could also fuel it. He was right though; I was powerful—more powerful than he knew, that was certain. But the Hurstons had all the money and connections in the world. I couldn't understand how one more mage like me, a rogue mage at that, could be of any help. Surely they had strong fire mage friends. "What do you need my help with?"

He sat on one of the chairs in front of the countertop and looked down for a minute before answering. When he did, his voice was soft, "My sister, Sarah, was abducted last week. My family is doing everything in their power to get her back, but we're not getting far, and we have very few clues. She was out with two friends. Her friends are now dead. Their bodies were recovered in the same place where her phone last logged her location. Her body wasn't left with the others, so we believe she's still alive. The only clue we have about the person who took her is that there were three streaks of glittering teal that almost looked like claw marks across both of her friends' chests." I managed to hold back my gasp, but it was several seconds before I remembered to breathe again. He'd just described the same marks as the ones that had been found in my house and on my parents the night they were murdered. I'd been looking for someone with information about what had happened to them for years. Now Charming was looking for the same person who had killed my family and he was asking for my help to find them. This was the closest I'd ever been to being able to reveal who, or what, had taken my parents from me.

"So you were in the tunnels trying to get information when I saw you the other night?"

"Yes."

"From Grog?" I asked, a note of doubt in my tone.

"Grog is known for having information if you pay the right price."

That was true, but the price usually came in a very unpleasant and deadly form. "He would have drained you dry before he ever gave you the information you wanted."

"I was willing to take that risk to get my sister home safe."

It was a stupid idea. His parents would have ended up with two dead kids that way. "That was risky, and wouldn't have played out well for you."

He met my eyes, cold and hard. "I had it under control, and I would have stopped him before anything serious happened to me."

"You would have *tried*," I said, my tone implying that he would have been very unsuccessful in the attempt.

"He'd already told me some information before you arrived."

That piqued my interest. "Like what?"

Charming shifted and grabbed a cookie off the counter. "That the person I'm looking for will be at the Mystic Ball this weekend. I need to find them. And I need a date who can help me do that." He looked up at me, his eyes darkening, "Preferably one who burns hot."

I raised my brows at that, certain he was referencing my magic, not the fact that he thought I was attractive. I didn't keep up with magic circle gossip, but from the little I had heard, Charming was a known player who dated incredibly beautiful women. He wasn't interested in me for anything other than help finding his sister. And I was considering using him for help finding the person who killed my parents. I needed to keep reminding myself of that.

The Mystic Ball was an expensive and ornate party held by magic's most elite every year. Charming would have never missed it because the Hurston family was one of the most highly respected magic families in the world. I'd heard about the ball, but I'd definitely never been invited. I didn't even know where it was held. Now Charming was asking me to go with him? I really hoped I wouldn't have to dance. "What makes you believe Grog's information?"

He took another bite of cookie. "Because Grog traffics in information. Plus, I paid him well for it and threatened him if he gave me incorrect intel." Of course he did. Because threats were second nature to someone with the power, money, and magic lineage Charming had. "My family is employing an investigation team, and I'm helping to facilitate their queries by getting as much additional information as possible. The information we have so far points to the fact that this involves someone, or maybe several people, in the magic community. We can't go to any of our family friends and mages we know for help. We can't trust them."

I almost snorted a laugh. "But you think you can trust me? You don't even know me."

He looked at me, pulling his bottom lip back with his teeth. I reminded myself not to stare. "Yes. I think I can. You haven't been part of the mage culture. You've grown your magic outside of it, not getting influenced by the politics. I don't know your story, but I imagine there's a reason for why you are where you are, and why you feel the need to help others, whether it be taking out a sweatshop, helping a stranger who seems like they're about to be killed by Grog, or simply finding other magic users in need of a home and shelter. You use your magic for good, and there's no one better than my sister. She needs help and I can't go to anyone else. Will you help me?" Charming asked. His eyes were soft and his voice sincere. It would be easy to fall for someone like that. Luckily, he wasn't always this endearing.

I furrowed my brow and looked at him closely, trying to ascertain the best course of action. Partnering with him would mean putting myself out there and risking my own life. More people would find out about my magic, and I didn't have the protections Charming did. I'd spent my whole life trying to stop that from happening, and keep people from finding out about my powers. And it wasn't just me I had to think about. I had no way to keep all of my friends safe from the Magic Harnessers. I didn't want them to become targets as well. But Charming had every resource on the planet available to him. There was a chance he could keep us all safe.

Previously, I had wondered who would win if we squared off. Now I wondered what would happen if we used our magic to work together. Could we really do it without killing each other? I wasn't sure. But this was also a huge opportunity for me. It was the closest I'd ever been to finding out who had murdered my parents. Charming had information and could get me into places I couldn't get to alone.

"My home, and my friends and I would all need protection from the Magic Harnessers."

"Done," he said immediately. "I can take care of that."

"What about after this is all over? How can I guarantee we'll have the security we need going forward once people know about my magic?"

"I'll have a security team put on you just like my family has. You won't have to worry."

"Indefinitely?"

He nodded.

Being rich and powerful sure made things easier. I wondered what that life would be like.

"What about the security team that was assigned to your sister?"

"She wasn't considered high risk and only had one guard. We've changed protocol now. Your team will keep you and your friends safe."

So the security obstacle was out of the way; I tried to consider if there were any others. I could only see one; it involved his sparkling blue eyes, alluring smirk, and the thick muscles that encased his frame —and that wasn't a problem I was ever going to tell him about. I'd just have to deal with the attraction on my own. This was my very best chance for being able to find the people who had killed my parents, and I wasn't going to pass it up because I was distracted by the circumference of his arms.

"Give me my shoe back, and we have a deal."

His lips slid into a slow smile. "Done," he said. "I'll send you a dress."

I shook my head. "I can get my own."

"You're sure?"

"I've been dressing myself for twenty-five years, I think I can manage."

He opened his mouth to say something undoubtedly snarky, and then closed it. Wise choice.

"Then I'll see you on Saturday." He handed me my shoe.

I took it, and hoped I'd made the right choice. If I hadn't, everyone I loved and everything I'd built could be at risk.

CHAPTER 3

A box addressed to me showed up on the doorstep the next afternoon. I took it inside and opened it. Another silver box with a pretty pale blue bow wrapped around it sat inside. I untied the bow and then gently lifted the top off of the box and gasped. A dazzling new pair of shoes. They were see-through with a three inch heel, pointed toe, and they glittered with blue and silver speckles sprinkled over the entire shoe. They almost looked like glass sparkling in the sunlight. I took them out of the box and slipped them on my feet, trying them out. They felt like I was walking on a cloud and they were a perfect fit. I stood in front of the full length mirror in the hall, putting my foot out and admiring the gorgeous slippers. A smile curved my lips. They had to be from Charming. He was the only one who knew I was going to the ball. At least he'd done something useful with my shoe and figured out my shoe size. I wrinkled my nose at the memory of the shoe theft and considered not taking the gift, but decided it was a peace offering. At least, that's how I was justifying it so I could keep the magnificent heels. Shoes were kind of my weakness. I loved them, and rarely had the money to buy a pretty pair, or the opportunity to wear them. I had one now.

"Holy crap!" Sway said, as she walked into the room with Lauren and Lexi. "Those shoes are amazing! Where did you get them?"

"I think Charming sent them," I said, turning to examine them from a different angle. I couldn't stop staring at my new glittery gift, and already loved them more than cake—which was *a lot*.

"Why?" Lauren asked, leaning against the wall. She hadn't been at home when Charming had arrived, but everyone in the house had heard about his Haven invasion.

"For the Mystic Ball."

All three sets of their eyes went as wide as saucers. "You're going to the *ball*?" Sway asked.

I nodded, and slipped the shoes off, placing them back in the box gently.

Three identical squeals came out of their mouths! "Oh my gosh! What are you going to wear?" Lauren asked.

"It has to be something exquisite!" Lexi said.

"Oh, it will be. Just leave that to me," Sway promised. Sway's magic gave her the incredible ability to weave illusions. They didn't last forever, but she was a master of clothing design, and she could conjure a heart-stoppingly beautiful gown out of thin air.

"You would do that for me?" I asked. I was more than grateful because despite my assurances to Charming, I really didn't have the time or the money to find a gown that would work for such a formal occasion. Charming had offered to send me one, but I hated relying on other people, and who knew what kind of dress he would have procured.

"Don't be silly," Sway said, waving me off like I would be crazy to think she wouldn't do it. "Of course I will. I would love to! You're going to be the most beautiful girl at the ball. You'll stop people in their tracks!"

My stomach clenched at the thought. I'd spent so many years trying not to be noticed that the thought of the magic masses seeing me, and someone possibly recognizing me, gave me serious anxiety. The worry started to spread and I immediately tamped it down with the thought of my parents. This was my opportunity. I might be able to avenge them soon, and if so, then this would all be worth it. And I had Charming's security crew to help keep us safe. Plus, it wasn't like I was helpless—as long as I wasn't up against a mage who could counter my powers.

Sway picked up one of my pretty, sparkling slippers and studied it. "Yes," she said, tilting her head and looking it over, "I can definitely make something that goes beautifully with these. You have to give him credit, he knows how to pick shoes."

I had to agree with her on that. I loved them.

Sway put her fingers to her lips, a small smile playing over them. I'll be back later. I have a dress to design.

I watched her walk away, a slight thrill going through me. I'd never been to a ball. I'd never even really been on a date. My whole life had been a series of firefights, trying to make sure I could survive, and trying to help others survive while I attempted to find the murderer of my parents. Getting dressed up and going out, even if there was an agenda behind it, made me excited and giddy. For the first time in years, I felt like I might be running toward something instead of away from it.

"Stop fiddling with the lace," Sway admonished as she brushed my hand away from the intricate scallops framing my sweetheart neckline.

We were in the car on our way to the address Charming had texted me earlier in the day. He'd sent a fancy SUV with a driver who was part of his security team to pick us up. When my friends in Haven had heard about the plan to help Charming find his sister, and possibly help me find the person who killed my parents, they'd all wanted to come along. I'd managed to keep the guest list to Sway and Perry. Bringing an entire platoon with me would draw unnecessary attention, not to mention that showing up at the Mystic Ball was basically a declaration of your magic power. At eighteen and nineteen respectively, Sway and Perry were the oldest of my friends, and had control over their powers. They were adults, and could make their own choices. I knew they could defend themselves and, to be honest, I felt more confident having them by my side. Sway was wearing an emerald dress that highlighted her curves and brought out her fiery hair. Perry had on a black tuxedo that managed to somehow make him seem less intimidating. He was six-foot-six so that was hard to do. I imagined Sway's magic had helped make that illusion happen.

I looked down at the fabric encasing my figure and still couldn't believe I was wearing it. My dress was incredible! I'd never felt so beautiful, or so self-conscious. It was form-fitting in a way I didn't think dresses could even be. I felt like I'd been sewn into it from my chest to my hips. I was worried that if I bent wrong, I'd break the seams. The gown flared out from my hips into billowy yards of satin and lace. The train trailed behind me like waves on the ocean.

"I've never worn anything like this before," I said, uncomfortably.

"Which is ridiculous because you were *made* for this dress!" Sway said, rolling her eyes. "You're drop dead gorgeous!"

I wrinkled my nose as I looked down at the pretty, dark blue lace overlaying a shimmering pale blue gown. The sleeves hung off my shoulders and the neckline showed a hint of my chest, emphasizing a brilliant square sapphire dangling from my neck. My earrings matched the necklace, and the colors all combined to bring out the blue of my eyes. My dark hair was curled and swept to the side so it hung over my right shoulder, and my makeup was a masterpiece of grey and pink shades, and incredible contouring. I'd barely recognized myself when I'd turned around and looked in the mirror an hour ago.

"I feel beautiful," I said, and didn't like the taste in my mouth that came with the admission. "It makes me uneasy," I admitted.

Sway gave me a look. "Good! You *should* feel beautiful because you *are!*"

I shook my head. "You're just good at illusion, and you're being nice."

Sway rolled her eyes so hard I thought they might roll out of their sockets, and swung her head to Perry. "Am I just being nice, Perry?"

Perry looked at me appreciatively. "She's definitely not being nice. Charming's going to lose it."

Sway giggled. "He totally is."

This time I rolled me eyes, fidgeting my hands in my lap. "He won't even notice." Did I want him to notice? I kind of did. But what did that mean? Okay, so I was attracted to the guy. I was adult enough to be honest with myself and admit it. He was an attractive guy. And what girl *wouldn't* want to be wanted? I was sure that was all it was. I wanted someone to look at me with desire and it wouldn't matter if it was Charming or some stranger on the dance floor. I felt better after my little internal assessment.

Perry snorted. "Oh, he'll notice. *Everyone* will notice. You'd have to be blind not to."

That reminder made me worried all over again. I knew coming tonight meant that I was putting myself out there and I, and my magic, wouldn't be a secret anymore. The people I'd run away from years ago would be able to find me again. I was older now and more capable, but it still left a knot in my stomach. I had Charming's word that he'd keep me, my friends, and Haven protected. I had no reason not to trust that. But I'd been hiding for so long that it was hard to just flip a switch and be okay with my magic going public.

We pulled up to the hotel the Mystic Ball was being held in. The building was a masterpiece of Victorian architecture. As we walked inside the lobby, a chandelier bigger than my entire bedroom hung from the ceiling. Every piece of furniture was antique, and probably cost a small fortune. The walls were wrapped in flocked wallpaper and the place practically dripped money. I took a deep breath, feeling totally out of my element. I needed to get over that because we had a job to do.

We walked into the hallway leading to the ballroom and were stopped at the door by a woman in a black formal dress. "Name, please?"

"We're guests of Storm Hurston," I answered.

She gave me an appraising look. I must have passed her test

because she looked down at her list. "Ah, yes. He's listed with a plus three. Can I have your names for the announcement?"

"Announcement?" I asked, confused.

"Yes, we announce everyone when they walk into the ball."

I froze, unsure about what to say. Sway and Perry both gave her their names and started through the door before looking back at me. I'd known going into this that people might realize who I was, but I hadn't planned on using my magic, or even my name. The goal was to get in, get the information we needed, and get out. But now it was more than that. If I gave my real name, everyone would know. I'd been in hiding ever since I'd run away to save my life. I wasn't sure if revealing my name was a good idea. My parents were dead, but there were others who still might be looking for me. At some point, the rumors would spread and the news would get back to people that I was still alive. I wasn't ready to let them know my real name, so I used the name I'd taken after I'd gone into hiding. "Hadley Scott." Hadley was my mom's middle name, and Scott was my dad's middle name. I couldn't keep using the name they'd given me, but this made me feel like I still had a piece of them as part of me.

She nodded, wrote down my name, and directed us through the doors. We stood in a line behind a curtain until our names were called. Sway and Perry went first, then the announcer said, "Hadley Scott." I walked into the room and stood at the top of the stairs, my heart racing. I pasted a fake smile on my face as I took in the ornately decorated room. The ceiling was drenched with flowers in various shades of pink. Crystals woven through the blooms glinted off of carefully placed lights. The flowers on the tables mirrored the flowers on the ceiling, only they were in round, slender vases with glass stems so thin I wasn't sure how they were holding the sheer weight of the arrangements. The room smelled like a spring garden, and looked like one too. It was the most spectacular space I'd ever been in, and I couldn't believe I was there—and couldn't imagine how much the décor had cost. It wasn't until I'd stopped staring at the room that I realized how quiet the crowd had become. I looked around and everyone had stopped what they were doing, their eyes focused on me. I couldn't have been more uncomfortable if I'd been standing there naked. My eyes swept the room, a multitude of gowns and tuxedos, faces that seemed familiar and some that didn't, staring back at me, assessing, judging. Magic users were celebrities within the mage world, so it wasn't a surprise that some of them would look familiar, but it was a surprise that any of them would ever be interested in me.

My eyes went over the crowd, searching for a friendly face. That's when I found him. My gaze halted like I'd been going a hundred miles an hour and suddenly hit the brakes. In the middle of the room, with a look of pure longing etched on his face, stood Charming. He was wearing a black tuxedo with a white shirt and cuff links that sparkled like diamonds—and probably were. He started up the stairs to greet me and when he reached the landing I almost gasped. His eyes looked like they were heated from within. "You look stunning," he said, whispering in my ear as he offered me his arm.

"Thank you," I murmured back, still feeling like this was all a dream. I put my hand in the crook of his elbow and let him guide me down the stairs.

Sway and Perry were waiting at the bottom. "You remember my friends," I said to Charming.

He nodded. "Thank you for coming."

"Thanks for inviting us. Just kidding, you didn't," Sway said, a hint of annoyance in her tone. "But thanks for getting us tickets after Hadley asked you to."

His eyes flashed with mirth that didn't seem entirely friendly. "You're welcome."

Sway met his gaze, totally unafraid and unwilling to stand down.

The hush was still lingering over the crowd and people hadn't stopped staring. Charming's interest in me hadn't helped that. I needed to change the subject before Sway said something she shouldn't and someone overheard. "Your family isn't here tonight?" I asked Charming.

He turned his attention back to me and shook his head. "My parents and our entire security team have been working non-stop trying to find out more information about where my sister might be.

But since we can't trust other mages, we haven't gone public with the news of her disappearance. The Hurston family is old in the magic world, and needed representation at the ball, so I was the best choice. Since I had the intel from Grog that this is where I needed to be, we decided to have me cover the ball."

The orchestra at the front of the room started playing a beautiful song. The melody was one I remembered my mom humming during my childhood. It brought back beautiful memories of her sitting by my bed at night, reading me a bedtime stories, and then humming as she lightly brushed my cheek with her soft fingers until I fell asleep. I yearned for those days, and often felt sad when I thought of the things we were both missing out on now. Growing up without a mother's guidance was difficult.

Storm noticed me watching the orchestra, my body swaying slightly to the music as I remembered my past. "Would you like to dance?" he asked.

Surprise washed over my face. I hadn't expected to actually dance. I'd thought we were just here to do a job. "I would love to, but shouldn't we be looking for the person who took your sister?"

He gave me a wink. "We will be."

"By dancing?" I asked.

He nodded, a smile playing at the corners of his lips, and took my hand pulling me onto the dance floor.

Sway and Perry grinned like fools behind me as I looked back at them over my shoulder. Everyone was watching us—the notorious Charming and the new girl in blue.

Charming reached around me, his hand like a warm compress on my back. His eyes were soft and full of heat. I could easily get lost in them and be happy—for a while at least. Then reality would come and I'd remember we were from two very different worlds and Charming would bring me nothing but heartbreak.

I looked around the room as we turned, trying to see if there was anyone I recognized and could name. This was a gathering of magic's elite; I should know some of them, or at least know *of* them. Aside from trying to place faces, I was checking for one person in particular. "Are you looking for someone?" Charming asked, watching me.

I turned my attention back to him. "Not anyone in particular, exactly."

The fact was that I actually was looking for someone. My uncle. I hadn't seen him in years, and had no idea if he'd be here. He didn't have magic—that I knew about, but he was associated with magic users, and there was a chance he could show up at the ball. If he did, and if he recognized me, Charming's security team was going to earn their paychecks.

"Not anyone particular, exactly?" Charming repeated, a question in his voice.

I lifted a shoulder, trying to make it seem like it wasn't a big deal but in reality, my heart was hammering a drum beat against my chest. "My uncle. There's a chance he could be here."

"And you don't get along with him?"

"No," I said flatly.

Charming's eyebrow went up like he wanted the rest of the story. I didn't want to go into that much detail.

"We haven't seen each other in years," I said. "Not since I was a child."

Charming cocked his head to the side and spun me around expertly before pulling me back into him. "Why not?"

"A multitude of reasons." I'd been in the throes of grief, a child desperate to understand what had happened to her parents, and struggling to deal with the realization that I'd never see them again when I'd found out that I would be living with my uncle and his sons, Mark and Kory—the same son who had tortured my little cat, Star. I hadn't stayed there long. The memories tasted bitter as I tried them out on my tongue, and quickly decided not to probe for more.

He nodded and we kept dancing. "I see my family frequently. Family is a big deal for the Hurstons."

I looked at him. "Congratulations." I tried not to let the words bother me. I hadn't had the luxury of a family until I'd created my own through my friends.

"Sometimes it's nice," he said, not picking up on my mood. "Other times it's annoying. But I love them."

Why was he telling me this?

"Do you want a family of your own someday?"

I stared, taken aback. "That's a really random and personal question. We hardly even know each other."

He lifted a shoulder in a half shrug. "Which is why I asked. I'm trying to get to know you." His lips formed a crooked, disarming smile that I didn't trust for a second. "It's just a question."

I considered it. I hadn't ever really thought about having a family of my own. My goal had always been to help people, and get revenge. Dating, relationships, family...those were things I'd never had the time to even contemplate. I didn't believe family meant blood. I'd created my own family, one that I loved very much. "I have my family. Sway, Perry, and all of my friends who live with me at Haven. They're the people who have been there for me my entire life. They'd take a bullet for me, and I'd do the same for them. It's a family I chose, and they make me happy."

He nodded, considering that. "But you could choose your partner as well, and have a family that included everyone."

Yes, I could. And maybe someday I would, but I hadn't really had a chance to think about relationships. I'd been too busy trying to survive my entire life, and keep my friends alive. "I haven't had much time to date, so that's not really on my radar."

"Do you want it to be?" he asked point blank.

I furrowed my brow and thought about it as we moved around the floor. I didn't know what I wanted. The only thing I'd ever been certain of was that I needed to find my parents' killers. "Maybe someday. I'm not sure."

He eyed me. "What's stopping you?"

I lifted a shoulder. "I have too many people I'm responsible for to take the time for me and my wants."

"Ah," he said, his tongue running slowly over his lips. "I can see how that would be difficult. But now you have a dedicated security team to help with some of that responsibility." He spun me again and this time when he pulled me back into him, I could feel every line of his body against my own. My heart sped up and he leaned in to whisper in my ear, "So maybe you need to make some changes."

My heart was thumping in my chest and I felt like I was in some weird twilight zone. The notorious Charming Hurston was interested in *me*? It was too unbelievable to comprehend. And then my bafflement abruptly turned to annoyance. Who did this attractive weather controlling mage think he was? Giving me life and love advice like he had some special insight into the secrets of the universe even though he wasn't much older than I was and he'd never had to struggle a day in his life. Just the other day he'd been stealing my shoe and infuriating me to no end! At what point did our relationship merge into him acting like he wanted to be my friend, and maybe even more than that? I tried to trace it and couldn't tell.

The air shifted slightly and Charming and I both looked up, noticing the change, but unable to pinpoint it. "Come on," Charming said, moving his hand from my back and lacing his fingers through mine.

He led me out the door into a beautiful garden area. A maze of flowers and leafy trees stretched before us, dotted by tiny lights that looked like fireflies flitting through the greenery. An asphalt walkway marked a path to navigate the gardens. I breathed in the fresh air. It was so much cooler outside, and I relished the breeze, though I was a little confused about why we weren't inside, trying to find out who took his sister. "Why are we out here?"

"Because I'm counting on the fact that the people we're looking for will follow us."

I stared at him. "Why do you think they'll do that?"

"Because the people who took my sister were interested in her magic. You're stunning, intriguing, and new and shiny. You wouldn't be here without magic and they'll want to know more about who you are, and what you can do."

"So you're using me." It was more of a statement than a question, but I was using him too.

"I think we're using each other." His eyes dropped, snagging on my lips. "They won't be able to resist you. I can't."

My cheeks pinked and I rolled my eyes to try and cover it. "You're being ridiculous."

He held my gaze, his eyes clear and focused. "I'm being honest."

I stared at him, trying to decide if he was really being sincere. I didn't see deception in his expression; instead I was faced with heat, focus, and determination. A flutter started in my stomach and the energy around us seemed to change. He moved closer to me, his hand still entwined with mine. His other hand came up and brushed the side of my cheek. I closed my eyes, reveling in the warmth of his touch and the feel of his body so close to mine. If he tried to kiss me now, I wasn't sure I'd have the self-control to stop him. And I wasn't sure I even wanted to.

"This isn't a good idea," I said, my voice soft.

"Mmm," he answered back, his fingers trailing along my collarbone. "Why is that."

"It would complicate things."

His lips slid into a slow, lazy smile. "I don't mind complicated."

A tingle ran over my lips and I licked them, trying to stop the anticipation. Charming's eyes caught on the movement. "My life is complicated enough."

"It doesn't have to be," he said, his voice gentle. "Let me help with that."

I blinked. The offer stunned me. I'd been on my own, responsible for so many people and taking care of myself for so long that the idea of having someone help me was hard to even wrap my head around.

"I have a lot of responsibilities."

He reached his hand up, a warm weight against the back of my neck and head. He leaned in, his eyes totally focused on mine. His lips were a hairsbreadth away as he whispered, "Let me help you." His mouth closed over mine, electricity flowing between us. His lips were silky soft as they moved with mine in a graceful dance, creating their own kind of magic. It was like the two of us were merging, our energies becoming one. I'd never felt like this before...I'd never wanted anyone. I hadn't allowed myself to want, or need, or think beyond my goals of vengeance. But I wanted this, and wanted him. Badly. And it was terrifying. Whatever this was felt a lot like need. I didn't want to need anyone. I'd built my life on being alone and not having to depend on anyone because last time I'd relied on other people, they'd been taken from me. I couldn't handle that heartbreak again. I pulled away.

"What's wrong," he asked, his hands resting on my waist as his eyes searched mine.

"I can't," I said, stepping back, away from his touch. Severing the connection felt like a knife slicing through me. I looked down and wished my life were different and I didn't have to stop this thing between us before it even really started. "This won't work."

"Why?"

Because it couldn't. Because I'd just had a glimpse into what my life could have been. I *wanted* a partner, and companion, and best friend I could always count on. I wanted this too much and it would break me when Charming inevitably left to go charm someone else and I was on my own again. I'd been broken before. I could get through it. But I wasn't going to put myself in that position willingly. "We're too different."

Emotion feathered across his face. "That's one of the reasons I want this...want you. You're different, and I love that about you. I love your fire, your independence, your fierce soul. I want it all. I want you, Hadley."

He'd just basically said he loved me. No one had ever told me that —not since I was a child. My heart constricted at his words. I wanted that too. Everything he'd said was perfect. But a relationship with Charming couldn't last. It wouldn't, and I knew it. I wouldn't do that to myself.

I shook my head slightly, and his jaw tightened. I could see that he was getting ready to launch into another speech that would try to make me reconsider. He might succeed.

"Hadley—"

I let my eyes fall to the floor and in that moment, the material of my dress shimmered. The beautiful gown Sway had made for me with her magic started to falter. "Oh no," I gasped.

"What is it?" Charming asked, worry lining his face.

"It's Sway," I said, pointing to the lace that was fading in and out in color from sapphire to white. "Something must have happened to her. She made the dress and her magic is weakening. She's either in distress, or someone is siphoning her magic."

CHAPTER 4

$\mathcal{I}$ reached down and picked up the gown so I could run, and took off into the ballroom. Charming followed behind me, right on my heels. I needed to figure out where Sway was. People stared as we ran out of the ballroom into the hallway. I'd always had a strange connection to my friends. I could feel them when they were around, I just needed to center myself and concentrate. I stopped in an arched alcove of the giant building and closed my eyes, breathing in and out slowly and rhythmically. After about a minute, I felt pulled down the hall. I followed my instinct and Charming followed me.

We turned down another hallway, then opened a door and went into a corridor. We were getting closer, I could feel it. That's was when I heard an urgent whisper from a room to the side of us. "Hadley!"

I swung my head in the direction of the noise. It was Perry. I ran and hugged him, so grateful he was there, safe, and unharmed. I never wanted to let him go. "What happened?"

He shook his head, his face sheathed with worry. "Sway was asked to dance by a few different guys. One of them seemed to like her a lot. Some guy named Mark." The hair on the back of my neck stood straight up and I tried not to overreact. There were a lot of Marks in the world. It couldn't be the same Mark I knew, my cousin. "Everyone saw us walk in with you, and then you left with Charming which made people even more curious. Everyone wanted to know who you were, and we were getting a lot of attention." I was angry with myself. I shouldn't have ever left them alone. Charming had thought we'd draw the bad guys out into the garden; instead, they'd zeroed in on our friends.

"Where was our security team?" I asked Perry, and slid my eyes to Charming whose face was also pulled tight with concern.

"All but one of them followed you out into the garden," Perry said.

"They probably thought we were the bigger targets," Charming said, grimacing. "I thought we were too."

So had I.

"The guy who stayed with us was monitoring us, but someone came up and distracted him. I don't think he saw Sway or I leave."

Charming's eyes narrowed and I could tell he was unhappy. "I'm sorry. I promised you safety and my security team screwed up. I will handle this after we find Sway."

I was frustrated, but mistakes happen. It sounded like this abduction was planned. The security guy had been distracted on purpose so that Sway could be taken. "Mistakes happen and I'm sure distracting him was part of the plan." I turned to Perry and asked, "What happened next?"

"Mark offered to take Sway to get a drink. I had a weird feeling about him, so I discreetly followed behind them. As they were walking away, another guy Mark had been hanging out with started following him too. Mark led Sway here, and then they all went into this room." He pointed to the large French doors in front of us. "I've been trying to decide how to attack. I thought about trying to find you, but I didn't want to risk the chance of them leaving and me not knowing where they'd gone. I'm a good fighter, but I don't know how many people are in there, and you know my magic doesn't work quickly."

Perry's magic was pretty incredible but the side effects hit people later. He was smart to not go in there alone. "You did the right thing," I reassured him.

I turned to Charming. "We know we have at least two people in there with Sway. Maybe more. Are you ready for this?"

Charming gave me an amused look. "I won't have a problem." And with that, he kicked open the door, his magic pushing out and the air spiraling around him like a hurricane he could control with laser precision.

We walked in to see Sway sitting in a chair, being held against her will by two men I hated with my whole soul: my cousins Mark and Kory. They were taller now, and they'd filled out, but their beady eyes and disgusting smirks were exactly the same as I remembered. Sway's face was a study in condensed rage, and I knew she was itching to get up and use some of her karate skills on them both. I would have happily paid to watch that fight, and would have liked participating in it even more.

Mark and Kory each gave me a terrible smile that was so awful I immediately wanted to wash their gazes off. "Long time no see, El."

"Yes," another deep, familiar, and horrifying voice said from the other side of the room. My head swiveled in his direction at the same time my stomach knotted.

I froze, paralyzed at the sight of him. My uncle, Robert Dodd. The man I'd run away from years ago, and hoped I'd never have to see again. My whole body ached with rage and fear as my mind raced. I was going to be sick—but not until I stopped Robert, Mark and Kory.

My uncle gave me an appraising look. "You turned into quite the lovely young lady. I see you changed your hair. It used to be long and blonde, like your mother's." I'd changed my entire appearance when I'd run away because I knew he'd be looking for me. My skin crawled at his visual appraisal and his words. "In fact, I wouldn't have known it was you at all if it wasn't for your name." He shook his head slightly. "You're pretty, but you never were the smartest. Using your mom and dad's names to create your fake name was a poor choice, El."

The more he spoke, the angrier I became. My real name was Ella Hart, and it made me furious that he'd used my nickname. That name was a name my parents had lovingly chosen and used. He wasn't allowed to use it too.

"Do you have any idea how long I searched for you?" he asked. "Years, Ella. Every time news about a fire mage came through the gossip circles, I would increase my efforts with the hope that we could find you, but you covered your tracks well. Until now. Thanks for making it so easy for me. Had I known I just had to take someone you cared about, I would have made more of an effort to keep your parents alive."

Blood drained from my face and I felt like I'd been stabbed. I knew my parents had been murdered by someone heartless, but I hadn't guessed that they'd been murdered by a family member. There couldn't be a worse betrayal. I felt faint and the icy prickles of shock started to set in. At the same time, I felt Charming's hand on my back, steadying me. His touch grounded me with support and I came back to the present. No. This was not happening again. I was not losing another person I loved. I would deal with my uncle and the revelation of who murdered my parents, but not until I saved Sway.

I wanted to kill him, slowly and with a lot of pain. But right now he was deliberately using my emotion to try and distract me. I couldn't let that happen. "Let her go," I growled through my teeth.

His eyes flashed with challenge and his lips lifted in a terrible way. "Come with me, and I will."

"No," Charming said, stepping forward. His voice was solid and brokered no argument.

My uncle laughed like Charming's denial was the funniest thing he'd ever heard. "Do you really think you can stop me from getting what I want, Hurston? Trust me, you can't. And neither can your family's security team and investigators combing everywhere from the tunnels in the city to the forest surrounding Everly looking for your sister."

Charming's eyes hardened with fury and he looked like he wanted to commit murder. "How do you know about my sister, the security team, and the investigation?" he asked, his voice dangerously soft.

My uncle lifted his shoulders. "Your sister has been missing for days. Everyone knows about it."

Charming eyed him. "No, they don't. We've told very few people and only our security team knows about the rescue efforts, or where the searches are taking place."

My uncle's lips spread into a smile that showed his teeth, and they looked ready to bite something in half. "Maybe your team isn't as loyal as you thought. I know a lot of things."

Charming's face morphed into a blank mask. It was the same face I'd seen him make in the tornado video right before he'd made the twister crumble into nothing. "Do you know where my sister, Sarah, is?"

My uncle lifted a shoulder in a half shrug. "I might."

Charming's hands clenched into fists and the air around him started whipping into a frenzy. I stepped back, trying to shield myself from some of the wind. "Tell me," Charming said through his teeth.

My uncle inclined his head in my direction. "Give me your girl-friend, and I will."

Anger flashed across Charming's face. He was absolutely seething. "You're the lowest form of human scum that has ever lived, Dodd. People aren't things. They're not made to be traded or given to anyone."

My uncle gave him a bored look. "Do you want to see your sister again, or not?"

Charming's expression shifted, determination mingling with fury. "If you think you can fight me, you're an idiot."

My uncle's lips curled into a twisted, evil smile. "Let's see how much of an idiot I am."

The air around us started to shimmer and in seconds, there were at least fifty versions of my uncle surrounding us, all smiling the same, evil smile. I couldn't tell the difference between them, and couldn't figure out who was the real one. My uncle didn't have magic of his own, and had always been angry about his lack of power. Since he wasn't born with magic, this meant he'd harnessed his magic from some other mage, in his own personal Jekyll and Hyde lab—something he'd been trying to perfect for years. Either that, or he'd paid the Magic Harnessers a great deal of money to transfer magic to him.

"Who did you steal your magic from, Robert?" I said, my eyes going around the room and trying to pinpoint who my real uncle was.

All fifty versions of my uncle laughed, creating a vile concert of noise. "A better question would be: who didn't I steal from? I've had goals for a long time. You know that, El. If you hadn't run away, I'd have your magic too."

Memories of my past and that awful lab sprung into my head and threatened to cripple me. I couldn't let that happen. I dug down into the well of anger that consumed me and pulled from the fury, determined to use my rage for fuel.

The fifty versions of my uncle all spoke at once. "I knew you had magic. So did your parents, but they weren't concerned until the night you tried to start poor Mark on fire after he was just playing with your cat.

"He wasn't playing with her," I snarled. "He was torturing her."

Robert shrugged. "Tomato, tomahto. When Mark came to tell us what you'd done, your parents were worried and discussed sending you to a school for mages so you could learn how to use your powers. That just wouldn't do for my needs. You were clearly a powerful mage to be able to use your magic at such a young age, and with no training. I knew if you were sent away, you'd be protected and I'd never have the chance to take your power from you. So I sent a shifter to abduct you, one known for his fierce protective instincts—because I didn't want you to come to me dead and useless—and one who was also incredibly strong and powerful. My shifter tried to get into your room that night, but couldn't. Someone had put an incredibly powerful protection spell on your door. When shifters can't complete a task, they get angry. So it went looking for another way to reach its goal. It found your parents and killed them instead. It was an unfortunate turn of events. I would have just as soon preferred to only take you and leave your parents alive, but it all worked out. Once your parents died, I became your legal guardian and got you anyway, like a gift from the universe wrapped up in a pretty little bow. In retrospect, I could have saved myself a lot of time and trouble by just killing them to begin with."

I stared at him, bile rolling in my stomach and wrath rising in my throat. "My parents' lives weren't things you could just discard."

He gave me a condescending look. "But I did."

My blood felt like it was boiling. I'd never been so angry in my life. I wanted to reach over and rip his heart out of his chest. I'd have to settle for burning him to death. If I could kill him twice, I would. We needed to save Sway and Sarah so I could.

He'd chosen the wrong mage to play his illusion game with. He didn't know the extent of my magic, but his trick was about to become useless. Fury surged within me; anger at my uncle for what he'd done, and how he'd ruined my life in multiple ways. Anger that he was trying to hurt Sarah in the same way he'd hurt me, and anger that he was threatening my friends and using them as a bargaining chip.

All of the versions of my uncle lifted their arms, pushing Sway toward my cousins, and the two of them took off, holding Sway's arms and legs so she couldn't wrestle away. Perry tried to catch them and Charming tried to slam the doors shut, but they were both a second too late. I wanted to take off after them and save Sway, but I couldn't. I had to stay and fight my uncle. I was the only one who could.

I focused my anger back on Robert, and all fifty copies of him. Flames danced in my eyes and fire burst around each version of him, surging up like a spiral around them. His face was a mask of anger, and as the fire continued, growing hotter, turning from orange, to blue and white, some of the anger was replaced with uncertainty and fear. The various fake Uncle Roberts' started popping out of existence as soon as they got too hot.

Charming held the doors shut with his magic to make sure no one else could get in or out. My uncle wasn't leaving here unless one of us let him.

I heard a creaking noise and looked up. Another chandelier hung above us, just like the massive one in the lobby. And it started to sway. Violently. Charming wasn't paying any attention to it.

"Storm!" I yelled, panic ringing in my voice. I pointed up and watched as the chandelier snapped. It all happened in slow motion.

Without even looking Storm *moved*, pulling me with him as he twisted out of the way of the chandelier, and raising his arms at the same time. A gust of wind came out of nowhere and captured the chandelier, setting it down gently on the floor. If it had crashed, we would have been crushed and the glass would have shattered, slicing us all.

Charming and I looked at each other, relief washing over both of our faces. Perry stood off to the side of us, his eyes wide with shock. I turned back to my uncle Robert, and my breath caught in my throat. One of the doors was wide open and he was gone. "Where is he?" I asked.

Fury radiated from Charming. "I couldn't hold the doors and the chandelier at the same time. He must have realized that and escaped."

My heart sank at Charming's words. I'd brought my friends with me and put them in danger, and now they were in even worse danger and it was my fault. I needed to do something to fix this, but had no idea where to even begin. I didn't know where they'd gone, or what they planned to do with Sway. I'd failed to protect the people I loved the most. How could I right such a massive wrong?

I looked around the room at the shattered glass, torn curtains, and destroyed furniture, and came to terms with reality. My uncle and cousins were gone. And so was my friend. I collapsed on the floor, my head in my hands.

CHAPTER 5

*M*y emotions were all over the place, despair and anger, hopelessness and determination. One minute I wanted to sob into my hands, the next minute I wanted to use them to fight my uncle and cousins until we were all bloody and I'd stopped them from hurting any other person ever again. Sway was my family, and now my uncle had her. He'd taken my family before, and now he was doing it again. I had no idea what he wanted Sway for, other than leverage. He wanted me, undoubtedly for my magic—he'd always wanted it—and hostages were helpful in getting your way. Knowing he had Sway brought back every horrible memory of losing my parents. And now I knew that I'd lost my parents and Sway to the same man—but Sway wasn't dead yet. That was the thought that pulled me from my despair. I would find Sway and I would fight to get her back because there was no way I was letting that malevolent man take any of my family again.

I got up, steel in my eyes, resolve coursing through me. I wouldn't let them have Sway, or anyone else. "Come on," I said, motioning for Charming and Perry to follow me.

"Where are we going?" Perry asked.

Charming was looking at something on his phone as he ran next to me. "We had a security team outside the hotel. They saw Sway in a car with your uncle and cousins as it sped out of the parking lot. My team has eyes on their vehicle. We're following, and we'll know where they're going."

Charming's security team was handy to have around. I already had a suspicion about where they were going, however. It was a place that haunted my nightmares. When my uncle found out I had magical powers, he'd been incredibly jealous. He'd always wanted magic, and wanted his sons to have it too. They didn't, but I did. He'd built a makeshift magic siphoning lab in the basement of his vacation home. It was only about an hour from the city, nestled into a quiet piece of land by the beach, and it was rarely used unless he needed it for his own nefarious purposes. He'd tried to take my magic there repeatedly with his own resources. And when it hadn't worked—because of his lack of experience stealing magic and my sheer anger and will, he'd decided to send me to the Magic Harnessers so they could take it for him. Magic siphoning was dangerous, painful, and often killed the mage the magic was being stolen from. I refused to let that happen to me. When I'd found out my uncle's plans to send me to the Magic Harnessers, I'd decided to run away to save my life. I'd never shown my uncle the extent of my magic—but I would tonight.

"I think he's taking her to his magic siphoning lab in the basement of his vacation home. I'm almost certain of it." I said as we got to Charming's car, a black Escalade with chrome trim. It shined like a diamond and practically screamed money.

"He has his own lab?" Charming asked, stunned. He got in the front seat and I jumped in the passenger side. Perry got in the back.

We sped out of the parking lot with Charming following the directions that were being sent to his phone from his team.

I nodded. "He wanted his own magic, and wanted his sons to have it too. None of them did."

"What about your aunt?"

"She didn't have magic either."

"Where is she now?" Charming asked.

"She died when my cousins were young."

"Of what?"

I'd never actually been sure. "They told us it was an accident, but now I wonder if that was really the case. She was a kind woman, but she wouldn't have stood for my uncle's magic obsession. My uncle is a lunatic and I wouldn't put murder past him. I don't remember her well because I was only four when she passed away."

Charming's eyes hardened and his anger seemed to be building even more. "I have no tolerance for people who hurt others."

Neither did I; I'd spent my life fighting against it.

I had a good idea of why my uncle wanted Sway—to use as a bargaining tool to get to me, but I still wasn't sure how Charming's sister fit into this, or what Robert wanted from her. "Why does he want Sarah?"

He pressed his lips together and slid a glance toward me, then to Perry. "If I tell you this, it has to stay between us."

I nodded in agreement and Perry shrugged and nodded as well.

Charming's grip on the wheel tightened, his knuckles going white. "She has a unique magic. Our family has kept it a secret for years, but she used it to help someone a month ago and we weren't able to completely contain the information."

"What is her power?"

He took a deep breath and then answered, "She makes the transfer of magic seamless."

I stared at him. "You mean she can perform a magic transfer on people without any Harnesser intervention?"

He nodded slowly.

"How long does the transfer take?"

"It's immediate."

I gaped at him.

"What's the success rate?"

"One hundred percent."

My mouth fell open even more. The transfer of magic had become a science that had been learned through years of trial and error. A gifted Magic Harnesser could control the amount of magic being taken, and most Magic Harnessers could take magic from mages and transfer it to others, but the process was long—days depending on the amount of power and type of magic being transferred—and painful, and it didn't always take. If his sister's magic had the ability to make the transfer of magic quick, easy, and painless, that could change everything. Everyone would want her...especially people like my uncle.

"That explains why my uncle wants her," I said. "He doesn't have magic of his own and he's been trying to get it for years. I wouldn't be surprised if he hired his own Magic Harnesser. Whatever we saw back there in the ballroom with the multiple copies of him was the result of a Magic Harnesser giving him that ability. If he has your sister, his powers could be limitless. He's had her for a week. I'm surprised he hasn't already forced a transfer."

Charming shook his head. "Her power only works if she's willing." His phone rang and he picked it up. "Good. We'll wait for your signal and then follow." He hung up.

Charming pulled to the side of the road a few blocks from my uncle's vacation house and came to a stop behind another black SUV that held some of his security team. It was a road I'd been on many times, and the memories of coming here and enduring the torture my uncle put me through while he tried to take my magic made my stomach clench.

"We're stopping here in case your uncle has his own surveillance. My team is already on the way to check out the perimeter, and we'll follow as soon as we get the call."

I nodded and tried to keep myself from going insane with worry. Less than five minutes later, Charming's phone buzzed and we started toward the house with Charming's security team.

They motioned us to the front door where we crept inside behind several armed guards. I looked around and remembered every part of the house. Not much had changed in the twelve years since I'd been here last. The compartmentalized layout was the same, and so was the décor, a mix of modern and classic. A layer of dust covered the surfaces of the furniture and the air smelled musty and stale. The home wasn't used much. One of the guys pointed to the stairs and we formed a single file line, quietly following them down.

When we got to the bottom, we were in an empty, large room. I pointed down the hall toward the back of the house. There was a door there that opened up into a large lab. In any other house, it would have been four separate bedrooms, but my uncle had made it into one large, horrible room of torture.

We could hear voices coming from inside. There were at least four people in there: my uncle, Mark, Kory, and Sway. I hoped Sarah was in there too.

The lead on the security team motioned for us to move. We did and he took a few steps back to get some velocity behind him, then ran and kicked the door as hard as he could. The door frame splintered and the door swung open as all of Charming's team pushed inside and we followed. The whole thing took seconds and as we descended on them, my uncle and cousin's faces were priceless, their mouths frozen open in shock.

Sway was tied to a chair, next to another girl who was also tied and hooked up to a multitude of wires. I heard a sound that could only be described as a growl come from Charming as he surveyed the room and his eyes landed on the two girls. The girl next to Sway was surely Sarah.

Charming motioned to his team and they moved forward like they were one person instead of ten, each movement precisely choreographed.

"I don't think so," my uncle said. He raised his arms and a transparent wall seemed to build between him and us. Charming's men ran toward it and were stopped in their tracks. They tried kicking and punching it, but nothing happened. One of them took his gun and shot at a corner, in an area where it wouldn't affect anyone if the shot bounced off the wall. The bullet hit the wall and dropped straight to the ground. My uncle laughed with victory, confidant he'd won this fight.

The anger that had been boiling inside me was back, and getting hotter. I couldn't let this horrible man win. Who knew what damage he'd already done to Sarah. I walked to the edge of the wall, examining it.

"There's nothing you can do, El," my uncle taunted. "The wall can't be penetrated by fire."

I looked at him and smiled slowly, danger glinting in my eyes. Fire wasn't my only trick.

I lifted my arms, palms out and focused every bit of my intention on my uncle and that wall. Flames started in my eyes, white hot, and then they began to build around the wall. I focused on the wall, testing a theory—my uncle's magic wasn't real. It was stolen from other people and even though magic could be transferred, it was never as strong as when the original magic holder used it. My uncle's magic was as fake as he was, and nothing more than an illusion he'd constructed. I specialized in burning up those falsities and I knew that I could do it to him too. The flames burned hotter and my uncle's face grew more and more concerned. The top of the wall started to crumble. I'd stripped him of the illusion and as soon as I did, the wall fell, scattering into hundreds of cinders smoldering on the ground, awaiting my next instructions.

My uncle's mouth fell open and he seemed paralyzed with shock.

"You never did know the extent of my magic, Robert. I never let you see it." Blue fire filtered my vision and his face became a mask of terror and awe. My voice came out as a roar, "I'll let you see it now."

I twisted my wrist, guiding the cinders toward him, circling him, their tiny pieces glowing with anticipation.

"My fire burns away illusions and I can see a person's true nature and reflect it back to them. Their true nature is a culmination of all the things they've done and lied to themselves about... things they've convinced themselves are true. I gather their illusions and the lies they've composed about who they think they are, and pull them away from the person. When that happens, the illusion bursts into flames. The cinders fall, turn to glass, and reflect the person's true selves back at them. They are the things people know deep down, but can't face. It often causes them to have a psychotic break because most people can't handle the truth." I eyed him. "I have a feeling you'll be one of those people, Uncle. Why don't we find out?"

With that, I let the fire rise. It burst up into a column of orange and blue flames that consumed him. He screamed, a sharp, piercing noise, not from the pain of the fire, but from the pain of being stripped of the fallacies he'd composed about who he thought he was.

As the fire died down, the ashes fell and the glass reflected his true self back at him. He was an ugly, horrible man with a heart as black as tar. Everyone's mirror was different; some were words, some were images, sometimes it was a combination of both. Words started forming in the glass. Murderer, kidnapper, liar, thief...all things he knew about himself, but refused to own or see the truth in.

My uncle's face crumpled into a defeated mess and he fell to the ground in a ball, sobbing. He was a broken man and I felt no remorse for making him feel that way.

Charming rushed forward to his sister and yanked the wires off her body. Perry ran to Sway and untied the ropes. Sway looked ready to kill someone. "Let me at him," she snarled.

Perry shook his head. "I don't think that's a good idea."

"It's an *excellent* idea," she growled. "Let me go!"

Mark and Kory started to move toward us, anger fanning their faces. Before they could take more than a few steps they both fell to the ground clutching their stomachs, their faces contorting in serious pain.

Perry's eyebrow went up. "Guess my magic kicked in faster than usual."

Perry's magic basically turned him into the karma police. Depending on how a person had lived their life, his magic could be a good thing, or a very bad one. He was able to make someone responsible for their own actions, and make them feel the emotions they'd caused others to feel. Based on how my cousins were writhing on the floor, Mark and Kory had a lot to make up for.

As soon as Sarah was untangled, she jumped up from the chair and grabbed onto Charming as tears leaked from her eyes. He wrapped her in a huge hug, his expression full of love and relief. "I'm so glad we found you," Charming said.

"Me too," Sarah said. "I wanted to kill that jerk."

"I don't think anyone would have minded if you did," one of the security guys said.

He took his mask off and I blinked. "Kerry?" I said, my voice baffled and my expression completely stunned.

His lips spread into a kind smile. "Good thing I gave you those shoes at the ball or I might not have found you."

I stared at him, dumbfounded. "You're the one who gave me the shoes?"

"Course I am. They were spelled so I'd be able to keep track of you. Did you think this knucklehead sent them?" Kerry asked, nodding toward Charming.

I looked between them. "Yeah, I kind of did."

The corner of Kerry's lips went up in a playful smile. "He has no taste. He would have bought you something awful."

"Hey!" Charming said, punching him playfully in the shoulder. "Be nice."

I was so confused. "Do you work for Charming?"

Kerry shook his head. "No, but we know each other. When he was wandering around the tunnels like a lost puppy with your shoe, I pointed him in the right direction."

Charming rolled his eyes. "I wasn't acting like a lost puppy."

Kerry put his thumb and forefinger up about an inch apart from each other. "A little."

I still didn't understand. "So you knew I was going to the ball with him? And you just decided to leave your tunnel post and join his security team for the night?"

Kerry lifted his shoulders. "Well, it's kind of in my job description."

"What's your job description?"

He gave me a look. "I'm your Magic Godfather."

I stared at him, incapable of making words for several seconds. "My what?"

"Magic Godfather." He said the words slowly, like he was trying to help my mind wrap itself around the information.

"One, I wasn't aware that Magic Godfathers existed, and two, I didn't know I had one."

"That's kind of the point. If we went around advertising our services, everyone would know who we are and what we could do, and we wouldn't be much help."

"How long have you been my Magic Godfather?"

He lifted a shoulder. "Since you were born."

How had I never been told about this? I'd never met Kerry until I ran away from my uncle Robert. Kerry was the first person I met my first night alone when I was seeking shelter, and he introduced me to the tunnels and showed me the building I later turned into Haven. "Does everyone have a Magic Godfather?"

"Not everyone, but your parents made sure you did."

"My parents?"

"They didn't know if you had magic when you were born, but they hired me as a precaution. They had me spell your bedroom to make sure you'd always be safe. None of us considered that there might ever be a threat to them as well. I'm sorry I wasn't able to save them too."

I stared at him again, my eyes blurring. "You're the reason my uncle's shifter didn't take me away that night?"

He nodded in a matter of fact way, like it wasn't even a big deal. My heart felt like it was going to burst. All of the emotions I'd been feeling seemed to crash into me at once and I flung myself at Kerry, wrapping my arms around his neck, tears falling silently down my cheeks. "Thank you for saving me."

"I always will, El. Always. I know you've felt alone for a long time, but you never were, I promise. I'm so proud of the woman you've become and how you use your powers. Your mom and dad would have been proud too."

I wiped tears as I stepped back, looking at the scene. My cousins and uncle on the ground, and my friends at my side. "What are we going to do with them?" I asked.

"The Mystic Commission is on its way and they'll take care of your uncle and cousins," Charming said. "Aside from kidnapping, they've broken several laws regarding magic harnessing and transferring. They'll be locked away somewhere they can't hurt you anymore."

His words were like a balm for a wound that had been gaping open for years.

"Thank you," I said, the release overwhelming me and lifting a heavy weight off of my chest.

"You're welcome."

I looked at Sway and Perry, relief shining through my tears. "Let's go home."

CHAPTER 6

*I*t had been a week since the Mystic Ball and the confrontation with my uncle. Charming was right. The Mystic Commission worked swiftly and had judged my uncle and cousins to be a severe threat. They were sent away to a prison specially built to contain mages in another state. Things had started to get back to normal at home. There were rumors swirling about Hadley Scott, the fiery eyed girl in blue who showed up at the Mystic Ball. I knew it was only a matter of time before I had to accept my place as a mage and live in the open with my powers. But I'd keep it a secret as long as I could. It was a relief to know that I was safe, and so were the people I cared about. I had my friends who were basically family, my own powers, and I had my very own Magic Godfather looking after me just in case I ever came across a situation I couldn't handle on my own. Charming had followed through on his word. Haven, and all of the people who lived there with me, had a security team. It hadn't helped much at the ball, but I'd take all the extra protection I could get to keep my friends safe.

The fall day was unseasonably warm on my walk home from work. As I passed one of my favorite parks, I decided to sit by the lake and reflect on everything that had happened during the past two weeks. The sky was pale blue, dusted with clouds, and the lake was a calm sheen, fish swimming peacefully below the surface while ducks floated aimlessly above.

I sat there and thought about life. Two weeks ago, I'd been living the same way I always had—fighting to reach a goal, fighting to stay alive and keep the people I loved safe. I hadn't known Charming, or revealed myself in the magic world. Now a simple stolen shoe had changed everything. The threats were gone for now, but as life went on and people realized Hadley Scott was actually Cinder, new threats would emerge. I'd gone back to work, and things in my universe had calmed down. For the first time in my life, I wasn't worried about who might be looking for me, or about spending all of my extra time searching for my parents' killers. I'd found the man who sent the shifter that had killed my parents, and murdered the friends of Charming's sister. According to Charming, the shifter had been located and subdued by the Hurston family security team. I reached my goal, and now I wasn't sure what to do with myself. My life had been so focused on one task—finding out who took my family from me—that I no longer knew my purpose. Maybe it was time for me to start living for me, instead of living for revenge.

My thoughts strayed to Charming. After we'd left my uncle's house, he'd called to check on me a couple of times. But that's the only contact we'd had. I wasn't sure what to think about that. There was definitely chemistry and a connection between us, and our kiss at the ball had heated me from the inside out before I'd pulled away because I didn't want to end up heartbroken. If everything I'd heard about him was true, he wasn't the relationship type. I'd never even allowed myself to think of a relationship before because I'd been so focused on finding my parents' murderers. Now that was taken care of, but the thought of starting a relationship for the first time, especially with someone like Charming—egotistical, stubborn, challenging, and so freaking hot, terrified me. Could I handle a relationship? Could Charming and I really make one work?

The glass-like surface of the lake was suddenly dotted with drops and fish started jumping. I looked up and saw his tall form, carved arms, and wide shoulders before my eyes landed on his perfect face. Charming was standing five feet from me with a bag of fish food.

It was like I conjured him out of thin air by thinking about him.

"Hi," I said carefully, wondering what he was doing here.

"Hi," he said back. "Come here often?" His eyebrow went up and then one corner of his lips slid into that alluring smile I'd come to think of far too often.

I stared at him. "That's a horrible line."

"It wasn't a line. I'm genuinely curious."

I looked out at the lake and the fish waiting for their benefactor to drop more food. "Sometimes I stop on my way home from work. It's a good place to think."

He inclined his head. "What are you thinking about?"

Him, but I wasn't about to admit that. "Life."

He dropped some more fish food and then moved toward me, sitting next to me on the bench. Less than three inches separated his leg from mine and so help me, I wanted to close the distance and feel his arms wrapped around me again. "Do those thoughts include anyone else?"

I narrowed my eyes. What was he getting at? "Like my friends?"

He leaned back against the bench and stretched an arm behind me. "Them too. But I was mostly thinking about me. Us."

I blinked. "*Should* my life thoughts and plans include you?"

He fixed his eyes on mine and I couldn't look away. "Do you want them to?"

It felt like butterflies had started a party in my stomach and my heart sped up. I lifted my shoulder, unsure how to answer. Yes, I wanted to see what this was between us. I wanted to have a relationship. But Charming wasn't the relationship type and I'd had enough heartbreak in my life.

"Why did you pull away from our kiss at the ball?" he asked.

I looked at him for several seconds before answering, "Do you want the truth?"

"I always want the truth."

I looked down, composing my thoughts before meeting his eyes.

"You're rich, privileged, and you have a reputation for being a spoiled playboy. I doubt you've ever had someone say no to you in your life."

"That's not true," he said, his tone mildly amused. "You've said no repeatedly, and kicked me with your shoe."

I gave him a look. "You deserved the kick."

He tilted his head and I couldn't tell if it was in agreement, or dissent. "The gossip columns aren't the best place to get accurate information about me. I dated a lot when I was younger, but I graduated with my master's degree a few years ago and I've been working with my parents, learning the family business. I go out occasionally with clients and take a date, but it's nothing serious. I haven't had a relationship in a long time. I haven't wanted one." He paused, holding my gaze. "Until now."

I stared at him, eyes wide. I hadn't been expecting that declaration, or his directness. It took me a minute to recover before I could answer. "I already told you that we come from two different worlds. I'm not used to your world, and don't know if it's the life I want. The magic world is full of power and politics. It's not a world I've ever wanted. I'm happy in the tunnels with my friends. I could keep being happy there."

He stared at the water for a long time, his face a calm mask. After several minutes he said, "You've spent your whole life trying to get revenge, and helping others. Your friends will always be there for you, that doesn't have to change, regardless of what else you choose to do in life, or with your magic. I hate to be the one to break this to you, but you might not have a choice about becoming part of the magic world. You were the talk of the ball, Hadley—or Ella," he said, raising an eyebrow in question. I didn't have an answer for him. "The hotel had security cameras that caught your magic on video. My security team was able to isolate the recordings, but we don't know who saw them before we did, or if there are any other copies. At some point, you're going to have to declare your powers." He turned to me, his eyes clear. "I'd like to be there to help you navigate the waters of the magic world when you do."

My heart surged at his admission. "Why?"

He licked his lips slowly, a wet sheen of temptation left behind. "I know what it felt like dancing with you, and then outside on the balcony. I've never felt that with anyone else. I want you in my life, El. If you want to be part of it."

I looked up and met his gaze. "I haven't had an easy life, Storm, and I've had enough heartbreak to last a lifetime. How do I know you're telling the truth and you're not going to hurt me?"

He pressed his lips together like he was thinking and then said, "I can't promise you I'll never hurt you, but I can promise you I'll do my best not to."

I wasn't sure if that promise was enough.

"Test me," he said.

"What?"

"Strip away the illusion and see who I really am, El. See if you can trust me, and if you want to be with me."

Striping the illusion away could be a painful process, or a pleasant one, depending on who the person was, and how much they'd lied to themselves. It wasn't something I did lightly. "You don't know what you're asking. It might not be a pleasant experience, Storm. Most people can't handle who they really are."

"I can," he said immediately. "Test me."

I bit my lip, studying him. He wasn't going to let this go. "Okay," I said. "There's a garden on the other side of the park that's enclosed and private. We can do it there."

We walked together and when we came to the entrance we went through a tunnel of flowers and leaves that opened up into a quiet, serene garden fragrant with blooming flowers and freshly turned soil. It was one of my favorite parts of the park. We stood on an area with brick pavers and I looked into his eyes, searching for any hint of reticence. I found a calm and quiet confidence instead. "Are you ready?"

He nodded.

I closed my eyes and raised my hands, letting my magic push onto him. The flames rose around him, a brilliant orange and blue, before the cinders from his illusion scattered to the ground. I gathered them, and pushed them toward him. Then waited for Charming's mirror to appear. It did, and what it reflected back shocked me. It was Charming, helping others, caring for animals, speaking for those who couldn't speak for themselves. He was good, and he was kind, and I knew he really would try not to hurt me. And I realized the truth was I hadn't needed my illusion breaking magic to tell me that. The only thing holding me back from him was fear, and I'd never let fear rule my life before. I wasn't about to start now.

He reached out and took my hands in his, the touch warm and reassuring. "Be with me."

I looked up at him, emotion clouding my vision, and flung my arms around his neck. His strong arms went around my back and I was sheltered and safe and my heart felt like it might burst in my chest. His lips found mine and told me everything my magic already had. This was a man who was truly good, and would do anything to make me happy. It was something I hadn't even realized I'd wanted, but now I didn't want to imagine life without it.

A gust of wind picked up and Storm used his magic to sweep the glass into a trash can. One piece fell to the ground. I bent to pick it up and looked at it, then started to laugh. Charming's brow went up with interest as he looked over my shoulder and then started laughing too. It was a picture of my shoe. "So you're not all good, Charming. Even my magic knows you're a thief."

The smile he flashed me could have lit up an entire city. "I'd happily do it all over again if it meant I got you."

My cheeks pinked and joy washed through me like a ray of white light. I put my arms around his neck and he returned the favor, wrapping his arms around my waist. "You were right," I said.

One of his eyebrows rose. "About what?"

"You said one day I'd ask you to capture me. I'm asking you now."

The corners of his lips kicked up. "And I'm never letting you go." His lips met mine and with them, the weight that had been on my shoulders my whole life lifted, carried by two instead of one.

Charming took my hand and I followed him through the garden tunnel and out into the world and our happily ever after.

ABOUT THE AUTHOR

Angela Corbett graduated from Westminster College and previously worked as a journalist, freelance writer, and director of communications and marketing. She lives in Utah with her extremely supportive husband, and loves classic cars, traveling, and chasing their five-pound Pomeranian, Pippin—who is just as mischievous as his hobbit namesake. She's the author of Young Adult, New Adult, and Adult fiction—with lots of kissing. She writes under two names, Angela Corbett, and Destiny Ford.

Join my newsletter to get a free book! <u>Click here</u>

For special sneak peeks and giveaways, follow Angela here:
www.angelacorbett.com

facebook.com/AuthorAngelaCorbett

twitter.com/angcorbett

instagram.com/byangcorbett

THE WRONG FOOT

ADRIENNE MONSON

THE WRONG FOOT

Paranormal Romance

by

Adrienne Monson

Proclamation to the kingdom from their liege, Prince Bastion:

Let it be known that every maiden in the kingdom is commanded to try on a glass slipper found at the ball given in my honor last eve. It is essential that all maidens make themselves available to my servants day or night. Whomsoever fits the petite slipper, I will wed by month's end.

~ So it is written, so let it be done

CHAPTER 1

elicia watched her father, Viscount Durand, pace through the modest parlor, his thick fingers rubbing each other as his brown eyes lit in thought. "The prince's men will be here at any moment." He dropped his hands as he continued his endless pacing on the worn rug.

Counting the four long steps before he was forced to turn, Felicia wondered at how her father could get so much exercise in the small room. She stayed still instead of tapping her foot like she wanted. "Father," she said with forced patience. "You and I both know that I'm not the young lady the prince is looking for. I stayed by your side for most of the ball." Something Felicia had learned to do in order to steer conversations away from people slighting the viscount, or trying to snare him in another bad investment. "I didn't dance once and I certainly never spoke with the prince."

But she'd watched him. Prince Bastion was easy to spot since he stood a head taller than most. She'd come to enjoy seeing him enter the room at the royal balls. Even the heat from the lamps and hundreds of bodies, not to mention the overpowering mix of body odor and flowery perfumes, could detract from the charisma that the prince exuded.

When that mystery woman had shown up, Felicia had assumed that they'd already known each other. They'd acted so familiar together, he touching the small of her back and brushing a finger across her jaw. After their third dance, she'd thought that they were betrothed and it hadn't been announced yet. Then, when they continued to dance every time after that until midnight, everyone gossiped of the scandal. The King and Queen had huddled close and whispered frantically as they glanced at their son dancing with the girl in the sparkling gown. Her blonde hair had been upswept with ringlets hanging down around her white smile and gleaming blue eyes.

Felicia knew that no one could mistake her for the mystery guest since she had average features topped with plain brown hair and brown eyes. Nothing nearly as exquisite as the beauty at the ball.

"That doesn't matter, girl. Don't you see?" Her father paused to look down at her, his sagging cheeks twitching. "This is our big chance! Everyone has been talking about how tiny that slipper is. It's bound to fit you."

Rolling her eyes, she glanced down at her petite frame. The ladies of the court often made snide comments of how she resembled a child – and didn't remotely look feminine enough. "Good thing no one will marry you dear," they'd say with exaggerated sympathy. "You'd never survive childbearing."

If anything, that blasted slipper will be too big for me. But she didn't bother saying that to her father. She could tell by the far-off look in his eyes that he'd reached that point in his head where reality was too unpleasant to acknowledge. His visions of grandeur never became more than just that – a vision; but he heartily believed every time that his next venture would be the thing to save them. At least the current situation didn't require her father to put up funds that they didn't have.

"Father, even if that slipper fit, you know I only want to marry for love."

"Not this again!" He glared, resentment shining from his pupils. "If you had accepted Brecklym's proposal, we wouldn't be here." He

ADRIENNE MONSON

placed his hands on his hips. "I don't care if he wasn't titled. Brecklym was the wealthiest merchant this kingdom had ever seen!"

Felicia had tried to explain last year when she'd denied Brecklym's proposal; she didn't love him. And he was older than her father. Not a life she would enjoy no matter how much money the man had, which meant she'd probably end up like her mother – something she'd vowed never to do. Plus he was a foreigner, which meant Felicia would not have been able to live nearby and watch over her father. Even though they were in debt, he'd still take out a loan to invest in poor schemes if she wasn't around to stop him.

She was the one to look after the viscount when her mother ran off with the blacksmith four years ago. If she married, her father could afford a new servant along with a valet. But they wouldn't be able to stop him from agreeing to money sharks and their schemes. Or to shield him from the slander and jabs that everyone relentlessly threw his way. People only saw him for his buffoonish failures. Felicia couldn't understand how they accepted him so warmly when her mother was with them, but be so cold in his darkest hours. He'd been devastated when Mother abandoned them for another, yet he was still the same man as before. Didn't anyone see that, or was respect only had from money?

If only Felicia's godmother were here, she could talk some sense into him now. But Lady Ella wasn't answering her letters. Felicia knew that her godmother left sporadically to find exotic herbs for her magical potions, though her father certainly had no knowledge of Lady Ella's activities. He could never keep a secret and Felicia certainly didn't want her godmother burned as a witch.

A loud knock interrupted them, freezing her father. A voice boomed through the front door. "Open in the name of the prince, heir to the throne!"

Despite her opinion that this was all a waste of time, Felicia's heart pounded faster as their only remaining servant, Tess, came into the hall from the kitchen and opened the door. She was suddenly aware of the worn furniture in the parlor, of the homemade potpourri she

190

had put out this morning to try to mask the smell of the previous tenant's tobacco habit.

Tess entered the parlor, her black hair smooth in its bun and her finest frock perfectly ironed, but Felicia could tell by her pale complexion and twitching fingers that their servant was nervous. She stepped to the side and Felicia saw the entourage come in. A young man, no more than eight and ten led the party. He kept his nose pointed toward the ceiling as he spoke. "It is decreed by Prince Bastion, the royal heir, that every maiden try on this glass slipper." He gestured behind him and another servant held up a gold tray showcasing a shoe that shined in the candlelight.

As the royal announcer continued, Felicia studied the elegant shoe. She'd heard all about the extravagance of the slipper, but seeing it was still awe inspiring. It wasn't just glass; gold lined the base of the shoe, then white and blue diamonds decorated the toe. Even the broken strap that hung limply to the side, crooked in the middle where the strap broke, looked like spun gold and didn't detract from the shoe's beauty. It screamed delicate femininity. *And money,* she thought with a sour note, *something we clearly lack. It's obvious I'm not the girl who wore that slipper.*

A third servant stepped out from behind and picked up the shoe. Felicia realized she hadn't been listening to the announcer as he explained about the decree. She straightened as the older man holding the slipper came toward her.

Glancing around, she realized that there were no female servants among the royal entourage. Eyes wide, Felicia glanced at her father for help. He met her gaze and shrugged.

No man had ever seen her ankles, let alone been close enough to touch them. Alarm swept through her core and the boning of her corset suddenly felt as though it dug too tightly into her ribs. The servant was kneeling in front of her now. He set down the slipper and reached for the hem of her gown.

It wasn't her place to speak, being a woman, and unmarried at that. But could she really sit there while her modesty was violated? Fingers shaking, Felicia pulled her skirt out of his reach. "Pardon me, sir," she said with forced politeness. "Would you please allow my servant to put the slipper on? I'm sure you can respect my desire for propriety."

The man narrowed his grey eyes at her. The silence that followed was strong enough to crack teeth.

Swallowing, Felicia wondered if they'd arrest her for impertinence. But she couldn't take it back now, and wasn't sure that she wanted to. *Am I the only maiden who protested? Surely someone else would want to protect their modesty.*

After a pause, the servant nodded once. "But I will need to watch closely, madam, and be sure that no trickery is involved."

Felicia straightened at the insult, but let it go. At least she'd have a woman touching her foot instead of a man she'd never met. Keeping composure, Felicia called, "Tess, could you please put this slipper on for me?"

Her servant swallowed, her eyes wide, and she glanced at the royal servants with fear, but came forward. The older man scooted to the side and held his hand out to help Tess to her knees.

Felicia softened when she saw that. *At least he's nice to Tess.*

Tess murmured a thank you and proceeded to reach under Felicia's dress to remove her plain, tan leather shoe. Felicia could see the tremor in her servant's hand when she picked up the immaculate slipper. Tess raised Felicia's skirt to her ankle.

Felicia's blood rushed to her face as the roomful of men watched closely. She felt as though she were a strumpet and couldn't believe that every maiden in the kingdom had suffered this humiliation.

"As you can see," her father said, interrupting her thoughts, "my daughter is going to marry the prince, for it was she who danced with him at the ball."

Brow wrinkling at his words, she looked down at her foot. The slipper was on it, sparkling and glittering in all its fanciful glory. It looked like it belonged there. She lifted her foot off the ground and gently shook it to see if the slipper would fall off. It didn't. The shoe fit perfectly and was surprisingly comfortable.

Everyone in the room gasped. Tess stared up at her mistress as if seeing her in a new light.

But that's impossible. Felicia had to special order her footwear, along with her garments, because of her petite frame. She thought she was the only woman who was so tiny in the kingdom, even the whole world. While she'd seen that the woman who'd danced with the prince was small, she'd never gotten close enough to see if they had comparable sizes. The thought had never occurred to her.

The three servants came alive and flitted around, their voices growing high with excitement. Felicia felt numb as she watched them take the slipper off and put it back on the tray. They practically danced as they gathered their things to leave. She wanted to put a stop to it all. *How can they all be so blind?* She was clearly not the right girl.

Tess put Felicia's leather shoe back on, then the royal servants crowded around and hauled her off the settee. They'd stopped speaking, but their excitement was still palpable... and suffocating.

"Wait." Her words drowned among the chaos as they shuttled her out the front door and lifted her into a royal carriage. The viscount plopped in next to her. "Father, we must stop this!" she hissed.

The door closed and they started forward with a jerk. Sweat pooled at the base of her spine as lavender wafted to her nose.

"Nonsense, girl," her father growled. "This is it! How can you even think to throw away this opportunity? We're going to be set for life. No more pesky budgeting. We can hire back all of our servants, maybe even buy back our old home."

"This isn't right, and you know it!"

Waving a hand, her father continued to look unconcerned. "Nonsense. You're a beautiful young lady. The prince will be thrilled to marry you."

Blinking, Felicia stared hard at her father, wondering if he'd lost his wits. "Father, my hair is brown. The other woman was blonde. My face is pale and hers was tan. I highly doubt the prince is going to go along with this farce."

His lips pulled down and his eyes narrowed in determination. "He sent out a proclamation to the kingdom, and by God, I'll make sure he keeps his royal word."

Sitting back, Felicia rested her head on her hand, wondering how this had happened. *What if I actually marry the prince?* She pushed the thought aside. She knew the prince would refuse her. But the idea of marriage… didn't sit well with her. Even when she'd discovered her father's poor financial state, she refused to marry for convenience – an argument she and her father still had regularly. The fact that Prince Bastion was, well, a prince, did not change the fact that she had worked hard to stick to her convictions. She'd rather stay unmarried than be stuck in a loveless marriage. *Besides, Prince Bastion will see that I'm not his mystery girl and send me away immediately, so there's nothing to worry about.*

CHAPTER 2

*T*he steps to the palace entrance loomed before Felicia. Her legs were stiff and she couldn't move. The five royal servants bounded forward, pulling her up the stairs. The youngest sprinted ahead, presumably to announce her directly to the prince.

When will this nightmare end? The viscount gripped her hand occasionally, as if he could pump his own enthusiasm into her.

Felicia's stomach cramped every time she looked into her father's eyes. Didn't he know that the prince would give them the boot as soon as he looked at her? *No, of course he doesn't.* Because her father lived in his head and assumed the rest of the world would go along. He always seemed so shocked when things didn't go according to his fancy.

But Felicia was a realist. No doubt Prince Bastion would throw them on their ear and take away their title for wasting his time. *And then how will we survive?* They'd been losing money consistently since her mother ran off. Every year, they'd had to let go another servant or three. It was to the point that Felicia'd had to wear the same formal gown to the prince's ball that she'd worn three times already. Thank goodness for Tess' seamstress skills and her godmother donating bits of lace to her. But the other nobles still knew and did all that they could to humiliate her with veiled comments.

Finally reaching the top of the stairs, the large doors were already opened. It was quite a walk to the Throne Room, and Felicia's knees threatened to give out with each step. Opulence in the form of exquisite paintings and gleaming chandeliers surrounded her. The corridor smelled of lavender soap and fresh flowers. On any other day, she would have delighted at seeing the clean beauty around her. But now, her stomach was sour with bile threatening to rise up.

They were still a ways from the Throne Room when none other than the prince himself trotted down the hall. The young servant was with him, a pleased smile on his face as he spoke to his liege. The prince's light blue eyes were aglow with anticipation. His long strides showcased how eager he was to reach them.

Felicia knew he wouldn't be thrilled once he figured out what had happened. *What kind of idiot says he'll marry a girl who fits a certain slipper?*

She watched as the prince and his servant approached. The others around her stopped and parted so she and her father were in the center. She'd never been this close to him. Even though she knew he was tall, it struck her how high he actually stood. Felicia probably came up to his shoulders, and her waist looked like it could be the size of his thigh. He held himself regally and moved with a certain grace that made it impossible to ignore.

The prince darted his gaze over her and the viscount, then continued to look at each servant. His smile slipped and he glanced around the hallway.

That's right, Prince. The real princess is hiding behind that tapestry, ready to jump out and yell surprise. Rolling her eyes, Felicia took her father's arm. It was only a matter of minutes before they'd be turned out.

"Well?" Prince Bastion boomed. "Where is she?"

The servants blinked and looked back and forth between Felicia and the prince. "Sire?" the young servant at his side pointed in her direction. "This is the woman whose foot fit the glass slipper. This is your bride."

Once again, Prince Bastion looked at her. This time his eyes inspected her from head to toe. His frown deepened as he lingered at her feet peeking out from the hem of her dress. "It's not her." He turned and said over his shoulder, "Keep looking."

"But, Sire," the older servant protested. "This was one of the last ones. There's a good chance she is the only one petite enough to fit the slipper."

"It's not *her!*" Though his back was still turned, Felicia saw the stiffness in his posture and the tightness of his fists.

Not wanting to be the subject of his ire, Felicia turned, ready to go home and back to her normal life. But no matter how much she pulled on his arm, her father wouldn't budge.

"Pardon me, sire," the viscount said hesitantly. "But, by your own proclamation, you are bound to wed my daughter."

Pausing, Prince Bastion turned and studied her father. His gaze rested on the boots that were fashionable three seasons ago. "I see." Jaw clenched, he bowed his head. "My apologies for the misunderstanding. I'll happily compensate you for this inconvenience. These men will show you to my treasurer and he'll take care of everything."

Her father's mouth dropped. The prince was once again walking away. Felicia nudged her father. "It's not so bad, right?" she asked. "At least we'll have money for next month's rent now."

Looking down at her, her father's lips thinned. He straightened his shoulders and spoke loud enough for everyone to hear. "I demand to see the king immediately."

This time the prince didn't bother to turn. "If you see my father, the inconvenience transfers to the royal family and you will not receive compensation."

Heat suffused Felicia's cheeks. *The nerve!* She didn't care that this man was royalty; his pompous attitude grated her spine. She certainly hoped she wouldn't have to marry him.

Viscount Durand stepped forward. "Take me to the king, then."

The prince was out of earshot, but the servants began to escort them forward.

Felicia couldn't bite her tongue for one more second. "No," she said firmly. "This has gone far enough. We are leaving. Now." She turned and slipped through the servants, but the older one who had given the slipper to Tess stopped her.

"Beg pardon, milady. But you may not walk the palace corridors unattended." He glanced at the viscount, who watched Felicia with an impatient frown. "You must stay by your father's side."

Sighing, Felicia's shoulders sagged and she trudged forward with her father and the servants. She knew some nobility attended court and would see the spectacle that would no doubt happen. She'd be hearing about this for months to come. *Maybe I should become a hermit so I don't have to attend any more soirees.* It wasn't the first time she'd had the thought. But her father insisted on attending social functions and Felicia couldn't allow him to go unattended.

The mood of the servants as they continued to the Throne Room was somber. All the excitement from a few minutes ago had fizzled into surliness. Prince Bastion had already arrived in the Throne Room and was occupying the chair next to his father when they entered. The servants took Felicia and the viscount to the back of a long line of people and left them there.

Smoothing down her day frock, Felicia glanced at the ladies in waiting. They stood to the side of the queen, ready to take care of her needs and were dressed in fine satins with jewels that shined across the room in the morning light like a stained glass window. Most of the people waiting in line in front of them looked to be commoners with wool clothes and greasy hair. They stood out from both classes, wearing nicer clothes than the commoners, but looking poor compared to the nobility watching the proceedings.

"Father," she whispered. "We can't win this battle. Time to go."

The viscount didn't move. "I know what I'm doing, girl. Mind your place and let me be." His shoulders were stiff and his posture unyielding. Felicia knew his stubborn streak all too well. There was nothing she could do to dissuade him.

Frustration threatened to choke her, but she swallowed it down. No way would she lose control in front of the royal family and everyone else at court. Taking a breath, she listened to the farmer pleading for soldiers to patrol his land and protect the crops from the borderliners.

The king listened patiently to the case and granted four soldiers to patrol daily in exchange for two percent of his crops. Felicia's brow raised at the decision. It seemed like a fair enough deal. Clearly it was in the farmer's interest to have the soldiers around to protect his farm and what the king asked in return was very reasonable.

The next man approached to air his grievance about an indentured servant he'd bought and felt that the auctioneer had conned him about the purchase.

Listening to all the people and their various difficulties fascinated Felicia. She was surprised at how many people came to court for such mundane things. *Can't the cobbler and the tanner work out their differences on their own? Why should the king have to tell them to stop harassing each others' customers?*

If she did marry the prince, would she be able to participate in helping the commoners that attended court? The idea intrigued her.

They slowly walked forward, getting incrementally closer to the front of the line. Many people had entered after them and Felicia knew that court would continue until late in the day.

Only two more men in front of them. Felicia's heart rose to her throat. *There's no scenario where this ends well for us.* What if the king evicted them? They were barely making ends meet as it was.

When it was time for her and her father to step forward, Felicia could hardly take in a breath. She trembled out a curtsy while her father bowed.

"Sire, I appreciate your time while you aid me in a most sensitive matter." The viscount held himself tall while still showing the utmost respect. Felicia was distracted by the imposing presence he held. Her godmother, Lady Ella, had told her stories of how her father was once known for commanding his way through any party. But Felicia had never believed it because she'd only seen her father as the brunt of everyone's jokes most of her life. But now, seeing the viscount hold himself tall and looking so calm and collected in front of everyone, she wondered if her godmother had been right after all.

"What is this sensitive issue you speak of, Viscount Durand?" The king leaned back, his grey eyes wandering over the people behind them in a bored fashion.

"It's about the proclamation your son sent out this week, Sire."

The king glanced back to the viscount with narrowed eyes. "What of it?"

The prince was staring at something in his hand. Felicia wondered if he even knew they were talking about him and his silly proclamation.

"He commanded that all maidens try on the glass slipper, Sire. So my daughter did as commanded."

The king's lips thinned. "I'm aware of what it said. I apologize if the slipper was too small for your daughter's foot, but the proclamation clearly states that the prince will only wed whomsoever can wear the slipper." He waved a hand as if dismissing them.

"But Sire," her father protested. "It did fit my daughter." The buzz around the room quieted. The king's full attention was suddenly on Felicia, the wrinkles on his forehead deepening.

"What's that you say?"

"It fit her foot perfectly. We were whisked away to the castle directly after, but the prince claims that he won't marry my daughter."

Face grim, the king slowly turned to his son. The prince glanced up, unconcerned. "It's not her, Father." The king glared. "I offered them compensation, but this man insisted on seeing you instead."

"Your Highness," her father stepped closer. "As you yourself said, you know what the proclamation reads. Was there a clause that perhaps I did not see? One that stated the prince could change his mind if a girl did, in fact, fit the slipper?"

"No, it did not." The king was stone-faced, but the prince finally perked up.

"You can't honestly expect me to marry her, can you, Father? Everyone knows her father is in debt. She's clearly a fortune hunter trying to take advantage of my predicament." When Prince Bastion pointed in her direction, Felicia felt every gaze boring through her. Gasps and excited whispers carried throughout the room.

She wished for a witch to appear and turn her into a mouse so she could scurry away. *Where's your magic when I need it, Godmother?* Anything was more preferable to standing in court and bearing this humiliating rejection. Even if everyone knew of their financial strains, to have it publicly announced was devastating.

As if reading her thoughts, the king clapped once. "Court is dismissed for the day. Everyone will please leave."

Stepping forward, Felicia grabbed her father's arm again. "Let's go," she murmured.

"You two," the king pointed at them, "will stay."

At least the prince can reject me more privately now. Of course, it wasn't that simple. Within the hour, everyone would know what happened. She could already hear the snide remarks of the courtiers who would pretend to offer sympathy. *Maybe I can convince Father to move to the country and become a farmer.*

CHAPTER 3

*A*fter everyone left, the king ordered that a receiving room be prepared with refreshments. The queen sent her ladies to oversee the details.

It was quiet as they stared at each other in the large room. The prince stood up. "Father, we are wasting time. This isn't the woman I danced with." He glanced at her, annoyance evident in his gestures. "My apologies, lady. I thought only one woman had as dainty feet as my love. But clearly I must put an amendment on that proclamation." He started walking away. "Consider the matter resolved."

Viscount Durand held up a hand. "I'm afraid it's not that simple."

The king frowned at his son's back. "Bastion, you will stay and deal with this disaster you've created."

Prince Bastion stopped and matched his father's glare. "I already dealt with it." He turned to Felicia's father. "I'm sorry my answer is not what you want to hear."

"No," the kind growled through his greying beard. "I'm sorry that *my* answer is not what *you* want to hear."

The prince blinked, his wide shoulders tense. "Pardon?"

"You are of my lineage, Bastion. We are royalty and must adhere to higher standards. That means you always keep your word. Always."

Eyes bugging out, the prince's mouth dropped. "You can't be serious." He glanced at his mother.

Felicia followed his gaze and saw the queen's pale complexion, making her red lips and blue eyes more striking. She put her hand to her throat before speaking. "Dearest, we promised him."

Standing, the king looked down at his wife. "Yes, we did. But he also promised when he sent out that damned fool of a proclamation. I told him not to do it, but you said he had to do whatever he could to find her. Neither of you were thinking rationally, and now look what's happened."

The queen's eyes narrowed and she looked at the prince with pursed lips.

Walking down the steps, the king held out his hand to the viscount. "Best get used to our spats if you're going to be a part of the family. We have many."

Her father grinned and shook the man's hand. "I'm honored, Your Highness."

"I'm not marrying her." The prince folded his arms as the corners of his mouth tightened. "You can't make me."

The king moved over to his son. "Try me." The warning lacing his tone spread goosebumps along Felicia's neck.

"If I may." The queen stood and sauntered gracefully over to them. "I'd like to see this slipper and be certain it fits on this girl's foot." Her blue eyes shined with skepticism as she looked down at Felicia.

Prince Bastion pointed at his mother, a smile forming. "Yes, of course. We must be sure it actually fits."

The queen gestured for a servant. When he approached, she commanded, "Have the glass slipper taken into the green receiving room." The servant bowed and exited. The queen gazed back at Felicia, a challenge etched in her haughty expression. "Shall we?"

Felicia straightened to her full height, wishing she could berate the queen for insulting her in such a manner. Instead, she nodded as regally as she could, showing none of the hurt and anxiety swimming in her stomach.

Together, they walked out a side door and down a smaller corridor. When they entered the receiving room, Felicia clicked her teeth closed. *I knew the royal family lived well, but this is beyond grand.* The room was larger than their townhome, and displayed beautiful paintings of fairies and magical forests that took up entire walls. The furniture was a rich, dark green. When Felicia sat in a plush chair, she was certain she could stay in the cushions for hours and never get uncomfortable.

A different servant came in with the slipper on the gold tray. Again, Felicia realized that there was no female to assist with the shoe. It took effort to speak up for her modesty the first time in her home, but now at the castle and in front of the royal family? Her resolve waivered until she met the blue-eyed glare of Prince Bastion. Her shoulders stiffened. *That spoiled prince isn't going to get a peek at my ankles!*

Before the servant reached them, Felicia stood. "Pardon me, but could we get a female servant to try on the slipper?" She looked at the king and the prince. "And I'd prefer to have my modesty honored as well."

"I knew it," Prince Bastion burst out. "It doesn't fit. And now you're trying to stall from being exposed to your deceit."

Forgetting all about using proper protocol, Felicia lost the reigns over her tongue. "Trust me, Sire, if I were to think of some elaborate scheme to come into money, it wouldn't involve having to see your arrogant face every day for the rest of my life."

Prince Bastion's cheeks became a mottled red and he opened his mouth. But before he could say anything, the king stepped in front of Felicia. "I can get a female servant for your comfort, but I must confirm with my own eyes that the shoe fits."

Lips twisting, Felicia nodded and sat, doing her best to tamp down her ire at Prince Bastion.

"Don't bother to send for another servant," the queen said. "I'll do it myself."

Felicia glanced up at the queen with her mouth open in surprise.

The queen took the glass slipper and knelt before Felicia, giving her a close view of the older woman's gold crown cushioned by thick blonde braids.

The room was quiet. Everyone seemed to be as shocked as Felicia at having someone of high rank kneeling before her. Blinking, Felicia wondered if this was some sort of twisted dream. The queen removed Felicia's leather shoe, her nose wrinkling as she placed it to the side. Then she put the slipper on Felicia's foot.

Frowning, the queen bent lower to inspect the fit.

Prince Bastion and his father also leaned in to get a better look.

Sighing, she pushed modesty aside and raised her foot higher, then shook it like she did earlier. There was no disputing that the shoe fit perfectly.

Prince Bastion's gaze strayed to her exposed ankle, his eyes warming. Flushing, Felicia quickly put her foot down and covered it with her skirt. Her stomach fluttered, but she couldn't if it was in a pleasant or ill manner.

"See?" Viscount Durand's smile was broad and beyond pleased. "Our family is also one that keeps their word. Now, shall we sign the marriage contract?"

"But Father," the prince protested, his expression outraged. "You can't honestly expect me to marry her. She's clearly here to rescue her family from financial ruin."

Stepping close, the king's face was hard as stone. "That wasn't a stipulation in your damned proclamation," he said in a low voice.

"Wait." Everyone stopped and glanced down at Felicia. Her spine trembling, she stood and looked at the king. "There are two weeks until month's end. What if Prince Bastion can find another whose foot fits this slipper, then perhaps he can choose his bride out of the other and myself." Of course, all of them knew who the prince would be choosing. Though Felicia didn't want to marry him, it still stung that the prince was so clearly repulsed by her. Perhaps he'd heard the gossip that she was a harlot, just like her mother. A vicious lie, but one he'd certainly believe.

Prince Bastion frowned, his expression confused and pensive.

Exhaling loudly, the king nodded. "That's quite reasonable."

Felicia nodded, ignoring the burning glare her father threw at her.

Viscount Durand cleared his throat. "Might I make a request, Your Highness?"

Stepping away from his family, the king turned to the viscount. "I'm listening."

"My daughter is not schooled in the ways of court." He bowed his head. "I realize that she may not marry the prince after all, but if she does, she'll need to learn much before she'll be ready to rule by your son's side."

"I can't disagree with that assessment," the king murmured.

"May Felicia stay in the castle and observe while we wait to see if the prince can find this other woman? She's a quick study and will be much better prepared if it turns out they will indeed wed."

The king's beard twitched as he thought. The queen and the prince, however, glared at Felicia's father. Felicia's chest tightened and she gripped the arms of the chair. *Thanks, Father. You've just painted a target on our backs for both the prince and the queen.*

Finally, the king held out his hand to Viscount Durand. "Sounds fair to me. Send her back here tomorrow and everything will be prepared for her stay." He glanced at his wife as if giving her a silent command to make the arrangements. The queen folded her arms and glanced away, her jaw flexed so tight that Felicia thought it might snap.

The viscount shook his hand and bowed his head. "Thank you, Your Highness."

***

The king commanded that Prince Bastion keep Felicia company while he and the viscount went over the marriage contract. Felicia sat stiffly while a maid served them tea. It was impossible to ignore the prince's brooding glare.

Felicia sipped her tea, wondering how things had gotten so far out of control, as the hot liquid formed a path down her chest and into her stomach.

"Why did you say that?" the prince asked.

Setting her teacup on a side table, she frowned. "Say what?"

Prince Bastion leaned forward, resting his elbows on his knees. "Why did you suggest I take more time to find another girl? You could have ensnared me into marriage today."

"I don't want to marry you," she said softly.

It was quiet in the room. Perhaps her declaration had hurt his feelings. The prince was likely not used to having women rejecting him.

"We both know that's untrue. Why else would you be here?"

Ire stiffened her spine. "You have the audacity to call me a liar?"

"Beg pardon, my lady." His tone dripped with contempt. "But a fortune hunter such as yourself isn't exactly trustworthy."

"Excuse me?" Felicia's voice was higher than ever before, making her sound like a child. Heat spread up her cheeks. "You do not know me, sir. I could be the epitome of virtue."

"Please." He folded his arms and leaned back as if it were obvious. "It's no secret that your father is struggling. Any money he once had has gone to poor investments. The only thing keeping you afloat is his paltry title of nobility. But that may only carry you through for another month or so." He shrugged. "So you pursued an opportunity with that small foot of yours."

Having her grievances over the last few years listed in such a casual manner hit hard in the gut. Her corset felt too tight and Felicia's fingers tingled with longing to slap the condescending look off the prince's face.

"And, no doubt, you think I'm exactly like my mother."

His eyes narrowed in confusion. "Who is your mother?"

Tension worked from her torso to her shoulders. "Don't toy with me. I'll not go into the sordid details of my mother abandoning us for your amusement."

The prince frowned, studying her. "She was the one who ran off with the town blacksmith?"

Instead of answering, Felicia stood and faced the window, glancing over the splendor. After she felt a fraction calmer, she said, "Playing ignorant doesn't become you, sir. Everyone knows the story and no doubt you're privileged to hear all the gossip in the kingdom."

"This may come as a shock to you," retorted the prince, "but I do my best to not listen to the gossip circulating through the nobility. I find there's only a grain of truth in the pile of dung people toss around."

Surprise made her head feel light, and she turned to look at the prince. His posture was stiff, but he looked sincere enough. The fact that the prince didn't listen to all the torrid gossip made her see him in a different light. "Well, still." Where was her witty comeback? Her brain was working too slowly. Without her mask of indifference and her wits to hide behind, she felt vulnerable. It wasn't a good feeling and anger rose to the surface. "If you had any wits at all, you would have made a completely different decree to find your girl."

The prince stood and glared at her. "She left her shoe behind, which is unusually small. It seemed the best way to find her was to fit the slipper back on her foot. How was I to know there would be another girl with extremely tiny feet?"

Felicia stared, her mouth open. "You didn't think that through at all!" she finally bellowed. "How could you command every eligible maiden in the entire kingdom to show her ankles to complete strangers and think that's okay? Why couldn't you have sent out a detailed description of your mystery princess and told everyone if they found her that they'd receive an award?"

Blinking, Prince Bastion's lips turned downward. "My idea seemed very romantic at the time," he muttered, rubbing the back of his neck.

Folding her arms, Felicia huffed. "I'm fairly certain that all the maidens who had to expose themselves on your behalf did not find that romantic in the least, myself included."

He turned as if to leave and Felicia couldn't stem her outburst as she raged to his back. "You know nothing, Prince. But how could you?" She gestured around the room. "All you've had is entitlement.

And you even shrug off the responsibility that supposedly comes with higher status. You're insensitive to anyone or anything that doesn't interest you and you judge others who do what they can to not fall into a pit of despair." He spun and she pointed a finger in his face. "For your information, I don't want to marry you, nor am I a treasure hunter. I care not for riches but for living a full and happy life." Her godmother would be tickled to learn that Felicia quoted her. "But you, you only think of yourself. You're not just selfish, but incomparably shortsighted."

His ears tinted red and his nostrils flared. "How dare you call me shortsighted?"

"I very much dare, sir, because you can't see anything outside of yourself!" Felicia realized she'd lost it. There was a part of her that was screaming to get herself under control, but her body, particularly her mouth, wasn't listening. She couldn't shut off this rant. "Do you not realize that you've ruined my life? You think I want to be stuck in a loveless marriage? Why do you think I'm unmarried?"

The prince frowned. "I had assumed... well that is to say, I believed no one had—"

She cut him off, not wanting to hear again how much the prince thought her undesirable. "This may come as a surprise to you, oh selfish one, but I had offers. While we are poor, we're still nobility and men wanted to marry into that title."

Prince Bastion's brows came together. "And you declined? Did they have no lands or money?"

"Yes to both, you insensitive buffoon!" Never had she raised her voice so much. The servants were staring at her as if she'd grown a second head. Felicia couldn't believe how much he'd gotten to her. She'd always tolerated the jabs and disdain from the rest of society, but for some reason, his harsh judgment had her screaming like a raving banshee. "I said no because I knew I wanted to marry for love or not at all. And your half-brained proclamation ruined all of that."

The room settled into an uneasy silence, with the servants staring at the floor as they shifted. Felicia turned and inhaled a shaking breath. Her anger was draining away, but now tears threatened. *He must not see me cry.* She knew he'd exploit her weakness and hit her while she was down, just like everyone else did.

"It seems my passionate nature has doomed us both then."

The king and her father entered, saving her from responding.

CHAPTER 4

elicia lay in her bed, beyond exhausted, but sleep eluded her and thinking of what the following day would be like bombarded her. She'd be moving to the palace tomorrow. Thankfully, her father agreed to let her bring Tess as her personal maid.

They'd finally left the castle after the king and her father drew up the marriage contract. Of course, no one would sign until the end of the month. But it was postdated so that they could marry as soon as the deadline arrived.

Prince Bastion hadn't said another word to her after their confrontation, nodding a farewell when they left. Her father had been jovial the entire way home, wanting to celebrate. Felicia had pleaded exhaustion and escaped to her room, but her mind whirled with her predicament.

When the first pink rays of light filtered through her curtains, Felicia got up and went about her morning ablutions. She had to wait for Tess to lace up her corset, so she stayed in her nightgown and robe, packing her valise with the items she wanted to keep with her. Tess would take care of the rest while she broke her fast.

Yawning, Felicia sat at her desk and penned a letter to Lady Ella. *Dearest Godmother,*

You would not believe what has happened these last couple of days. Pure madness, I tell you. And it's not only my father this time. The worst part? His fantasy has become reality and I'm being sent to the castle to wed Prince Bastion. The man despises me, and I can't say I express any affection for him, either. The one thing I wanted in life was a marriage filled with love, where I could share my life with someone else and be happy. How can I accept this fate when it goes against everything I've yearned for?

What am I to do? You must visit me. I need your wisdom and your guidance. I can't imagine being a princess. Me, of all people. With the ridicule I've endured over the past four years, I doubt I'd be able to get anyone to obey my commands. Especially since the prince and the queen both loathe my very existence.

Please see me at your earliest convenience. Just go to the castle and ask for the imposter pretending to be the princess. They'll know exactly whom you're speaking of.

Your most devoted goddaughter,

Felicia Durand

Sealing the letter with hot wax, Felicia printed the name Ella de la Roche and left it on the desk. Tess would know to send it when she saw it.

As if summoned by her thoughts, her maid entered the room and helped Felicia change into her best dress. It was still drab in comparison to richer nobility, but the dark blue complimented her complexion and contrasted well with her brown tresses.

Viscount Durand was already downstairs and bursting with energy when Felicia entered the dining room.

"Father?" Felicia eyed him as she put eggs and kippers on her plate. "You rarely get up before noon, and even then, you take a full hour to wake."

The viscount laughed. "Well, this is no ordinary day, is it? You move into the castle and will be married in a fortnight!"

Sighing, she sat at the table to eat. "You're assuming the prince won't find the other girl. He probably will."

"No, no." He sat across from her. "I feel it in my bones. This is going to work." He reached over and patted her hand.

Felicia looked down at her plate so he wouldn't see the derision she felt. It was difficult not to remind him that those words were spoken each time he'd made a poor investment.

He sat back. "Besides, if it doesn't work out with the prince, you have two weeks to meet other nobles who frequent the castle. You can work your charms to get one of them to marry you."

This time she did look up, and let the exasperation she felt show. "Really, Father? Have you not heard anything I've said when I turned down other suitors?"

Shrugging, the viscount pulled out a small canvas bag of tobacco to fill his pipe. "I was likely too irate with you to listen. Especially with the last one." Who had been extremely wealthy.

Felicia didn't understand why her father couldn't comprehend her desires. She'd thought that of all people, he would support her in this. Her mother had been so unhappy in her loveless marriage with the viscount. That misery had led to the most selfish act of running off with her "true love" and leaving a daughter and husband behind to deal with the mess.

Forcing a bite of cold eggs in her mouth, Felicia let the matter drop, trying to push away all the hurtful remarks and jabs she'd had to endure since then.

Will life be different if this farce of a wedding actually takes place? Would the other nobility try to be friendly with our elevated status? No, she decided. That was something unrealistic, like her father's fancies. They never came true. *Except you might marry the prince.* But Felicia still hoped that she'd get out of it. Being a spinster was much more desirable.

The trip to the castle was much better this time, since Felicia could ride her own horse and enjoy the fresh air. She didn't care much for being stuck in a stuffy carriage, even the nice royal ones.

No one in the royal family received Felicia upon her arrival. A groom led her horse away while an older woman led her and Tess through the maze that was considered a hallway to her chambers. Two servants trailed them with her luggage.

The servants exited the chambers, leaving Felicia and Tess to

wonder at their new living quarters. Everything screamed extravagance, from the silk sheets on the spacious bed to the plush rugs lining
the apartment. Felicia's anteroom was larger than her father's parlor.
And the closet was already filled with new gowns. Vanilla and rose
drifted over the smell of the fire blazing in the fireplace, making her
shoulders relax.

Under different circumstances, Felicia would have savored every
bit of newfound opulence. But the situation soured everything,
making luxury salt in her fresh wound. No amount of satins and
jewels would cover the fact that the prince didn't want her, or that the
queen disapproved of her, and that she wanted nothing to do
with them.

Hopefully her godmother would be able to visit soon. Ella de la
Roche was the closest thing to a mother that Felicia had, and she
craved the guidance that the witch would offer.

Felicia was in the middle of directing Tess's unpacking when there
was a knock on the door and a high, feminine voice called, "Open. In
the name of the queen."

Stomach dropping, Felicia nodded for Tess to answer. The door
swung in to reveal three ladies in waiting and their queen behind
them. They glided into the room as if floating on air, scanning Felicia
with raised brows and sneers. The queen held her countenance in
check, though Felicia could feel condescension oozing from her.

Turning out her best curtsey, Felicia murmured her respects to the
older woman with the jeweled crown on her head.

"Making yourself at home so quickly, I see." The queen held her
head high and frowned at Felicia.

Trying not to roll her eyes, Felicia was unimpressed. She was
shorter than everyone; people looking down their noses at her had
stopped intimidating her since she was fourteen.

"I'm enjoying my new chamber, Your Highness. Thank you for
your kind inquiry."

The queen blinked.

Felicia fought a smile. *Two can play at this game.* Of course, the
queen wouldn't know that Felicia had had to learn quick retorts over

the last four years. Otherwise, she'd have been eaten alive at every social outing that she and her father attended.

Sauntering to the wardrobe, the queen fingered a pink gown. "These are a bit large, but I'm sure that with all the luxurious food you'll partake of here, you won't need to have them taken in."

"On the contrary, Your Majesty," Felicia said in her most flattering voice. "I could never esteem myself to meet the advanced appetite of one such as yourself."

The ladies in waiting gasped. The queen didn't move; she watched Felicia with narrowed eyes, as if seeing her for the first time. She dropped forced politeness and squared her shoulders. "While this little visit is quite amusing, I'm here to inform you that you will be shadowing me this afternoon. To observe and retain the information you'll need to understand your duties *should* you become the princess."

Bowing her head, Felicia kept an air of distant politeness. "Of course, Your Majesty. I will do what I can to learn quickly."

"We shall see." With that, she swept out of the room, her ladies glaring at Felicia as they followed their queen.

Once Tess closed the door behind them, Felicia sank into the closest chair, exhaling loudly.

"What are you thinking, Milady?" Tess whispered. "You make enemies with the queen before you're even wed."

Felicia shook her head, her brows pulled together in thought. "No, Tess. The queen wishes to make enemies with me. I had to show her that I wouldn't be easy prey." She waved a hand. "That woman may be royalty, but she's no different than all the other nobles with their double entendres and snide remarks behind my back."

Sighing, Tess went about unpacking Felicia's things.

Now that she was at the castle and her first confrontation over with, the long night from before was catching up to her. She lay on the soft, feather mattress and closed her eyes.

Next thing she knew, there was tapping at the door and the shadows in the room had grown longer.

Tess came into view. "The queen requests your presence, Milady."

Bolting upright, Felicia touched her hair. It was a mess, of course.

"I'll fix it." Tess already had a brush and was pulling out wayward pins and placing them where they belonged.

Felicia didn't bother glancing in the looking glass and darted out of the room, following a servant sent to fetch her and brushing wrinkles out of her best gown.

They arrived in another receiving room, this one decorated in pinks and whites. The queen sat with perfect posture, slowly sipping her tea, golden light kissing her pale gown. When Felicia entered, the queen raised one arched brow.

Heat rushed to Felicia's cheeks, knowing that the queen and her ladies in waiting scrutinized her every move and found her decidedly lacking.

"Thank you for joining us," the queen said. Her eyes narrowed in on Felicia's feet and she realized that she'd forgotten to put her shoes back on.

I've been walking through the castle in only stockings! All her mental preparations for how to handle the queen suddenly flew out the window. Recognizing the damage was done, Felicia held her head high and sat across from the queen with all the dignity she could muster.

"May I ask why you've decided to forego footwear?" A tick in the queen's jaw twitched as she asked.

Felicia wouldn't give her the satisfaction, though it was clear that they both knew what had happened. Waving a hand, Felicia showed indifference. "The king told me to make myself at home when I arrived at the castle." She shrugged with deliberate nonchalance. "I find it much more comfortable walking around in just my stockings when I'm at home."

"So which am I to believe? This story you feed me now or your pretended modesty yesterday when you tried on the glass slipper?"

Legs tense, Felicia made sure it didn't show. "I'm being perfectly modest right now. My dress is just the floor length." When the queen continued to stare at her, Felicia ignored the tremors along her spine and forced a delicate sniff. "Now, did you send for me or not?"

Chin lifting, the queen glared. "Of course I did. It's time to instruct you on your potential duties."

Felicia tried to ignore the judgmental looks from the ladies in waiting as she listened aptly to what the queen had to say. While the older woman made side remarks in every other sentence, Felicia found the information quite useful. She hadn't realized just how many duties a queen had to attend to. *No wonder she's grumpy all the time.*

Once the queen finished her instructions, but certainly not her insults for the day, Felicia wasn't sure she'd be able to remember everything.

"You shall sit with me tomorrow when the English ambassador and his wife come." The queen held up a finger. "But you may not speak a word. Only observe."

A servant entered and announced that dinner was served. Everyone stood and followed the man. Unsure of what to do or how to find her way back to her chambers, Felicia trailed behind, fully aware that the whispers from the group of ladies a few feet ahead were about her.

CHAPTER 5

Supper turned out to be a small affair. The king welcomed Felicia warmly, telling her that she should consider herself part of the family soon, but Felicia felt too much an outsider. And there was still the hope that she'd get out of this whole mess. She wasn't sure if this mystery princess could be found, but the woman had to be close enough to attend the ball in the first place.

In the meantime, she had to do her best to learn about a queen's duties and remember how to navigate her way through the castle. If she'd had any money, she'd have tried to bribe the servants to report to her on the prince's progress, but she'd have to rely on Tess instead. Her maid was friendly enough that Felicia hoped the royal servants would include her in their gossip.

Instead of a large table, they were seated at a small cherry wood one with only six chairs around it. The king was sitting at the head, the queen across from him. The prince was nowhere to be seen, and Felicia chose a seat that was right in the middle to not show any favoritism. Though she was definitely more comfortable around the king than his wife.

"Where's Bastion?" the king questioned when their first course was served.

A sweet-smelling dressing covered a plate of freshly picked greens, sprinkled with cherry tomatoes.

"Where do you think?" The queen lifted her head as if to challenge her husband.

Felicia looked over to see the king's lips pressed together tightly beneath his beard. "The damned fool," he muttered, then pointed his fork at the queen. "It's your fault, you know. You've been filling his head with fantasies instead of teaching him about duty."

Dropping her utensil on her untouched greens, the queen stared hard at her husband. "I've been giving him hope. He has the power to be happy; something I never had."

The king shook his head and went back to eating. Felicia suspected this was a dialogue they engaged in frequently.

The next course was served. Felicia savored the spices rubbed into her duck. *At least there's one benefit of living in the castle.* Though it didn't justify Felicia living in misery the rest of her life.

She tried not to think of her own parents as the king and queen glared at each other. Her mother had pretended to be happy for her father. And her father had believed it. Felicia resented her mother for catering to the viscount's fancies. Perhaps if he'd known how miserable her mother had been, something could have been done. Maybe her mother wouldn't have felt the need to leave without a backward glance.

As soon as it was polite to leave, Felicia excused herself and wandered the castle, still only in her stockings. She was trying to figure out how to find her chamber, but every corridor she turned down seemed unfamiliar. *Where are all the servants?* She didn't run into a single one as she wound through the labyrinth of hallways, and the guards intimidated her too much to ask them where to go.

She finally saw a balcony and walked out into the night air. The view overlooked the kingdom, showing an entire village. *Oh great.* Felicia's room faced the forest; on the opposite side of where she was now.

Frustration and fatigue nipped at her and she leaned onto the balcony. She decided to stay out there and enjoy the view for a moment. She'd never seen her large village from this vantage point. Wind caressed the errant strands of hair around her neck and Felicia closed her eyes, enjoying the feeling.

"What, pray tell, are you doing all the way over here?"

Gasping, Felicia jumped back and stared at the figure in the dark. "Me?" she asked, recognizing the prince's voice. "I could say the same of you. Anyone with manners would have announced themselves instead of quietly watched me like a mouse in the shadows."

Rising from his seat, Prince Bastion came into the dim light. Felicia couldn't see the blue of his eyes, but noted the suspicion that shined from them. "It's well known that I like to sit on this particular balcony in the evenings. I wasn't sure if you were looking for me."

Mouth dropping, Felicia guffawed. "So you decided to spy on me to determine my motivations. Why not simply ask?"

"Beg pardon, my lady." His tone dripped with contempt. "But I don't trust you."

"Then you're in good company. I don't trust you, either."

He held his hands out to the side. "I've nothing to hide."

Turning to the balcony, Felicia rubbed her forehead. "Neither do I, sir. Can I please enjoy the view in peace? Your stubborn inclination to paint me as a lying fortune hunter is exhausting."

The prince gave a long sigh and leaned onto the balcony next to her. "I'm sorry."

Straightening, she stared up at him. Those were the last words she expected to come out of his mouth.

He met her gaze. "I confirmed your story about turning down other suitors. They were rich and you still said no. I was wrong to think so lowly of you."

It took a moment for Felicia to collect herself. "Thank you." She returned her gaze to the scenery and they stood in silence, though the animosity was difficult to cling to now.

"Why?" Prince Bastion asked after a few minutes.

Her lips twisted. "Why turn down those suitors when they could save me from financial ruin?"

He nodded.

Shaking her head, she laced her fingers together. "I doubt you would understand."

"Then help me to." He folded his arms. "I've been trying to puzzle it out all day. First you give me hope by suggesting I take the next fortnight to find my love, and then I discover you're not seeking any fortune. I'm quite flummoxed over you."

Shrugging, Felicia searched for words to explain. Finally, she decided to be forthright. "I don't want to become my mother."

Prince Bastion tilted his head. "You're afraid you'll run off with a blacksmith?"

Biting down a scathing retort, Felicia did her best to not spark another argument between them. "She was so unhappy in her marriage that she was willing to leave her family for another man." She faced the prince, revealing things she'd only confessed to her godmother. "I grew up feeling loved by both my parents, sir. I wanted for nothing. I knew my mother wasn't in love with my father, but she made a good show of it. When she left, she never even said goodbye to me. I wonder if she'd ever really loved me or had just put on a good face." Emotion clogged her throat and she coughed. "I couldn't bare it if I did something so cruel to my own children."

A tear spilled down her right cheek and she dashed it away.

Large hands rested on her shoulders, then turned her around. Felicia watched as the prince took in her state. "I'm sorry, Felicia." His lips thinned as if to ward off his own emotions.

His sincerity touched her. Felicia let out a sigh, her shoulders dropping. "Me too. It was not my intention to come between you and your love."

His face softened, his blue eyes warm. "I'm beginning to realize that."

The emotions churning between them had somehow changed. No longer was there accusation and animosity, but more of a comradery, like they were fighting a battle together instead of against each other.

Prince Bastion leaned forward as if he would embrace her, but he pulled back, like he'd just remembered himself.

They stood for an awkward moment, Felicia feeling embarrassed with her deep fears exposed.

His hand came up and she placed her own in his palm, feeling the heat of his fingers, the smell of sandalwood wafting from him. Very slowly, Prince Bastion leaned forward while keeping a direct gaze on Felicia. Her chest hitched with an unknown anticipation as his lips made contact with her knuckles. Something about the action drained all the tension she'd felt. She wished he had embraced her the way it looked like he'd wanted to.

He pulled away, his demeanor lighter. "Now that we've cleared things up between us, I have another question. If you weren't looking for me, then what are you doing on this side of the castle? It's inappropriate for an unmarried maiden to walk the men's ward, especially unchaperoned."

Gasping, Felicia glanced fearfully at the door. "I didn't know. That is to say..." She stared at the floor. "I got lost." She laced her fingers together. "I can't find my way to my chamber."

Prince Bastion released a belly-filled laugh, transforming his face into one of softer planes. He wiped the corner of his eye, then held out his arm as he continued to chuckle. "Then let me be of service, my lady."

Hesitating, Felicia placed her arm in his as he led the way back into the castle.

"I may only know entitlement."

Hearing the prince's tone of self-depreciating tone, Felicia cringed at the words she'd yelled at him yesterday.

"But along with that comes a complete knowledge of this castle." He smiled. "I can help you learn your way around here, if you'd like."

Blinking at his kind offer, Felicia found herself wondering how things would have been between them if he'd not judged her so harshly. "I'd appreciate that. Thank you, sir."

They went down a set of stairs and Felicia recognized some of their surroundings like the gold pedestals showcasing red flowers and the painting of sailors forging through a lightning storm.

"It would be my pleasure. I feel the need to make it up to you, considering I ruined both of our chances at happiness."

He was joking, but the truth behind his words stung. Felicia paused. "Prince Bastion, are you still looking for her?"

His smiled dropped. Slowly, the prince nodded.

"I won't protest, should you marry her over me. I'll convince my father to drop the matter." She bit her bottom lip. "If you have a chance to marry for love, you should take it."

The prince's blue eyes lightened to near grey, and he bowed his head. "I cannot tell you how much that means to me, my lady."

They stopped in front of her chamber door. He squeezed her hand before dropping her arm and stepping back.

She gave a small curtsy and straightened to see Prince Bastion staring at her toes. "Where in the world are your shoes?" He didn't look upset, but there was an intensity in his expression that she couldn't read.

"Well…" Heat crept up her neck as she explained being late to meet his mother and forgetting to put shoes on during her mad rush.

Once again, the prince released a deep laugh. He continued to chuckle and clutched his stomach. "I'm glad I ran into you tonight." He straightened and gazed down at her. "You've cheered me up more than anyone else could have. Sleep well."

She forced herself not to linger in the hall and watch his retreating figure. When his defenses came down, he was a better man than she'd originally thought.

CHAPTER 6

*T*he rest of the week carried on in a similar fashion to Felicia's first day, with the exception that she remembered to wear her shoes before leaving her bedroom. Handling the queen's rude insinuations and the tittering whispers of her ladies in waiting was getting old.

It was difficult work, conveying only regality and elegance. Though Felicia had to admit that dealing with the rude nobility for most of her adulthood had primed her for these very situations. For instance, when she met the queen and her ladies in the royal receiving room, Felicia contained her ire as the queen presented Felicia with a gift.

"I thought it perfect for you," she'd said as she motioned for a servant to bring in a medium-sized box. "I believe this will suit your royal status." The servant placed the box at Felicia's feet and she looked inside to discover and beautifully polished chamber pot. "This throne should fit your petite frame just right."

Felicia had fumed inside until it felt like her blood would boil out of her ears. But she smiled, knowing that there was nothing to be done about her flushed cheeks. "Thank you, your highness," she'd said overly sweet. "I shall think of you whenever I use it."

The tittering ladies quieted, their eyes wide. The queen had also gone quiet, then had announced it was tea time and fled the room.

Or when she'd shadowed the queen receiving the English ambassador and his wife, Felicia displayed only the best of manners, smiling politely while the queen made veiled insults against her.

"I find that having my wife with me for public appearances helps the common folk see me as more of a human being than a political figure," the ambassador had said as he patted his wife's hand affectionately. "It's quite a useful tactic to help soften their hearts toward me." The two had smiled at each other.

The queen took a dainty sip of her tea and quirked her lips upward. "How sweet. It's so nice to see a husband and wife who love each other. Something I'd hoped to have for my son."

The ambassador raised his eyebrows. "Hoped? You no longer wish this happiness for your boy?"

Sidling a glance in Felicia's direction, the queen's nose wrinkled and she turned her attention back to the ambassador. "I'm afraid it's out of my hands now."

The ambassador's wife frowned as she glanced between the queen and Felicia.

Felicia had plastered on a polite expression and pretended not to feel any resentment at the comments.

Presently, Felicia was wondering the hallways, using the map that Prince Bastion had drawn for her. His servant had delivered it the next morning after they'd resolved their differences. Felicia knew most of the layout now, and was certain she wouldn't get lost again.

As she was passing one of the receiving rooms, she heard her father's deep rumbling voice. Her spirits lightened and Felicia realized that she'd missed him terribly. She paused her steps and turned to enter when she heard other men's voices.

Felicia frowned, realizing it was a gentlemen's gathering and it wouldn't be prudent for her to enter.

"I thought that mine closed because there was no more copper to be found," her father said.

"That's what they believed, but we're certain there's more veins just waiting to be mined down there," came another voice that Felicia didn't recognize. "Rumors are that if we can dig deep enough, we might even find some gold."

Fury rose to her chest and Felicia clenched her jaw. *No Father. You cannot buy into their obvious lies!*

"Well." That familiar hopeful and dreamy tone entered the viscount's voice. "That would be a good investment, indeed."

Fingers shaking with anger, Felicia prepared to open the door and step into the room. She didn't care if it was against social standing. She wouldn't sit there and allow these sharks to take money from her father. Money he didn't have and they certainly didn't need any more debt.

Before she could twist the knob to open the door, however, Prince Bastion's voice drifted through the wood. "That could be a fine investment," the prince said, his tone bored. "But I have it on good authority that there are other investments that are more certain. Viscount Durand, would you care to join my father and I this afternoon? We're going to meet with the royal financial advisor. I daresay he can steer you in the right direction of where to place your funds."

Felicia held her breath as she waited to hear her father's response.

"I would be most obliged, Your Highness."

She exhaled and felt tension in her neck melt away. Smiling, Felicia continued on her way, comforted to know that Prince Bastion was looking out for her father. It was such a relief, to let someone else handle those kinds of things. So much so, that Felicia couldn't stop a small smile forming, even when she joined the queen and her ladies for more instruction.

CHAPTER 7

The following day, Felicia finished her eggs and headed to the queen's receiving room. She'd had tea with her father the day before. He'd been in great spirits, telling her of all the king and prince had advised him to do with investments. Everything the viscount told her had sounded practical and she had high hopes that he could actually pull himself out of debt if he followed their advice.

Felicia had wanted to thank the prince, but he wasn't at dinner again. She hadn't seen much of Prince Bastion since her first night, and Felicia wondered if he was scouring the countryside himself now, desperate to find his princess. The prospect of him not finding the other girl gave Felicia a mixture of confusing emotions.

She realized that she was enjoying her time at the castle. She was beginning to understand the intricacies of politics and had even grown fond of the king. He was harsh and very blunt, but fair in his judgments. And he showed appreciation for Felicia's opinions, asking to give her input on issues discussed at dinner.

"I would that Bastion had your insight," the king had said one evening. "You're able to look at every aspect of the puzzle before deciding the conclusion." He shook his head. "Bastion doesn't take the time to think like that. He's too fiery and hot-tempered." He glanced down the table at his wife, who pretended deep interest in her vegetable bisque. "Just like his mother."

Felicia had observed no censure in his tone. Rather it was something like affection. She blinked in surprise. Could it be that the king loved the queen, even with her sour moods? The queen certainly acted as though she were stuck in a loveless marriage.

Thinking back on that dinner, Felicia walked down a hallway, contemplating the idea of one-sided love. *Is that what's in store for me if I marry the prince?* She didn't love Bastion, but Felicia was already softening toward him. If they wed, she would take her vows seriously, even if it was fashionable for the nobility to engage in affairs. Felicia hated the idea of being stuck with a husband who carried on affairs of any kind.

"What could possibly be weighing on your thoughts so completely?"

Jumping at the voice right next to her ear, Felicia batted at the prince's arm.

He laughed, and she tapped his shoulder for good measure. "Where is your entourage to announce you wherever you go?"

"Beg pardon, Lady Felicia," he said while trying to hide a smile. "I truly did not intend to startle you. As for my entourage, they know that I don't like having extra shadows while in the comfort of my own home."

Heat suffusing her cheeks, she glanced down, smelling his familiar scent of sandalwood. "Oh. You're forgiven, Sire." Felicia looked up to see the prince studying her, his blue eyes tracing over her cheeks to her lips, then back up to her eyes. It gave her time to obverse him in return, to pause and appreciate his strong, square jaw and the playful dimple on his left cheek.

"What were you thinking about when I so rudely interrupted you?"

"Well, um…" Her mind worked, but Felicia couldn't think of a good lie. "I'd rather not say."

His eyebrows shot up. "Now I must know."

Felicia resumed walking, hoping that Prince Bastion would let the matter drop.

He matched her pace. "There's something you should know about me if this marriage actually happens."

Frowning, she wondered how serious he was about the possibility of their marriage. It mirrored her own musings too closely. "What is that?"

He smirked. "Once I get something into my head, I can't let it go. And I want to know what you were thinking about."

She waved a hand. "It was nothing of consequence, really. Just embarrassing."

"You should also know that I love embarrassing details about people I find interesting."

She paused in her stride and met his gaze. "You find me interesting?"

Prince Bastion shrugged. "Of course. It's not every day I meet a lady who isn't throwing herself at me."

Disappointment pulled the corners of her lips down. "Very flattering indeed." Moving to continue, she stopped when the prince touched her arm.

"That didn't come out right." He took a breath. "What I meant to say is that you're one of the few women I've met that thinks about more than position and power. I've seen you with my mother. You understand how to navigate social situations, my father keeps talking about how quickly you're catching on to politics, yet you have no ambition to use your position to force this marriage with me." He stepped closer until she could feel his citrus breath on her cheek. "I find that quite fascinating."

"Oh." It came out breathless and Felicia bit her lip.

Prince Bastion watched the movement and his eyes unfocused.

They stood there, their faces inches apart for several seconds. Felicia's heart sped up and her palms tingled.

Blinking, the prince broke whatever spell was brewing between them and cleared his throat. He held out his arm and she accepted it, feeling the heat of his skin through her gloves and his sleeve. "You were telling me what you were thinking about earlier," he said as they continued toward the throne room.

"Really?" she feigned ignorance. "I've already forgotten."

"You're not seriously going to make me ask again?" His eyes widened and his mouth turned down in a ridiculous pout.

Laughing released some tension Felicia didn't even realize she'd been holding. "Fine, fine." She lowered her voice. "I was merely contemplating whether one could find happiness in an arranged marriage."

His eyebrows shot up. "Deep pondering indeed."

Glancing away, she shrugged. "Well, you already know I don't want to become my mother. But is it possible to be put on the same path as her and make different choices? I favor my father's looks, yet we don't think alike at all. Perhaps I won't mimic my mother's behavior if I'm unhappy. Besides," she waved a hand, "I don't hold her beauty and I'm already a social pariah so it's doubtful that another man will even come into my life down the road."

They approached the doors to the throne room and a guard was just about the open them when the prince waved him away. "You may not have the fashionable beauty that women are vying for these days." He touched her cheek. "But your beauty is even better. It's a perfect reflection of who you are as a whole. And I agree with your musings; you are a strong woman, Felicia. Your choices will belong to you and you alone."

Felicia didn't know how to respond. His finger trailed down to her chin and then dropped to his side. She stood, unmoving as Prince Bastion nodded to the guard and the doors opened. The prince led her to the area portioned off for the queen's ladies and took his seat next to the king.

The ladies-in-waiting's rude whispers didn't bother Felicia that morning. She didn't have to pretend like their demeaning comments didn't affect her. She was too occupied with what had happened between her and the prince. *This changes nothing. He's still scouring the countryside for the woman he loves, which isn't you.* But even that thought didn't dampen her mood.

CHAPTER 8

*T*he next morning, Felicia was putting on one of her newly tailored gowns when a servant knocked on her chamber door. Tess opened it and then came back, a smile on her face. "I think you'll want to receive this visitor, milady."

Felicia didn't know what to make of her maid's expression. "Who could it possibly be?"

She opened her mouth to reply, but Lady Ella de la Roche swept into the room, her satin gown flowing around her with its usual elegance. "Bad time, Dearie?" Lady Ella's skin was smooth, even as she raised her eyebrows in concern. Her oval face was slim and show-cased perfect, high cheekbones. Felicia had no idea how old her godmother was. The woman appeared to never age and looked like she could be as young as thirty, yet her eyes held all the wisdom of someone who was ninety.

Felicia opened her arms wide, breaking into a grin. "Godmother!"

Lady Ella returned the smile and sauntered forward to give Felicia a hug. "Sorry it took me so long to visit." She leaned back and held Felicia's shoulders, her eyes scanning the girl from head to toe. "But you don't look worse for wear. In fact," She brushed gloved fingers through Felicia's hair. "You look wonderful. I can't remember the last time your cheeks held such color."

Smirking, Felicia waved a hand. "My face is almost always red, Godmother. You know that."

"This is not the same thing, child. You look great. Healthy. Life at the castle suits you." She straightened and clapped once. "Now Tess, could you arrange for refreshments to be brought up? My dear goddaughter and I have some catching up to do."

Tess bowed her head and rushed out the door.

Lady Ella walked over to a cushioned chair then sat. She motioned for Felicia to sit on the settee opposite of her. "Now, what in the world has happened? How did you become betrothed to the prince? You said this was one of your father's schemes? It doesn't seem like something he could accomplish."

Felicia proceeded to tell her everything that had happened from the time of the infamous ball to the present. Her godmother's mouth popped into an "O" at least three times during the recount. Once finished, Felicia sat back and studied Lady Ella. "How did you not hear about the prince's proclamation? Everyone gossiped about it for weeks."

Tess came in with a tray and set up a table between them.

"I was abroad." Lady Ella picked up a cup of tea and took a delicate sip. "I left the night of the ball and only returned yesterday."

Picking up her tea, Felicia noted that there were lemon cakes on the tray and smiled at Tess's retreating form. Lemon cakes were her favorite.

"There is something of import you need to know about this situation," Lady Ella was saying as Felicia picked up the cake dusted with sugar. "The night of the ball—" She stopped and stared as Felicia took a big bite of the cake.

With her mouth full, Felicia chewed and quickly swallowed. "Not to worry. I promise I eat with more feminine grace in front of others."

"No, it's..." Lady Ella closed her eyes, her lips pulled down in a frown.

Felicia knew that look. Her godmother's magic linked her to the spirit world and they were communicating, trying to tell her something. Curiosity piqued, Felicia finished off her cake and sipped her tea, waiting for Lady Ella to be lucid again. Deciding it would be another minute, she reached for a second lemon cake.

"No!" Lady Ella's eyes were open wide. She gripped Felicia's hand before it could reach another cake. "Tis poisoned."

Shock sank through her head and she placed a hand over her stomach. "Are you certain?"

"Yes. The spirits just told me." Pulling off her gloves, she felt Felicia's forehead. "Lemon cakes are your favorite. Anyone who knows you would know that you'd eat them."

Her tongue numb, Felicia blinked back tears. "Am I going to die?"

Her godmother narrowed her eyes. "Not with me around." She steered Felicia into bed. "Try not to move much; it will help prevent the poison from spreading quickly. I must go home and get some of my herbs."

Felicia knew that Lady Ella would also be casting spells in the privacy of her dark room. She'd probably bring a nasty potion to drink down, but Felicia knew that her godmother's white magic was powerful and should work.

Sweat broke out along the back of Felicia's neck at the same time that her stomach churned in a painful cramp.

"It's begun. This is a strong poison indeed." Lady Ella stepped away from the bed. "Don't worry, Dearie. I promise to make everything right." She stopped at the threshold, calling for Tess. When the servant finally arrived, she instructed, "She's been poisoned. Do not leave her side – not for anything – until I've returned. And don't let any of those ridiculous doctors give her their nonsense tonics."

Tess spoke to her in a panicked tone, but Felicia couldn't comprehend what she said.

The rosy pinks of the tapestry in front of her started to swirl. Felicia blinked, but that made her vision turn blurry. The cramping came back and spread lower in her stomach. *Please hurry, godmother.* She was too frightened to think that Lady Ella wouldn't return in time to save her.

Fever erupted within the hour. Tess sent a servant to bring wash-cloths and a bowl of water. The damp towels only made Felicia's teeth chatter with cold. She couldn't find a comfortable position and writhed constantly. Everything in her body ached.

"There, there, Mistress." Tess's voice shook.

Time blended into restless dreams and Felicia wasn't sure what was real and what wasn't. The prince came in, his face drawn with concern. "Why haven't you administered any tonics to her?" he demanded of Tess.

Her maid bowed deeply. "Her godmother knows a remedy for this type of poison. She's gone to fetch it and will be back any moment."

Bless you Tess, for not outing my godmother. Who knows what would happen should the prince discover Lady Ella de la Roche was a witch.

A large hand touched her shoulder and she moaned. The hand withdrew and she wondered if she imagined the touch. She pulled the blankets over her for warmth, her teeth clicking.

More time elapsed. The queen appeared and laughed. "That's what you get when you try to rise above your station." Then she turned into Lady Ella. "I'm going to fix this, Dearie. I promise." Felicia knew they were hallucinations, yet it seemed so real.

Felicia flopped her arms at her sides, sweat trickling down her hairline. A small, cool hand touched her forehead. "Wake up, Felicia. You must awaken and drink this."

Blinking, everything was blurry. Felicia couldn't focus on the woman before her. "Mom? Are you taking me to heaven now?"

"Not if I have a say in the matter," said a firm, male voice. Strong arms lifted her into a sitting position and then a cup was placed at her lips.

"Drink up, Dearie," instructed Lady Ella.

She opened her mouth and took in the hot liquid. It was bitter and rancid on her tongue. Felicia coughed, spewing the potion over her chin.

"Stop that now," the man commanded. "Lady Ella says you must drink it all. It will save you." The arms supporting her pulled her forward a little more until he slipped behind her. Felicia leaned back and rested against a strong, defined chest. His arms came around her and helped her sip the medicine.

Felicia slurped it loudly, forcing herself to swallow past a catch in her throat. Each time she took a sip, she paused to cough, trying not to retch.

"That's it," the prince soothed.

Once the cup was empty, she fell against Prince Bastion, gasping and exhausted.

Sleep came over her once again, but less feverish this time.

CHAPTER 9

*F*elicia woke with stiff limbs. She couldn't remember what had happened and wondered if she'd been in a carriage accident. Perhaps dragged several miles by the horses for good measure. Salty body odor reached her and she grimaced. *That can't be me smelling so awful, can it?* Yet her skin felt sticky with dried sweat.

Shifting, her muscles protested the movement and she groaned.

"Are you awake, Milady?" It was Tess. She was sitting in a chair next to Felicia's bed.

"It would appear so," Felicia rasped. Her mouth was dry. "How long was I sleeping?"

Tess went to a side table and poured a glass of water for her mistress. Then she helped Felicia sip it. Ignoring the burning in her fatigued muscles, Felicia drank every drop.

"I'm so glad you're up," Tess gushed. "We weren't sure if Lady de la Roche's potion had come in time." She sat and stared at Felicia with solemn eyes. "It took her until the day after you took the poison for her to find the right spell. She came in wearing the same dress she'd had on the day before and dark circles under her eyes. Your father was here too. Lady de la Roche sent him home early this morning to rest."

She grabbed Felicia's hand. "I'll send word to her and your father right away. They'll be so relieved."

Felicia watched her maid as she rose and exited the room. Tess looked worse for the wear, herself – with puffiness around her eyes and her hair limp in a sloppy bun.

It wasn't long before the door opened again. But instead of Felicia's loyal servant, Prince Bastion strode in. Unlike Tess, his hair was perfectly combed back and his attire impeccable. His eyes, however, were bloodshot and his stride hurried.

"You're finally awake." The broad smile lit his face and showcased perfect, white teeth.

Pulling the blankets up to her shoulders, Felicia nodded. "I asked Tess how long I was asleep, but she was too excited to answer me."

"It's been three long days," Prince Bastion replied. "You'll have to forgive her. I don't think she's slept much that whole time." He sat in the chair Tess had vacated. "We've all been quite worried about you."

Felicia's eyes widened. "I was out for three days?" She glanced at the window, with the drapes open to let in the sunlight. "What time of day is it now?"

Prince Bastion leaned back. "Around noon."

She took in his slouch and the tired lines around his mouth. "Aren't you supposed to be holding court with your father?"

He shrugged. "Tess had specific instructions to signal me the moment you woke up."

Processing the information, Felica's forehead wrinkled. "Are you saying that you got up and left your father in the middle of court? That's open to the public right now?" When he nodded, she chuckled. "I bet he's not very happy with you right now."

Prince Bastion didn't return her smile. "Actually, he's fine with it. He's almost been as worried about you as I have."

The pain in her body melted a little. "You've been concerned about me?"

He glanced away. "Well, you were at death's door. How could that not concern me?"

She tucked some ratted hair behind her ear. She wished that she didn't look such a mess. "If I died, you would have been free to marry your princess with no complication." The comment gave her pause, wondering if the queen had had a similar thought. *But even she wouldn't stoop to murder...would she?*

"Felicia, it wounds me that you'd think of me in such a callous manner."

Looking up, she could see that she'd struck a nerve. Prince Bastion's blue eyes lit with stormy emotion and his lips pressed into a thin line.

"I didn't mean to offend." She placed a hand over his. "You'll have to forgive me, sir. I'm so practical in my thoughts that even the morbid comes to mind."

Jaw clenched, he squeezed her hand. "Call me Bastion. And perhaps this is my doing. I haven't given you any opportunity to get to know me." He looked deep into her eyes. "I may be many things, Felicia, but I'm loyal. You and I have established a comradery and I will always honor that."

Felicia swallowed down the emotion that was thick in her throat. "Thank you, Bastion. And I know you have strong moral character. I truly didn't mean to bring that into question."

With the conversation complete, Felicia expected Prince Bastion to return to court. But he stayed at her bedside and they talked. He told her about his exploits of thwarting his tutors in order to sneak out and ride ponies. She told him all about her mother and the happy childhood she had. Felicia was all too aware of the prince holding her hand as they visited. He didn't seem to want to pull away and she was happy to let them remain connected.

She wasn't sure how long they would have gone on that way, but they were interrupted by her father and godmother.

"I knew you'd be alright," her father exclaimed, his face open and warm as usual.

Prince Bastion stood and offered the chair to Lady Ella, who graciously accepted it. She smiled at Felicia, her face wan. Opening her arms, Lady Ella leaned over and they hugged.

"Thank you for saving me, Godmother," Felicia whispered.

"I'm just glad it worked, Dearie."

When they separated, Felicia's father sat on the other side of the bed and patted her head, just like he did when she was a child and had done something to make him proud.

Prince Bastion quietly snuck out as Felicia conversed with her newest visitors. She caught his eye as he exited and the prince nodded to her with a brief smile.

Felicia didn't get out of bed until the following morning. There was still stiffness and fatigue in her body, but she simply couldn't abide another day lying down. Tess brought her a light breakfast. Felicia stared at the eggs and orange slices.

"What's wrong, Milady?"

Clearing her throat, Felicia scattered the eggs on her plate with her fork. "How will I know if they've been poisoned? How can I take another bite without the fear that it could be my last?"

Tears spilling down her cheeks, Tess rushed to Felicia, kneeling in front of her. "Please forgive me! I only turned from your tray to heat the water for tea." She shook her head, her nose running. "I had no idea, Milady. I was thrilled when they had lemon cakes because I knew they were your favorite. But had I known..." She broke off, her chin trembling.

"Oh, Tess! I never even thought to blame you." Slipping onto the floor next to her maid, she embraced her. "I know it wasn't your fault. You'd never do anything to hurt me."

Wiping her eyes, Tess stood and helped Felicia back into a chair. "But to answer your concerns, I ate a bite of each item before I brought your tray up." She gestured to herself. "As you can see, I've not taken ill, so the food should be fine."

Chills of fear covered the back of Felicia's neck. "No." Her voice had never been so firm. "I'll not have you risking your life like that."

"It's only temporary. Prince Bastion is hiring a test taster for you today."

The information sunk in, making her stomach clench. Felicia looked down and forced herself to take a bite of the eggs. She didn't like the idea of anyone testing her food for poison; should something happen, their death would be on her conscience for the rest of her life. However, it was comforting to know that it was safe to eat her food now. *Does that make me a bad person?*

The walk to the queen's receiving room felt longer than before. Felicia's muscles protested each step, but she knew it wasn't a physical ailment that made her drag her feet. She didn't like the suspicion that niggled in the back of her brain. It couldn't be true that the queen had tried to poison her. She also did not want to fight with the queen and her lackeys anymore. It was exhausting.

If I married Bastion, this would be my life. Every day I would have to engage in verbal battle. The thought only made her slow her pace even more.

"You look like a sheep going to slaughter." Prince Bastion strode toward Felicia and picked up her hand, kissing the back of it. Citrus and sandalwood wafted from him and Felicia breathed in as much as she could without him noticing.

Bastion stood back and inspected her. "Though I must say you look much improved."

A blush spread over her cheeks and Felicia looked down. "Shouldn't you be in the throne room with your father, holding court?"

"Yes, I'm on my way." Bastion leaned back and yawned, not bothering to cover his mouth. Though the lack of gesture was certainly rude, Felicia somehow found it endearing. "I admit that I could sleep the entire morning away if I could."

"Really?" Wrinkling her nose, Felicia shook her head. "I couldn't bear it. I'm not the kind of woman to sit idly."

Tilting his head, Bastion's blue eyes lingered over her face. Felicia wished her godmother could put a spell on her that would make it so she could know what the prince was thinking.

"And yet you're on your way to sit and observe my mother as she entertains the nobility's inner circle."

Felicia shrugged. "I can't say I'm looking forward to it, but I fulfill my duties."

Bastion held up a finger. "And that is why you looked so forlorn just now." His eyes sparkled. "What if I whisk you away to keep me company while I have to sit through another tedious morning in the throne room?"

A smile tilted the corners of her mouth. "Prince Bastion, are you trying to rescue me?"

The prince's lips twitched, making his dimple show, but he kept his expression solemn. "Why, no. It is I who needs rescuing. And if my request happens to help you as well, then all the better."

This time her smile turned into a grin. "Well, how can I say no to that?"

Bastion held out his arm and she accepted. They walked to the throne room together.

Felicia paused when the doors were in sight. "But I'm supposed to sit with your mother's ladies. She's not holding court today. Where will I sit?"

The prince waved away her concern. "With me, of course. You can't very well keep me company across the room."

Her brows tugged together. "But won't that confuse the public? We're not officially engaged. And if you find your mystery princess, we won't wed and there will be all kinds of rumors."

Stopping and looking down at her, Bastion smiled ruefully. "Has anyone told you that you overthink things?"

Felicia stiffened. "Only my father. Every day of my life."

"I didn't mean to offend, Felicia. I'm only trying to encourage you to relax. I promise everything will turn out just fine."

She still felt wary, but followed Prince Bastion. He led her to a chair next to his throne and helped her sit before seating himself.

All eyes were watching them with intense curiosity. Even the king glanced over as he listened to a farmer listing a grievance.

Flustered, Felicia turned her attention to the farmer and pretended that it didn't bother her to be the center of attention.

Once again, Felicia was impressed with how fair the king seemed to be. He ruled firmly, yet decreed resolutions to help with the common folk.

Bastion discreetly tapped her forearm. Felicia leaned closer to him so he could whisper to her. "I'm bored."

A giggle bubbled out and Felicia coughed into her hand to cover it. Once recovered, she whispered back. "Why? There should be plenty of drama here to keep you occupied."

The prince rolled his eyes at her. "You actually listen to everything being said?"

She stared at him. "Of course. Are you saying that you don't?"

Looking ahead at the next person speaking with the king, Bastion continued to whisper to her. "What's the point? My father takes care of everything. I'm only here for appearances sake."

"That couldn't be further from the truth," she quietly admonished. "You're here to observe and learn. To be your father's apprentice, as it were."

His expression didn't change.

"Bastion," she tried again. "When your father dies, you'll rule in his place. You need to be around and even participate so you'll be ready for that eventuality."

Prince Bastion threw her a sidelong glance. "You sound just like him. He's always saying that to me."

"That's because it's true."

He looked uncomfortable. "Some of his rulings... I don't agree with. If I take his place, I won't make the same decisions as him."

Felicia wanted to touch his hand, but forced herself to be still. "Just because you're different from the king doesn't mean you'll be a bad one. You must rule in a way that suits you. I'm sure your father dictates differently than his father did."

Bastion turned to her, his face soft and eyes warm. "I suppose you might be correct." He smiled.

Felicia's heart fluttered pleasantly and it took everything to break the eye contact with him, to lean back in her chair. She didn't listen to much after that. She was too distracted by the thought of what a wonderful king Bastion would make. And of the kind of husband he'd be.

CHAPTER 10

The days blurred together with Felicia working alongside the queen to entertain important guests and joining Prince Bastion every morning at court. While it felt that she and Bastion were becoming closer, the others in the castle treated her more poorly than before.

It wasn't just the queen and her ladies in waiting who created cutting undertones within conversations; even some of the royal servants made snide remarks under their breaths. Felicia did her best to not be phased by others of the realm insinuating that she somehow faked the slipper fitting on her foot. Everything from sleeping with the prince and the king to cutting her toes off slipped into conversations.

Keeping her face placid, Felicia merely smiled and clung to topics of the weather or the latest fashions coming into season. She'd be lying to herself if she said their condescending remarks didn't hurt, but she'd dealt with this behavior her whole life and knew that she couldn't show her pain. The people of the court were like vipers and would strike if any chink in her proverbial armor was visible.

One evening, Tess brought a beautiful dress made of cream taffeta and dark blue velvet to Felicia's room.

Reaching out a hand, Felicia enjoyed the smooth, soft textures. The bodice had beadwork set in the pattern of diamonds. "This is beautiful," she exclaimed.

Tess smiled. "I had quite a bit of help, but I'm very proud of how it turned out."

Felicia's brows came together. "What did you make this for? There aren't any balls coming up for months."

Her servant blinked several times before bursting out in giggles. "Have you truly forgotten? You're to be married in five days."

Eyes widening, Felicia sat on the bed behind her. "You're right. How could I have let that large detail escape me?" Shallow breaths suddenly plagued her, and Felicia wished she could take off her corset.

Tess shrugged. "I suppose you've been a bit preoccupied."

"And how could the prince not have mentioned it when I saw him last night?" Felicia assumed he'd have sulked to her about it. The opportunity for him to find the woman he truly loved was quickly dwindling. "What if this actually happens?" She stood and walked the length of the room. "This entire time, I assumed he'd find that mystery princess and that I'd quietly back away. The prince already guided Father's investments. We'll soon be out of debt. It all fell into place so perfectly."

"Have you lost your wits?"

Shocked at a servant speaking to her in such a manner, Felicia stopped and stared at Tess.

The maid's nostrils were flared and her eyes shined with emotion. "You are the perfect woman to be the next queen." She walked to Felicia and put her hands on her shoulders. "And don't you dare tell me that Prince Bastion feels nothing for you. I've seen the way he looks at you. This is meant to be, Milady. It's time you accepted it."

Felicia's mouth worked. Open, closed. No words came out.

"Now, let me help you out of your clothes so you can try on the wedding gown."

CHAPTER 11

*W*andering the halls the following afternoon, Felicia chewed her lower lip. She'd never sought out the prince before. He spent nearly every morning holding court with his father, and had been joining them for dinner each evening this last week. But she had no clue what he did with the rest of his day.

If I really thought we were getting married, would I have tried to get to know his routine, get to know him *better?* Yes. She would have plunged herself into learning all that she could about him. Yet even still, they'd grown close. She woke each morning with excitement to join him in court. She loved seeing the mischievous smirks he threw her way, and his puppy dog eyes when he got bored – as if she were the only one in the world who could save him.

She liked it when he leaned over and asked her thoughts on whatever problem was being presented. He'd listen attentively and it always made her feel pleased when his face would turn into admiration for her opinions. He made her feel strong, beautiful... important.

Shaking her head at herself, Felicia knew that she had to speak with Prince Bastion. She had to know if he'd run away or do something drastic to avoid the marriage. But the king had threatened to marry him by proxy if he attempted anything of that nature.

Maybe I should ask Godmother to turn me into a pumpkin or something. Then the prince wouldn't be stuck with me anymore. If she were truly willing to sacrifice herself, she'd jump from the highest turret. Unfortunately, she valued her own life too much to do that. And… the idea of marriage to Prince Bastion didn't repel her like it did before. But she still wasn't sure if she actually wanted to marry him. If he loved her, it would be an easy decision.

"What are you doing in the royal family wing?" The queen demanded, pulling Felicia from her thoughts.

The queen was standing in a doorway gilded with gold, her ladies noticeably absent. An empty glass was held loosely in the older woman's grasp, but Felicia could smell the hard liquor wafting from it. That was no mild sherry or port.

The queen narrowed her eyes. "Come to inspect your future chamber?" She sniffed, pulling her chin up. "If I had my way, I'd never have to look upon your wretched face again."

Felicia blinked. The queen had never said something so frank. She was always passive with her hatred. "Unfortunately, we don't get much say in our own lives, do we?"

Tilting her head, the queen folded her arms. "As a matter of fact, I control quite a bit around here. If you're truly sticking around, you'd best get used to it."

Straightening to her full height, Felicia stepped closer. "You mean that ridiculous guilt trip you hold over your husband's head?"

The lady's lips parted and her cheeks paled.

"Yes, it's clear as glass how you manipulate him." Felicia pointed in the matriarch's direction. "So you were forced into a marriage you didn't want many years ago. Time to move past it. Besides," She waved a hand. "You married not just a king, but a man who treats you with respect. Who listens to you and allows you to manipulate him just because he loves you."

The queen stepped back, a hand coming to her throat. "What did you say?"

Putting her hands on her hips, Felicia took another step forward. "I'm saying you should be grateful instead of clinging onto this trite bitterness. It could have been worse and you could actually be happy if you chose to."

Shoulders stiffening, the queen narrowed her eyes. "You think you know me so well after only a couple of weeks living here? You know nothing." She stabbed a finger into Felicia's chest. "You are a fortune hunter, taking advantage of my son's weakness. Well, let me tell you something. Even if you do marry, the prince will resent you for it the rest of your days. Every time he looks upon you or touches you, he'll think of his true love and hate you a little more each day." The queen breathed heavy. "And when he does find her, because he's tenacious enough, I will give my blessing for him to house her in this castle as his mistress right next to your chamber!"

Stomach trembling from the verbal attack, Felicia found no words for rebuttal. The queen was right, and the truth stung more thoroughly than a thousand honey bees. She blinked back tears, wondering how she could leave with her dignity intact.

"Mother." The deep growl of Prince Bastion came from down the hall. "That's enough."

The queen exhaled a shaking breath and turned to her son. "Bastion, I was merely—"

"I know what you were doing," he interrupted as he walked closer to them. The tips of his ears were bright red and his blue eyes stormed fiercely. "I said, that's enough." He placed a large hand on Felicia's shoulder. The touched soothed her more than she could have imagined. "I will not have you treating my betrothed in such a manner. Do you understand?"

In that moment, Felicia saw the kind of king Bastion would be. One who was passionate, but also honorable and loyal.

The queen stared at her son, the wrinkles around her mouth prominent as she frowned. Without saying another word, she moved around the couple and stormed down the hall.

The shaking moved from Felicia's stomach to her knees and she teetered.

Prince Bastion pulled her into his chest and patted her back. "I'm sorry," he muttered. "I'm afraid my selfish behavior of late influenced her in a most deplorable manner."

Breathing in the scent of sandalwood coming from him, Felicia's shoulders relaxed. "It's alright." She leaned away and his hand fell from her. "It was spoken harshly, but she only told the truth." The tears were back, but she met his gaze anyway, refusing to let one drop spill. "You would resent me if we married." Sniffing, she wiped her eyes. "We're supposed to wed in four days time. You haven't told me if you've found your mystery princess." She paused and looked up at him. "Have you?"

His mouth pressed into a thin line and he glanced away.

"I didn't think so." She took a deep breath. "Bastion, what your mother said... I cannot abide infidelity." She looked at his shoes, too uncomfortable to meet his gaze for this conversation. "If I marry – anyone—I plan to keep my vows, and I'd ask that my husband reciprocate that." The hall was so quiet that she could hear the material of her gown whisper as she shifted. Heat spread through her chest as she waited for a response. She wished she could take back the words, pretend like it wasn't an issue for her.

"Felicia," the prince said softly. "I would never want to cause you pain." He cleared his throat. "My mother raised me with the idea that I would marry for love. It's something she made my father promise her when I was very young. Whenever I thought of marriage, it never occurred to me to be unfaithful."

Grimacing, Felicia wondered if she'd always wonder about this other woman who had captured his heart so neatly.

His gloved fingers grazed her cheek. "If we do marry, I promise to be faithful."

She met his solemn gaze. "Even if you find her after we wed?"

Prince Bastion blinked slowly, the corners of his lips turned down. He opened his mouth to speak, but a servant came running down the hallway. "Sire, your horse is ready and the guards are mounted, waiting to leave at your convenience."

Still looking down at her, the prince closed his mouth and nodded. "I must attend to some business. But I promise that I'll seek you out tonight to discuss this further." He cupped her cheek and leaned in. "There is something I want to tell you."

Swallowing, Felicia nodded, wondering what he needed to talk to her about. As soon as he left, she brushed her cheek, already missing the heat of his touch.

CHAPTER 12

Though the castle was as large as a village, Felicia could feel the walls closing in on her, making it impossible to think. She was supposed to sit with the queen and watch her entertain the Spanish ambassador but she sent Tess to the stables to order a horse readied for her instead.

She needed to be with someone she trusted, who had wise counsel and a sturdy shoulder to cry on. Felicia hoped Lady Ella would forgive her rudeness for not sending word ahead, but she had to see her godmother as soon as possible. *Besides, knowing her witchy powers, she's probably already expecting me.*

Smiling at the thought, she went to the stables and mounted a fine white stallion. Tess and two guards were already on their horses, ready to follow their mistress. Felicia shook her head. *Something else I'd need to get used to if I marry Bastion – having guards escort me every- where I go outside of the castle.*

It was only a thirty-minute ride and Felicia's chest swelled at the sight of her godmother's villa. It was atop a hill, giving a perfect view of the castle and the three villages between them. Felicia had always admired the grounds, filled with flowers of every color and smell. There were also many trees surrounding it. She'd grown up climbing their branches as her mother and Lady Ella visited, wishing for a brother or sister to play with. Nostalgia washed over her as she entered through the gates and went up the drive.

A servant was waiting to take her stallion and Felicia was certain that Lady Ella had accurately predicted this visit.

She followed the butler into the villa, to the front parlor, where Lady Ella sat with a tray of steaming tea and various cakes and scones.

Felicia half-smiled and sat next to her godmother, hugging her tightly as soon as the butler left.

"What's the trouble, Dearie?" Lady Ella poured a cup of tea and handed it to Felicia.

Straightening, she accepted the cup. "It feels like everything is so wrong, Godmother." She proceeded to tell her everything that had happened that day, including her suspicions of the queen being behind the poisoning and all her fears of marrying a man who could never love her, and possibly break his vows.

"Are you certain he could never love you? Your first impression of the prince was less than flattering, after all. And now you look like you're falling in love with him."

Lips twisting, Felicia glanced away. "I'm not in love with him." She looked up at her godmother with large eyes. "And while we've become friends, I doubt very much that he'll ever come to love me. And even if he said he did, how could I believe it when I was the one to take him away from his true love?" Her head dropped into her hands. "I wish he could just find her and that I didn't have to go through this farce of a union."

Lady Ella paused, studying her intently. "Are you certain? Because I got the impression that you're well suited for each other. And I believe you'd make a remarkable queen."

Felicia stared. "You too? Tess somehow got it into her head that the prince has feelings for me." She shook her head, hysterical laughter bubbling up. "Nothing could be further from the truth, Godmother. We've formed a friendship, but that's it."

Frowning, the Lady stared into her teacup as she stirred. "I'm most disappointed on your behalf to hear that. I'd hoped things would work out." She met Felicia's gaze. "Do you truly mean it? You have no feelings for the prince whatsoever?"

It was Felicia's turn to pause. Closing her eyes, she thought hard before replying. Her godmother was good at reading faces and if there was a trace of untruth, she'd pounce on it. Sighing, she opened her eyes and said, "I can't say that there are no feelings toward him. I've come to care for and admire Bastion. Is it love?" She opened her mouth to say no, but couldn't bring herself to say it. *I can't love him, can I?* "It doesn't matter. Because Bastion doesn't regard me in that manner. He only loves the mystery princess." She swallowed past the lump that suddenly formed in her throat. "And whether I love him or not is irrelevant. He should be happy. And being with her would make him happier than anyone else on earth."

Her godmother exhaled slowly as she leaned back, her face troubled. "I had hoped everything would work out for the best. I thought I'd read the tea leaves correctly, but it turns out I was only half right."

"What do you speak of?"

She opened her mouth, paused, then closed it. After a moment, her lips formed a determined line. "Come with me." Lady Ella stood and walked out of the room.

Confused, Felicia hesitated before following.

Her godmother went down the corridor that led deeper into the villa. They walked up a flight of stairs and into an unused bedroom with white linens covering the furniture. Lady Ella lifted a white linen off the wardrobe and opened it to reveal a stunning gown made of silver silk and adorned with white and gold diamonds. Reaching in, she lifted a glass slipper Felicia was all too familiar with.

"But, I don't understand." She took the shoe and traced a finger over the gemstones. The bottom of it was coated with dry dirt. "It couldn't have been you he danced with." Her godmother had magic abilities, but certainly she couldn't transform herself. *Could she?*

"No, Dearie, it wasn't me." She opened the curtains to let in the descending light. "You're not my only goddaughter."

Felicia's head snapped up and she tightened her grip on the slipper so that it wouldn't drop and shatter. "What's this?"

Lady Ella shrugged. "I happen to be godmother to several children. Twelve, in fact." She walked over and pulled a linen off of a settee to sit. "Most of them have their parents still, so there's not much required of me. But one girl, Cynthia, is in a poor situation. Her father died and her stepmother and stepsisters treat her cruelly."

Gesturing to the empty bedroom, Felicia asked, "Why not bring her to stay here? You've got plenty of room."

"Believe me, I've offered several times. But she has a strange sense of obligation. My guess is that her stepmother is the last connection to her father, so she's reluctant to leave."

Stomach tensed, Felicia wondered where this was going. She had an idea that it had everything to do with the glass slipper in her hand.

"One day, she came to me in tears. Her stepsister had driven away a suiter that she'd hoped to marry." Her godmother waved a hand. "I came up with this foolish idea to make this gown and send her to the ball. If she wanted to marry, there were many eligible men she could meet there. I told you I went abroad, just before the ball, so I didn't know what had happened until my return."

"She's the one that Prince Bastion fell in love with that night." Felicia's jaw was numb, making it difficult to annunciate her words properly. "And he hasn't been able to find her because..." She stopped. "Why hasn't he been able to find her? The proclamation stated that all unwed maidens try on the slipper."

Lady Ella sniffed. "My guess would be that her insufferable stepmother kept her from trying it on. Probably hid her when the entourage came to their home." She shook her head. "I've tried calling on Cynthia three times and the stepmother gave me silly excuses and practically ran me off. I'm quite worried about her. The tea leaves give off the impression of darkness whenever I try to read them on her behalf."

"Poor girl." Felicia blinked, a swirl of emotions boiling in her stomach. "Godmother, why didn't you tell me? We could have resolved this whole situation as soon as you'd returned."

Lady Ella shrugged, looking down. "I was going to tell you. But that was the day you'd been poisoned. And then I spent all that time making a cure." She met Felicia's gaze. "When I returned, I watched the prince nurse you. He stayed by your side to let Tess rest."

Eyes widening, Felicia's head felt light. "He did?"

"Indeed." Her godmother watched her closely as she continued. "When I saw how intent he was on taking care of you... well, I thought he was falling in love with you. So I decided not to say anything and see if you two would want this union after all."

Felicia's legs were suddenly too weak to hold her. She stumbled and sat next to Lady Ella. There was a seed of hope wanting to sprout within her, but reasoning saved her and she squashed it, turning on Lady Ella. "Godmother, how could you be so fanciful to mistake concern for love? That's something my father would do. I thought you more practical than that."

Sitting back, her godmother put a hand to her chest. "Felicia, you've never spoken to me in such a manner."

"I've never had to." The anger gave her strength and she stood, glaring down at the older woman. "I always thought you to be practical, like me. But you not telling me about this because you wanted to see if the prince fell in love with me?" Stopping, Felicia drew in a long breath. "I'll never compare. I saw her at the ball, Godmother. I'll never compare with her." Tears blurred her vision. "He doesn't want me."

"He never said that." Lady Ella's voice filtered softly through the room.

"He didn't have to." Wiping her eyes, Felicia stiffened her spine with resolve. She would end this nightmare once and for all.

"Give me the name of this cruel stepmother. She may be able to run you off, but she certainly can't do that to Prince Bastion." Her stomach clenched in grief, but she kept an impassive face.

Lady Ella studied her for a moment with her lips pursed to the side. Then her shoulders sagged and she answered, "She's Barroness Duveroux and lives in Prevairy village."

"The village closest to the castle?" Felicia guffawed, some tension releasing with it. "She was right under his nose this whole time."

"Indeed." Lady Ella stood. "I'll see you out." She walked down the stairs and paused on the landing. "Dearie, I understand that you're not happy with me right now, but I'll always be here should you need me. Your situation isn't as dire as Cynthia's but you're always welcome to move in here. Perhaps be my travel companion."

Warmth sifted through the pain in her chest and tears threatened again, but this time they stemmed from love. "I certainly can't stay mad at you for very long." She reached out and squeezed her godmother's hand. "Thank you."

CHAPTER 13

elicia had intended to go straight back to the castle and let Bastion know about his mystery princess, Cynthia. But curiosity compelled her to head straight to the woman's home. She wanted to see exactly what kind of woman could so thoroughly capture the prince's heart.

With Tess and her two royal guards, she rode to Prevairy village. Tess asked around for directions to the Baroness' home and they found it quickly.

The sun was well in its descent when they finally arrived. One of the guards helped her down, then volunteered to knock. Felicia gratefully accepted. Hopefully a man in royal uniform would get her past this horrific stepmother Lady Ella spoke of.

The servant that answered was a young woman who looked to be her own age with a petite frame similar to Felicia's. Before the servant could utter a word to welcome them, Felicia stepped forward. "You're Cynthia, aren't you?"

The girl's blue eyes widened and she looked between the guards and Felicia nervously. "What can I do for you, Milady?"

"I know it was you who danced with the prince at the ball a few weeks past."

Cynthia jumped and glanced throughout the house like a bunny looking for a predator. She came outside and closed the front door, stepping close enough that Felicia could smell dirt and lye wafting from her. "What do you know about that?"

Tess and the two guards eyed Cynthia. Felicia could see speculation stirring in their expressions.

"We have the same godmother, Lady Ella de la Roche. She explained everything."

Cynthia's complexion paled to match her light blonde hair. "What do you mean to do with this information?" The girl glanced back at the house. "My stepmother will beat me when she finds out."

Felicia shook her head. "I certainly didn't come to tattle on you." Seeing the perfect complexion on Cynthia, and her large blue eyes, Felicia knew she could never match up to this beauty. Even if Felicia looked her finest, she'd still be considered wanting next to Cynthia in her rags.

The girl's head snapped up and her eyes narrowed as she studied Felicia's face.

Felicia's throat suddenly felt tight, but she forced herself to get out the next words. "I am here to help you meet the prince." She then explained about how her foot was the one who fit the glass slipper and she didn't want to force the prince to marry someone he didn't love.

Cynthia's tongue darted out before she responded. "That's mighty noble of you, Milady. Most women in your position would probably never tell the prince they know where I am so they could still marry him." She glanced suspiciously at the guards. "Some would even try to kill me so he'd never be able to find me."

"I don't know if I'd call it noble," Felicia looked aside. "Just trying to do the right thing, I guess." But her heart pulsed and she realized she resented being here. She resented this young woman for being what the prince wanted. For being more than she could ever measure up to.

"Does the prince really love me as you describe?"

Felicia clenched her jaw against the pain thrumming in her chest and forced a nod. Blinking at Cynthia, she noted the thoughtful expression and how the young servant glanced back at the house. "Do you return his devoted affection?" The question was difficult to utter and she steeled herself for the response. *But even if Cynthia doesn't love him, does that mean that I want to be his consolation bride?*

Cynthia plucked at her skirt. "How could anyone not return affection to a prince?" She met Felicia's gaze. "He would rescue me from my dire situation. How can I deny something so fortuitous?"

Frowning, Felicia's forehead wrinkled as she studied the other woman. "But he is not the only means of relief from your predicament. You know that, don't you?" She thought back to Lady Ella saying how she kept trying to get Cynthia to move in with her. "If you don't love Bastion, you can be our godmother's companion and travel with her."

Cynthia wrinkled her nose. "I love Lady Ella. She has been the only one in my life to show me love and caring since my father died, but I couldn't accept her charity." She shrugged. "I did for one night, and that ended up being more of a fiasco than I could have imagined."

Frustration mingled with perplexion rippled through Felicia. "You truly believe that staying here and being abused is a better choice than living with our godmother? Lady Ella is a good woman. She would take you in out of love, not charity."

Folding her arms across her stomach, Cynthia's expression shuttered tighter than Felicia's best corset. "The prince would be taking me in out of love. He would not take me to his castle out of charity. That's what I want."

Felicia took a step back from the girl's forceful tone. Out of habit, her face turned to indifferent politeness and she nodded. "Certainly. I shall report back to Prince Bastion. You can expect him to come here at first morning's light."

The rude exterior Cynthia exhibited melted away and she smiled while bowing her head. "You are most generous, Milady. I will never forget your kindness."

"You're mixing up the meanings of charity and kindness," Felicia snapped before she could reign in her tongue.

Cynthia stepped back. Felicia felt guilt rise up at the wary expression on the girl.

No more words could be uttered, but Felicia managed a stiff nod before retreating to her horse. Her heart sank when they arrived at the castle. This would be her last night residing here. Her last time to see Bastion.

CHAPTER 14

*A*s soon as Felicia entered the castle doors, a young servant ran to her. "The prince has been looking for you for hours." He turned to another servant to fetch the prince to the blue receiving room and then led Felicia straight to it.

Her breath hitched as she contemplated why Bastion was so intent on speaking with her. There was an intensity emanating from the servant, like something important was going to happen.

Unable to sit, she paced the large room while she waited for the prince. It felt as if a lifetime had passed before he finally entered, though she knew it was likely only a few minutes.

Bastion came directly to her, a fire shining from his blue eyes. "Where have you been?" He hugged her tightly.

Felicia gasped at the unexpected embrace, then relaxed and rested her head on his shoulder, breathing him in and savoring the moment.

"I had thought you ran away because of what my mother said to you." He reached up and stroked the back of her head, loosening the pins in her hair.

Pulling back, Felicia met his gaze. "I'm not the sort to run away, Bastion." He smiled, and it warmed her to the core. "I visited my godmother." She was about to explain everything, but Bastion took over the conversation.

"Of course, I should have guessed." He grabbed her hand and led her to a chair, then helped her sit. "I can tell you highly favor her."

"Yes. We're very close." She frowned. "Though there is some news that she neglected to share with me until this afternoon."

"I'm sure you'll work it out." Bastion knelt in front of her and began pulling on her glove.

"Bastion? What are you doing?"

He grinned as he continued to release each of her fingers, letting the air caress her skin. "You'll see." Her hand bared, Bastion brought her knuckles to his lips and kissed along their length.

The sensation of his full, warm lips over her naked skin tingled all the way to her toes and Felicia closed her eyes. "What's gotten into you?" It came out breathless and not at all censuring as she'd intended it.

"Felicia, there's something I want to ask you." Bastion released her hand to pull a small pouch off of his belt. He upended it into his hand to reveal a delicate ring showcasing a large sapphire surrounded with little white diamonds.

Felicia froze, wondering if she were hallucinating her deepest fantasy. *Drat, I'm turning into my father.* Blinking, Bastion was still kneeling before her, holding the ring for her to see. "Oh my," she breathed. "Bastion, it's magnificent."

She saw his fingers tremor as he slid the glorious ring onto her finger. "Felica, will you marry me?"

He said it exactly how Felicia would have fantasized. The moment was perfect, with his large hopeful eyes drinking her in. But Felicia wasn't her father – she knew better.

"Bastion, don't you intend this ring for another?"

His hand closed over hers. "No," he said firmly, staring into her eyes. "I do not."

The intent look he gave made Felicia's belly quiver in a strange, pleasant way. In a way that made her want to believe him, but logic wouldn't allow it. "What about your mystery princess?"

"I stopped looking for her." Bastion stood and pulled her up so she was once again nestled in his arms. "I have spent weeks scouring the countryside looking for a girl that I knew for only one night." He pulled back and looked down at her, affection pouring off of him. "And then I came home to you. Felicia, I have been getting to know you. I see you and the way you handle my mother, the way you watch the king and how you learn politics so quickly. You're more adept at ruling than I am and I've been raised for it my whole life." He leaned toward her until their foreheads touched. "You're perfect for me. More of my match than any stranger in a sparkling gown."

Each word resonated in her chest until hope and love enveloped her. Felicia swallowed down her emotions. "Truly?"

"Truly." Bastion pressed his lips to hers, lightly at first.

Her mouth tingled at his touch and she moaned. Bastion returned the sound and pulled her closer, deepening the kiss until his tongue danced over her lips.

Felicia pulled away, gasping. "Oh my." She giggled. "I didn't realize it could feel like that."

Chuckling, Bastion kept his hands around her waist. "Like what?"

"Like…" she searched for the right words. "Like, I could be so alive and die happy at the same time."

Bastion smiled, his gaze warm. "I like this side of you. I haven't seen much of it."

The comment pulled Felicia straight back to reality. Frowning, she pulled out of his grasp and turned. "This isn't right."

She felt his hand on her shoulder, the warmth of his fingers seeping through the material.

"I don't understand."

She had to tell him. Knew that it was the right thing to do. She'd promised Cynthia that she would. And yet, being here with Bastion expressing his love for her changed everything. *But he didn't actually say he loved me, did he?* She wondered if he was coming to accept the inevitable and was trying to make it seem like it's what he really wanted. *If he really wanted to be with me, he'd still choose me after I tell him of Cynthia's whereabouts.* And yet, she knew he wouldn't choose her.

"There is something I must tell you." Her voice quivered.

"What is it?"

Her chest was tight and her shoulders stiff. But she turned to face Bastion, clasping her hands and doing her best to appear placid. "I found your mystery princess today."

Breath whooshed out of the prince and his mouth dropped open. "You found her?" He chuckled. "Why am I not surprised that after I look for weeks, you go out for one afternoon and find her."

Felicia wasn't sure how to feel about his response. "She's living as a servant to an abusive stepmother, Bastion. In Prevairy village. I believe she's waiting for you to come and rescue her."

His smile slipped and he continued to watch Felicia. She wished to know what he was thinking. She couldn't read his expression. If she didn't know any better, she'd think he was contemplating something. *But what choice is there to make? Of course, he'll want Cynthia.* The thought made Felicia want to curl on her side and wallow in depression, but she refused to let Bastion or anyone else see it.

"I see." His tone was sober, his manner calm. "Well, then, I shall go and take care of her at once." He walked to the door but paused before opening it. "Please don't leave the castle. Promise you'll wait for me?"

The agony she felt at his words was intense. The insult of him bringing home another woman and asking her to wait for him was like being pulled apart on the rack. "Of course," she said stiffly.

When he left, Felicia bent over and drew in a shaking breath. She needed to find Tess and have her pack up their things. She might have promised Bastion that she would wait until his return, but she'd leave as soon as that obligation was fulfilled.

CHAPTER 15

Felicia helped Tess pack up. Though it was servant's work, it distracted her from the empty pit gnawing at her heart.

Tess kept glancing at Felicia's trembling fingers as they worked together, but didn't say a word. The servant left to send a note to her father, so he'd be ready for their arrival. Felicia almost didn't want to face him. She could already see the look of disappointment. It was tempting to stay with Lady Ella instead, but Felicia needed to get back to her life. The one boon was that her father had made some good investments from which he was already gaining an income. Soon, they'd be out of debt.

There wasn't much that she'd brought, and Felicia certainly didn't want the beautiful gowns provided by the castle, especially the wedding gown that Tess had made. *Let Cynthia have them all. We're the same size anyway.* The thought made her chest squeeze tightly and Felicia closed her eyes to stop the tears that wanted to erupt.

"The defeated look of a gold digger," the queen's snide voice penetrated the room.

Shoulders sinking, Felicia wondered if she kept her eyes closed, then maybe the old bag would go away. A rustle of skirts came closer, along with slippered footsteps. Apparently not. Steeling herself, she opened her eyes and saw the queen towering over her with a smug smile pasted on her tastefully rouged lips.

"My servants told me the wonderful news that my son finally found his true love. That he's bringing her to the castle as we speak." She glanced at the bed and Felicia's valise. "My thanks to clearing this room out so quickly. Honestly, I was expecting you to fight this." The queen's voice deepened with condescension. "Ah, but your daddy isn't here to fight your battle again, is he?"

A hundred different insults filtered through Felicia's mind in rapid succession. She knew she could respond with a cutting remark, something that would hit deep. But to what end? The queen was right – she was defeated, just not in the way the queen meant. "Goodbye, Your Highness. Try not to poison this girl like you did with me."

The queen's face went pale and she took a step back. "What do you mean?"

Studying the older woman's reaction, Felicia knew she'd been correct. If the queen hadn't poisoned her, the woman would have retorted something rude. "I mean exactly what I said. If Cynthia is poisoned, I'll not hesitate to send word to Prince Bastion of your involvement." Without bowing, she stepped past the older woman.

The queen placed a hand on Felicia's wrist. Felicia was surprised to see her haughty exterior melted away. In its place stood a woman with fearful eyes and a pained expression. "I did not intend for you to die."

Felicia pulled her arm away. "What exactly did you intend?"

Letting out a frustrated noise, the queen shook her head. "I'm not certain really. I was simply trying to make you miserable. One of my ladies gave me a tonic and she said it would make you sick for a few days. When I heard how close you came to dying…" She glanced away, but Felicia saw tears pooling before the older woman could hide it. Then she straightened and blinked, returning to her usual demeanor. "Well, I dismissed my lady and you are well, so there's nothing more to discuss, is there?"

Felicia stared at the queen, a mixture of pity and anger swelling within her. A petty prank almost killed her. The queen may have felt bad, but she certainly wouldn't apologize to Felicia. She noted the lines around the older woman's eyes. Those weren't wrinkles of age, but of bitterness. Felicia resolved to never let herself become like that. "Let go of your hatred," Felicia said softly. "You'd be surprised at how happy the king might make you."

A wrinkle formed between the queen's eyebrows and she frowned.

Shrugging, Felicia spun around and walked swiftly down the hall. She moved fluidly, now knowing the layout of the castle. Her gaze lingered on the hall that led to the throne room. She would miss the daily politics and sitting with Bastion. His sly glances and mischievous smiles. A sigh escaped and she quickened her pace.

Felicia focused on the doors at the bottom of the stairs. She'd be out soon, back to her old life, just as she'd wanted. Only now, it was the last thing she desired. Sadness weighed down her steps but she plowed forward. The prince would be back soon. She'd wait for him as she'd promised, say goodbye, then be on her way. *I just need to stay composed until then.*

Tess appeared with her valise. They were halfway down the stairs when the front doors to the castle opened. The cool night air drifted toward Felicia and toyed with the hair at the nape of her neck.

The prince and his entourage entered. Bastion's gaze went straight to her, his eyes widening. Then he glanced at Tess, the luggage in her hands and his lips flattened.

Swallowing, Felicia wondered how she'd be able to say goodbye without breaking into a fit of tears. But she wouldn't allow Cynthia or the queen see her fall apart now.

Bastion leapt up the stairs faster than a racing stallion, his eyes a stormy grey.

"You're leaving?" His tone was low, like he could barely contain his temper.

Pushing down the urge to grab his hand and soothe away the hurt she saw in the set of his jaw, Felicia clasped her hands together. "Of course."

"You promised you'd wait," he bit out.

"Yes." Felicia nodded. "I had planned to wait for you before I left."

His expression was flat while his blue eyes raged like a tempest. "Why?" he grated out.

The tension rolling off of him made her shoulders tighten painfully. "I don't understand."

"Why are you leaving?"

She stared, her breaths growing shallow. "You're going to make me say it?"

It was his turn to appear confused. Then he narrowed his eyes while he folded his arms across his chest. "Yes, dammit. You will say to me why you're leaving after I proposed."

Felicia's gasp was drowned by several other's. She hadn't realized that Bastion's servants were at the bottom of the stairs, watching them openly. She noted that everyone was still. The queen and the king were even watching above, leaning over the balcony and hanging on every word.

Bastion leaned in close. "You said yes, Felicia. Have you changed your mind?"

Blinking, Felicia wondered if she was dreaming. "But..." She leaned back and pointed a finger at him. "That was before I told you."

His hands came over her shoulders and she could tell his frustration was barely coiled. "Explain. Now."

The confusion and agitation rose within her until she pushed his arms away. "I told you where to find your true love!" she shouted. "And then you left. You left me and went to her." Tears spilled over her cheeks and she dashed them away, cursing her emotions. "How could you expect me to stay after that?"

She stared at her hands, willing herself to gain her composure back, not wanting to see the rejection coming. But when Bastion chuckled, her head shot up.

The prince was laughing, his body suddenly relaxed.

Humiliation and disappointment swelled. He was laughing at her? At her pain?

Sobering, Bastion grabbed her and pulled her to him for a deep, hard kiss. Felicia melted when she tasted him, felt the pressure of his mouth on hers. She wanted to savor the moment, until she realized that they were in front of an audience and that he wasn't making a lick of sense.

Pulling back, she went to the step above. "What in the world are you doing?" she gasped.

Not looking at all contrite, Bastion pointed to the front doors, which were now closed. "Do you see Cynthia here?"

She looked around, seeing that only the prince and his servants had entered with him. "Well, no..."

He laughed some more. "I rescued her, as you bid me. But I am not in love with her."

He stepped up, closing the gap between them. "I informed her that my true love was waiting for me at the castle. And then the maiden Cynthia asked me to take her to Lady Ella's villa." He grabbed her hands and held them against his chest. "And then I raced back home to be with the woman that I love." His face leaned toward hers, his warm breath blowing against her lips. "The woman that I want to marry and spend the rest of my life with." He kissed her again, softly this time. "Please stay, Felicia," he whispered against her mouth. "Rule the kingdom with me. Now that you've been in my life, I cannot imagine it without you."

Tears spilled over her cheeks once more. The love she felt for Bastion was too powerful to contain. She laughed and cried at the same time, collapsing into Bastion's chest. She breathed in his familiar scent. She couldn't believe that she'd be able to be with him every day. That he wanted her by his side. "Yes, Bastion." Looking up at him, she smiled through her tears. "I love you. I want to spend the rest of my life with you."

"I love you, too." He smiled, then kissed her again.

Felicia was certain she could get lost in his kisses, in his touch. She wanted the moment to last forever. But it ended all too soon when the king cleared his throat.

They pulled apart as if water had been thrown on them, though Bastion was smiling unrepentantly.

Felicia turned to see the king standing with the queen only a few steps above them. "Congratulations, my boy," the king said. "I've never been more proud of you than in this moment." He smiled broadly. "But you two still need to be wed before you can behave like that for all the world to see."

Bastion and the king laughed heartily. Felicia watched the queen as all four of them walked up the stairs and deeper into the castle. The older woman wouldn't look at Felicia, and her face was stiff with no expression. Felicia wondered if it would be a battle between the two of them forever. Then she looked up at Bastion. He was smiling down at her, looking as happy as she felt. She would handle the queen. Bastion was worth it.

THE END

ABOUT THE AUTHOR

Adrienne Monson is an award-winning hybrid author who has been hailed by MSN as a "vampire expert". She has always had a voracious appetite for reading and enjoys all kinds of fiction. While she is primarily known for her vampire novels in the Blood Inheritance Trilogy, she also writes historical romance, dystopian, and other genre mash-ups.

Join her readers club or find out more about her other books at http://www.adriennemonson.com/.

You can also follow her on Instagram

(https://www.instagram.com/adriennemonson/) or Facebook (https://www.facebook.com/adriennemonson/).

www.adriennemonson.com

facebook.com/adriennemonson

instagram.com/adriennemonson

TIME AFTER TIME

ANGELA BRIMHALL

TIME AFTER TIME

Historical Fantasy

by

Angela Brimhall

CHAPTER 1

TRYSTS AND TRAGEDIES

*E*very girl secretly dreams of meeting their own prince at one time or another and I was no different. Illusions of gold-flecked eyes, broad shoulders, and a commanding presence had ebbed in and out of my nightly dreamland excursions from the time I was twelve years old. So, when I heard the messenger arrive this morning with a summons for Father to negotiate a new royal trade agreement with the king, I bounded out of bed to dress.

I wonder if today will finally be the day he lets me go inside the castle and meet the prince.

"Are you ready yet, young lady?" Father hollered up the stairs.

Hands shaking, I jammed the laces of my ankle boots into their eyelets, tied a bow, and pinched my cheeks to put color in them.

"Coming," I yelled, then hurried to grab the leather satchel with my sketchbook and chalks, just in case.

"Going with Father to the castle again?" a voice called out behind me. I turned to see my new stepsister Ophelia giving me the evil eye. My cheeks burned. I tried to paint a friendly smile on my face before my eyes darted to the ground.

"I don't know why he always chooses you. It's like he doesn't even consider us his daughters." She curled her upper lip and scrunched her nose as if something rotten had wafted up her nostrils.

"It's tradition," I explained, trying to placate her. "When my mother was alive, she sent me with him a few times to keep him company. I've been going with him since she died."

Ophelia narrowed her eyes. "Well, *my* mother is still alive. Perhaps I should speak with *her* about starting a new tradition, now that we're all part of the family."

Father appeared at the top of the stairs, his eyebrows knitting together, face drawn. Moisture beaded in my scrunched hands and I swallowed.

He'd overheard.

"Ophelia, I didn't realize you were interested in accompanying me. I'll make it a point to save you the seat on my next trip. We're still getting to know each other, aren't we?"

My stepsister's glaring eyes never left mine.

"Indeed. Thank you. That sounds grand, Father." She turned and disappeared back into her room.

Father cleared his throat and reached for my hand. "Come, Ella. We mustn't be late." I took it, deliberately taking deep breaths to calm my hummingbird heart.

As we galloped across the countryside, Father at the reins as always, the cool fall air tasted sweet. Flocks of birds dipped, diving inside the wisps of clouds pressed against the morning sky, their songs permeating the air with soft prattles.

"Birds are heading south for the winter," Father observed, flicking the reins to encourage the horses to move faster. I pulled Mother's shawl around my shoulders, trying to trap body heat to fight off the small shiver tingling up my spine.

We rounded two giant boxwood hedges on the corner of the king's estate and headed down the long dirt road, loose rocks churning up from the rolling wheels.

"Will King Francis have you traveling during the winter months again? You nearly missed our first Christmas together last year. Lilith and the girls were dancing on their heels, waiting for you to return with their gifts."

"Yes," Father sighed, then laughed. "Lilith surely has a spirit and mind to know what she wants, and those girls—I, uh, wanted to apologize for the way your stepsister behaved toward you this morning. Ophelia had no right to talk to you that way. I'll speak to her."

This wasn't the first time. If you only knew, Father.

"It's okay. This marriage has been an adjustment for all of us. I overheard her talking to Gisella about their previous stepfather when I was watering the garden on Sunday. Their last experience with a new family was quite unpleasant. I'm sure Ophelia's just trying to protect her and Gisella's interests. Perhaps even prevent Lilith from being hurt again. I understand it's going to take some time to get used to the whole idea of another new family."

"My Ella, you're always so generous with your charity." Father turned around and flashed me his legendary smile. The way his graying mustache curled when he grinned always made me laugh.

I giggled and opened my mouth to tease him, but as the castle came into view, my throat tensed in anticipation. The gray marble stone caught the early morning light just enough to give off a glimmering sheen. My knee bounced and my toes curled inside my boots as we approached the ornamented wrought iron gate. I tipped my head out of the carriage window, searching across the lush grounds, then peered into the windows for a glimpse of Prince Greyson.

Father stopped the horses and tied the reins. "I won't be long, Ella. The king and I have a little business to attend to, then we can get back home. Lilith told me she was anxious to go into town. The ladies at tea informed her yesterday that a new shipment arrived at the dress shop. With Christmas coming, the party invitations will start circulating. She won't hesitate to accept."

I blinked, pretending to rub a speck of dust from my eyelid to mask my rolling eyes. He noticed but didn't comment. He just smiled.

I agreed to be understanding when you married her. I never said I appreciated her ostentatiousness.

"Of course, Father. I'll be waiting."

He turned to leave, then paused and returned, an even wider grin on his playful face. My stomach swooped and I licked my lips.

He's going to invite me in. I'm finally going to get my chance to see the castle and maybe even the prince.

"Ah, yes. I almost forgot." He dug in his bag and retrieved a small crystal-blue paper box wrapped with pink ribbon. "To pass the time," he said, giving me a knowing look.

My heart dropped a little as he meandered down the pathway and through the castle entrance. For years I'd wished Father could read my mind or somehow realize how much I longed to be at his side and see what he saw.

I looked down at the lovely package sitting in my lap. Even though I was somewhat disappointed about staying outside in the carriage, excitement bubbled at the prospect of Father's new gift. I bit my lip and held my breath as I opened the pretty box. A brand-new set of chalk lay in a rainbow of deep, brilliant colors on a bed of deep blue velvet.

He's always brought me pastels before. What a wonderful surprise.

I pulled out my sketchbook and searched the misty grounds of the royal estate for any sign of Prince Greyson. With the tip of my index finger I smeared the new robin-egg-blue chalk across the top sheet of blank white parchment, smoothing it in small circles to spread the color. The new stick wobbled in my trembling fingers, making odd streaks. I blew out a long breath, not realizing I'd been holding it in.

The first time I had sketched the prince was five years ago, just after my thirteenth birthday. The sky had sobbed great streams of rain that morning, but the surge stopped just as we'd arrived at the castle. The air was rich with the scent of wet earth and grass. Father had just returned from a three-month errand. However, the king sent a message to the house just one week later for another extended trip. I'd pouted, not wanting him to go, vocal about what I thought of the king and his errands. Father had guffawed, then rustled in his bag.

"Perhaps this will buy me and the king some forgiveness," he'd said, a twinkle in his raven eyes as he presented me with my first sketchbook and chalk set. "Why don't you find something to sketch while you're waiting with the horses and I'll be right back."

I'd glared at him as he made his way to the castle, a teapot still whistling inside me. But as Father walked under the wide wooden threshold of the entrance, Prince Greyson had emerged, greeting him with a friendly hello.

The rough edges of my mood smoothed away.

Dizziness had sailed across my consciousness. My lungs pumped, fighting for breath as if I'd sunk underwater. I watched his slow saunter and steady cadence as he made his way down the pathway. It sent a swell of nausea flooding across my already taut stomach. I nearly lost the eggs and ham we'd eaten that morning.

The prince had headed across the grounds in my direction, and as he caught my eye, a flash of heat rose from my toes, burning the nooks of every square inch inside me. I ducked inside the carriage, waiting a few moments before peeking again around the side of the curtain to see him heading for the large stable on the east side of the castle. As he disappeared inside, my slender fingers flew across the new parchment capturing every detail.

I've never forgotten that day.

Although I always hoped to accompany Father inside the castle, I didn't necessarily mind tending to the horses and carriage on the road outside the gates. Most times waiting meant gifts: new parchment, a new sketchbook, imported charcoals, and of course the guilty pleasure of spying on the mysterious prince.

On our visits, it was rare for me not to see Prince Greyson riding his horse in the meadow or practicing his fencing on the veranda, but today, the grounds were empty of his presence. I stared out across the vast gardens and fountains, contemplating, but decided to sketch the many windows staring back at me from the stone and glass castle.

I wonder where he is, what he's doing? What it would be like to live behind those walls, inside those windows; to see the marble halls and gold-leafed walls of the castle? How would it feel to dine inside the huge ballroom, feel the prince's embrace as we dance until midnight at a ball?

A voice in the distance floated across the air and stirred me out of my reverie. I poked my head out to see where the noise was coming from and forgot the new box of chalk lay in my lap. It tumbled to the carriage floor, shattering the sticks into broken nubs. I sighed and popped the door open to gather what was left of the chalk pieces. The only stick still intact rolled out into the road.

"Of course," I mumbled. Cursing under my breath, I stepped out from the carriage and scuttled into the road to retrieve it. As I bent over to retrieve the chalk, the rapid clomping and loud snorting of a horse thundered behind me.

"Macadamis! Easy boy! Whoa!"

I whipped my head up to see Prince Greyson barreling around the fork in the road on his spooked stallion.

"Watch out!" I screamed and jumped back, pressing myself against the carriage. He yanked the reins hard right to avoid crushing me. The jittery horse reared up and bucked him off. The prince's body sailed through the air, then collided with the shoulder of the dirt road behind the carriage. He rolled twice and smacked his head on the rods of an iron fence.

The Windsor Grey flew past the carriage and down the road, kicking up clods of dirt in his wake. I ran to the prince, fear clenching my throat. A wide stream of crimson blood pulsed and oozed from his dark hairline. He groaned, writhing back and forth, muttering incoherent words. I tore off a piece of my dress and knelt beside him, pressing the wad of fabric against his wound.

"Are you al-alright?" I said, stuttering over the question. I leaned down closer to his face.

"You fell off your horse."

"Mmmph." Prince Greyson mumbled, his hot breath feathering up my cheeks. He blinked, trying to focus his pale green eyes on me. He licked his full lips.

"Prince Greyson?"

"As beautiful as your father said," he whispered, his gaze so drawn into mine that I could see myself in his dilated pupils. Quivering fingers reached up and caressed my bottom lip with a tender stroke.

Time paused for a sacred moment.

His eyelids fluttered. He convulsed twice, then his head fell to the side.

"Miss!"

I shot up to see a mass of uniformed guards flooding through the tall iron gate, a large burly man with a heavily medaled coat commanding the charge.

"What have you done to the prince?" the man bellowed, beet-purple streaks coloring the pale skin under his blond mustache.

I stood and put my hands up.

"N-nothing!"

A group of guards swooped in, scooped the prince's body off the ground, and hurried to the castle. The commander and whom I assumed was his junior stayed.

"Commander Drake—" The young guard attempted to speak, but the commander cut him off.

"Get to the castle and inform the king of the prince's injury. I'll deal with this."

The guard threw me a look as if to apologize, then turned and ran for the castle.

The commander stared at me, eyes blazing. "I asked you a question. What did you do to the prince?"

I waved my hands side to side. "I didn't do anything. I was trying to help him. His horse bucked him off and—"

"Royal blood stains your hands!" he yelled, spit flying from his mouth onto my nose. I examined my hands. Crimson smears dripped down my fingers into my palm. I clenched my fists and pulled them to my side.

"Yes, but I was only helping. I would never hurt him or anyone." I backed away from him, my eyes darting around, looking for anyone who could attest my innocence.

The huge man launched at me and grabbed my arm, squeezing it. The vein on his left temple swelled and his eyelid twitched.

"Just where do you think you're going? You're coming with me," he demanded.

I saw a blur of color. I turned to see Father headed right for us.

"Get your hands off my daughter. What's going on here, Commander Drake?"

The commander's grip loosened on my arm but he didn't let go.

"Your daughter?" He glared at me, then turned back to Father with a smug grin. "We found her kneeling over Prince Greyson. He was unconscious, and she has royal blood all over her hands. I'm taking her to the king."

Father bared his teeth. "No. I said, get your hands off my daughter." His tone was low and threatening, something I'd never heard before.

Commander Drake stared at Father with a strange aggression that confused me, as if they were old enemies. "Move out of my way or I'll have you arrested as well. Believe me, it would give me great pleasure to do so," he snarled.

Father launched at him, swiping at the arm that held me. Commander Drake let go and swung at Father's face catching him on the corner of his chin. I watched stunned as he fell backward, cracking the back of his head into the metal hub of the carriage wheel. The sudden reverberation of the carriage startled our horses. They reared up and lurched forward in a rapid sprint. The motion of the back wheel turning hooked Father's coat onto the loose hub rivet. My jaw fell agape as they dragged his trapped body down the rough road.

"Buck, Jasper—stop, stop!" I darted after our carriage, screaming for the horses to stop, choking on the roiling dust clouds. I ran, utterly helpless, watching Father's limp body toss back and forth across the pitiless road. Once the horses reached the edge of the road by the hedges, they slowed, then came to a halt. Father's body lay still, the collar of his torn coat flowering deep red.

"Father, no!" I collapsed on my knees at his side and put my hand against his chest, waiting for it to rise, but felt no movement. I shook him. Nothing. I continued to shake him, punch him, screaming his name over and over—but he didn't move.

He was gone.

"Oh no, no, no, no, my Papa," I gripped his jacket in my fists and buried my head in his chest.

I vaguely remember the shaken commander pulling me off Father's broken body. He forced me to walk to the carriage and helped me inside. The same guard who tried to help me earlier came to report the prince's condition.

"The prince is still unconscious. The royal physician is tending to his wounds." The guard noticed Father's body in the road and made to run for him but Commander Drake yanked his sleeve and pulled him back.

"There was an unfortunate accident with their carriage. Her father was killed. I need you to accompany this girl back to their estate and inform his mistress. Upon your return, have the body loaded and taken to the home for burial."

As the guard took the driver's seat and reins, the commander leaned into the window, snarling in a barely audible voice. "If you ever speak of what happened here today, I'll have you arrested and imprisoned for your father's death."

I have little memory of the journey. The only thing I could think of was the look on Father's battered face as he lay in the dirt. I vaguely recalled the quiet guard walking me to the door when we arrived home where he lied to Lilith, telling her there'd been a terrible accident on the way to the king's castle and Father was dead.

The moment the door closed on the informing guard, Lilith, Ophelia, and Gisella turned on me. My family convinced themselves I was somehow responsible for Father's death because I was with him. Although the ultimate wrong remained in the commander's unexpected violence, sorrow weighed on my heart.

Matters became worse each day following his death as debtors came and went, informing us of unresolved contracts and deals that fell through in Father's absence. Each visitor whittled down the inheritance he left us, carving my already hardened stepmother into stone.

At first, I believed the anguish at losing the man she dearly loved incited her increasing coldness toward me. However, it became noticeably obvious as the money disappeared that my stepmother had married my father for his wealth. Without Father to support us, the estate soon fell into ruin. The luxuries she and my stepsisters had become used to over the short span of their one-year marriage vanished.

The day before Christmas Eve, the last of the housemaids and servants left to find other employment. Sobbing at the thought of their plight I stood at the door and watched them leave. Soon after Lilith sat me down in our dining room to talk.

"As you know, the last of the debtors came to settle your Father's debts this morning. I let all of our servants go, as we have no money to pay them." She patted her upper lip with the corner of her mono-gramed handkerchief. She'd aged significantly over the months since Father's death. Bitterness and resentment told their story in the lines on her forehead and the dark circles under her eyes.

"My life has not been pleasant, Ella. I will not bore you with my past, but I can tell you I found hope in my union with your Father, both for myself and my daughters, in spite of you. I had one year, one *year* of happiness. I just got comfortable here in this town." She gestured over to the window, then stood and rubbed the skin over her right eyebrow.

"I'm so sorry, I . . . it was an accident." I longed to tell her the truth—that it wasn't me who had taken Father from her. But I didn't dare to confess the secret I'd been forcibly commanded to bury.

"Stop talking," she barked. I flinched. She stared at me, a slow burn roiling behind them. "As I said, I had to relieve our servants of their duties this morning. I don't believe it would be fair to punish my daughters with the responsibilities and care of the estate when their second chance at a good life was stolen by you."

"But . . ." I gasped. My lungs constricted. The room spun.

"As of today, the burdens of the house are yours. It will be your penance for our suffering. Come now, there will be much to clean and prepare. It's Christmas. I'll not have my daughters feel the sting of our loss on their favorite holiday."

She left the room without another word. From that moment on, I worked day and night to please my stepmother and take care of my two stepsisters' every whim.

Lilith, Ophelia, and Gisella took every opportunity to remind me I was to blame for Father's death and their indigent living conditions. During the long hours of daily toil, the events of what happened that day with the prince looped over and over in my mind. After the initial shock of Father's death wore off, I couldn't help but resent the prince and feel the remorse of my part. Father would still be here with me if Prince Greyson could've controlled his horse that day and I wouldn't have had to jump to his aid and help him.

That thought haunted me for months.

In the time of my profoundest sorrow and pain, late at night when I finally retired to bed, I would hum Mother's favorite song and picture her embracing Father as he entered heaven. For comfort, I envisioned them looking down to praise me for acting on what they always taught me—*do good and good will be returned to you tenfold.*

I struggled to come to terms with recognizing how doing that one act of good could possibly profit me in kind when it ended in such tragedy. But over time, I came to accept Prince Greyson could no more have prevented the events of that day than I could've. Deep down, I accepted that helping the prince was the only thing I could've done—because it *was* the right thing to do.

Resentment and regret began to fade and the few precious moments the prince and I shared glimmered like gold on the edges of my heartbreak. Although it seemed silly for me to admit, I secretly clung to the look in his eyes and the complemented whisper because that was really the only happiness I had left. It was the only thing in my life that shone with the possibility of returning the good I'd done back to me. That single memory was the only bright star in the darkness of my loss and gave me hope of redemption when my resilience faded.

CHAPTER 2

SERVITUDE

"Mother, she ruined the glaze on the rolls on purpose."

Gisella threw her linen napkin on the floor, then picked up her plate and vehemently shoved it at Lilith. "Taste them. The glaze is scorched."

Ophelia grabbed the half-eaten roll from Gisella's plate, her sausage fingers sinking into the soft dough, and chomped down on the corner. She made a face, then spit out the half-chewed portion.

"Yes, Mother. Scorched. Just like she said. I'm positive she did it on purpose. Like everything she does to us." She narrowed her eyes and licked her lips. "Like burning my sash with the hot iron, the other day." She turned to her sister as if to invite her to join in.

"Yes. Like killing our new father," sneered Gisella.

Her harsh words made my stomach sour, reopening the raw wound in my heart that never seemed to heal. It was Father's first birthday in heaven, and my homage to him was to make his favorite food. I'd risen hours earlier than normal. I'd labored over those rolls and painstakingly followed the recipe in his honor. If he'd have been here, he would have consumed at least three, like he used to, and complimented me with each bite.

"It's amazing you can even remember to blink or breathe,

Cinderella. Your ineptitude knows no bounds. Pitiful. I'm utterly disgusted, yet not surprised that you've ruined such a simple recipe. If I *were* paying you, today would be your last day in this house. But alas, due to your father's untimely death, we're forced to put up with you." Lilith clicked her tongue, then stood.

"Come girls, we have much to do today. Let's leave this pathetic servant girl to her chores. I have a surprise for you when we get to town."

Lilith headed for the doorway, paused, then brushed her shoulder against the potted plant on the edge of the secretary. My heart dropped as I watched Mother's ornate vase tumble to the floor, exploding dirt and the budding plant all over the rug. Lilith dug the soles of her velvet shoes into the dark soil and cleared her throat to signal her daughters to do the same. As they left the room, tracks of sodden mud and crushed leaves scattered in their wake.

I pressed my fist to my lips, fighting back the flood of tears clouding my vision. I knelt on the ground and as I began picking up the pieces of the shattered vase, Mother's voice echoed inside my ear. *Broken things are just things, Cinderella. All that matters in life are the people you love and those who love you in return.*

My broken heart begged me to hear her, to allow her words to comfort me, but the porcelain shards in my hand were a sore reminder that no love resided for me within these walls. The only love I could ever hope to have in this life seemed to exist in another time and place.

Scrubbing the dirt-tracked floors took most of the day. This, in addition to my other chores, stole the snippets of the time I usually relied on to complete the garden and farm tasks. With the sun setting, it meant working into the fading light to feed the rest of our animals. I heard Lilith's cruel words repeat in my mind, and it threatened to wear me down. I tried not to let it get to me but no matter how many times the sun rose or set, the pain of having watched my father die continued to haunt me. In the cold of last winter just after he died, I tasted his tears on the snowflakes as they melted on my lips. I saw his kind face in the clouds during this spring's sunny days, and I heard his laugh ride in upon the breeze as it tickled the brittle fall leaves these past few weeks.

I missed him so much.

I closed my eyes and thought of Father in heaven with Mother to bring me a semblance of peace. In my mind, they laughed together as she handed him a roll with extra glaze. Father ate it, then licked his fingers. Mother admonished him on his manners like always, and they smiled at each other. The image helped to ease some tension from my shoulders. I felt a little comfort, but it soon faded.

I walked out into front yard and made my way to the dirt road to dump the scrub bucket. Muddy water, fragrant with peat moss and bark, slopped from the silver can as I poured it into the gravel just outside the front gate. After Lilith smashed my mother's planter, she and my two stepsisters tracked the dark soil and plant skeleton not only down the hall but throughout the entire house.

Lilith and the girls had hurt me so much over the past year it was beginning to numb me. The anger and resentment I'd have felt months ago at the intentional act seemed dim, almost lost in the physical pain I was in. Each beat of my heart pulsated through my swollen fingertips. My back ached down into my legs as I shook the dirty dregs of water from the base of the bucket. Only minutes before, Lilith and the girls returned from town. She made it quite clear she was expecting supper soon and my daily chores weren't even halfway finished.

I wanted to cry but I pressed my jaw tight to hold it in. I needed to stay strong, if only for my sanity.

"Psst."

A hissing voice from the thicket of butterfly bushes startled me. Gasping, I dropped the bucket. It clanged and crunched on the wet gravel. I whipped around to see if Lilith's sharp face appeared in any of the windows, then turned back to see my only friend peeking out from behind the bush, her hand over her mouth. Her apple cheeks glowed. I could tell staving off the belly full of laughter threatening to erupt from her was proving difficult. The tendons in my neck tensed and pulled on my already sore shoulders.

"Anjelina. What are you doing here? Lilith will skin me alive if she catches you."

I gestured for her to follow me, and we scampered across the garden into the barn. I swung the door closed after I stared at the windows and doors of the house for any sign of Lilith and the girls. My throat pulsed as I swallowed over and over.

"I'm so sorry, Ella. I didn't mean to scare you, I'm just so excited." Her eyes lit up like a sunburst.

"Shh. Keep it down." I said, but couldn't help cracking a smile to see her so giddy.

Anjelina giggled between gritted teeth. She jumped up and down like an excited toddler. "I came to bring you this," she whispered, shoving a roll of parchment stamped with the blue royal seal into my hand. "Read it. Read it. You aren't going to believe it."

Curious, I untied the silver ribbon from around the scroll and rolled it open.

King Francis and his honored son, the Prince of Wallachia,
cordially invite all maidens of the kingdom over the age of seventeen to join them
in celebrating his coming of age at a grand ball on the 31st day of October.
The gallant Prince Greyson wishes to choose a maiden to accompany him
for the evening. As such, we request you wear your most exquisite finery and present yourself at the castle at 8:00 p.m. Please RSVP

The words rose from the page, as if speaking directly to me. A swell of capricious excitement roused, only to be overshadowed by a pang of sorrow that bubbled in a pool of bitter acid and settled into my heart.

A ball, a grand ball at the castle of the king for all *the maidens in the kingdom includes me. But how can I even think about going?*

I stared down at the parchment again, the events of that fateful day one year ago flashing in my memory.

"Ella, are you alright?" Anjelina placed her hand on my arm. My dear friend and neighbor from the time we were old enough to walk, she remained my only friend after Father's death. Lilith, Gisella, and Ophelia, of course, didn't approve of my having any sort of friendship, so our secret encounters were few.

"Yes," I cleared the emotion from my throat. "This sounds lovely for the maidens of our kingdom. Are you planning to attend?"

She gave me *the look.*

"Ella, it says all the maidens over the age of seventeen. *All* the maidens. You know what this means, don't you? Prince Greyson is looking for you. You saved his life that day. This is his way of contacting you."

I huffed.

I want to believe you, Anj, I really do. But I'd be more of a fool than I already am.

"Anj, he was delirious, and I didn't save his life. I just helped him until real help came. He wouldn't be looking for me. I doubt he would even recognize me if he saw me. I mean, look at me."

A piece of greasy hair fell into my face. I swept it back behind my ear and inspected a piece of stray straw under my foot. Anjelina put her hands on my shoulders.

"Yes, he would, and you're going. I'll help you. Mother has loads of beautiful gowns. Let me sneak you into the ball. You know I can do it. My cousins Jacque and Gus are chefs in the royal kitchen. They have a lot of friends there. I know they can help me pull this off."

I eyeballed my foot again and noticed a smudge of manure across the toe of my scuffed, dirty shoe.

"Come on, you're already so beautiful. Once I'm done adding my special mix of sugar and spice, you'll not only get the prince to remember you but the entire castle will be clamoring for a dance with you."

She caressed my matted hair and put her finger under my chin, gently pulling it upward. I turned from her, the rank smell of the barn and the day's chores wafting from my clothes. I fidgeted with a tear in my skirt.

"Anjelina, you know what Lilith would do if she found out I even considered attending this ball, let alone carried through with it. She would—"

She snorted and waved her hands in the air. "Lock you up and throw away the key? Yeah, yeah, she's evil and malicious and could ruin your life." Her arms flailed in the air in all directions. "Well, look around, how much worse can it get? She's made you her slave, and there's nothing you can do about it. You know what I think," said Anjelina, rolling her eyes. She took the scroll of parchment from my hands. "I think you're afraid of what could happen if you did go. You and the prince had a moment. I'm positive he'd remember you. You could be his soulmate, you know live happily ever after? Get away from this horrible place and that poor excuse for a woman."

I saw the fervor in Anjelina's eyes and I dearly loved her for it. A spark of hope ignited in my heavy heart. I wondered if we could really pull it off. If, somehow, the prince would remember me. If, by some crazy miracle, I could escape this life of servitude and guilt, somehow forgive myself enough to give happiness a chance.

"I'll do it," I said and hugged her. "I'll do it."

CHAPTER 3

SECRET STASH

*A*njelina and I planned to meet at her house after Lilith and my stepsisters retired for the evening. I pretended to be finishing chores in the kitchen far past my normal bedtime to avoid being caught when it came time to meet her. Every nerve in my body teemed with anticipation and anxiety as I lay on a worn blanket next to the dying fire in the kitchen, watching orange embers fade from the charred wood.

The wind outside slithered into the house through alcoves and split wood paneling. The smell of fall mixing with the soft smoke from the fire infused the house. Although fall continued to mark itself my favorite season of the year, the days growing shorter and colder meant more work for me. The brutality of last winter made me cringe.

Life the past year wore on me day after day. The tragic loss continued to tear me up, and although the cost bore much, when I saw that parchment with Prince Greyson's name, a sliver of hope for something more awoke inside my heart for the first time since that day. Like Anjelina said, what if Prince Greyson did remember me? What if he chose me at the ball? What would that mean for me?

A blistered log broke inside the fire, sending glowing ash up into the chimney. A puff of warmth blew against my face, reminding me of my father's breath. I wondered how he'd feel knowing I blamed myself, and if he'd want this life for me or if he would rejoice at the opportunity the ball presented me. The question inside my head answered itself the moment I thought it. Of course, he'd be pleased. He'd even encourage me. He had even spoken of me to the prince. Everything he ever did for me or my mother meant to bring us security and happiness.

I sat up and listened hard for any stirring or sign from Lilith and the girls but heard none, aside from the creaking of the eves and the owl hooting outside in the evergreen. I wrapped Mother's old pink crocheted shawl around my shoulders and tiptoed outside.

The full moon lit the grounds with silver beams, easily lighting my way to Anjelina's estate. The darkness generated new vision and life to my growing hope. Things always seemed peaceful at night to me, as if my reality were different, calmer. Silence enveloped the shadows and quieted the odd repetitive sounds of life, bringing a sense of serenity not known to me during daylight.

When I approached my friend's home, I could already see her pacing. I found myself smiling, gratitude swelling inside for her ever-present enthusiasm.

"Ella, come on. I already asked Mother if you could borrow one of her old dresses. I've got them in the cottage out back."

Anjelina grabbed my hand and we ran to the cottage like young children sneaking off to cause trouble. She lit a few candles. In the flickering light, I could see an array of satin, brocade, chiffon, and organza in a multitude of colors.

"I don't want to tell you what you should wear on the most important night of your life but I think . . . this one," she rustled in the pile and pulled out a silvery-blue ball gown. "Yeah, this is it. I just know it. It's meant for you. I remember it was your mother's favorite color."

She held it up, biting her lip. As the candlelight burst into the crystal beads rolling over the bodice, the dress appeared to take on a life of its own. I reached out, breathless at its beauty, and caressed the satin sleeves, mesmerized at the dancing sparkle.

"Do you like it?" whispered Anjelina.

"It's perfect," I breathed. "Absolutely perfect." I bounced up and down on my toes, allowing myself to feel joy for the first time in over a year. I imagined Mother looking down on me, sighing, a tear falling from her eye.

She'd have loved the dress.

I started envisioning the different twists and braids I could sweep my hair into. Father had given me a strand of Mother's pearls after she passed. I'd kept them hidden in the attic in a small wooden box. Finally, I had somewhere to wear them.

Anjelina squashed me in a tight embrace and squealed quietly into my hair. "Then it's yours. When Mother gave me this pile of dresses to choose from, I envisioned you the moment I saw it."

A deep sense of appreciation swelled within me. I reached out and grabbed her up in my arms, hugging her. We twirled around twice. I had one person left in my life who knew me as the person I used to be. Anjelina woke that inside me tonight. If there was such a thing as a fairy godmother, she'd have been it.

She squeezed me enthusiastically then pulled away and again rustled through the pile of dresses.

"I'm going in this," she said. Anjelina held up a deep purple taffeta gown, layered with black lace and silver pearls.

"You'll look breathtaking in that one," I gasped. Her sharp angled cheekbones, bright blue eyes, and soft chin made her look cherubic.

She laughed and held the dress up to her, spinning around like a giggly ballerina.

"I'll have my pick of the men at the ball. All but one." She winked.

I gazed down at my blue dress, wanting to live inside the dream and fantasy of a perfect night with the prince, but reality brought me back to the present. Anxious trepidation started clawing at my stomach. Pulling this off would be impossible.

"How is this going to work? You know Lilith won't allow me to go." I peered up at my friend.

She dropped her dress atop the pile and put her hands on her hips.

"Well, I was in the market with Mother today after the royal messenger dropped off our invitation. She insisted on buying me a new ruffled slip for my dress. So, while in the dress shop I saw Lilith and your stepsisters shopping for their gowns."

She scrunched her nose and set her jaw.

"I overheard them talking about the ball when the tailor was hemming Gisella's dress. Lilith used the last of your family's gold pieces to buy the most expensive dresses from the dressmaker. She kept hounding them about how to act and what to do to catch the prince's eye. I mean seriously, how in the world could one of those two cows—"

"Focus," I said, stifling a snigger.

"So, the herd of horrible hags dressed from nose to hoof will be leaving your house at 7:30 p.m. to arrive at the castle. After they leave, I'll help you gussy yourself up to perfection in this beauty so you can be ready at 8:30. I've arranged with my two cousins to have a royal carriage sent for you."

She reached out and took my hands.

"No one is going to stop this, Ella. Meeting the prince that day on the road was destiny. The stars aligned, marking you both. Stars *don't* make mistakes. He's yours and you're his. Tomorrow night, sparks are going to fly."

She grabbed my hand and we began waltzing around the room. All I could think of was how it would finally feel to have Prince Greyson's hands around my waist, to feel the beat of his heart against mine. For so many years I observed him from afar—sketched his angled face, strong jaw, and broad shoulders. Tomorrow, I'd see them up close.

"You'll kiss under the moon and stars. He'll confess his undying devotion to you and whisk you away from your life of slavery into the castle, where you'll get married. You'll have gorgeous fat babies and do *whatever* princesses do."

We stopped and she eyed me, her face as serious as I've ever seen it. "Because, Ella, your father's death was *not* your fault. Forgive yourself. Stop punishing yourself for an accident that was out of your control. You're a good person, the most loving, sweet, hardworking person I've ever known. We've been friends since forever. I love you.

You do deserve to be happy, and it's what your father and mother would've wanted. So, be happy, Ella."

A lump of emotion rose in my throat. I swallowed three times to get it to go back down. I nodded, not being able to speak. I'd never told her about what happened, only that there was an accident. She knew Lilith, Ophelia, and Gisella blamed me for it. I wanted to tell her the truth so many times, I just couldn't dig up the courage for fear somehow the commander would find out.

Anjelina folded the gown and placed it in a large dress box.

"Now, take this dress and get home. Work your butt off for the last time tomorrow, then be you'll be off to the ball. Tomorrow night is going to be magical," she said shoving the box into my arms.

"Are you sure your mother doesn't mind?"

"Honestly, when Mother found out about the ball, she had me gather these to see if you liked any of them. If she wasn't with Father at Lord Christensen's fall feast, she'd be here fussing over you like she always does. I know she'd be proud to have you wear it. She loves you like a daughter."

A flood of gratitude and adrenaline pulsed through me. When she hugged me goodbye, she had to pat my back to signal me to let go of her. Anjelina pushed me out the door, chortling. I hurried across the grounds. I turned back to see her waving enthusiastically. I hugged the box to my chest, promise glimmering like a beacon of heavenly light. I imagined myself at the ball, Prince Greyson's arms hugging me, tossing me around the ballroom; the exquisite tones of the royal symphony filling my ears; the smell of food, flowers, and perfume scenting the air.

Tomorrow, my life is going to change.

CHAPTER 4

PRIMPING AND PRISSING

Gisella and Ophelia bellowed at the top of their lungs from the upstairs hallway, screaming at me to bring the baby roses for the finishing touches on their elaborately coiffed hair.

My stepsisters not only bragged about the ball at breakfast that morning, they reveled in the fact my stepmother insisted I not attend. Primping them for the night's festivities perpetually engrossed Lilith's attention. I ran back and forth, braiding and curling, fluffing, and tying.

But I didn't care.

My dress secretly lay under the blankets in my room in the attic. Each time one of them shrieked at me, I closed my eyes and focused on the crystal-green stare of the prince as he gazed deliriously into my face, hearing the whispered compliment floating off his perfect lips as I cradled his head on the road that day.

I prayed he'd remember me.

Night came fast. Although my joints and muscles ached from running up and down the stairs all day, my insides jittered with electric excitement. So many facets of tonight could be life changing but could also go awry.

An exasperated inner voice continuously chirruped in my ear

every spare moment I had to take a breath. *What if I get to the ball and Lilith catches me? What if my dress doesn't fit? What if Jacque and Gus couldn't get the carriage? Worst of all, what if Prince Greyson doesn't recognize me or remember me?*

Whenever I heard that voice in my head, Anjelina, in her lovingly obnoxious way shouted over it. *"Lilith won't catch you, I'll be there to distract her. You've got the best figure in town and that dress will hug your curves like a glove. I've got dirt on Jacque and Gus, they'll deliver. And if you think the prince could forget your adorable face, you're delirious."*

"Cinderella, where are those roses?" Lilith snarled as she approached me from the foyer.

The clock chimed 7:15. I woke from my internal conversation into reality, meeting her piercing black-brown eyes as they bore straight into mine.

"Right here, Stepmother. I was just getting them."

Lilith smirked and waved her hand. "Come, sit on the sofa. I'd like to have a word before we leave."

Butterflies pirouetted like tiny ballerinas on the lining of my stomach as I followed her. She took a sip from the steaming china tea cup in her hand before she sat, then placed it on the table.

"I remember the first day your father spoke of you. We were sitting just outside the portico of The Maison Shariff, waiting for our table. Your name rolled off his tongue as if it were the most reverent name in our language. He loved you, child."

A mixture of feelings sent tendrils into my core—longing, pain, love.

"Do you ever wonder if he looks down from heaven seeing you still alive and cries because you took him from his new wife and daughters?"

Shock poured into my stomach showering sparks of cool fire, igniting and silencing the innocent dancing butterflies. Sweat beaded on my lip. I chewed the inside of my cheek.

"Because, I know he does. I see him sometimes, in my dreams, reaching out for me. I was the love of his life. Our love story just began to flower when you stole his life on the road that day and left me here to mourn him alone. He finally had the family he wanted, the one he deserved. Yes, child he loved you, but he loved me more."

She took another sip from her hot tea, her fingers trembling.

"You didn't mention attending the ball today after Gisella brought it up. I found it quite odd that you didn't ask permission to attend with your sisters. I wondered what was in your mind girl, but no matter."

She licked a drying drop of tea from the corner of her mouth and clasped her hands together in her lap. "Now, I know you don't have means for a dress or any other fancies, but that friend down the road, the insufferable one, she would help you." She raised her eyebrow as if she already knew I snuck out last night. My heart smashed against my ribcage so hard I was positive she could hear it struggling to escape and the echo would give me away.

"I—"

Lilith's face flushed. She pursed her lips, blew a long breath, then leered like a wolf just shedding its sheep's clothing. "Shh, girl. I'm talking now. I just want you to know that I appreciate you not asking. I see that you acknowledge your fault, the part you played in your father's death. I'm happy to know you understand that attending the ball would not only disgrace my beloved husband's memory but would put a black mark on our name. And that will… Just. Not. Do." She paused in between each of the last words, pronouncing them with such ferocity each syllable punched me in the gut.

"So, we've agreed, yes? There will be no duplicitous attempts to attend King Francis's ball tonight."

My tongue stuck to the roof of my cotton mouth. Even if I'd wanted to, I couldn't speak. I swallowed, nodding my head once more. Lilith stood with stiff grace, sipped the last dregs of her tea, and reached out to hand me the cup but let it go just before I secured it. The second to last cup of Mother's china collection shattered into shards of porcelain on the wooden floor. My heart broke with the ceramic mint-colored cup. One more of the physical memories of my parents dashed to bits.

"Get those roses up to my daughters first, then get that cleaned up. Our carriage will be arriving any moment."

A sob choked in my throat but I wrestled it down. My stepsisters would rain hell down on my if they saw me cry. A few months ago, Ophelia found me crying while hanging laundry on the line outside the back door. She approached me as if to comfort me, then slapped my wet cheek. She told me to stop blubbering and get on with the laundry because she wanted to wear the sodden lavender dress to tea that afternoon.

I left the smashed tea cup on the floor. When I arrived in the girls' bedroom, they stared at me, clearly annoyed by the delay. Gisella clicked her tongue and studied me.

"Cinderella, you are useless, truly. I don't know why Mother bothers with you at all."

I set my jaw, grinding my back teeth to keep from crying, and wove the roses into Ophelia's hair first, then Gisella's. They talked the entire time about who would talk to the prince first and what they would say. Echoes of Lilith's words banged around inside my head, each of them hammering my hope and heart to dust.

A knock echoed from the door. They squealed. "The carriage is here!"

Just as they left, I caught the last of Gisella's sentence, "Love is false, will never stay. The only man worth salt is the one who will pay." They both giggled and rushed down the stairs.

A twinge of pain seared my finger. I studied my finger and noticed a rose thorn protruding from it. I pinched my fingertips around it and yanked it out. Wine-red blood oozed up to the surface. I closed my eyes. Flashes of my father's crumpled, bloodied body peppered the dark canvas. Pain I'd felt only once before as I pounded Father's still chest enveloped me. Floods of the horrible things my stepmother and stepsisters chanted at me day and night squeezed in on me from all sides. I bent, then reduced into a heap on the floor.

CHAPTER 5

THE GLASS SLIPPER

"*I* had a feeling," said the most musical voice I've ever heard.

I sniffed and saw Anjelina standing above me, the base of her enormous purple gown filling the entire bedroom.

"Come on, let's get going."

I shook my head and buried my face in the floor again.

"Nope, that's not going to work. We've got to get you ready, Ella. Suck up those tears. Give me your hand."

I peeked my head out from my hands to see her reaching down for me.

"No, you don't understand. I shouldn't go. I can't go, I just can't. Lilith said if I went to the ball, I'd disgrace my father's memory and our family."

Anjelina sighed a long, dramatic sigh.

"Ella, she just said that because she doesn't want you to go. She knows if you're there, her pig daughters won't have a chance." She grabbed my hand and yanked me up.

"Where's the girl with the twinkling eyes I saw last night? The girl who visited the royal castle? Who memorized and sketched every inch of the castle grounds, the one who's *destined* to win the fair prince's heart?"

She wriggled and adjusted her slip, then squatted down and put her hand on my cheek.

"I know it's been hard on you. I can't imagine what you must have been through. But this is your chance to change things. To find out where the rest of your life will take you. Don't tell me you picture yourself serving those three witches until they're old and gray?"

For the first time in a year, I truly realized what I'd become. The strong brave girl who loved life, the one Mother and Father raised to have courage and self-confidence, had shrunken into a near life-less shell—doing what she was told, letting sadness and grief bury the light inside of her. I pictured myself ten years older. I saw a lonely spinster who watched her only dear friend marry and start a family. A sad broken woman whose only lot in life was continuing to serve her cruel, wicked stepmother and stepsisters who weren't even blood. Something inside of me clicked, as if my thoughts forced a switch on in the very back of my brain. Gears started moving inside of me, clicking and turning, waking me from a mechanical stupor.

I sat up and rubbed my eyes. "No. I'm not going to let them treat me like this anymore. Father's death wasn't my fault. I've let them convince me I'm less than the dirt they track inside the house. I don't deserve this. Father and Mother would never want this for me. You're right. I'm sorry, I just forgot who I was the past year. I *am* going to the ball. I'm going to take my life back."

Anjelina licked her lips and slapped my shoulder.

"That's my girl. Now, where's your dress? I'll go get it."

"In the attic, under some blankets."

Her eyes widened in shock. "They have you sleeping in the attic now? If I wasn't a lady, I'd spew all the bad words I'm thinking right now."

Anjelina stormed out of the bathroom in a fluff of purple and black. I bathed, scrubbing the dirt from my face and the grease from my snarled hair. The irons were still hot from the last curls I put in the girls' ponytails, so when Anjelina returned, she helped me twist and curl my hair. We talked it out, and just like the girl I loved, she had me in stitches with her impressions of the stepsisters trying to woo the prince.

"What shoes am I going to wear?" I said, realizing the only pair I had were the dingy dirty shoes I did the chores in.

Anjelina's face fell slightly.

"Oh, oops. I completely forgot about that. Do you have any you could wear with a dress?"

I gawked at my bare feet. "No, all of my shoes have been ruined over the past year."

"Well, it's no never mind. The dress is long enough, not a soul will even notice, unless the prince literally sweeps you off your feet."

We both broke out into a fit of laughter, then went on twisting and braiding my hair. The clock chimed repeatedly, signaling each quarter hour until finally it struck 8:30. After Anjelina put the last pin in my hair, I twirled around, feeling the skirt of the gown lift from the floor, soft air tickling my ankles. The chiffon sleeves rubbed against my arms, releasing the rose scent from the soap off my skin.

Never had I felt so strong, beautiful, and determined.

"Your carriage will be here any second. I need to get back to my house and head to the ball. I promise you, cross my heart, that I will find a way to pull Lilith and the other two away from the prince long enough for you to approach him. Good luck, Ella. You truly look stunning. He will remember you, don't you worry. Hey, you won't forget about me when you're the queen, will you?"

An odd sensation like déjà vu rose from the bottom of my feet to the top of my head as she finished her sentence. The words she spoke resonated with me in such a strange way it stole my balance. I teetered to the side, grabbing the vanity for support.

"Ella, are you okay?" Anjelina raised an eyebrow as she walked back into the bathroom.

"Yeah, yeah. I'm fine. Lilith and the girls had me running all day. I've been pretty emotional. I think I'm just tired."

"Are you sure you're okay, do you want me to stay until the carriage gets here?"

I put my palm in the air. "No, I feel fine now. It was nothing. Just a weird wave of lightheadedness. You go so you can ride with your mother to the ball and announce yourself."

Anjelina hugged me. "Alright, see you there. Good luck, Ella. Find the prince. Trust in fate. Your life is about to change for the good."

We both hurried down the stairs but as she reached the front door a knock sounded.

"Hmm. Just in time. Good ol' Jacque." She skipped down the rest of the stairs and pulled the knob. As the door swung open, a footman stood on the porch in a lavish suit, an ornately wrapped box in his hands. Another wave of déjà vu swept over me and I closed my eyes to stave off the spinning.

"Miss Ella?" he said to her and bowed.

Anjelina sniggered, "Nope," then she snuck past him and ran for the gate.

I descended the rest of the stairs and approached the door. "I'm Ella."

The footman handed me a box wrapped in gold paper and ribbon. "We must hurry to the castle. No one must know I'm gone. You can open your gift on the way."

"What is this, who's it from?" I questioned as he handed it to me.

"I have no idea who it's from. A woman gave it to me. She told me to give it to you just before I left the castle. Let's go, miss, please. I said you can open it on the way. Come, I'm doing a favor for Jacque and Gus. I did owe them one, but if you don't hurry, I'm sure to lose my job."

I followed him as he scuttled to the open door of the carriage, and he helped me inside. As we rode, a little too fast for my liking, I peeled the wrapping from the box on my lap, curious about its contents and who'd sent it to me.

I tipped the lid off the bare box. The moonbeams cascading through the carriage window caught the facets of two glass slippers lying on a black velvet bed inside, exploding them with silvery light. A small note nestled just inside the corner of the box scrolled in curly gold writing bore my name. I opened the small note, but there was no signature inside. It simply said, "For the ball."

Breathless at the generosity of the gift, I lifted one of the slippers out. The design exceeded any jewel. It sparkled and glowed as if it were a living, breathing object. The unique cuts across the top came together at the rounded toe, creating what appeared to be the hands of a clock at midnight. I inspected the slipper's edge where the two points met. Ever so slightly, the numeral twelve rose from inside the glass. I noticed he same design etched into the other slipper's toe as well. I noticed a few deep cracks on the bases of each heel, but figured it was likely part of the design and dismissed it.

I wondered if perhaps Anjelina's mother sent the gift. Warmth enveloped me from the inside out as I took off my scuffed, frayed shoes and slipped on the glass heels.

Now I'm complete—from head to toe.

"We've arrived, Miss Ella."

The carriage stopped. A pocket of time escaped. There was no memory of the ride to the castle.

The footman, eyes darting back and forth, offered his hand to help me out. Then he took off running, calling back and waving at me as he ran.

"Goodbye, miss. I must say, I do hope the prince chooses you."

I blushed as he disappeared behind a tall hedge.

Alone, I peered up at the majesty of the landscape before me. Constellations of stars crowned the spires of the castle. Never in the many visits with Father had we come during the night. Ambient light luminesced from the stacks of windows shining out into the darkness. Hundreds of candlelit lanterns dotted the grounds, beckoning the evening visitors forward on winding paths.

The scene stole my breath away.

Father, Mother, I hope you can see me and are looking down, happy I'm finally taking my chance at happiness.

I proceeded forward on the lighted path closest to me. As I climbed the winding trail, the sole of the slippers hugged my feet as if made of soft satin pillows instead of glass. For a moment, I hoped by some miracle my mother sent them, but I knew that couldn't be so. Perhaps, like they say, I had angels watching over me.

Violin and cello music floated out from the open doors as I approached the castle threshold. The doorman stared. "My, my, young lady. You must hurry inside. You are quite late for the festivities, but all is not lost. Dinner is finished, but the king just struck up the orchestra."

He bowed and gestured for me to enter.

"Yes. My apologies. Thank you, kind sir."

I stepped into the foyer. The smell of roasted meat, onion, and garlic along with the warm savor of bread yeast drifted into my nose. My mouth watered, remembering the times when Father and I would eat such grand feasts with Mother. Consumed with the chores and preparations for my stepsisters, time hadn't allowed for me to eat today. I was indeed disappointed to have missed the grand feast.

The doorman appeared at my side, noticing my hesitation.

"The ball is to your left, my lady." He pointed down the hallway that forked off the foyer where dazzling light shown across the parquet floor from the open door at the very end.

He leaned down close to me. "The prince still hasn't chosen his maiden, perhaps he's been waiting for you."

As he finished the last word, dizziness and fog swept through me. I lost my balance. The room spun like a top. I squeezed my eyes shut, flinging my arms out to brace my fall. A pair of strong hands grabbed my waist before I hit the ground, tilting me upward.

I forced my eyes open. Blurs of brilliant color spun in every direction and disorientation set in. When I came to myself I realized I was inside a ballroom, at the edge of the dance floor. Couples danced, locked in twirling embraces in front of me. The hands on my waist moved away and a warm body nudged up next to me. I glanced up to meet the surprised light emerald eyes of Prince Greyson. My chest constricted. My head swam. I rubbed my forehead trying to get my bearings.

"Are you alright?" he asked, his eyes narrowed in concern.

Time had somehow jumped forward, whisked me from the hallway into the ballroom. I wondered if I had truly worn myself to the point of delirium with my chores and readying the girls for the ball.

"Is that a yes?" he questioned, a broad grin spread his lips. Speechless, I batted my eyelids several times and nodded. He chuckled. "I may have had a sip too many of my champagne at dinner as well."

He began to laugh and I joined him. The beats of the music changed. A new, more upbeat melody rang out. His eyes lit up, although I could see fair bit of apprehension behind his calm demeanor.

"I wonder if you would care to dance?" he said, holding out his white gloved hand.

"Uh huh," I said, then realized my mouth was open like a gaping fish. I casually pulled it shut. I took his hand and he led me to the dance floor. As he slid his fingertips around my waist and took my hand, my heart beat so fast, I wondered if it could take flight—dive from my chest like a hunting falcon. Heat rushed into my cheeks. Another surge of dizziness hit me.

Don't pass out, pull yourself together, girl. This is what you've dreamed of since you were twelve. Get it together, get it together, get it—

"So," the prince cleared his throat and chuckled. His nervousness seemed to match my own, and yet it was somehow charming, endearing.

"Yes?" I said, my voice still shaky. I peered into his face. Every muscle and organ inside me ignited, sending a shockwave of cool fire into my limbs. I could barely catch my breath in my fluttering lungs.

"I'm sorry," he laughed as if embarrassed. "I'm usually more articulate." He spun me gently across the floor. "I meant to ask your name."

"Oh," I smiled. "It's Cinderella, but I usually go by Ella."

"Ella," he breathed, pulling me into him a little tighter. His chest pressed against mine. My knees went weak.

"My name is Greyson," he said as if he didn't realize I'd recognized him.

"Yes, you are. I mean, I know. This is your house, uh, c-castle. You're the prince, right?"

Did I just stutter?

Greyson chortled, "Oh, yeah. I guess I am. Is it that obvious? I told Father I didn't want to wear this sash tonight. I wanted to blend in."

"It makes you look sort of handsome. I, um, think the sash is great." *Wow. Graceful, Ella.*

"Thank you. You as well. Not handsome. I didn't mean to say you were handsome. I meant you're beautiful, you *look* beautiful as well." He closed his eyes as if to wish he could rewind the conversation and start over.

"Thank you, Prince Greyson." I giggled.

"Please, just call me Greyson." He spun me around quicker than before and as we danced our bodies moved in sync, as if we knew one second beforehand which way the other person was going to lean or turn. The music rushed over the crowd, pitched chords coming to life in the magical air. When the end of the song came and the next symphony started, the notes plinked inside my ears. A rush of déjà vu pummeled me. I twisted the wrong way and lost my footing, falling into Greyson. He slowed us down, searching my face.

"Ella, you look a bit pale." He steered me near the edge of the dance floor and stopped. "Was I turning you too quickly? That dance can be a little tricky."

Nausea clenched my stomach. I backed away from him, then stumbled forward. Instead of colliding with him, my hands met a solid railing of marble. Cool evening air hit my face. I examined my surroundings. The ballroom had disappeared. We were standing out on the balcony staring over the grounds. Like the ride in the carriage and the conversation with the doorman—a chunk of time had just disappeared.

"Perhaps we should sit down somewhere. It doesn't seem like you're well."

Greyson's fingertips grazed the small of my back and I turned to see a concerned look on his face. Embarrassed, I stared at the ground. "I'm so sorry, Greyson. I don't know what's happening to me. I know it sounds crazy but it's like certain things keep feeling familiar, like I'm reliving a moment. Then time jumps forward and suddenly I'm in a different place. I know that doesn't make any sense."

He's going to think I've gone insane. I'm ruining this. We just barely met.

His brow furrowed. A knowing look settled across his face. He took my hand in his and gently squeezed. "Will you please come with me, Ella? I have something to ask you."

"Yes," I said. Curiosity piqued as he guided me off the balcony. We filed around the outside of the ballroom and through a side door. I prayed he wasn't taking me to one of the guards to have me dismissed, especially not Commander Drake.

We walked down a candlelit passageway and then through another door. The tang of rose, lilac, and gardenia flavored the night air as we entered a secret garden. Beams of glittering moonlight shown in through the breaks in the tall bushes. An ornate swing hung from an old, wide chestnut growing in the middle of the grove.

Now completely alone with the prince in such a beautiful place, knowing he wasn't turning me into the guards, I relaxed. I saw him observing my reactions and became very aware of the electricity in the air between us.

We could've torched the entire kingdom.

Everything seemed crisper, more alive—the glisten of soft condensation on the body of the leaves, the dampened music from inside the castle vibrating, a nightingale singing in the distance.

"Are you feeling better now? Would you like to swing?" Greyson offered, flashing his enchanting smile.

"Yes, I'm feeling a bit better. Thank you, I'd love to," I said returning a smile.

I sat back on the thick board and held fast to the braided rope as he pushed me gently.

"You said you wanted to ask me something," I said still anticipating his question.

"When I saw you walk into the ballroom tonight, you seemed very familiar. We've met before, haven't we?"

Words caught in my throat, and I had to force them out.

Is he having the same déjà vu I am, or is he talking about the incident on the road?

I wasn't sure how to answer him so I decided to focus on the latter.

311

"Yes. My father used to work with yours, he managed some of the royal property contracts."

Greyson stopped pushing the swing. He came out from behind to face me, his cheeks streaked with a pallid glow.

"What was your father's name?"

A lump rose in the back of my throat and I realized I hadn't spoken Father's name out loud since he died.

"Roger. His name was Roger Hammerstein."

Another knowing look exuded from his narrowed eyes and he nodded his head. My body suddenly felt strange, hollow. I tried to shake the rising feeling of déjà vu, but it pulsated inside me like another heartbeat, separate from my own. I'd recited Father's name to the prince before and seen his reaction but how could that have been? Somehow, somewhere, we'd talked about him before but he was the only one who'd spoken on the road that day.

How could he possibly know? This is the first time we've ever had a conversation.

"Does this seem familiar to you at all?" he said, his tone wanting. He gestured at the garden.

"It feels like parts of it do, but I can't remember." I pinched the bridge of my nose and moistened my lips.

Greyson perched on the grass in front of me. He rubbed his forehead and sighed.

"Everything that happened tonight from the moment I saw you walk through the ballroom doors until now seems like a waking dream. I'm positive I've lived these moments with you before. Most importantly though, I remember how we *first* met."

I started playing with the beads that came to a point on the base of my bodice.

That's the only memory I'm sure of right now.

"Ella, I wanted to thank you for helping me on the road that day after my accident. When I woke three days later, no one would tell me what happened. All they would say is my horse, Macadamis, got spooked and bucked me off. My skull ached, but I kept remembering a compassionate, lovely face staring down at me, soothing me.

Everyone worked hard to convince me I was just delirious, that my mind played a trick on me because of my concussion. But I couldn't shake the feeling there'd been someone there—a girl who helped me."

He plucked a blade of grass and started working it over.

"So, I began to ask around. All the guards seemed jittery, afraid to talk about it. They avoided me, and I thought their behavior quite strange. Why would they act like this over such a simple question?"

A chill fingered up my spine and wrapped tendrils around my ribs, clamping down my stomach.

He remembers me, but no one told him what happened to Father that day.

"Well, I'm not the type to give up. I let it rest for a few months, allowing for time to soften the anxiety over the subject, then began asking again. I questioned the servants, whenever I could get them alone. Finally, one of the stable boys confirmed my suspicions. A girl *had* helped me that day. I wasn't crazy. My mind hadn't played a trick on me."

Greyson grinned.

"So, I convinced my father to hold this ball. I hoped when I sent the invitation, you would come. I wanted to meet with you, talk to you, show you my appreciation," he said, his tone steeped in emotion and gratitude. "I knew I'd recognize you if you came. How could I forget the charming face of the girl frequenting my dreams and waking fantasies? My only fear was that you wouldn't come."

He rubbed the back of his neck and blushed.

"But it seemed my fear was unsubstantiated because you walked through that door tonight, more beautiful than I even imagined. Only . . . when I saw you standing there, searching over the crowd, floods of strange memories poured into my mind. I saw us dining and dancing together. I even saw myself pushing you on this swing. We've spoken about the stars, our late mothers, even your cruel stepmother and stepsisters. All of this has happened before—the ball, this garden, the swing. Everything. Many times."

His eyes met mine and longing stretched from his gaze. He pulled me in.

"Do you remember being here with me before?"

I tried to draw up any sort of memory or experience, but I knew what my answer was already.

"There were a few times tonight where certain things rang a bell and felt familiar. I've had strange spells of dizziness and déjà vu all evening." My cheeks and ears felt hot. "But I'm sorry to say, nothing with you so far seems familiar."

Greyson rolled up on his knees, then stood. He offered his hand and I took it. He pulled me up and cradled me in his arms. We began to sway back and forth, dancing under the watching moon. I wanted to forget the odd phenomenon unraveling, just live in the moment with him—drink in his woodsy scent, melt into the warmth of his chest, and relish his embrace. I longed to accept for the first time in over a year in his arms I was safe and cared for. I wanted to lose myself in this refuge. It'd been so long since I'd had human contact that wasn't cruel or violent. I would've given anything to force my mind to settle into this dream coming true, but confused thoughts racked my brain, interrupting the live fantasy.

How can I not remember him when other things have triggered my memory? What are these time lapses? Why is this happening?

Greyson slowed to a stop and pulled away. The corner of his mouth rose in a coy grin. My palms moistened, and the ends of my fingers trembled as he stood over me, capturing me in his intense gaze. He reached up, grazed my cheekbones with his fingertips, then ran them over my upper lip. The blood inside my heart launched like a startled grasshopper, then vaulted through my arteries, laced with drawn adrenaline, sending exhilarating sensations to the edges of my limbs. He leaned in, our noses almost touching. His sweet hot breath bathed my face in warm delicious air.

"Perhaps you'll remember this."

Our eyes met for a brief second, then his closed. The bell tower of the castle began to chime with loud bongs, reverberating over the muffled music of the ballroom. I anticipated the feeling of his lips against mine. Then everything faded and bled into darkness.

CHAPTER 6

THE CLOCK STRIKES TWELVE

The clacking of glass on marble echoed in my ears as my feet pounded the floor. Confusion jarred me, and I opened my eyes to see the open front door of the castle, not Greyson's lips, rushing up to meet me. I burst through it and found myself on the pathway I'd followed to get to the castle earlier.

Greyson and the garden were gone.

The bell in the tower continued to echo through the cooling air, chiming over and over. I whipped around to see the clock. The hands met each other on the twelve.

Three hours had passed since I arrived.

Light and color swam like pinwheels in my peripheral vision. All I could think of was getting back home. Hair tickled my bare back, flying wildly behind me as I jogged down the steep stone steps leading to the road.

What are you doing?

I tried to force myself to stop running, but the urge to return home compelled me with such vivid potency it forced me forward. I was on its leash. For the first time tonight, fear overrode confusion, piercing me to my core. The events of the evening were no longer strange—they were terrifying.

Greyson's shouts rang through the air behind me. "Ella, no! Please, come back. I can't lose you again."

The pleading in his voice struck a chord in my heart, so I turned to see him standing at the precipice of the stairs. A look of devastation and longing carved into his perfect face. His voice challenged the pull dragging me away, but it didn't hold enough power. I continued to run, hearing his frantic shouts fade as the distance between us grew.

The clang of the clock tower struck its last. Midnight fell as I reached the edge of the royal property. Time skipped again. I hurtled down the road in the direction of my house. Bewildered and frightened, I whipped around to look behind me. With the focus off my direction, I caught my heel in a large divot. The tendons in my ankle twisted and the glass of the heel on my right foot crackled and splintered. I tumbled to the ground, colliding with the unforgiving gravelly dirt.

Both the slippers vibrated, sending peculiar inviting sensations up through my legs, into my body. Vivid memories of the night's events frolicked inside my head; Anjelina coaxing me to dress for the ball; the doorman's courteous smile as he greeted me at the door; Greyson's handsome face leaning close to mine—the musk of his cologne popping onto my tongue as I opened my mouth to receive his kiss.

A dark hooded figure breached the trees just across the road. The comfortable, soothing vibration turned to pain. Shocking stings shot from the base of the slipper, scrabbling like razored tendrils up the same pathways. I tried to cry out but my throat seized.

The figure approached me slowly, its head tilted, savoring the scene. I writhed as searing agony electrocuted my body from the inside out. Convinced death had surely come for me, I closed my eyes and begged for my heart to stop, for this shadow to deliver me from the earth into my parents' arms.

Then I thought of Greyson—the pleading emanating from his hurt eyes, the slight pout on his lips, his crestfallen shouts for me to turn around. I rolled over to face the shadow now hovering over me.

Whatever this was, I would fight it.

A cold voice rasped from under the hood. "How many nights must we do this, Ella, before you learn to stay where you belong?"

The figure reached for the slippers still clinging to my feet and yanked them off. The moment they left my soles, the struggle within dissipated. Darkness encased me as my feet iced over and I faded into sleep.

CHAPTER 7

FAMILIAR CHORES AND SPEECHES

"Mother, she ruined the glaze on the rolls on purpose."

Gisella threw her napkin on the floor, then picked up her plate and shoved it at Lilith. "Taste them. The glaze is scorched."

I opened my mouth to protest that I would never have burned the glaze on Father's favorite rolls on his birthday. A swell of nausea and déjà vu swept over me. A flash of memory pulsed and I recalled similar mornings when Gisella accused me of this. The thoughts seemed to cling to the inside of my mind like a cobweb on the corner of a wall.

So strange. I only make these for Father's birthday. She couldn't have accused me of this before. This is the first birthday we've had without him.

Voices from the table chattered back and forth but were unrecognizable, as if they were underwater. I moved my attention to Mother's vase on the stationary. I saw it falling to the ground, splitting open, spilling dirt all over the floor. I reached over and steadied myself against the threshold of the doorway. My vision waned and turned black.

The clang of a bucket on the ground woke me. I stood feet from our stone wall in a puddle of filthy mud-seeped water. The gentle breeze on the air chilled me. A pale buttery orb hung low on the horizon, preparing to dip itself in the pool of dark blue rising to swallow it for the night. I grabbed my head with both hands. Flashes of this scene along with many others reeled through my bending mind.

I've done this before. Many times.

I watched the butterfly bush in anticipation of Anjelina peeking her head from the branches. When I saw her lean out I placed my hand across her mouth.

"Shh. Come with me."

Her eyebrows raised into her hairline. She furrowed her brows. I grabbed her hand and yanked her to our barn. She sprinted behind me, nearly tripping on the large pumpkin vines curling up through the garden. The moment we reached the barn stalls, I snatched the scroll from her hand and tore it open. Anjelina huffed and put her hands on her hips.

"Hey! I was going to show you that. What in the world is going on, Ella?"

I ignored her and read the calligraphy penned across the parchment aloud:

King Francis and his honored son, the Prince of Wallachia,
cordially invite all maidens of the kingdom over the age of seventeen to
join them
in celebrating his coming of age at a grand ball on the 31st day of October.
The gallant Prince Greyson wishes to choose a maiden to accompany him
for the evening. As such, we request you wear your most exquisite finery and
present yourself at the castle at 8:00 p.m. Please RSVP

She cleared her throat and pulled the scroll from my hand.

"You're acting so weird. What's gotten into you? I've never seen you this . . . ruffled."

I gaped at her, my insides whipping around like a sizzling summer wind. The words rolling around on my tongue fought to break free, but I was afraid to say them out loud.

I didn't want to admit to my fears.

"Ella, tell me," she coaxed and put her soft manicured hand on my arm.

I collapsed onto the milking stool, hiding my face in my hands

"I think I'm going crazy, Anj. I've seen this scroll before. I cleaned up the exact same mess in my house before, dropped that same bucket. I've even talked to you in this barn about the ball before, more than once. More than ten times." I exhaled, pulling my hands from my face. "I can tell you what you're going to say next. List every single event that happens in the next two days."

Anjelina stared at me with a worried look for a few moments, then her frown curved upward.

"Ella, those horrible women have worked you into delirium. Let me guess. You haven't eaten today. You've worked those slender fingers of yours to the bone and beyond. You need some sleep, my dear friend. A healthy meal and a restful night's sleep."

I stood and grasped her sleeves, laden with anxiety.

"I'm telling you, Anjelina. I know what's going to happen. You're going to convince me to sneak over to your house tonight so you can let me borrow your mother's blue gown for the ball. You tell me your cousins Jacque and Gus owe you a favor. They send a carriage for me. The footman gives me a pair of glass slippers to wear. I end up at the ball tomorrow and dance with Prince Greyson. He almost kisses me. Then the clock starts chiming. I start running and I fall. The glass slipper cracks. A figure in a hooded cloak comes to steal them, and I—"

I slapped my hands over my face as scores of images pepper my mind, a raging storm of watery recollection, each droplet containing a memory that repeated once it hit: scrubbing the plant soil from the rug, picking up Mother's broken vase, emptying the bucket.

"I'm remembering today and tomorrow, the past and future all at the same time. I've repeated them. Not just once before, but—a hundred times."

Anjelina's eyes widened. She smacked her hand over her mouth. She leaned against the work bench and stared at me.

"Do you believe me?" I whispered, praying she wouldn't run from the barn to call the lunatic wagon.

"Actually, yes I do. You're my best friend. I know you would never lie." Relieved, I fell into her open arms. She hugged me fiercely, then pulled away and grabbed my hands.

"When Mother received the invitation and I read it, I knew your wicked stepmother and those horrible stepsisters of yours would forbid you to go. I've been setting those gowns out all day. I've already sent the message to Jacque and Gus to arrange your carriage. I came over here to show this to you, hoping I could convince you to go. There's no way you could've known about that."

She escorted me to the barn doors.

"I've got to get back or Mother will be missing me. We'll figure this out, Ella. I promise. Go back inside, finish your chores."

Anjelina gave me her famous devilish look, winked, then hurried through the garden and disappeared behind the stone wall.

Still shaking, I went inside to start supper. As the stew bubbled in the cauldron over the fire, an inconsistency in the repetitive events troubled me.

If I'm repeating the same two days over and over again, why aren't the others having the same experience I am? Why doesn't Anjelina remember repeating this day? Why haven't Lilith and the girls complained about the strange phenomenon? What was different about today? What had happened last night that forced me to remember?

My stomach flip-flopped, full of angst and strangely enough— excitement. The only person who remembered was Prince Greyson. He'd been desperate for me to remember too.

A voice from behind me caused me to jump and flip the soup spoon, dousing the front of my dress with hot drippings.

"Don't scorch the supper, Cinderella. I'll not be eating two burned meals today. Didn't Mother tell you? We're celebrating."

I turned around to see Ophelia staring at me, mocking malice ebbing inside her deep brown eyes. Gisella appeared behind her and butted in front.

"King Francis announced a ball in Prince Greyson's honor. Mother

321

took us shopping for dresses today. But she told us there wasn't enough of our dead Father's money left for four dresses, only three. So you won't be going."

They sniggered and marched out of the kitchen, waggling their large buttocks behind them, proud they'd pulled one over on me.

But I knew about the ball. I knew everything that was going to happen.

I stirred the stew, the savory steam joining the mist forming in my eyes. Never since Father died had the girls left an opportunity to bring up my father's death in any conversation. That memory, mixing with the confusion and frustration about this repeating time rocked my composure.

For the first time since Father died, waves of anger emptied into my core. All this time, I'd been tormenting myself for playing a part in his death, acting the victim. I allowed Lilith, Ophelia, and Gisella to rub my nose in my ever-present guilt. The past year was composed of nothing more than daily punishments—both emotional and physical. I willingly allowed Lilith to take advantage of me, giving me all the responsibilities of the house, the chores, everything because I'd resigned myself to a life of slavery.

No more.

I couldn't bring Father back but in that moment, I embraced the truth of what happened. *It was an accident. If anyone was to blame, it was Commander Drake. I'm giving myself permission to let go of the past and allow fate to embrace me. Prince Greyson remembered me. In his arms, with his love, I could be free of this hell and hold the commander responsible for Father.*

My way out was clear, tonight was my last night of servitude. When I attended the ball tomorrow night, nothing would keep me from Greyson. I turned to dish up the stew for Lilith and the girls, but pain surged through me like a jolt of lightning. My knees buckled. I plummeted into a heap on the floor. Pressure thronged me from every direction, threatening to squeeze me to death. I wrestled with the invisible force, trying to free myself. Then the pressure ceased, and a delicate wind tickled my face. I opened my eyes to find myself standing on the veranda, Greyson's hand clutching mine.

"We've been here before, haven't we?" he questioned.

Once the shock of finding myself at the ball again dissipated, I answered.

"Yes. Several times."

He turned to me, and I surveyed his quizzical face. His Adam's apple bobbed. He swallowed and squeezed my hand. "What's happening to us?"

CHAPTER 8

DISCOVERIES

"Come with me," I said. I pulled him from the veranda. We ran around the crowd of twirling guests, and I scanned across the sea of color to find Lilith and my stepsisters engaged in what seemed like a passionate conversation with Anjelina and her mother. I caught sight of Commander Drake eyeing them. White-hot hatred struck me to my core. My heart ricocheted so hard against my sternum I could barely breathe. Pain and pressure again surged through me. Looming darkness on the edge of my vision threatened to tear me from the present into the past.

Begging whatever this curse was for a few more seconds, I barreled through the side door, dragging Greyson behind me into his secret garden. I had to get him alone, I needed to tell him everything I knew, everything I remembered before the time loop reset again.

The swing hung from the large oak as it had done so many times before. I headed for it to recreate the many scenes I now so vividly remembered in this garden, praying time would allow for a short conversation. I had to find out what he remembered this time.

Just before I reached the swing, my right foot caught on an exposed tree root and the cracked heel of the glass slipper broke free.

I tumbled forward. Greyson caught me mid-fall. When he pulled me upward, the broken slipper tumbled from my foot.

Time stopped.

The feathering melody of the violins and cellos in the background ceased. The excited chatter from the exquisite guests fell into silence. Not even the chittering crickets chirruped. The only thing I could hear was Greyson's breath, panting softly against my cheek.

He gently put me down, and we stared around the garden. The flittering flames on the candles inside the lanterns stood at attention. The crimson gold leaves falling from the surrounding trees bent in strange ways having stopped halfway through the air on their journey to the ground.

"Ella, the slipper," Greyson gestured to the fallen shoe lying sideways on the still grass. A rainbow of color twisted up from the toe, a kaleidoscope of strange but mesmerizing shades. The sole pulsed as if a true heart beat inside the inanimate object.

"What is that?" I breathed and bent down to touch it.

"Don't disturb it, Ella. I don't want you to get hurt."

I couldn't take my eyes off the whirling colors. Pictures began to form inside the growing rays of light. A euphoric tingling sensation filled my body and hinted if I waited for only just a moment, perhaps I could recognize them. Greyson gently put his hand on my shoulders and turned me toward him, then framed my face in his hands pulling my attention from the glittering lights. I gazed up into his eyes, the spell from the color diffusing.

"Ella, who did you get these from?" he gestured to the slipper.

"The footman who brought the carriage said a woman gave them to him. She told him to give them to me as a gift. There was a card inside the box, but all it said was 'for the ball.'"

He breathed an exasperated sigh.

"Well, let's get the other one off you. Their beauty is deceiving. I get the feeling there's something very wrong with them."

"No. Whenever both slippers are off my feet, I fade into blackness and wake up to repeat yesterday."

Greyson pointed to the fractured slipper. "Well, the other one is broken now. Perhaps that changed things. Let's see what happens."

He bent down. I lifted my foot up, and as he pulled the slipper off me, time suddenly jolted and started again. We were standing in a different position as if another time loop repeated. The interruption of the stark silence and our repositioning startled me. Music, laughter, and chattering filled the air. The leaves fell to the ground. The crickets played their song.

"How strange," I muttered, staring at the slipper in his hand.

"Indeed," said a raspy voice from behind the trees. The hooded figure I saw last night appeared from the thicket to the left of the swing, two other hooded bodies flanking on each side. Greyson dropped the slipper and reached for the sword strapped to his right hip, but he wasn't quick enough. The larger of the two accomplices ran at him. Both of them were knocked to the ground. The second accomplice grabbed the slippers, and the leader came for me. They threw me over their shoulder. I tried to fight, but the arms that cinched around my legs held tight like vice grips.

I could hear the struggle between the hooded figure and the prince. I kicked and wriggled to free myself but it was of no use.

"Greyson! Greyson! Get your hands off me!"

"Stop kicking," the voice said gruffly.

My captor was a man. But who?

He raced across the royal grounds and headed for a carriage waiting just outside the gate. I continued to fight, but his hands held me fast. We reached the carriage, and he chucked me inside, closely following in after me.

The clock on the bell tower began to strike.

"It's nearly midnight. We have to get both of the slippers back on her, then take them off at the same time or the day won't reset," the figure growled. He slammed me into the corner of the bench and yanked my legs downward, intertwining them with his own to keep them steady.

The hooded figure holding the slippers jammed the good slipper onto my left foot. Searing pain jolted up my leg like before. Floods of memories sailed through my mind, reeling so fast I could barely see them. A flurry of strange sensations weaved through me.

"Hurry, the other one."

As the tall figure made to shove the broken slipper on my foot, they crumpled at my feet, the prince towering behind them with raised fists. I regarded Prince Greyson, his lip bloodied, blue streaks flowering on the swelling lump above his left eye, relieved he was here.

"Greyson, you've alive," I squealed.

He threw a fist at the man holding me. The head of the hooded figure cracked against the door of the carriage. His arms loosened and he collapsed on top of the other person on the ground. Greyson grabbed my hand and helped me out of the carriage. My chest heaved as I panted.

"The slipper, it's hurting me. I want to take it off but I'm afraid we'll be back to where we started. Who are these people?" I whimpered. "Why are they doing this to us?"

Greyson swooped me up into his arms, cradling me.

"I need to get you back to the castle. My father will help us figure out what's going on."

He carried me across the grounds and we headed for the face of the castle I remembered from my childhood. I recalled how I used to memorize and sketch every inch of the lit windows, draw the bubbling fountains dotting each side of the entrance while waiting for Father to do his business with the king. The irony of our situation boggled my mind.

"We'll figure this out, Ella. I know that we're meant to be together. I've dreamed of you so many times. I love—"

Greyson lurched forward, his arms falling slack. I tumbled to the ground and rolled, every part of my body bending in abnormal ways. The prince toppled just to the side of me, unconscious. The large hooded figure from the night before, the one who attacked Greyson in the garden, brandished the broken glass slipper from the carriage. His hood slipped and fell from his face. I recognized Commander Drake.

327

"We need to set this right. One of these days, you'll figure out that this is not meant to be and stop fighting your fate."

He approached me. Fat fingers wrenched my ankle and jammed the broken slipper onto my foot, then ripped off both the slippers at the same time. In the distance, I heard the clock on the bell tower of the castle chime, then fall silent. I reached for Greyson. My fingertips barely grazed his jacket before the stars above me blurred. My eyes rolled back into my head, bathing my vision in silky blackness.

CHAPTER 9

CAUGHT UP IN A NEW DAY

"*M*other, she ruined the glaze on the rolls on purpose."

Gisella threw her napkin on the floor, then picked up her plate and shoved it at Lilith. "Taste them. The glaze is scorched."

I blinked rapidly, hearing my stepsister's whiny voice echo inside my ear, repeating itself.

The glaze is scorched. The glaze is scorched. The glaze is scorched.

"No!" I screamed and launched at her. I ripped the cinnamon roll from her hand and chucked it across the room.

"Cinderella, how dare you!" roared Lilith.

I stared at her wide eyes and gaping mouth. Ophelia and Gisella also gawked speechless, mouths hanging open like carp plucked from the river.

"This can't be happening again!" I shrieked and darted from the room. Shouts and commands followed behind me, but I didn't care. Memories from yesterday—or tomorrow or whenever it was—were still fresh in my mind. I could hear the music of the ball, feel the satin of Anjelina's mother's gown pressed against my skin, still feel Prince Greyson's heart patting against my cheek as I nuzzled against his chest after the melee in the carriage.

Today, none of the memories blurred. I could recall the past, evoke every moment of the endless times I'd relived these two days.

What changed?

I burst from the door of my childhood home and raced down the street, hoping to find Anjelina home. The fall air bit at my cheeks, cooler as the early morning sun still climbed across the new blue sky. My muscles ached from the tumble I took last night when the prince dropped me, but I didn't care. I pushed harder until I reached my best friend's porch.

"Anjelina," I hollered, pounding on the door. "Anjelina! Anjelina!"

Their butler answered the door. I pushed past him.

"Miss Ella, what do you think you're doing?" he called after me.

"Where's Anjelina?" I yelled whipping my head around the foyer then up the grand winding staircase.

I need you, Anjelina. Where are you?

"Miss. The royal messenger just delivered an invitation to a ball tomorrow night. Her grace and Miss Anjelina have left for town to shop."

Without a word, I elbowed past him and ran for town. I needed Anjelina's help to get to the castle. I had to speak to Prince Greyson. If he remembered everything that happened last night, we could try to figure out what was going on, who was behind this bizarre curse, and how to stop the time loop.

Tired and ragged, I crossed the town border. Hundreds of people milled around, no doubt having received the invitation for the ball. I scanned the harried crowd, hoping to see Anjelina or her mother, but I didn't recognize a soul in the sea of faces until I caught the eye of Commander Drake. His eyes bore into mine, and he marched his way through the crowd.

Fear sent spikes of cold ice into my stomach. I turned to run, but a hand grabbed my arm from behind and a shrill voice whispered in my ear.

"Don't you dare move, Ella."

Shocked into stiffness, I recognized the voice of my older stepsister, Ophelia. Her fingers dug into my already bruised arm. A needle-like pinch jabbed into my back. I cried out.

"If you try to run, I'll run this knife clean through you."

I bit back the scream readying to explode from my mouth and pressed my lips together. Sweat moistened the back of my neck. I shivered.

The commander approached us. Seeing him again this close was like a living nightmare. I saw his fist slamming into my father's chin and heard his head smacking the carriage wheel. I remembered Commander Drake's cruel directive to keep quiet or he'd have me imprisoned.

"Follow me and keep quiet, Cinderella. You know, it's a joy to be a part of destroying the girl of the man who stole my childhood love from me. It seems fitting."

Shock and understanding flowed through me, answering the question I asked myself the day my father died. This was why they'd been old enemies.

Ophelia shoved me forward into the commander, and he took my wrist and guided me through the bustling crowd to the largest of the royal carriages on the west side of the square. The steel end of the sharp blade still edged into my back as Ophelia followed close behind. Thoughts of betrayal and utter disbelief melded with the horror of what they were going to do with me. In this enormous sea of people, not one of them recognized what was happening to me. The excitement surrounding the upcoming royal ball kept them all entranced in their own worlds.

"Get in," the commander said as we reached the carriage. The door opened, and Gisella peered at me from the dark shadows, a sneer on her ugly fat face. I stood there, another bolt of shock and awe coursed through me.

A sharp pain stung my back as Ophelia dug the point of her knife into my flesh.

"Go on," she commanded.

I hopped onto the stair, then ducked into the carriage.

"Well, this is a real mess you've gotten us all into, isn't it, *Sister*? If you hadn't broken that slipper, we would have eventually had a happily ever after." She reached across and slammed a handkerchief over my mouth. Sour fumes accosted my nostrils and tongue. I fought against her clamp hold, but she held it true. White spots dotted my vision, and the last thing that flashed through my mind was Gisella's evil smile.

CHAPTER 10

LOVE IS FALSE

*A*loud bang woke me from unconsciousness. My eyelids fluttered. The capillaries in my brain pounded with fierce pain each time my heart pulsed. I tried to speak, but my swollen tongue stuck to the back of my front teeth. The inside of my mouth was as dry as stale bread.

"Good, she's awake."

I recognized Gisella's voice. I tried to move, but my hands and feet were tied at the wrists and ankles.

"Sit her up," commanded Ophelia.

Gisella waddled over and gripped my shoulders, yanking me up from the hardwood floor. A dull ache pulsed in my lower back where Ophelia punctured me with her knife. I realized we had returned home. We were inside the attic. The commander was no longer with them.

Black velvet sky flecked with glittering silver stars painted the glass windows. Candelabras stacked with flickering candles lit up the walls. A slumped figure sat, tied to a chair in the far corner. I blinked my eyes several times to focus. My throat constricted when I realized who was there.

Greyson.

"Ophelia, what in the world do you think you're doing? You kidnapped the prince?"

"You shut your mouth and listen up or I'll go and slit his throat right now."

Even though the unforgiving floor dug into my bruises I nodded, afraid to move or make a peep, not knowing if she was telling the truth and still had her knife.

My stepsisters pulled up two dusty chairs and sat in front of me, both of them staring down observing like I was a mouse caught in a cage.

Ophelia pursed her lips and smoothed her kinky blonde frizz.

"I want to tell you a story. Once upon a time, when we were young, we had a mother and a father who adored us. Our family lived in the smallest home in our village. We never had much money, but there was love. Father often told us that love conquered all. He taught that even if you had every gold piece in the world, it didn't matter, as long as you had love."

Gisella peered up at Ophelia, sadness overshadowing her normally impertinent demeanor.

Ophelia continued. "When we were eight, our beloved father contracted consumption and died, leaving us destitute. Mother, although heartbroken, worked odd jobs to support us. We barely ate and lived in an abandoned barn. She promised us that one day, when her savings could buy the finest clothing, she would travel with us to the next kingdom. She'd find a wealthy man and convince him to provide for our future."

I stared over at Greyson—his head lolling on his shoulder, cheeks blanched. I wondered if he was alright.

Ophelia narrowed her eyes and snapped her fingers. "I want you to look at me and pay attention when I'm talking to you." She pulled the knife out of her skirt pocket and set it on her lap. I straightened up, staring at her.

"The years of the dark underground of nightwork took its toll on Mother. She pounded into our heads that wealth and fancy meant more than anything else in the world, especially love. Whenever a village boy would catch our eye, the whip came out and cost us both uncomfortable seats for weeks. With each lash, she forced us to repeat the same line: *Love is false, will never stay. The only man worth salt is the one who will pay.*"

I stared at Ophelia's taut face. A black shadow of hate fell over it.

"When we were eleven, Mother took us to our neighboring kingdom of Britannia to seek a rich man who could take care of us."

Gisella cleared her throat, interrupting Ophelia. "By some miracle, Mother charmed a very wealthy importer."

Ophelia licked her lips. "Indeed. She did find a man—a beautiful, charming, rich man whom she married. Going against what she'd taught us, over the next four years she fell for his charm. She believed it to be true love. We got stupidly comfortable in our life with our new father. Hope filled my heart that perhaps with this newfound money, Gisella and I too could find someone we could love."

Gisella's face pinched and pink flourished in her cheeks. "But we soon learned our mother's wisdom ruled out. Love *was* false, and it *didn't* stay. While overseas to procure more goods for his import business, another much younger woman from a distant land turned his eye. Upon his return with her, our new father threw us to the street like trash, leaving us to once again fend for ourselves."

Ophelia smirked. "But Mother was no fool. She'd kept gold hidden from our new father, away from the manor. Enough for us to travel and buy new finery. So, we headed here, into Wallachia. Word reached her of a widower who worked as a successful tradesman for the king. She watched him for many days, even followed him back to his estate."

Fury ate at my stomach at the thought Lilith had tricked my father. The dislike I had for her grew into loathing as Ophelia revealed more lies and deceit.

"It became clear his wealth exceeded all of our hopes. He was much wealthier than the importer, only second to the king and prince themselves."

She gestured behind her to Greyson. I ground my molars trying to keep quiet, eyeing the knife still cradled in her lap.

"The opportunity she dreamed of presented itself. Soon our mother wooed, courted, and married your father."

Angry inflammation pulsed through my back, legs, and buttocks from sitting on the floor for so long, but it was nothing compared to the fire now blazing in my heart.

Father married Lilith because he wanted me to have a mother. He married that despicable, horrible, disgusting liar for me.

I wanted to launch up at my two stepsisters and slap both their faces.

Gisella gestured around the room. "Life in your estate became quite comfortable for us. Our new father spent so much money doting over and spoiling us."

Ophelia's face hardened. She interrupted Gisella's thought. "Just before he died, Mother even admitted to me that the forbidden bud of love started to blossom again for this man because of his generosity and kindheartedness toward us all. Oh, there was no doubt the largest portion of his heart belonged to you, but she thought as long as it was a daughter, not another woman, she could live with it."

Gisella sneered and pointed her finger at me. "Everything was perfect until you killed him. You ruined everything."

"Yes, Sister. *She* ruined it all." Ophelia crowed and waved her hand in the air flippantly. "All our happiness perished like a summer storm. I never imagined Mother's luck would fade three times and her marriage to the richest tradesman in the kingdom would end up leaving us destitute once again. After overhearing the last debtor come to take all but the last hundred pieces of our gold, I ran from the house into the woods to get away for a few hours to think."

A thought popped into my head. I remembered Ophelia disappearing a few weeks ago. Lilith was furious and the fight they had after she returned could've been heard by the dead. I wondered where she'd gone.

"While in those woods I met someone who would fix our problems. The price seemed worth the prize."

I couldn't hold back, the word just flew from my lips

"Who?"

Ophelia eyes shined and a Cheshire grin drew across her mouth from cheek to cheek.

CHAPTER 11

TRUE CONFESSIONS

"Commander Drake and I have been seeing each other in secret for quite some time now. I'd told him about our tragic past and the destitute circumstances we were living in. When I cried to him about the debtors, he promised he would help us. I knew if I could get close to him and get him to trust me, I could use him to get to the prince and in turn the means to save us from poverty. I did him some little favors and he's convinced we've grown quite close."

The thought of Ophelia with that man made my skin crawl.

"Commander Drake eventually told me about what kind of a person our new father was. He regaled the story of his adolescence and how the attention of the one girl who'd loved him from childhood was unjustly stolen by a foreigner whose family settled in Wallachia. He also told me how you went to Prince Greyson's rescue that day at the castle and he'd seized the opportunity to get even with the man who robbed him of his happiness. I was angry with him at first for taking his life, but soon realized he only did us a favor. With your father out of the way, I had a chance to go for a bigger purse."

I squeezed my fists, digging my fingernails into the soft flesh of my palms, loathing growing ever deeper for her and the commander.

"I asked him about Prince Greyson, curious now to find out about how to get close to him. The commander complained that he kept talking about this mystery girl who helped him that day. How he was obsessed with finding her. After the prince talked the king into having a ball to find this girl, I realized I had to step in and do something about it. After all, I'd endured my time with the commander only to get to Prince Greyson, and I couldn't have you getting in the way."

She retrieved a box from under of her chair and pulled out the glass slippers.

"My slippers? You were the woman who gave them to the footman?" An assortment of emotions churned inside me. I wanted to rip her head off.

Ophelia smirked and dangled the good slipper from her finger. "Not just pretty little spoiled girls like you have fairy godmothers—or at least commanders who know the town witch."

I stared at the ugly, horse-faced girl looking down at me, amazement at the sheer audacity and resourcefulness she'd managed. Ophelia had never been nice to me, but the hollowness of her wretched heart, the lengths she went to in order to construct such an elaborate plan genuinely shocked me. I wondered what it had truly cost her to meddle with dark magic.

"You said the prize was worth the price. What was the price? I was already your slave. I have no money, I've lost both my parents and have nothing, just like you used to." I questioned.

A loud voice behind her shouted at us. "I can tell you."

"Greyson," I whispered. Hot tears filled my eyes, and I finally let them fall. Sobs choked in my throat. I was both overwhelmed with relief he was okay and racked with such horrible guilt at getting him involved in the terrible situation.

"The slippers have reset the time loop so many times the past few days. This isn't the first time we've been in this attic. There are things you don't remember that I do. Ophelia sold her soul to that witch. She realized she was never going to get close to me, or my money, through Commander Drake. After I announced the ball to look for you, she had that demoness create the magic slippers for insurance. But she couldn't get it to work, because something happened to me on the road that day you helped me. I'd already begun to love you. The magic wasn't able to erase the feelings I already had. Reliving day after day has just proven that true love like this endures."

Ophelia's face flushed red. She gripped her knife and stood, throwing the chair backward. She stalked toward Greyson. "I will have your money one way or another. I refuse to live in squalor anymore, refuse to suffer and endure another move to another town. If my stupid mother can't find or keep a decent man to provide for us, I'm going to have to do it. Clearly, no matter how many times I've tried to keep you two apart, you're drawn to each other. No matter how many balls those slippers reset, you end up together. So, I'm going to have to do something to change that."

Ophelia walked behind Greyson. She grabbed a handful of hair, yanked his head back, and jabbed the point of the knife into his throat. She stared straight at me and smirked. "I realized that as long as one of you is still alive, I can reset the day but it will still end up the same. If you're dead, then I can start over." She looked down into Greyson's face. "I can work on your father instead. Then I won't have to worry about this little kismet between you and my worthless, pitiful stepsister."

"Leave him alone," I choked, my throat constricted from the successive sobs. Greyson tried to pull his head away but she punctured his neck. He yelled out. Bright red blood pulsed out of his neck, soaking his white linen shirt and the royal sash hugging his shoulder.

"No! Greyson!" I screamed.

Ophelia examined the blood dripping from the end of her blade. "I told you. Love is false, will never stay. The only man worth salt is the one who will pay. Well, love can't stay now, and the prince will surely pay. So, I guess in the end he was worth his salt, just like I thought he'd be. It won't take long now. I've severed his artery. I'm going to make you watch him die. I doubt it will be as tortuous as having to watch you two gallivanting and flirting at the ball over and over again, but I truly hope so. Then, you're next. Midnight is almost here, and a new day will start."

"Ophelia, what are you doing?" yelled Gisella. "This wasn't part of the plan."

"I told you last time, I was going to do whatever it took to fix this."

I turned to Gisella, pleading, "Gisella, help me get the slippers back on. We need to reset the day. Help me, please. I'm begging you. Help me save the prince."

My stepsister stared down at me from her chair, her face the color of newly fallen snow. Strawberry blonde locks hung in strings across her cheeks and forehead. She looked frazzled, confused. "But you broke them, Ella. They're not working right. Ophelia's never taken it this far. I don't know what will happen if you reset the day."

"Please, Gisella. Ophelia's gone mad. She's killing him. She's going to kill me. You have to help me stop this!"

Ophelia crept forward, the point of the bloody knife sticking straight out.

"If you try to put those slippers on her, I slit your throat too, Gisella. I told you, I'm fixing this. And I'll do it with or without you."

Gisella stood to face Ophelia.

"How dare you threaten me. I'm going to get Mother. She'll put a stop to this. You've gone too far."

Ophelia charged her and sunk the blade into her gut. Gisella's eyes widened. She fell backward, collapsing on the floor next to me. Shock reverberated through me, and my sobs stopped. Ophelia turned and stared daggers at me, blood dripping from her hand. I scrambled on the floor away from her but struggled to move farther than a few feet with both my hands and feet tied. She lunged at me. I kicked out, slamming her in the stomach. She doubled over and toppled backward.

I struggled to reach the glass slippers on the floor next to the chairs, seeing Ophelia squirming, trying to roll over and get back on her feet. Blood pounded in my ears as I worked the rope on my hands, trying to free myself. Gisella groaned next to me and reached out. "Let me help . . . you."

I cinched over to her and felt her fingers working the knot over.

The grip on my wrists loosened. I was free. I hurried to untie the rope around my ankles.

Ophelia got to her knees and whipped her head over at us. She growled and got to her feet. I launched forward, trying to grab the slippers, but she kicked them away. I grabbed her leg and yanked it hard. She teetered and stepped sideways to regain her balance but tripped over Gisella's chair and went crashing into the floor again. The knife clanged as it skidded across the floor. Ophelia lay still, not moving.

The clock began to strike once more.

Midnight.

I clambered up and inspected Greyson. His face was pale, his head lolled forward. The entirety of his shirt and sash soaked clear through with dark blood. Gisella lay in a pool of her own scarlet blood, her eyes closed.

The clock continued to chime it last strokes. I had seconds left. I ran for the scattered slippers. I didn't know if they would work now they were fractured and damaged, but I had to take the chance. To save Greyson and Gisella. To make things right again.

I shoved the broken slipper on my right foot. Sharp pain seared inside of my skull. I made to grab my head but jerked against the restraints. White light strobed. My eyelids fluttered. Scenes from the events of the past few days looped in rapid spurts. The ball. The blue ball gown. The swing. The slipper. The mysterious figures. Town square. Commander Drake, Ophelia, Gisella. The attic. Greyson. Blood. Over and over and over. The pressure inside my head grew until I thought it would explode.

I fought it, reached for the other slipper and slid my toes into it just as the last stroke of midnight struck. Every nerve in my body surged, pitching in pain so excruciating it stole my breath. Then a wave of euphoria came over me like the time between sleep and a dream. The memories inside my mind slowed into what looked like a long rectangular mosaic, then shattered into a thousand pieces.

CHAPTER 12

FRACTURED TIME

"*E*lla, how do you like your new sketchbook and pastel chalks?" Father looked back at me from the driver's seat, his playful eyes dancing, anticipating my answer. It was quite odd, I felt like we'd been here before.

"Well?" he said, a little uncertainty in his tone.

Confused, but not wanting to hurt his feelings, I spoke, "I love them, Father. Of course, I love them."

My arms and legs felt as light as a feather, as if we were only floating above the seat, not sitting on the cushion. The thoughts inside my mind swirled around—blurry and unclear. I tried to focus on something but it tired me. I closed my eyes, feeling the carriage underneath me rocking back and forth. The horses clip-clopped in a steady cadence for only a few minutes, then slowed and stopped. I opened my eyes and turned to see we were in front of the royal castle.

"I need only just a few minutes to speak with King Francis. This new assignment seems fairly typical. Just a jaunt over to Britannia and back. Try out the new chalks. The king's grounds seem especially colorful this spring. I'll bet you can make an impressive landscape sketch."

I nodded, blankly staring across the grounds, working to focus my mind. That name sounded familiar.

Britannia. Britannia.

"Stay here and watch the horses, I'll be back before you know it."

Father winked at me, then turned and sauntered through the scrolled wrought iron gate. I closed my eyes again. A feeling of foreboding vibrated inside of me, as if something were about to happen, yet I couldn't quite put my finger on it.

I heard someone shouting in the distance. I peeked out of the window and my new box of chalk tumbled to the carriage floor. The sight of the broken chalk made me lightheaded. I'd seen this pattern of broken chalk before in a long-ago dream. I opened the door and a stick of bright yellow chalk rolled out into the road. Feeling I shouldn't but being drawn to it, I stepped out of the carriage and wandered into the road to retrieve it. As I bent over to pick up the chalk, chaotic sounds and shouts echoed behind me.

"Whoa, Macadamis! Whoa, boy."

I stood and watched dazed as Prince Greyson flew wildly at me on an enormous Windsor Grey, pulling the reins and shouting commands. When the horse saw me in the middle of the road, he reared backward, tossing the prince onto the road, then bolted past me in a blur. The thoughts inside my head still swirled but were beginning to become clear. I remembered that horse. I remembered the prince falling to the ground.

"Prince Greyson," I shouted and hurried to his side. A sizable crescent-moon-shaped gash gaped open above his left eye, spilling precious crimson blood down his taut cheekbones. I scrambled to tear off the hem of my dress, wadded it up in a ball, then knelt by the prince's side and held it fast to his bleeding head.

The prince groaned and rolled his head back and forth.

"It's going to be okay. Stay still. Shh, stay still."

He stopped moving his head and opened his eyes. The bright green of his irises mesmerized me as if they were a spinning hypnotic tool. He reached up and caressed my lips. "I remember you," he whispered, his tongue sitting on his top teeth, breathing out the syllable slowly. Then he leaned up, opened his mouth, and deeply kissed me.

The memories swirling in my head focused hard and came crashing into the forefront all at once. Father's death. Lilith, Ophelia, Gisella. Anjelina. The gown. The many balls. The slippers. Ophelia stabbing Prince Greyson and Gisella. Watching them both die. The images flipped before my eyes like a picture book, then the book closed.

Time fractured, bringing us all back into the past.

And saved us.

We both pulled away from the kiss at the same time. The surprise and shock I felt reflected back at me in his eyes.

"Ella." He cupped his hand on my cheek.

"Greyson," I whispered.

Then I leaned down, kissed him again with fevered passion, and melted into his strong arms.

CHAPTER 13

NO TIME LIKE THE PRESENT

*N*o matter how many times the sun rose and set, the joy of having Greyson at my side never ceased to enchant me. In the cold of last winter, we danced and kissed as the snowflakes melted on our lips. I heard his charismatic laugh ride in upon the breeze as it tickled the amber leaves of fall, and I saw his adoring face reflect the sun when we rode through the spring meadows today.

I love him so much.

From the balcony of our bedroom, I gazed down at the newly planted gardens across the royal grounds, bathing in the rose and gold rays of the setting sun, and put the finishing sweeps on my landscape sketch with the last nubs of my pink and yellow chalk.

I watched Greyson fencing with my father, and I couldn't help but chuckle to myself. Father insisted he could take him without any training. I noticed he was having to eat his words.

After that day on the road all our memories from the fractured slipper returned. Father asked King Francis to banish Lilith and Gisella, and he's taken up residence in the castle. Greyson immediately removed Commander Drake from the royal guard and had him imprisoned after he led him to the witch who supplied him with the cursed glass slippers. Greyson never mentioned what he and the king did with her or Ophelia, and I never asked.

King Francis held a magnificent ball to celebrate our engagement the following week. After Greyson pushed me on the swing for a great while, we actually got to finish our dance in the secret garden. All the surrounding kingdoms came together for our grand wedding one month later. Anjelina stood by my side as my lady-in-waiting, and I vowed to become his Ella forever. The time I've spent with Greyson has been the happiest time of my life. His gracious kindness and tender love reflect his true royal nature, and we share a kindred friendship of love and respect.

Today marked our one year anniversary, and I had a very big surprise for him. I set my easel aside, brushed the chalk off my skirt, then leaned over the balcony.

"Greyson, Father, come inside. I have a gift for both of you."

Greyson waved in acknowledgment, and I went back into my room to wash the chalk off my fingers. My hands were shaking so bad I could hardly get the soap off them. Butterflies whipped like a cyclone around the lining of my stomach. I was so nervous I could hardly breathe. I paced the room, biting my lip in anticipation, sweat beading on my forehead.

"Ella." Greyson walked in and headed straight for me. "You look so nervous. Is everything okay?"

"Yes," I laughed, a little louder than I meant to. He smiled and laughed too, then raised his left eyebrow and stared at me with those bright green eyes.

"You said you have an anniversary gift for both me and your father? Will you give me a hint or shall we wait for him? As long as it's not a pair of magic glass slippers, I'll be happy."

We both chuckled.

"Well, it was hard to think of what to get for you since you're a prince and you have everything you always wanted."

Greyson blushed.

"Since I have you, that's true. I do have everything I want."

I walked up to him and took his hands in mine. "Well, I have something special that I'm sure you don't already have."

I pressed his palms against my stomach. His eyes grew to the size of a tea saucer, and his jaw gaped wide in surprise.

"Happy anniversary, Greyson."

THE END

ABOUT THE AUTHOR

Angela Brimhall grew up trying to decide whether she liked romance or horror novels best. She graduated college with a BS degree in health, but decided she'd much rather experience the drama of life through her characters. She received an MFA in English and creative writing from Southern New Hampshire University and is a member of the Sigma Tau Delta English Honors Society, Romance Writers of America and Horror Writers Association. She lives in the heart of a city between two mountains with her husband, son and four dogs where spired castles dot every hill and fairy tales really do come true.

www.authorangelabrimhall.com

f facebook.com/authorangelabrimhall

We hope you enjoyed Fractured Slipper! We would love to have you leave a review on your favorite retailer!

Keep in touch with us and get updates about the next Fairy Tale Ink installment at www.FairyTaleInkBooks.com.